ST. MARTIN'S

MINOTAUR

MYSTERIES

Other titles from St. Martin's MINOTAUR Mysteries

ST. MARTIN'S PAPERBACKS is also proud to present
these mystery classics by Ngaio Marsh

ST. MARTIN'S PAPERBACKS TITLES
BY DONNA ANDREWS

Murder with Peacocks
Murder with Puffins

MURDER
with PUFFINS

DONNA
ANDREWS

St. Martin's Paperbacks

MURDER WITH PUFFINS

Copyright © 2000 by Donna Andrews.
Excerpt from *Revenge of the Wrought-Iron Flamingos* copyright © 2001 by Donna Andrews.

ISBN: 0-312-97886-3

Printed in the United States of America

St. Martin's Press hardcover edition / May 2000
St. Martin's Paperbacks edition / June 2001

St. Martin's Paperbacks are published by St. Martin's Press, 175 Fifth Avenue, New York, NY 10010.

10 9 8 7 6 5 4 3

ACKNOWLEDGMENTS

With thanks:

- To Dad, for inspiring Meg's dad.

- To Mom, for being nothing whatsoever like Meg's mother. (Well, except for the bit about the coconut.)

- To Stuart and Elke, for holding your wedding on Monhegan.

- To Monhegan and its residents—although a hurricane and a homicide must seem poor thanks for your hospitality.

- To Ruth Cavin and the crew at St. Martin's, and to Ellen Geiger of Curtis Brown, for helping steer me through the perils of publishing.

- To my friends and family everywhere, including the Misfits, Queen Bees, Teafolk, Wombats, fellow writers, and fellow readers.

CHAPTER 1

My Puffin Lies over the Ocean

'I see land ahead," Michael said.

"I'm sure they said that often aboard the original *Flying Dutchman*," I replied, my eyes tightly shut.

"No, really; I'm sure of it this time," he insisted.

I kept my eyes closed and didn't relax my death grip on the rail while the ferry's deck bucked and heaved beneath my feet. The rain and spray had soaked me to the bone, but I wasn't going into the cabin unless the swells grew dangerous. Way too many seasick people inside. Of course, those of us on deck were seasick, too, but at least out here the wind kept the air fresh, if a little damp.

"The next time I have an idea like this," I mumbled, "just shoot me and get it over with."

"What was that?" Michael shouted over a gust of wind.

"Never mind," I shouted back.

"I really do think that's land ahead," Michael repeated. "Honestly. I don't think it's another patch of fog."

I debated, briefly, whether to look. My seasickness seemed a little less intense if I kept my eyes closed. But if an end to our ordeal was in sight, I wanted to know about it. I opened one eye a crack and peered in the direction Michael pointed. To me, the vague shape ahead looked like the same ominous cloud bank we'd been staring at for hours. Maybe it made him feel better to think he saw land. Maybe he was trying to make me feel better.

"That's nice," I croaked, and closed my eyes again, blotting out the gray sky, the gray sea, and the disturbing lack of any clear line of demarcation between the two. Not to mention the gray faces of the other passengers clinging to the rail.

"We must be getting close," Michael said, sounding less confident. "Monhegan's only an hour off the coast in good weather, right?"

I didn't answer. Yes, normally it took only an hour by ferry to reach Monhegan, where we planned to stay in my aunt Phoebe's summer cottage. But there was nothing normal about this trip. If Michael still believed we'd reach dry land soon, I wasn't going to discourage him. Even though deep down I knew that we really *had* boarded the *Flying Dutchman* and were doomed to sail up and down the coast for all eternity, or at least until we ran out of fuel and had to be rescued by the Coast Guard.

"Well, maybe not," I heard Michael murmur.

I pried my eyes open to check on him. He stared out over the water with a faint frown. I felt a twinge of jealousy. I probably looked as ghastly as I felt, but even in the throes of seasickness, Michael was gorgeous. A little paler than usual, and the hypnotically blue eyes were a bit bloodshot. But still, were I an artist, looking for just the right tall, dark, handsome cover model for a nautically themed romance, I'd look at Michael and shout, "Eureka!"

"I'm sorry," I said instead. "This was a bad idea."

"It'll turn out all right," he said with a smile. Only a faint ghost of his usual dazzling smile, but it made me feel better. "But next time we set out on an adventure, let's remember to check the weather first, okay?"

Well, that was encouraging. At least he was still talking about "next time." And next time I took off on a trip with Michael, I promised myself, we'd go someplace warm and tropical, where the nearest large body of water was the hotel swimming pool. Not on a boat in the middle of the Atlantic—well, several miles off the coast of Maine anyway. Hurricane Gladys had now headed out to sea and now subsided to a mere tropical storm, but if I'd bothered to check the Weather Channel before Michael and I set out for our weekend getaway, I could have picked a more promising spot. In fact, I could probably have done better just by sticking a pin in a map.

"It's a deal," I said, smiling back as well as I could. He put his hand on mine for a few seconds, until another wave hit the boat and he had to grab the rail again. But I felt better. Mentally anyway. Physically . . . well, I was trying to ignore another set of warning signals from my stomach.

"Meg Langslow? Is that you?"

I opened my eyes and turned, to see two figures standing to my left, both wrapped from head to toe in state-of-the-art rain gear. They looked like walking L. L. Bean catalogs and were probably toasty warm and reasonably dry underneath. I tried not to resent this.

"Yes?" I said, peering through sheets of rain at the small portion of their faces visible under their hoods.

"Meg, dear, don't you remember us? It's Winnie and Binkie!"

"Winnie and Binkie?" Michael repeated.

I finally placed the names. Mr. and Mrs. Winthrop Saltonstall Burnham, aka Winnie and Binkie, owned a cottage on Monhegan Island and were old family friends. Childhood friends of my grandparents, if memory served, which made them fairly ancient by now. And yet there they stood, two sturdy round figures in yellow slickers, seemingly undisturbed by the driving rain, the frantic rocking of the boat, and the near–gale force winds.

"Bracing, isn't it?" Winnie said, throwing out his chest and taking a deep breath, which was at least one-quarter rain.

"Don't mind him, dear," Binkie whispered, noticing my reaction. "Rough weather always makes him a little queasy, and he likes to put a brave front on it."

"Oh, I don't mind the crossing," Winnie said. "I'm just hoping the weather doesn't spoil the bird-watching."

"Bird-watching?" Michael said. "You're going out to Monhegan in the middle of a hurricane for bird-watching?"

"Yes, aren't you?" Winnie asked.

"It's been downgraded to a tropical storm," Binkie said. "And this is the fall flyover season."

"Oh, of course," I said.

"The what?" Michael asked.

"The fall flyover season," Binkie explained. "Monhegan lies right in the path the birds take when they migrate north and south. There's a short time every spring and fall when the bird-watching reaches its peak, and birders come here from all up and down the Eastern Seaboard."

"We have a cottage on the island," Winnie said. "We've been bird-watching here for fifty-three years." He and Binkie exchanged fond smiles.

"But if you're not here for the bird-watching, why are you going out to Monhegan?" Binkie asked.

"We wanted to get away from things," Michael put in. "Get some peace and quiet."

"Some what?" Winnie shouted over a gust of wind that had evidently carried away Michael's words.

"Peace and quiet!" Michael shouted back.

"Oh."

They still looked at us with puzzled expressions. I sighed. I wasn't sure I even wanted to try explaining.

The trip had seemed so logical a few days ago. My romance with Michael had reached the point where we wanted to spend a little time alone together—okay, a lot of time—just at the point when neither of us had a place to call our own.

As a bachelor professor of theater in a college town with a chronic housing shortage, Michael had lived in relative luxury for the last several years by renting houses from faculty members on sabbatical. This year, alas, his landlords had suddenly realized they couldn't afford to spend a year in London—not with their seventh child on the way.

They'd been very nice about letting Michael sleep on their sofa until something else turned up, but it was no place for the logical conclusion to a romantic candlelight dinner. We'd already ended enough dates watching Disney videos and dodging blobs of peanut butter.

And I was temporarily homeless, as well. Subletting my cottage and ironworking studio for several months to a struggling sculptor had seemed like a good idea at the start of the summer. I'd known I would be down in my home-town of Yorktown, organizing three family weddings; and with my career as an ornamental blacksmith on hold, I could use the rent money.

But when I tried to move back in, I couldn't get rid of my tenant. He was in the middle of an important commission; he would ruin the whole piece if he had to move it; he needed just one more week to finish it. He'd been need-ing just one more week for the past six weeks.

So I was still staying at my parents' house. Mother and Dad weren't there, of course; they were off in Europe on an extended second honeymoon. But the house was filled with elderly relatives. They'd come for the weddings and stayed on to watch the legal circus unfold as the county built its case against the murderer whose identity I'd man-aged (more or less accidentally) to uncover.

That was another problem. I'd become notorious. I couldn't go anywhere in Yorktown without people coming up to congratulate me for my brilliant detective work. More than one romantic candlelight dinner with Michael had been interrupted by people who insisted on shaking my hand, having their picture taken with me, buying us drinks, treat-ing us to dinner—it was impossible.

"Too bad we can't just run away together to a desert island," Michael said after one such interruption.

Inspiration struck.

"Actually, we can," I said. "What are you doing next weekend?"

"Running away to a desert island with you, evidently," Michael said. "Did you have a particular island in mind?"

"Monhegan!" I said.

"Never heard of it. Where is it?"

"Off the coast of Maine."

"Won't that be cold this time of year?"

"The cottage has a fireplace. And a gas heater."

"Cottage?"

"Aunt Phoebe's summer cottage. Actually, it's an old house. And hardly anyone stays on the island after August; it's too rugged." Which meant we wouldn't have half a hundred neighbors and relatives looking over our shoulders and reporting who said what to whom and how many bedrooms were occupied.

"What about Aunt Phoebe?"

"It's a summer cottage, remember? Which she isn't using, partly because summer's over and partly because she's having much more fun down here, waiting for the trial and keeping me awake with her snoring."

"And she won't mind if you use her cottage?"

"She wouldn't mind if she knew, and she won't have to know. Dad has a spare key. She's always inviting us to go up anytime. We haven't for years, but the whole family knows they have an open invitation."

"And how can we be sure the whole family won't be there?"

"In September? Like you said, it's cold this time of year. Besides, most of the family finds it a little too Spartan for their tastes. Mother won't go at all; she refuses to go anywhere that doesn't even have electricity, much less ready access to a deli and a good hairdresser. Michael, this is not a tropical paradise. But it's empty, it's free, and there's nobody else around for miles except for a few dozen locals who winter there."

"I'm sold," he said. "I can't skip Wednesday night's faculty meeting, but I'll get someone to cover my classes for the rest of the week, come by for you early Thursday morning, and we'll drive up."

As I said, it seemed like a good idea at the time. Even the two flat tires that stranded us in a Motel Six near the New Jersey Turnpike for the first night of our getaway hadn't dimmed our enthusiasm. But standing there on the deck of the ferry, I wasn't sure any of that would make sense. I focused back on the present, where Winnie and Binkie were still patiently waiting for an answer. From the way they looked at us, they probably thought we were on the run from something.

"Well, things were so hectic down in Yorktown, and I told Michael about what a great place Monhegan was for getting away from it all," I said finally. "I didn't really stop to think how far past the season it is."

"Yes, you've had quite a time," Winnie said. "We had a note from your father when they were in Rome, and he mentioned your detective adventures. You'll have to come over for dinner and tell us all about it."

Michael winced. I could almost hear his thoughts: So much for anonymity and privacy.

"Yes, that's a wonderful idea," Binkie said. Then her smile suddenly vanished, and she flung her hand out to point over her husband's shoulder.

"Bird!" she cried.

Winnie whirled, and they both produced gleaming high-tech waterproof binoculars from beneath their rain gear. They plastered themselves against the boat rail and locked their lenses on their distant prey. I couldn't see a thing. I glanced at Michael. He shrugged.

I had assumed that the other passengers clinging to the rail were seasick, like us, and either optimistically hoping the fresh air would make them feel better or pessimistically placing themselves where the weather could take care of the inevitable cleanup. But up and down the rail, a forest of binoculars appeared, all trained on the distant speck.

"Only a common tern, I'm afraid," Binkie said. "Still, would you like to see?"

Under Binkie's guidance, I managed to focus on a small black dot atop a distant buoy. Even with the binoculars, you could recognize the dot as a bird only if you already knew what it was.

"Poor thing!" Binkie said "Imagine being out in weather like this!"

I didn't need to imagine; we *were* out in it.

"Oh, there's another tern at three o'clock!"

Dozens of binoculars swerved with the uncanny accuracy of a precision drill team. Binkie redirected my binoculars to another, closer buoy. This one definitely had a morose bird perched on top. I deduced that terns must be closely related to seagulls; this looked like just another seagull to me. The buoy gave a lurch, and the tern had to flap its wings and scramble to keep its footing before hunching down again. It cocked its head and looked at the boat. In the binoculars, it seemed to stare directly at me. It shook its head, pulled it farther back between its shoulders, and looked so miserable and grumpy that I identified with it immediately.

"Poor thing," I said.

"Oh, they're fine," Winnie said. "Coming back very well."

"Coming back from where?"

"Extinction, dear," Binkie said. "Things looked very bad for them at the beginning of the century, poor things, but we've managed to turn that around."

"We have several hundred nests on Egg Island, and, of course, nearly a dozen pair of puffins," Winnie said. "If you get a chance, you should take the tour. The boat leaves from Monhegan and anchors off the island for several hours."

"In the spring, love," Binkie said. "I imagine they stop

running after Labor Day. The puffins would be mostly gone by now."

"True," Winnie said. "But if there are still a few puffins there, perhaps we could arrange a special tour for Meg. If the weather lets up a bit," he added, glancing up.

I forced a smile and handed Binkie her binoculars. The weather would have to let up more than a bit before I'd set out from Monhegan again in a boat. But if by some misfortune Winnie and Binkie succeeded in convincing a suicidal boat captain to take them out puffin-watching, I'd find some excuse.

"Just what is a puffin anyway?" Michael asked.

I winced. Dangerous question. The Burnhams and several nearby birders pulled out their field guides and began imparting puffin lore.

If I'd been explaining, I'd have said to keep his eye out for a black-and-white bird about a foot high that looked like a small penguin wearing an enormous clown nose over his beak and bright orange stockings on his feet. The birders did a good job of describing the beak—a gray-and-yellow triangle with a wide red tip—but they went into too much detail on the chunky body, the stubby wings, the distinctive, clumsy flight, and the precise patterning of the black-and-white feathers. I doubt if Michael needed to know quite so much detail on how to tell immature puffins from other birds he'd never heard of, or if he cared in the slightest about puffins' breeding and nesting habits. When Winnie and another birder began competing to see who could more accurately imitate the low, growling *arr!* that the usually silent puffins make when their nests are disturbed, I groaned in exasperation.

"Don't worry, dear," Binkie said, patting me on the shoulder. "It always gets a little rough when we're this close to the harbor."

"Close to the harbor?" I said. "You mean we'll be landing soon?"

"Thank God," Michael muttered. I wasn't sure whether the ocean or the bird lore made his exclamation so fervent.

And sure enough, within minutes we saw the ferry dock. Quite a crowd of people stood on it with great mounds of luggage. More birders, I supposed, since at least half of them peered through the rain with binoculars. Like the birders on the boat, they scrutinized the gulls that wheeled overhead—hoping, I suppose, to spot a rare species of seagull. The two sets of birders also scanned one another. As we approached the dock, they began pointing, waving, and calling greetings.

"Good Lord, Binkie, look who's on the dock," Winnie said. "Just beside the gift shop."

"Oh no, not Victor!" Binkie exclaimed. "How awful! I did so hope we'd seen the last of him."

"No such luck," Winnie growled. "Turns up like a bad penny every few years. Wonder what the old ba—scoundrel's up to this time."

"Never borrow trouble," Binkie said. "We don't know for sure that he's up to anything."

"Like hell we don't."

I peered at the dock, wondering who Victor was and how he could possibly have aroused this much animosity in the normally mild-mannered Burnhams. But without binoculars, I couldn't see many details; if the docks held a sinister villain twirling his mustache or sporting cloven hooves, I couldn't spot him.

"Oh, look, Dr. and Mrs. Peabody," Binkie said—no doubt to distract Winnie from his irritation with the nefarious Victor. "What rotten luck; they're leaving just when we're getting here."

"I wouldn't count on it," Winnie replied, inspecting the Peabodys through his binoculars. "I overheard the captain speaking rather sharply to someone over the radio. Said he'd never have set out if they'd accurately predicted the size of the swells."

I was glad Winnie hadn't mentioned this until after we could see the dock.

"You think he'll ride out the storm here, then?" Binkie asked.

"If he has any sense," Winnie replied.

"Luck was certainly with you two," Binkie said, turning to Michael and me. "You very nearly missed the boat!"

The boat picked that moment to make a sudden free-fall drop into the trough of a wave.

"Lucky us," Michael muttered.

CHAPTER 2

The Puffin Has Landed

"So this is Monhegan," Michael said as he stood in the middle of the dock, inspecting the landscape.

I was relieved to see that he looked better already. Entirely due to being back on dry land, I was sure. Certainly nothing about our surroundings would cheer anyone up. Did the Monhegan dock always look this seedy and run-down, I wondered? Or were the weather and my queasy stomach still coloring my view of things?

After the boat docked, we had the usual mad scramble to sort out the enormous piles of luggage. Michael and I were luckier than most; the birders tended to favor battered rucksacks and ancient suitcases covered with peeling travel stickers from unpronounceable foreign birding meccas. Our more sedate urban luggage was comparatively easy to spot.

"What next?" Michael asked when we had all our gear.

"Next, we negotiate for someone to take our luggage to the cottage."

I pointed to the island's half a dozen pickup trucks lined up, fender-to-fender, on the dock, with their tailgates open toward the arriving crowds. Beyond the trucks, a steep gravel road, already swarming with birders, led up toward the village proper.

"The two hotels each have a pickup truck to take their guests' baggage," I said. "If you're staying at a bed-and-breakfast or a cottage, you hire one of the freelance pickups to haul your stuff."

"Just our stuff?" Michael said. "What about us?"

"We walk," I said. "Unless you want us to get a reputation as lazy city folks."

Michael and I stood back, though, until the logjam of birders cleared. Which didn't take long: As soon as the birders realized the ferry wasn't going anywhere, they all panicked and scurried up the hill. Birders who had planned to leave set out to reclaim the rooms they had recently vacated before the newly arrived birders checked in. The new arrivals hurried after them to wave their confirmation letters and credit cards before their stranded colleagues established squatters' rights.

Within minutes, the dock lay deserted. The few travelers, like Winnie and Binkie, who owned cottages and didn't have to worry about someone else displacing them had gone into the small shop at the foot of the hill to drink hot tea and catch up on the local gossip. Lucky that Michael and I weren't staying in a hotel; I didn't think I could have beaten even the oldest and most arthritic birder up the hill. We declined an invitation to join the Burnhams and found ourselves alone on the dock, surrounded by mountains of luggage higher than our heads.

"Are they all just going to leave their luggage here?" Michael asked.

"Why not?" I said. "Who would steal it, and where could they possibly hide it if they did? There's no getting off the island until the ferry starts running again."

We found a truck with room for our larger bags, and paid the exorbitant hauling fee. Despite my warnings, Michael tried to talk the driver into giving us a ride.

"No room," said the driver. His broad face looked vaguely familiar. He was about my age, which meant if he was a local, I'd probably played with him as a child. Or, more likely, beaten the tar out of him for picking on my much younger brother, Rob, if my memories of some of the other children we'd played with on the island were accurate. His clothes smelled of cigarette smoke and beer, and he had a seedy, furtive air that made me wonder, just for a moment, if letting him have our baggage was really a good idea.

"We could wait till you come back," Michael said.

"Not coming back," the driver replied. "Not for a while anyway. You could walk there sooner."

"I'm not sure my friend is up to the walk," Michael said, putting a protective arm around me.

I did my best to look frail and in need of protection as the driver peered at me. I could tell I wasn't succeeding. Which didn't surprise me; when you're nearly five foot nine, people tend to look at you and think, Sturdy. Unless you're model-thin, which I'm not. Even with Michael looming half a foot taller beside me, I obviously didn't look like the driver's idea of a damsel in distress.

"She's getting over a broken ankle," Michael said. "She's not supposed to overdo it."

I switched from frail to suffering stoically. The driver still wasn't fooled.

"Only a quarter of a mile," he said. "Ain't even uphill most of the way."

With that, he jumped into the cab of the truck and gunned the engine.

The truck took off, spinning its wheels a little before the tires got enough traction to climb the steep slope up from the docks. Little blobs of mud spattered us.

"Bloody little weasel," I snapped. "Bad enough he wouldn't give us a ride—"

"Don't worry," Michael said, wiping a bit of mud out of his left eye. "It'll wash off by the time we get to the cottage."

"Yes, it is beginning to drizzle a bit more heavily, isn't it?"

"We follow him?"

I glanced over. Michael was staring up the hill.

"Strange," I said. "The hill didn't seem as steep when I was a kid."

Michael chuckled.

"I remember it always used to drive me crazy how long it took for us to get to the cottage from the docks."

"Oh great."

"But that was mostly because Dad insisted on stopping to talk to everyone along the way. We'd take two or three hours, sometimes. But really it's only a fifteen-minute walk."

"The sooner we begin, the sooner we'll get warm and dry," Michael said, hoisting his carry-on bag to his shoulder. "Lead on, Macduff."

We trudged up the hill. Ahead of us, we could see the last two birders hiking stoutly toward the crest. The rest had no doubt reached their hotels or bed-and-breakfast lodgings long ago and were now watching whatever birders watch when the weather deprives them of their natural prey.

At the crest of the hill, we turned right on the island's main thoroughfare—another dirt and gravel road, but this one slightly better maintained. It wound through a seemingly haphazard scattering of buildings, most made of weather-beaten gray boards. I tried to see the place through a stranger's eyes, and cringed. You forget little details over time, like how many yards contained untidy stacks of lobster traps in need of mending. Or how the utilitarian PVC pipes that brought water down from the central reservoir lined every road. I could see Michael darting glances around, and I suspected he was wondering why the devil we'd come all this way to such an unprepossessing place. The picturesque charm of the island definitely came across better on a sunny summer day than in the wake of a fall hurricane.

The drizzle had escalated to a light shower by the time we turned down the lane to Aunt Phoebe's cottage. About time; a little later and we'd have had to stumble along in the dark. Monhegan has no streetlights. And Aunt Phoebe thought repairing the ruts in her lane a citified affectation, which made finding your way in the dark a nightmare.

Only it wasn't dark. I could see light ahead of us—coming from the house. And was that music playing? I felt a twinge of panic. Surely Aunt Phoebe hadn't rented it, had she? She was always so adamant about having it ready at any time the family wanted to use it.

"Someone's already here," Michael said.

"No one's supposed to be," I said. "Maybe it's just the cleaners. I know Aunt Phoebe has someone local come in every two weeks or so to keep the place from getting too dirty."

A burst of laughter rang out from inside the cottage.

"Wish I enjoyed cleaning that much," Michael said. He shifted his carry-on bag from one shoulder to the other.

I noticed that the rest of our luggage hadn't arrived yet. Michael's attempts to bribe the driver into giving us a ride had probably irritated him to the point that he'd make sure ours was the last off the truck. He might even pretend to forget about it until the morning, with our luck. I sighed.

"Well, there's no sense standing out here wondering," I said. I marched up the steps, ready to deal with whatever the cottage contained—burglars? Squatters? Cleaners who had gotten into the bar and decided to hold an impromptu hurricane party?

I squared my shoulders and knocked firmly on the door.

CHAPTER 3

All My Puffins

No one answered. I waited briefly, then knocked again.

Another burst of laughter greeted my knock.

"What's going on in there?" I called.

Still no answer.

"Well, here goes," I said.

I flung open the door.

The cottage was empty. But someone, obviously, had been there, and not very long ago.

"I guess someone was expecting us," Michael said.

Evidently—but who?

We looked around. A fire crackled briskly in the fireplace. Enough candles burned in various parts of the room to cast a warm, romantic glow. Both sofas were piled high with down pillows and fuzzy afghans. Two teacups stood on the coffee table, and a hint of steam and a faint odor of jasmine indicated that the quilted cozy concealed a fresh pot of tea. A battery radio sat on the mantel; as we stood there gaping, a final burst of laughter signaled the end of a commercial and an announcer with a beautiful spun-silk baritone voice assured us that W something or other would now continue with its Friday-night light classical program. The strains of "The Blue Danube Waltz" filled the room.

"Hello?" I called.

I stepped inside. I could smell something cooking. Right now, my stomach objected strenuously to this, but, even so, I could tell that when I'd fully recovered from the ferry ride, whatever was going on in the kitchen would turn out to be intensely interesting. A bottle of champagne stood on the table, beads of sweat running down its sides, with a corkscrew and two glass flutes nearby.

"You know, this is a lot less primitive than you described it," Michael said, dropping his bags by the door. "In fact, now that we're off the boat, I think I'm starting to like this place."

He looked around appreciatively. The place did look its best by candlelight. The living room was two stories high, with stairs curling around one wall, leading to a balconylike upper hall, off which the three bedrooms opened. Downstairs, under the bedrooms, were a large bathroom and a larger kitchen. I remembered the place as tiny and cramped—which it usually was in the summer, with every bedroom filled, a carpet of sleeping bags in the living room, and a typical hour-long wait to use the bathroom. But for two people looking for peace and quiet and a place to get away from it all, the cottage suddenly looked like a palace.

"Let's worry about the luggage later," Michael said, sitting down on one of the sofas and patting the cushion beside him. I joined him, and for a few minutes we sat there in silence, enjoying the warmth, the music, the whole ambiance.

Although I did wonder who had opened up the cottage and set everything up for us. Had Winnie and Binkie made a quick call from the gift shop and sent some helpful neighbor over? Or had Aunt Phoebe noticed the missing key, done a head count, and decided to arrange a lovely surprise? Whoever it was, they had my thanks. In my exhausted state, I kept remembering the version of "Beauty and the Beast" in which the disembodied hands set the table and served dinner, and I wondered if something similar had happened here.

No matter, I thought, sinking back against Michael's arm. This is heavenly.

The door suddenly opened with a bang.

"I'm back!" caroled a voice.

Michael and I whirled about in astonishment.

"Dad?" I said.

My father stood in the doorway with a load of wood in his arms. Water flew everywhere as he shook himself like a dog.

"Meg!" he cried. He dumped the wood on the hearth with a thump, then enfolded me in a soggy bear hug. "What a wonderful surprise!"

"You think you're surprised," I muttered. "You have no idea."

"And Michael," Dad added. "How grand! Margaret, come look; it's Meg and Michael here to join us."

Mother appeared at the top of the stairway, delicately suppressing a yawn, carrying her embroidery and a European fashion magazine.

"Meg, dear," she cried. She floated gracefully down the stairs and bent over to kiss my cheek. "This is so nice! And how lovely to see you, Michael."

Not a single improbably blond hair had strayed out of place, and she looked, as usual, as if she could replace any of the models in the magazine on a moment's notice.

Just then, I heard a loud pop, and something whizzed past my nose and bounced off Michael's chin.

"Sorry about that, Michael," Dad said, waggling the champagne bottle. "Nothing broken, I hope?"

"No, I'm fine," Michael said, rubbing his chin.

"Here we go," Dad said, handing Mother a glass of the champagne and taking a sip from his own glass. "Would you two like any?"

"No thanks," Michael and I chorused. I closed my eyes. I wasn't quite ready to watch people eating and drinking.

The door slammed open again.

"Well, I see the ferry's in," said Aunt Phoebe, appearing in the doorway with a dripping canvas tote in each hand. "You've missed dinner, but there's plenty of leftovers. Smithfield ham, potato salad—"

"No thanks," I said.

"Maybe later," Michael added.

"Hell, they just got off the ferry; they're probably sick as dogs," cackled Mother's best friend, Mrs. Fenniman, appearing behind Aunt Phoebe with her own pair of tote bags. "Leave them in peace till their guts stop heaving."

Although Mrs. Fenniman was absolutely right, I wished she hadn't emphasized the word *heaving* quite so forcefully. My stomach gave a queasy lurch, as if to say, Okay, time to pay attention to me.

"Is the ferry going back tonight?" came a voice from above our heads. I looked up, to see my brother, Rob, standing on the upstairs landing, rubbing his eyes as if he'd just awakened.

"My God," I said. "Is everyone in Yorktown up here? Yikes!"

I jumped as something cold and wet touched my ankle.

"What the devil is Spike doing here?" Michael asked, looking down at the small black-and-white fur ball at my feet. Although Spike was Michael's mother's dog, he had never liked Michael. He looked up for a moment, curled his lip at Michael, and returned to his favorite pastime of licking me obsessively. He didn't seem to mind the mud.

"Your mother asked me to baby-sit him for the weekend," Rob said. "And when I had to drive up here, there wasn't anything I could do but bring him along. You want to take charge of him?"

"Thanks, but you'll probably get back to Yorktown before I do," Michael said. He didn't like Spike any more than Spike liked him. Of course, Spike didn't really like anyone but Michael's mother and me. And I'd never figured out why he liked me. The feeling certainly wasn't mutual.

"True, I'm heading home as soon as possible," Rob said. "Speaking of which, I'd probably better get my bag and head down to the ferry."

"I doubt the ferry's going anywhere tonight," I said. "And trust me, if it was, you wouldn't want to be on it. For a tropical storm that's heading out to sea to die, this one still has a lot of life left in it."

"That's because it isn't heading out to sea to die," Mrs. Fenniman said, pouring herself some tea. "It just went out to sea long enough to pick up steam. It's back up to a hurricane again and has turned around to take another run at the coast."

"What?"

"It's true; I just heard it on the radio," Mrs. Fenniman said with the good cheer she usually displayed when she had managed to scoop everyone else with news of a scandal or disaster.

"Oh great," Rob said. "I guess that means I'm stuck here for the duration."

He threw himself down on one of the couches and assumed a martyred air. Along with Mother's slender height and aristocratic blond looks, he'd inherited her talent for self-dramatization.

"Don't be gloomy," Dad said. He stood before the hearth, apparently trying to set the back of his pants on fire. His short, round form and the way the firelight played on his bald head made him look like a mischievous gnome. "Look on the bright side," he added. "After all these years, we'll finally get to see what really happens here during a hurricane!"

"Yippee," Rob mumbled without enthusiasm.

"Oh dear," Mother murmured.

"Don't worry, Margaret," Aunt Phoebe said. She had shed her dripping rain gear and was tying a green-and-orange-flowered apron over her stout khaki-clad form. "We've got plenty of food and fuel. We may have to rough it for a bit, but we'll come through just fine."

Mother looked relieved. After all, she knew better than anyone that Aunt Phoebe's idea of roughing it meant using the checked gingham napkins instead of the starched linen, and that the caviar might be tinned instead of fresh.

"Time we got busy," Mrs. Fenniman said. She had donned a flowered apron identical to Aunt Phoebe's, though it looked odd over her usual black clothes and scrawny frame. The two of them hefted their tote bags and disappeared into the kitchen.

"We can go out on the cliffs at Green Point and actually see the storm hit!" Dad went on. "Won't that be fantastic!"

"Oh, James, you mustn't!" Mother protested.

"Won't that be dangerous?" Michael asked. I looked at him with astonishment and more than a little dismay. He sounded as if he might actually be considering Dad's suggestion. Much as I adored my father, I'd always sworn never to get involved with someone who did the kind of crazy things Dad did. And yet, there it was again: I could see on Michael's face that same look of lovable but daft enthusiasm. Oh dear, I thought. Dad had spread a small map of Monhegan over the coffee table and was scribbling madly on it—apparently trying to calculate the best spot to await the hurricane's arrival. Michael leaned over to watch.

"Count me out," Rob said. "I have to work on Lawyers from Hell."

Mother sighed. The whole family was still anxiously waiting to see if Rob had, by chance, passed the bar exam in July. Since he and his bar exam review group had whiled away the summer inventing a role-playing game called Lawyers from Hell instead of doing anything that even vaguely resembled studying, the odds were slim.

"I really ought to be back in Yorktown working on it," Rob said. What he meant was that he wanted to be back in Yorktown talking about bits and bytes with Red, his new girlfriend, who was helping him turn Lawyers from Hell into a computer game.

"How on earth did you get here anyway?" I asked, taking Rob aside.

"We came over on the ferry yesterday," he said.

"Well, I figured out that much," I said. "I meant, what are all of you doing up here in the first place?"

"Dad called to say they were flying home from Paris and could I meet them at Dulles Airport," Rob said. "Their plane got in very early yesterday morning. And Aunt Phoebe and Mrs. Fenniman hitched a ride up to Washington with me so they could catch a flight to Maine to go birding. But the flight got canceled because of the hurricane, and instead of going back to Yorktown, Aunt Phoebe convinced Mother and Dad to come up here with her. What are you doing here?"

"Looking for a little privacy," Michael put in.

"Good luck," Rob said with a snicker, and slipped out of the room—probably to call Red and indulge in a little long-distance whining. Or heavy breathing.

Well, Rob isn't the only one doomed to disappointment in his love life for the immediate future, I thought, glancing at Michael as I sat back down beside him. Here I was, sitting with the man of my dreams on an overstuffed sofa by a roaring fire, just as I'd imagined in my fantasies about this weekend. But having to share the experience with my entire family took a lot of the fun out of it.

I felt guilty about resenting their presence. They were all trying so hard to make us feel better. Of course, this meant that every five minutes one of them would pop up with either a new remedy for seasickness or a new tactic for preventing pneumonia. And I'd taken a head count and compared it to the number of bedrooms and figured out that I'd probably be sleeping on one of the sofas.

"Now the phone's out," Rob announced, shuffling back into the room and throwing himself on the other sofa.

"Usually happens in a storm," Aunt Phoebe said, shoving a cup of herbal tea into my hands.

"I wouldn't mind so much if I could just use my laptop," Rob said.

"Can't you just run it on battery?" Michael asked.

"I could, except the battery's old; it only holds about a fifteen-minute charge," Rob said. "And it takes me ten minutes to boot up and figure out how to open my word processor."

"I tell you what," Dad said. "Let's run an extension cord up to the Dickermans' house. I'm sure they wouldn't mind."

Whether the Dickermans would mind or not was irrelevant; I doubted they could resist Dad when he got his mind set on doing something.

"Ugh," Rob said, and sneezed. A patently phony sneeze, I thought; obviously designed to serve as an excuse for not sloshing out in the rain with Dad. But it served its purpose. Mother, Aunt Phoebe, and Mrs. Fenniman immediately turned their full attention to medicating Rob. I took advantage of the distraction to pour my herbal tea into an already-moribund potted plant.

"Come on, Meg; you can help me run the extension cord," Dad said, picking up a flashlight. "You, too, Michael. Fresh air will do you a world of good."

I didn't really want to go back out into the rain. I wanted to curl up someplace quiet and sleep for a few years. But it didn't look as if I'd get any peace and quiet in the cottage for a while, with Aunt Phoebe and Mrs. Fenniman arguing about the weather and trying to pour their potions and philters into me. Not to mention the way my stomach reacted to the smell of all the food. Maybe fresh air was a good idea. I sighed, then got up and followed Dad and Michael to the coatrack beside the kitchen door, where we rummaged through a rather random collection of rain gear. We finally found slickers for all three of us, though Michael's was too short, mine nearly dragged the ground, and Dad's was glow-in-the-dark pink with lime green and yellow spots.

Then we repeated the rummaging, this time in the garden

shed. Underneath a hand-cranked ice-cream freezer, a collection of antique life jackets, a gas grill, odd parts of three unmatched croquet sets, and several dozen mildewing stacks of *Life* magazines from the forties and fifties, we finally unearthed three bright orange industrial-weight extension cords.

"That should do the trick," Dad said, and we set off for the Dickermans' house.

I'd forgotten how dark Monhegan nights could be. In clear weather, you could see three times as many stars as in the city, and the sight of the moon rising over the ocean could inspire even me to poetry. But when clouds obscured the moon and stars, as they did tonight, you could really understand the deep-seated human tendency to fear the dark.

The darkness relented only slightly when we passed by our nearest neighbors, with whom Aunt Phoebe shared her treacherous, muddy little lane. Like Aunt Phoebe, they had only oil lamps and gas appliances. Some residents ran their own small electrical generators—including, apparently, the Dickermans—but these contraptions were noisy and generally less reliable than the old-fashioned alternatives—not to mention so expensive that their owners tended to keep their wattage low to avoid bankruptcy.

The flashlight wasn't much help, and I felt strangely comforted by the luminous glow of Dad's raincoat as he bobbed along ahead of us.

Suddenly, just as we reached the head of the lane, the glow disappeared.

"Dad?" I called, and hurried to reach the point where I'd last seen the glow-in-the-dark raincoat. I tripped over something large and hard and fell flat on my face in the gravel road.

"Your luggage is here," Dad said. The glow hadn't disappeared entirely, I realized; it was now—like me—horizontal.

"Are you two all right?" Michael said, coming up beside us.

"I will be if you take your foot off my hand," I said, trying not to make it sound like an accusation.

"Sorry," he said. "I can't see a thing."

"Damn that little weasel," I said. "He might at least have run the luggage up to the house."

"Maybe he was scared of getting stuck in the mud," Michael suggested.

"Well, we can take it up on the way back," Dad said. "Let's get up to the Dickermans' house before they go to bed."

The Dickermans, to my surprise, were thrilled to have Dad run a power cord down to our house. Of course, Dad had forgotten to mention that this was a commercial arrangement, the Dickermans being the founders and owners of the Central Monhegan Power Company.

"I didn't know Monhegan even had a central power company," I said. "Of course, it's been several years since I've spent much time on the island," I added hastily, seeing the hurt look on Mr. Dickerman's broad, friendly face.

"Well, really it's only one generator," Mr. Dickerman said. "Quite a bit larger than the ones individual households and businesses use, of course."

"And a bit quieter, obviously, if you've got it anywhere around here."

"Oh, it's noisy enough, but we've put it up on Knob Hill," Mr. Dickerman said. "It's pretty much out of the way up there, and the noise doesn't bother folks as much. Jim does most of the work on it; he's always been handy that way, Jim has."

"And so nice that he's found something to do without leaving the island," Mrs. Dickerman put in. She was a sweet, motherly person; I never could figure out how she and her mild-mannered husband had managed to produce so many rowdy and unpleasant sons, at least half a dozen of them. "All my other birds have flown the coop, but Jimmy's happy as a clam, staying here with us, where he can tinker with the generator. Does you good to see how happy he is, up at the electric plant, when he's working on those machines of his."

"Don't forget Fred," Mr. Dickerman put in.

"Fred's only here between jobs," Mrs. Dickerman said. "You remember Jimmy, don't you, Meg?"

I did, actually, with something that approached fondness—he was the one Dickerman of my generation who wasn't loud, extroverted, and an inveterate bully. The worst had been Fred, whom I now recognized as the driver of the truck and kidnapper of our luggage. But Jimmy had been a small, intense, bespectacled little boy, whose main interest in life was taking things apart. He and Dad got along well that way, although, unlike Dad, Jimmy could also put the things back together again. When he felt like it, which was seldom. I wondered how much time the Central Monhegan Power Company's generator ran and how much time it spent disassembled for maintenance, enhancements, and general tinkering.

"Maybe if she sees how useful the electricity can be, Phoebe might see her way clear to hooking on," Mr. Dickerman suggested.

"Maybe," Dad said. "But then again, you know what a traditionalist Phoebe is."

"She is that," Mr. Dickerman agreed. "We could have used her here this spring, when the town council was squabbling over what to do about Victor Resnick's new house."

"Victor Resnick? The landscape artist?" Michael asked.

"That's the one," Mr. Dickerman said. He didn't sound all that fond of the local celebrity, and I suspected Resnick was the Victor Winnie and Binkie Burnham had been so dismayed to see on the docks.

"Monhegan has quite a lot of famous artists," I said

aloud. "One of the Wyeths lives here, too; or at least he used to. I forget which one."

"I thought Resnick had moved to Europe," Dad said, frowning.

"Came back last fall and built himself a new house," Mr. Dickerman said. "A real eyesore. Ought to run the bastard off the island."

"Frank!" Mrs. Dickerman scolded.

"Well, they ought to," Mr. Dickerman said.

Dad seemed unusually subdued as he and Mr. Dickerman finished hooking up the extension cord and making the arrangements for payment. He was deep in thought during the whole return trip to the cottage—which wasn't exactly a bad thing. Instead of returning by the road, we had to run the extension cord as directly as possible to Aunt Phoebe's—which meant slogging through the Dickermans' overgrown backyard, followed by a brier-filled gully, and then the cord barely reached the living room. Even in our debilitated state, Michael and I probably managed it much better by ourselves than we would have if Dad had insisted on taking an active hand.

Rob pounced on the cord with glee, hooked up his computer, and began tapping away on the keyboard—though whether he was doing useful work or merely composing an e-mail he could send to Red when the phone lines returned, I had no idea. Dad took advantage of the power supply to hook up his portable CD player and put on his beloved Wagner. And then he scurried out of the room again, after turning up the volume enough that he could hear it from anyplace in the cottage. From anyplace on the island, probably; lucky for us the phones were down, or ours would have rung off the hook with noise complaints.

I glanced at Michael to see how he was taking all this. At least so far, he seemed more amused than annoyed. That was one of Michael's charms: his tolerance for my father's eccentricities seemed as great as mine.

Possibly greater, I thought as the orchestra sank its teeth into a loud, rousing passage of the overture.

The opera was just hitting its stride when the music stopped in the middle of one of Brünnhilde more appalling shrieks.

CHAPTER 4

A Portrait of the Puffin as a
Young Man

In the sudden absence of Wagner, we heard Aunt Phoebe's voice bellowing in the kitchen.

"Never would have come out here in the first place if we'd had any idea we'd run into that son of a—"

"Sshh!" Mrs. Fenniman hissed, and then, a little louder, she called out, "What happened to the power?"

"Oh dear," Mother said, looking up from her magazine. "Not the generator already?"

"I hope I can save in time," Rob said, fingers flying over the keyboard.

"Maybe someone tripped over the cord," I said. "We should go see if—"

"Damnation!" came a voice just outside the windows.

"I don't think you'll have to go far," Michael remarked.

The music came back on, almost drowning out the loud footsteps stomping up the porch steps. Carrying Michael's and my suitcases, Dad appeared in the doorway with blood running down his face from a cut on the top of his head.

"James! What happened?" Mother cried, leaping up.

"Tripped over the extension cord," Dad said. "Don't fuss; it's not serious. Scalp wounds do bleed a lot."

"The suitcases," Michael said, rushing over to take our luggage from Dad. "I'm so sorry; I forgot they were there. I should have gone back for them."

"Not to worry," Dad said. He picked up his black doctor's bag and scurried off to clean up his cut, with Mother trailing in his wake.

Dad brushed off all our attempts at sympathy.

"I'll be fine," he said when he returned, sporting a picturesque dressing on his head. "I'll just sit here and listen to my Wagner and I'll feel better in no time."

After that, of course, guilt prevented us from even asking him to turn it down a little.

Dad hummed and conducted with his fork quite happily for what seemed like an eternity but must have been only an hour or two. Fortunately, before the neighbors showed up at our door bearing torches, like the villagers in a bad horror movie, the power went out again.

"Probably just someone else tripping over the extension cords," Dad said.

We waited for a few minutes, but no sounds of cursing came from the yard.

"I suppose I'll have to follow the line up to the Dickermans," Dad said with a sigh.

"I don't think so," I said, peering out a window. "The Dickermans' house is dark. And listen."

Everyone cocked their heads and listened intently for a few seconds.

"I don't hear anything," Mother said finally. "Just the wind."

"That's just it," I said. "I've heard this persistent rhythmic humming noise ever since we got to the island. I thought the hurricane was doing it. But now I realize it's the generator."

"She's right," Aunt Phoebe said. "I've complained to the town council about that noise. You don't notice it as much when a hurricane's approaching, but in normal weather, it's a menace. Much more peaceful like this, when the generator stops."

Deprived of his Wagner, Dad decided he was tired, and Mother agreed that perhaps an early night would be a good idea. Since by my calculations they'd covered more than three thousand miles by plane, boat, and automobile over the last forty-eight hours, I wasn't surprised. And the thought occurred to me that if the rest of the family got tired and went to bed, Michael and I might still rescue some shreds of our romantic evening by the fire.

Unfortunately, no one else seemed the slightest bit fatigued. Aunt Phoebe and Mrs. Fenniman were still out in the kitchen, cooking under the soft glow of the oil lamps. Rob wandered about restlessly for a while. Eventually, I could hear him opening the trapdoor and letting down the ladder to the attic. He scuffled around up there for a while, then reappeared with an armload of old volumes.

"What are those?" Michael asked.

"Photo albums that Aunt Phoebe likes to keep around at the cottage," Rob said. "She says when people have electricity, they're too busy with TV and computers and stuff to look at old photos."

"Well, she's right, isn't she?" Michael said. "What were you doing before the power went out?"

Rob shrugged sheepishly and picked up an album.

"Actually, Rob usually does spend time with the photo albums," I said. "It must be the charm of seeing variations on your own face, wearing so many old-fashioned hairdos and clothes, Rob."

"You could be right," Rob said. "Look at this. Great-Uncle Christopher."

He held up a picture. But for the handlebar mustache and dandified Edwardian clothes, you could easily have mistaken it for a picture of Rob.

"He looks rather dashing in the uniform on the next page, too," Michael said. "World War One?"

"Yes," Rob said, assuming a solemn air. "Poor Uncle Christopher!"

"He never came back?" Michael said. Rob shook his head and sighed, as if the whole thing were a tragedy from which the family had never recovered.

"Yes," I said. "Killed in a brawl in a French bordello, apparently; though they made up something else to tell his mother."

Michael laughed, and Rob looked as insulted as if I'd impugned his character, instead of that of our late and little-lamented great-uncle. He pointedly buried his face in the album. Michael picked up another volume and began to flip through it.

"Don't you enjoy the albums, too?" he asked. "Seeing your face through history and all that?"

"I suppose I would, but apparently I look like Dad's side of the family," I said. "None of the pictures look much like me."

I didn't mention the other reason: that looking in the albums usually triggered a temporary but acute resurgence of the inferiority complex I'd fought all my life. Far too many of my female ancestors had been tall, thin, aristocratic blondes, like Mother; and the albums contained far too many pictures of them surrounded by the swarms of beautiful, wealthy, and sometimes famous men who'd courted them.

The album Michael had picked up, for instance. Looking over his shoulder, I could see that it held hundreds of photos from the late forties and early fifties, all neatly arranged and held in place with old-fashioned black paper photo corners. The early pictures, featuring the angelic preadolescent Mother, were bad enough. But looking at her at thirteen, when she'd already acquired a figure and a flock of admirers, I could feel myself fighting off those old feelings of inadequacy.

It helps a little that none of the men were as gorgeous as Michael is, I thought, looking fondly at him and curling a little closer. And that many of them ought not to have allowed themselves to be photographed in swimsuits, although I suppose I was applying today's fitness standards to bodies not considered unattractive fifty years ago. Perhaps the kind of lean, tanned, muscular body modern women consider attractive in a man would have been a dead giveaway, back in those more class-conscious times, that its owner earned his living from some kind of badly paid manual labor.

But still; seeing picture after picture of Mother surrounded by half a dozen obviously smitten men—well, it got depressing. And the occasional suitor whose face appeared a little too often, who always wangled a place right beside Mother in the group shots, who occasionally managed to ditch the crowd and have his picture taken with Mother, as a couple—for some reason, they made me anxious. I couldn't help wondering if but for some strange accident or other, she might have married one of them. And where would I be then?

"I think some of them have fallen out," Michael said, coming to a page with several empty sets of corners.

"More likely, they're pictures Mother considered unflattering," I said. The other nearby pictures were all of Mother posing in a two-piece bathing suit. While the suit looked demure enough by today's standards, I suspected that forty-odd years ago, it had been daring enough to give my grandfather conniption fits.

We stayed up for a while, looking at the albums—at least Rob and Michael were looking, and I was half-dozing against Michael's shoulder. Even after Rob yawned his way upstairs with an album under his arm, Mrs. Fenniman and Aunt Phoebe kept bustling in and out of the living room at frequent intervals to make sure Michael and I weren't getting ill. Michael finally said good night. He found about a dozen excuses to pop back downstairs when everything seemed quiet, but we finally gave up trying to find a few moments alone together and said an awkward good night, with Mrs. Fenniman at our elbows, pressing cough lozenges into our hands.

If I hadn't been doomed to spend the night on the sofa, I'd have felt very sorry for Michael. He was sharing with Rob what we referred to as "the children's room"—a former walk-in closet fitted with a set of rickety bunk beds half a foot too short for either of them. Far from ideal, but since no one could reasonably expect Aunt Phoebe or Mrs. Fenniman to scramble into an upper bunk, they were stuck with it.

I made a bed for myself on the less lumpy of the two living room sofas. But I didn't get to sleep right away. Mrs. Fenniman and Aunt Phoebe continued their culinary efforts until well past midnight. Either they planned to invite the whole island over very soon or they expected to be stranded for a very long time. Both prospects appalled me.

They kept trying to talk me into sleeping on a floor pallet in their room. Since Aunt Phoebe's snoring had helped inspire my flight from Yorktown, and Mrs. Fenniman was just as bad, I resisted their suggestions with every argument I could muster, including the pretense that I still felt dizzy from the ferry and didn't want to risk the stairs, which let me in for another round of foul-tasting herbal remedies.

They finally tramped up to bed, still arguing about whether Hurricane Maude or Hurricane Ethel had been the most devastating storm to hit the island in previous years. After another hour or so of people stumbling in and out of the bathroom, dropping their flashlights, barking their shins on things, and swearing with varying degrees of verbal ingenuity, the house finally settled down and I dropped off to sleep.

I'd probably gotten a whole hour's sleep by the time the Central Monhegan Power Company's generator started up again. And I'd have slept through that easily if Dad, while trying to turn his Wagner off, hadn't turned the CD player's volume dial the wrong way and cranked it up to the maximum.

My second awakening of the morning was quieter, although no less nerve-racking. I woke up realizing that I needed to go to the bathroom. Luckily, before I leapt off the sofa, I noticed a small, warm weight lying on top of me. Spike.

Because I'd once rescued him from dire peril, Spike had decided I was the one person in the world he liked, other than Mrs. Waterston. Unfortunately, since his memory was as bad as his temper, Spike periodically forgot who Mrs. Waterston and I were. Which made him more dangerous to us than to the people he didn't like. At least they could keep their distance. He was always trying to climb into our laps to be petted, which brought us within easy chewing distance when he suddenly decided to mistake us for the dreaded mail carrier.

Mrs. Waterston took this a lot more philosophically than I did. Why couldn't Michael's mother have adopted a cat, for heaven's sake, instead of an overbred nine-pound dust mop?

I knew from experience that Spike was a lot more likely to bite you if you woke him up suddenly than if you let him wake up at his own pace. And you learned to give him a wide berth for the first hour or two, until he'd had his walk and his breakfast.

I lay there, growing increasingly uncomfortable as Spike slumbered, unbelievably loud snores issuing from his tiny pushed-in nose. Finally, around dawn, he heard Aunt Phoebe rattling pans in the kitchen and ran off to see if it was raining food in there.

"You look tired," Michael said over breakfast.

" 'The Ride of the Valkyries' is not my idea of a lullaby," I said, frowning at Dad. "It's a wonder I have any hearing left, as loud as that damned thing was."

"Remarkable speakers, aren't they?" Dad said.

"Hurry up with breakfast," I whispered to Michael. "We need to talk."

"Okay," Michael said—a little too loudly, for he found he'd agreed to a second helping of Mrs. Fenniman's undercooked grits.

"Well, the damned storm's stalled again," Mrs. Fenniman announced.

"Is the ferry running?" Rob asked.

"I said stalled, not gone away," Mrs. Fenniman replied. "Just close enough to keep the ferry from running, but not close enough to bother us much. Not yet anyway. Looks like we'll have good weather for another day."

I glanced out at the gray sky and the faint but steady drizzle. Yes, this would be Mrs. Fenniman's idea of good weather.

Michael and I managed to escape the house without anyone else tagging along, although Dad insisted that we each shoulder a backpack filled with several pounds of survival gear that we might need if we got lost for a few weeks. And Aunt Phoebe gave us a long list of errands she wanted us to run down in the village.

"You'd think the village was in Siberia," I complained as we finally escaped down the lane. "It's not as if it would take them ten minutes to walk down here themselves."

"If it keeps them happy," Michael said. He looked a lot more rested than I felt, and when he shook the water out of his hair, he resembled a hunk from a commercial for deodorant soap. I could feel my hair, initially frizzy from the damp, being matted down by the rain; no doubt I'd soon resemble a drowned rat.

"How did you sleep?" I asked.

"Your brother snores," he said.

"So does Spike."

"Spike doesn't talk in his sleep."

"Did Rob say anything interesting?"

"No, and if I hear another word about Lawyers from Hell . . ."

"I'm really sorry," I said. "It's all my fault; I should never have suggested coming here."

"Let's make a deal," Michael said. "I won't blame you for anything that goes wrong if you promise to stop apologizing for bringing me here. After all, if my damned car hadn't had those two flats, we might have spotted them before boarding the ferry the day before yesterday, and we could have changed our plans and found a bed-and-breakfast on the mainland."

"It's a deal," I said.

"So let's go down to the grocery store and see if they still have any of the things your aunt wants."

"We should probably hit both grocery stores," I said as we squelched down the road.

"Both grocery stores? How can an island this small possibly support two grocery stores?"

"The two of them together are smaller than a Seven-Eleven back home. And they serve slightly different clientele. There's the upscale grocery store—in that salmon pink building with the turquoise trim," I said, pointing down the road. "Caters more to the artists and the summer people; probably does a lot less business this time of year. Sells Brie and whole-grain bread from an organic bakery on the mainland. Nice selection of wines. The place that looks like a bait shop is the other grocery. More like a general store, really. Bologna and Wonder Bread, and a good variety of beers. They do a lot more steady year-round business, I should think."

"Let's start with the down-to-earth place," Michael said. "There's something obscenely decadent about eating Brie in the eye of a hurricane."

Decadent or not, it sounded perfectly lovely to me, but Michael was obviously getting into the spirit of things, roughing it here on the island, so I didn't argue.

"Actually, since we already have more food than we'll ever eat, I thought we could leave the grocery store till later," I said. "Maybe we should start with our other mission."

"Other mission?"

"Finding you a room of your own. One without a roommate."

"One where I might possibly entertain a friend without

being interrupted every five minutes to drink another cup of herbal tea?" he said, raising one eyebrow.

"You've got the idea."

"I like the way you think," he said.

CHAPTER 5

These Puffins Were Made for Walkin'

We tried. We really did. The Monhegan House's three dozen rooms were filled with birders. The Island Inn was full, as well. Overflowing, in fact. I'd forgotten about the oversupply of birders.

"We've called up everyone on the island, trying to find rooms for them all," the owner of the Island Inn explained. "We even have a bunch of birders camping out down in the church."

"Well, so much for peace and quiet and privacy," Michael said. "I assume on an island this size, everyone has a pretty good idea who has a vacancy and who doesn't?"

"On an island this size, everyone has a pretty good idea who's running low on corn flakes and toilet paper," I said. "I think we can take it as a given that there's no room at the inn. Any inn."

So by 9:00 A.M.—an hour when I normally prefer to be fast asleep—we had already given up on our search. We sat for a few minutes on a soggy wooden swing on the front porch of the Island Inn and watched the pedestrians hiking up and down the streets. The rain had temporarily slacked off to a mere icy mist, and both birds and birders made the most of it. I only caught fleeting glimpses of the birds, but I was getting to know the plumage and feeding habits of the common New England bird-watcher pretty well.

Actually, at first glance, it was hard to tell the locals from the bird-watchers. Everyone had some kind of waterproof footgear, with the unfortunate exception of Michael and me. Rain ponchos and down vests were commonplace.

I wondered if it had occurred to any of them how many birds had given their all to fill those vests.

But while most of the locals scurried about with canvas tote bags full of supplies and bits of lumber for boarding things up, the birders carried enough waterproof surveillance hardware to equip a squad of Navy SEALS. Binoculars, telescopes, cameras, tape recorders, video cameras—you name it, they had it.

Every couple of minutes, a troop of birders would swarm up the steps of the inn and ask us where we'd been and what we'd seen and whether we'd spotted the kestrels up on Black Head yet. When we explained that we hadn't been anywhere or seen any birds and thought the kestrels up on Black Head had enough company already, they would look at us oddly and slip inside to refill their thermoses with hot coffee.

"Apart from going back to the cottage and listening to more Wagner, what else is there to do on the island?" Michael asked.

"We could stroll through the village and see the sights," I said.

Just then, Fred Dickerman rattled by in his pickup truck, leaning on the horn, while a quartet of birders sprinted just ahead of his bumper. Monhegan has no sidewalks; any pedestrian walking in the road when a truck approached was expected to step aside to let the vehicle pass. Or jump aside, if the driver was Fred. Most truck drivers took it slowly when they went through the village, but Fred evidently enjoyed chivvying tourists into puddles and brier patches.

"Reminds me of running before the bulls at Pamplona," Michael remarked as the birders finally reached a wide spot in the road and hurled themselves to safety.

"Oh, have you actually done that?"

"No, and I'm not about to start now," he said. "Doesn't look too restful, strolling through the village. Anything else?"

"Mostly healthy, outdoorsy things like hiking around the circumference of the island."

"All right, let's hike," Michael said, standing up and holding out his hand.

"You've got to be kidding. In this weather?"

"It's not actually raining now, and the weather's going to be a lot worse in a few hours," he said. "Let's go and see the sights before it gets bad."

"You're serious, aren't you?"

"Why not? At least once we've done it, when the birders ask us if we want to go to the South Pole with them to see the penguins, we can say, 'No thanks, we've already circumnavigated the island.' "

"Okay," I said. "You're on."

I could tell after the first fifteen minutes that circumnavigating the island was a lot less fun to do than to brag about afterward. But I wasn't about to confess that I couldn't handle it, so for the next hour or two, we squelched and slopped up and down the muddy parts of the trail and inched our way gingerly over the rain-slick rocky parts.

And invariably, every time we paused, panting, to catch our breath, a covey of middle-aged or elderly birders would breeze past us.

"I always thought bird-watching was a sedate pastime," Michael said as we took temporary refuge beneath a rocky outcropping that sheltered us from the worst of the drizzle. "These people could probably ace an Iron Man competition."

"Yes. Stirs up all my deep-seated feelings of inadequacy," I said, panting slightly.

"Oh, I don't know," Michael said, putting an arm around my waist. "You look pretty adequate to me."

It wasn't exactly the tropical beach of my dreams, but this was the closest I'd gotten to being alone with Michael since we'd arrived on the island. I snuggled closer, and he bent his head down toward mine. Then he froze.

"Why are those people watching us through their binoculars?" he muttered.

I followed the direction of his eye.

"I think they're looking at that bird at our feet," I whispered back.

"Why? Is that some kind of rare and exotic bird?"

I glanced down. The bird was moderately large, light brown, with a black-and-white mask over its face. It had bits of red and yellow on its wings, and the end of its tail had been dipped in yellow.

"How the devil should I know?" I said. "It looks like a paint-spattered female cardinal; cardinals certainly aren't rare."

"Damn," Michael said, a little more loudly this time.

The bird, whatever it was, took flight.

The three birders removed the binoculars from their eyes and stared at us accusingly.

"That was a Bohemian waxwing," one of them said.

"Did you get any photos?" the second asked.

"No," said the third. "They frightened it off before I got the chance."

"Oh, you mean that bird with the yellow-tipped tail?" I asked.

The birders nodded and frowned at us. Madame Defarge looked more kindly on her victims.

"We've seen them around here a lot," I said.

"They're quite rare in this part of the continent," one of the birders replied.

"Yes, that's what I was telling Michael," I said. "How rare to see so many Bohemian waxwings here. If you just stay quietly where you are, you'll probably see dozens."

With that, Michael and I fled down the path, until we had rounded a corner and could collapse in gales of laughter.

"Bohemian waxwings?" Michael spluttered. "That can't possibly be a real bird."

"I'm sure it is," I said, peeping around the corner. The three birders had hunched down by the path and were on the alert, scanning the landscape through their binoculars, one looking left, one right, and the third straight out toward the ocean.

"Come on," I said. "Let's get out of here, in case the Bohemian waxwing has flown the coop completely."

We giggled intermittently over the antics of the birders for the next hour or so. But the day got colder and damper, and every time we rounded a headland that I thought would bring us to the end of our journey, we'd encounter another stretch of path. And another flock of birders.

In one place, I spotted the remains of a campsite back in the trees, some distance from the trail.

"How odd," I said. "Let's go take a look at this."

"What's so odd?" Michael asked. "Looks like someone camped here."

"Definitely," I said, using my foot to rake leaves away from a charred spot. "You can see where they had a fire, right here, and they buried something over there. Garbage, I guess"

"Beer cans, mostly," Michael said, looking down at the trash-disposal area. "Someone had quite a party."

The unknown campers had buried their empties on the side of a hill, and the heavy rain had washed away a good deal of the covering dirt, exposing a vein of silver-and-blue aluminum cans.

"Definitely odd," I murmured.

"Yes, I should think conditions back in the village are primitive enough to satisfy even the most discriminating masochist. What kind of nut would come all the way over to this side of the island for even more Spartan conditions?"

"Well, I'm sure some people want to," I said. "But it's illegal. No camping permitted. To protect the fragile eco-system on the undeveloped side of the island. And definitely no open fires. Normally, they're very quick to chase off anyone who tries."

"Maybe they did," Michael said. "Whoever did it is long gone."

Still, I couldn't help fretting as we hiked, and looking for further signs of neglect or environmental damage. I thought of summers past when Dad, Aunt Phoebe, and the rest of their generation would denounce some new change to the island. I'd thought them tiresome, a little cracked on the subject of keeping Monhegan unspoiled. And yet, here I was, fretting about the same thing.

At least until my energy began to flag again.

"Maybe it's my imagination," I said, stopping to pant. "But the path around the island seems longer than it did when I was a little kid."

"Your father used to let you walk around this path?" Michael said, peering over the edge of a precipice to the surf crashing twenty feet below.

"Let us? He'd insist on it. He thought it was good exercise. If we didn't voluntarily hike around the island every few days, he'd drag us along on a nature walk."

"And he was never prosecuted for child abuse? Amazing. I hope he at least insisted that you learn to swim before turning you loose on these cliffs."

"Technically, yes; though I don't see what good swimming would do anyone who fell off the cliffs. The undertow could drag away a small submarine, and if the undertow didn't get you, the waves would pound you to death against the rocks."

"What a vacation paradise," Michael said, chuckling as we resumed our hike. "I see why he brought you here; the place is as escapeproof as Alcatraz. He wouldn't have to worry about you sneaking over to the mainland and getting into any trouble."

"We managed anyway," I said. "The sneaking over to the mainland part anyway; we never could find much trouble when we got there. But you can reach the mainland quite easily if you know someone with a small boat. Not in weather like this, of course."

"Oh, the weather's not that bad," Michael said. "Great weather for sitting around by the fire."

"Sorry. Hiking wasn't that good an idea, was it?"

"Nonsense. It was a great idea," Michael said, smiling over his shoulder at me before turning and beginning to climb the next hill. "The scenery's fantastic, and when we get back to the cottage, I'll appreciate the fire all the more."

If only we could appreciate it by ourselves, I thought, pausing for a moment to enjoy the view of Michael's long legs as he jumped over a small gully that interrupted the path. Perhaps if all the rest of the family went hiking. But no, the weather would soon be too foul for hiking. And anyway, Mother never hiked. Turn her loose in a mall, or, better yet, on a street lined with quaint boutiques and expensive shops, and she could walk combat-trained marines into the ground, but here on Monhegan, there wasn't much shopping, even in the summer. How could we possibly get Mother out of the house? I sighed.

"Tired?" Michael asked, looking down at me. I shook my head.

"Just figuring where we are," I said. "It can't be too much farther. I'm sure we're getting close to the village."

"You said that an hour ago," he said, chuckling.

"That was wishful thinking," I said. "Now that I've gotten my bearings back, not to mention my second wind, I know exactly where we are. Just over the next hill we're going to see a quaint little shack that's been converted to an artist's studio. It's on a headland with one of the most spectacular views of the island."

"Over this hill?" Michael said. He had reached the top and paused to catch his breath.

"Yes. Look a little to your right. You should be able to see it peeping through the trees."

"Yes, that's quite a quaint little shack."

I reached his side and looked down, expecting to see one of my favorite rustic Monhegan landscapes. Instead, I saw a glittering, spiky forest of steel beams and glass plates.

"Wrong hill again?" Michael said.

"No, it's the right hill. I recognize the view, at least what little we can see of it behind that monstrosity. What the hell is it anyway? Some horrible new piece of weather equipment from the Coast Guard?"

"A rather large and very modern house," Michael said.

He was right, of course; when I'd stared at it a few minutes, the jumble resolved itself into something resembling doors, walls, and windows.

"I wonder how in the world they got permission to build it," I said. "The town council is very conservative about new development. It took Aunt Phoebe two years to get permission to expand her deck."

"We did hear the Dickermans saying that someone's new house was an eyesore."

"Yes, but around here, that just means someone painted the house the wrong shade of blue," I said. "Or painted it at all, instead of just allowing it to fade to the usual, tasteful weather-beaten gray. This is more than an eyesore; it's an abomination."

"I don't think the house itself is all that bad," Michael said, squinting at it. "Not my cup of tea, but you have to admit it's striking."

"True," I said, sighing. "Anywhere else I might actually find it interesting, although I can't imagine living in something that bare and modern. But here on Monhegan, it's completely out of place."

"No argument from me," Michael said.

"I was going to suggest stopping to enjoy the view, but I've changed my mind," I said. "Let's hurry up and get past that eyesore."

"Fine by me," Michael said.

We started down the hill, Michael again in the lead. I was craning my neck, trying to see something of sea and sky beyond the abomination, and mentally composing scathing letters to the town council, when—

"Look out!" Michael yelled. He ran back up the path a few feet, knocked me to the ground, and threw himself on top of me. I heard a sharp noise somewhere, and then a lot of sand and pebbles sifted down on us from higher up the hill.

"What's going on?"

"Some lunatic is shooting at us!" Michael said.

CHAPTER 6

They Shoot Puffins, Don't They?

Another shot rang out. Wonderful, I thought; now I know what getting shot at sounds like. Michael flinched, and I thought for an awful moment he'd been hit.

"Are you all right?" I asked.

"I'll be fine as soon as I know we're out of gunshot range."

"Excellent idea," I said. "Let me up; I can't get out of gunshot range with you on top of me."

"Right," he said. He jumped up, pulled me to my feet, and began dragging me up the path.

"Hang on a minute," I said, looking back over my shoulder when we got to the top of the hill. "He's not shooting now. Let's see what's going on."

"Keep your head down, then."

We both crouched on the path, peeking over the top of the rise at the lunatic below: a tall, gaunt man, all angles and elbows, with a bushy beard and long gray-streaked hair that looked as if he'd attempted, with limited success, to cultivate dreadlocks. He wore a baggy, shapeless, partially unraveled fisherman's sweater over paint-splattered olive corduroys. He stood with his left hand on his hip while his right held a long gun—a rifle or a shotgun, I supposed. He wasn't aiming it at anything, but he looked ready to. He stared up the path as if waiting for us to emerge again. If he planned on standing there with the gun, he'd have a long wait.

"He looks familiar," I said.

"Don't tell me he's one of your relatives?"

"Good heavens, no!" I said. "Do you really think my relatives would do something like that?"

Michael didn't answer.

"Okay, some of them *might* be crazy enough to shoot at the tourists, but none of them would have the bad taste to build that house."

"You have a point there," Michael said, chuckling. "So what do we do now?"

"Good question," I said. "We could turn around and go back the way we came."

"God no," Michael muttered. Perversely, it made me feel a little better that he hadn't enjoyed the last few rain-soaked, mud-infested hours of hiking quite as much as he'd pretended to.

"Let's try to talk to him, then."

"Talk to him?"

Just then, the man started up the path toward us.

"Damn," Michael said, "We'd better turn back after all."

"Don't come any closer!" I shouted.

The man with the gun ignored me.

"Stay where you are! I mean it!" I shouted, and lobbed a baseball-sized rock down at him. Well, not directly at him—I could have hit him if I'd wanted to—but in his general direction. Close enough to get his attention.

The rock bounced and tumbled down, taking quite a collection of pebbles and sticks with it. The man stopped and then backed up a few paces. I grabbed another rock and held it at the ready.

"Why the hell are you shooting at us?" I yelled.

"This is private property," he yelled back. "You're trespassing!"

"Trespassing?" I shouted. I stood up, ignoring Michael's frantic gestures. Foolish, perhaps, but somehow I didn't think that the man was going to shoot us. Not in front of witnesses. I could see a flock of birders peeking out of the woods at the other edge of his property, snapping away with their cameras.

"Trespassing?" I repeated. "Excuse me, quite apart from the fact that this trail has been a public right-of-way for generations, and assuming you do have some legal claim to keep people out, which I very much doubt—and I assure you that I intend to investigate very thoroughly—quite apart from that, were you planning to post any signs, or were you just going to kill off anyone not psychic enough to guess that you don't want them hiking here?"

"Meg," Michael said. He tugged on the leg of my jeans. I shook him off.

"There's a sign right there—" the man began, raising his hand to point and then stopping when he saw there wasn't a sign after all. "What the hell have you done with my sign?"

"Don't look at us," I said. "We just got here."

The man snorted in exasperation. He walked forward a few paces, then leaned his gun against a tree and reached down. He pried a battered sign out of the mud beside the path, picked up a large rock—possibly the one I'd thrown at him—and began hammering the sign back into the ground.

"I'm not kidding," he said, looking up from his work. "I'm fed up with people trespassing. And people knocking down my signs. I've served notice that this is private property, and I intend to enforce it."

"Well, serve notice a little more visibly from now on," I said, dodging Michael, who had despaired of making me crouch down again and was trying to put himself between me and the lunatic. "And speaking of serving notice, exactly who are you anyway? I'd like to know whom I'm going to ask the police to charge with attempted murder."

"You know perfectly well who I am!" the man shouted. He threw the rock in my direction, then reached for his gun. I quickly followed Michael's advice and we ducked behind the crest of the path, but instead of firing, the man stormed back toward the house. I suppressed a giggle; he was getting himself even grimier than before, stomping through the mud like that. And when he slammed the door, I burst out laughing: the huge, pretentious—and, no doubt, expensive—front door didn't fit quite right. Perhaps all the dampness had warped it. He had to spend several minutes wrestling it closed, his struggles clearly visible through the sweeping glass wall and slanted glass roof of the entrance hall.

"I'll refrain from saying anything about people who live in glass houses," Michael said. "But they shouldn't shoot rifles at people, either."

"And they definitely shouldn't live this close to the ocean," I said, giggling. A seagull had just flown in from the ocean, banked gracefully over the house, and landed, with a clumsy thud, on the glass roof of the entranceway, which was somewhat sheltered by the rest of the house from the full brunt of the wind. Several other gulls followed, and enough bird droppings coated the glass to show that this wasn't the first time the birds had discovered this refuge. The lunatic suddenly appeared behind the glass of the entranceway, causing both Michael and me to jump. The gulls, however, stared down unmoved as he thumped with a broom handle on the heavy plate glass beneath their feet.

"Serves him right," I said. "I hope that creep has to wash all those windows every day."

And he certainly had a lot of windows. In addition to the main house, we saw a smaller glass building nearby. A studio, apparently; while off-white curtains screened the lower six feet or so of its glass walls, from our place on the hill we could see the tips of several easels peeking over the top of the fabric. Even the nearby woodshed, while not made of glass, looked considerably newer, not to mention more expensive and stylish, than most of the actual houses on the island.

"Who on earth could possibly afford to build a place like this on Monhegan?" I wondered aloud. "Do you have any idea how much it costs to bring supplies and workmen over here?"

"Well, whoever he is, I'm sure he can afford to pay for a lawyer," Michael said. "Let's go back to the village and file charges against him."

"No sense tempting fate, though," I said. "Let's retrace our steps a bit; I think I can find a shortcut through the interior of the island."

As we retreated along the trail, I saw a flash of lavender disappear around a rock ahead of us. Somebody else watching our encounter with the mad hermit, no doubt. I nodded with satisfaction; it looked as if we'd have plenty of witnesses.

My shortcut didn't seem much shorter than going all the way back around the island, but at last we arrived at the village.

"I don't recall seeing a police station," Michael said. "Where are we going to report that lunatic?"

"There isn't a police station," I said. "They call the police over from the mainland when they need them. But a local resident acts as constable until the police arrive. Let's go into the general store and ask who it is."

We squished down the main drag until we reached the general store, then squelched up the front steps.

"I remember him," I said, pointing to a sign in the window that said JEBEDIAH BARNES, PROPRIETOR. "His family's run this place for two or three generations now."

"That's good," Michael said. "Maybe he'll remember you; otherwise, we may have a hard time making him believe what just happened."

The store was blissfully warm inside; an old-fashioned potbellied stove burned full blast, and a small crowd of local residents sat or stood around the stove, drinking coffee and listening to what sounded like an all-weather radio station. Hurricane Gladys still hovered offshore, according to the announcer.

Michael headed for the coffeepot while I strode over to the counter where the storekeeper stood.

"Where do I find the constable?" I asked him.

"You're looking at him," he said. "Jeb Barnes. What can I do for you?"

"I'd like to report an assault," I said.

CHAPTER 7

I Fought the Puffin and the Puffin Won

At the word *assault,* Jeb Barnes's jaw dropped, and the desultory conversation around the stove stopped cold. I could almost hear their ears turning in our direction. Jeb glanced nervously at Michael. He'd jumped to a very wrong conclusion, obviously; but at least I'd gotten his attention.

"Some lunatic fired a gun at us," I went on. "I realize you probably can't do anything until the storm passes and the ferry's running, but I'd like to make a report now so you can contact the mainland police as soon as possible."

"Fired a gun at you?" Jeb repeated. "Where?"

"We were trying to follow the public path around Puffin Point," I said.

The constable closed his eyes and sighed. Michael handed me a steaming cup of coffee and put some money down on the counter.

"Resnick again," said one of the locals by the stove.

"Crazy bastard," said another.

"Going to kill someone one of these days," said a third.

"He's done this before?" I asked. "And you haven't done anything?"

"We've formally warned him he has no right to block the path," Jeb Barnes said defensively. "And we're looking into the possibility of a lawsuit about that pile of junk he calls a house. We can't do anything about the alleged shooting incidents. No one who lives here wants to tick him off any more, and none of the damn fool tourists want to stay around to testify, so we haven't found anyone willing to press charges."

"Well, I will," I said. "I'm self-employed, so I can arrange my schedule to be here for the trial. And I'm sure Aunt Phoebe will let me use the cottage when I come back."

The constable sighed again. Here I was, offering to press charges against his biggest local scofflaw, and he wasn't acting the least bit grateful.

"You're Phoebe Hollingworth's niece?" he asked finally.

"Meg Langslow," I said, holding out my hand. Jeb Barnes shook it with obvious reluctance.

"One of them Hollingworths," I heard one of the locals mutter. "They'll take him on."

I was glad to see Mother's family name was still a force to be reckoned with here on Monhegan.

"Yeah, they're all crazy enough," agreed another local.

Well, I couldn't exactly argue with him. I heard Michael make a noise that sounded like a cough but had no doubt started out life as a chuckle. I decided to bring him onstage. Why should I have all the fun?

"And this is Michael Waterston, a family friend. I'm sure Professor Waterston will also want to press charges."

"Naturally," Michael said. "What a pity I haven't been admitted to the bar in Maine."

I had to hand it to Michael: he carried that off beautifully. Jeb Barnes turned pale.

"What about that cousin of yours in Bangor?" I said, picking up on the improvisation.

"He doesn't practice anymore," Michael said.

"Oh, I like that," I said. "Elect the guy to the legislature and suddenly he's too good to represent us common people."

"He has to avoid conflict of interest," Michael said. "But as soon as the phones are working again, I'll give him a call; I'm sure he knows someone who can help."

"You've got a cousin in the legislature?" asked one of the locals.

"A very distant cousin," Michael said.

Our joke had backfired, big-time. We spent the next half hour listening to a point-by-point analysis of a bill pending before the state legislature that Monheganites considered the last hope of preserving their lobster industry. By the end of the discussion, I still didn't understand the issue, but I had grasped that if anyone asked me where I stood on the lobster bill, I should express enthusiastic support for the town proposal and apologize for not being a registered Maine voter. Either that or turn tail and run the minute they brought up the subject.

We finally escaped, after Michael had promised to fill his cousin in on the details of the Monhegan bill. I had to admire the way he'd changed the conversation every time anyone tried to ask which legislator his cousin was. It wasn't as if we could make a name up; Maine had fewer than two hundred legislators, and the townspeople knew exactly how every one of them felt about their bill.

"And another thing," Jeb Barnes called out, following us out onto the front porch of the store. "Don't you listen to that Resnick fellow. He's got investments in foreign lobstering interests. Been spending a lot of money trying to kill our bill."

"Considering that he takes potshots at us whenever we get near him, it's not very likely we'll discuss it, now is it?" I said. "Don't forget to file my complaint with the mainland police if the phones come back up."

As I suspected, this sent Jeb scurrying back into the store.

"Everyone's quite impassioned about this lobster thing," Michael remarked.

"Well, it is the main local industry," I said.

"I thought that was tourism."

"Okay, the other main local industry. And no one's going to get all worked up about anyone preying on the tourists; they're not in short supply."

"But what am I supposed to do if someone corners me and asks about my cousin?"

"We'll ask Aunt Phoebe; she's sure to know a legislator on the right side of the issue, and she'll persuade him to adopt you."

"Speaking of your aunt Phoebe, shouldn't we get back to the house?"

"You want to go back to the house?" I said. "We'll be cooped up with my family soon enough when the hurricane actually hits. Do you really want to get a head start?"

"Well, it is warm and dry there," Michael said, pulling up the hood of his parka.

"It's warm and dry in the house," I said. "But right now I doubt if they'd let us stay inside."

"Why on earth not?"

"Look around you," I said. "What do you see?"

"Birders," he said automatically.

"Aside from the birders."

Just then, Fred Dickerman drove by at his usual break-neck speed. We leapt into some bushes by the side of the road while a flock of lady birders squawked and scattered like geese before his honking horn.

"The natives are getting hostile?" he asked.

"The natives are busy." I pointed out the half a dozen locals boarding or taping their windows, trudging back from the grocery stores with bags and boxes of supplies, and frantically trying to tie down or carry indoors every object smaller than a Volkswagen.

"With the exception of that crowd of old-timers killing time in the general store, you're right."

"If we go home now, Aunt Phoebe will find half a hundred chores for us to do, most of them outdoors," I said.

"And those same chores won't be waiting for us when we get back?"

"With any luck, she'll manage to get Dad and Rob to do quite a few of them while we're gone."

"So what should we do?" Michael asked. "I'll tell you straight out—I'm not up for another hike around the island, even if it wasn't infested with armed lunatics."

"We're going shopping," I said. "Monhegan has a few artists' studios and craft shops. You're not going to go back to Yorktown without a present for your mom, are you?"

"Now that's a good idea," Michael said.

We spent the next hour inspecting the remarkable number and variety of CLOSED FOR THE SEASON signs in the windows of the island shops and studios. Some of them were genuine works of art in their own right, but I wasn't having a lot of fun viewing them on water-soaked, locked doors or through rain-splattered windowpanes while my feet remained firmly planted in the mud.

At one point, we actually saw Victor Resnick stalking down the street in a disreputable mackinaw that made him look more like a scarecrow than ever. We ducked behind a building until he'd passed.

"He doesn't have his gun," Michael reported, peering around the corner. "If I were the constable, I'd tackle him now."

"I wouldn't count on it, though," I said, getting up the nerve to poke my head out.

Resnick stood in front of the general store, talking to someone—a young Asian man.

"Who do you suppose that is?" Michael said. "Doesn't have binoculars, so I doubt he's a birder."

"Definitely not a birder," I said. "He's wearing a necktie underneath his raincoat."

"The men at the general store did say something about Resnick having ties with foreign lobstering interests," Michael said. "Maybe he's from some Japanese seafood conglomerate."

"That's possible," I said. "Although around here, the word *foreign* just means 'not from Monhegan.' But he definitely looks corporate."

Resnick's discussion with the corporate man had grown heated. They stood nose-to-nose, both talking and gesturing furiously. Resnick's complexion grew redder and redder, and he shook his finger in the Asian man's face. Obviously, our visitor from the East hadn't heard about Resnick's readiness with firearms; he gave back as good as he got. A pity the wind, rain, and surf kept us from hearing what they said. Well, if the argument turned violent, we'd have plenty of witnesses, I realized. I could see at least three other people hiding behind nearby buildings, although I had no idea whether they wanted to avoid Resnick or eavesdrop on his conversation.

Suddenly, Resnick whirled and began striding down the street the way he'd come—toward us.

CHAPTER 8

The Little Puffin Around the Corner

"Oh my God, he's coming this way," I whispered. We both jerked back, but not so far that we couldn't see what went on.

"You can go to hell for all I care!" Resnick shouted over his shoulder.

The Asian man opened his mouth as if to reply, then stopped, took a deep breath, and shoved his hands in the pockets of his raincoat. He stood there for a few moments, staring after Resnick, then turned on his heels and began walking in the other direction.

About then, Michael and I scurried around the corner of the building to avoid Resnick. When we peeked out a minute or two later, both he and the Asian man with the necktie had disappeared.

After that brief flurry of excitement, we resumed our shopping quest and finally ended up down by the ferry dock in the only gift shop still open—probably because it doubled as the island-side office for the ferries.

We flung open the shop door, shook ourselves like large dogs, and said good morning to the shopkeeper and her one other customer. The shopkeeper was a stout sixtyish woman, sensibly dressed in boots, jeans, and several layers of sweaters. I couldn't remember her name—probably a subconscious form of revenge, since during my last visit to Monhegan I'd tried, without success, to get her to sell my ironwork in her shop.

The other occupant was a rather odd-looking woman in her forties, dressed in a peculiar multilayered medley of black, purple, and violet, topped with a limp lavender-trimmed straw hat. Not one of the birders, obviously; probably an artist or craftswoman.

"My God," Michael said, looking round. "Is the puffin the state bird here or something?"

He had a point; the shop was a puffin lover's paradise. Puffin posters, puffin T-shirts, puffin sweatshirts, puffin key chains, and so many stuffed toy puffins of all sizes that the place looked like Santa's workshop on December 23.

"We're very proud of our puffins," said the shopkeeper. "Maine is the only state in the union that actually has nesting puffins."

"Yes, so Meg's aunt Phoebe has told us," Michael said, breaking in to stem the tide of puffin lore.

"Oh, you're Meg?" the shopkeeper said. "I didn't recognize you; it's such a long time since you've been here. Your father's told us about all your detective adventures this summer."

I winced. I should have known that my mystery-buff dad couldn't spend five minutes anywhere without bragging about his daughter, who had actually solved a real live murder. Listening to Dad, you'd think any minute I'd quit my career as a smith and open up a detective agency.

"You know, we never did finish those arrangements for selling some of your ironwork here in the shop," the woman went on.

I snapped to attention. A more accurate statement would be that I'd never convinced her my occasional summers on the island constituted enough of a local tie to warrant my inclusion in the "Crafts of Monhegan" section of the shop. But if my past summer's adventures had made me notorious enough to interest her, thus opening up a profitable new market—well, I wasn't about to let the opportunity go to waste.

In minutes, the shopkeeper and I were deep in discussions of the quantity and type of merchandise she thought she could use and whether she would buy them outright or take them on consignment. Michael wandered off to inspect the puffin paraphernalia, and after a few minutes, the woman in lavender picked up her purse.

"Bye, Mamie," she whispered, and slipped out of the store.

"Oh, I'm sorry," I said. "I didn't mean to drive a customer away."

"Oh, she's not a customer," Mamie said. "That's one of our other island celebrities. That's Rhapsody." From the tone of voice, I suspected Rhapsody was one of those people who strenuously resisted admitting that they owned a last name. And that she was somebody I ought to have heard of.

"Rhapsody?" I said.

"You know, she does the children's books. They call her the 'Puffin Lady of Monhegan.' "

"Oh, the Happy Puffin Family," I said.

"That's right," she said, beaming.

I hadn't actually heard of the Happy Puffin Family before, but though my detective skills are overrated, they were sufficient to let me spot the giant display of Happy Puffin Family books right beside the cash register.

"I keep meaning to read one of her books," I said. "I'm sure my sister, Pam, has some around the house for her kids, but I never find the time when I'm home."

"Oh, they're wonderful!" Mamie exclaimed.

While Michael continued to inspect puffin tea towels and puffin ashtrays with a suspiciously serious look on his face, I poked through the display rack. Evidently, the Puffin Lady was reasonably prolific; the shopkeeper had at least a dozen titles displayed.

Even as a child, I had what Dad called a "deplorably literal streak." When presented with a book that was part of a series—*The Borrowers*, for example, or *Little House on the Prairie*—I would insist on beginning with the first in the series and working my way through in order. I therefore examined the copyright dates and passed up *Puffin in the Rye* ("The Happy Puffin Family Visits a Farm!") *The Daring Young Puffin on the Flying Trapeze!* ("The Happy Puffin Family Visits the Circus!"), and *Snow Falling on Puffins* ("The Happy Puffin Family Goes Sledding!") in favor of the original volume, *Hark the Herald Puffins Sing* ("Christmas with the Happy Puffin Family!").

I hoped the Puffin Lady's artistic and literary skills had improved over time. I wasn't much impressed with either in her first opus. The puffins looked vaguely inauthentic—either she didn't draw all that well or perhaps she had taken liberties with their anatomy to make them more anthropomorphic. Or perhaps it was the props and costumes. She liked decking the poor birds out in brightly colored bits of human clothing, or having them carry things like yo-yos and lollipops. They were colorful and eye-catching. But she hadn't succeeded in making them all that appealing, as far as I could see; in fact, they looked faintly reptilian. I saw more charm in one mass-produced plush stuffed puffin from the gift shop than in Rhapsody's whole book.

It was the beaks and the eyes. The puffins' beaks might be picturesque and unusual, but they weren't designed for expressing human emotion. Whatever charm the Puffin Lady had tried to create with cute little props and costumes, she hadn't managed to make those huge cartoonlike beaks look any different. Happy, sad, angry, or surprised, the puffins all had the same lack of expression. And the eyes—maybe it's just me, but I've always found birds' eyes a little cold and alien. You get the feeling they're off thinking strange, fluttery little splinter thoughts; and you hope it's all about seeds and nuts and where to find a birdbath, and not something like acting out in real life their great-great-grandfathers' starring roles in *The Birds*. Maybe I'd done her artistic skills an injustice. Rhapsody had captured everything I disliked about birds' eyes so accurately that a chill went down my spine.

"You're not really thinking of buying that," came a voice, interrupting my thoughts.

I looked up, to see one of the birders, a matronly woman who had both the inevitable binoculars and a pair of reading glasses dangling over her ample bosom, not to mention a camera hanging by a strap from her wrist. I wasn't sure, but I thought she might be one of the birders who'd snapped pictures of the lunatic shooting at us, so I resolved to be as polite as possible.

"Just trying to see what the fuss is all about," I said. "She seems such a local celebrity."

"I can't for the life of me see why," the birder said. "It's not as if she's particularly good at it."

Actually, I agreed, but the birder's bullying manner irritated me, so I said only, "Oh, really? How so?"

"Her stuff's shockingly inaccurate," the birder said with a sniff. "Shoddy research all around. Worse than useless from a scientific point of view."

I looked back at the brightly colored page, where the Happy Puffin Family was sitting down to Christmas dinner. The little Puffins, complete with napkins tied bib-fashion around their necks, looked eagerly toward their mother— you could tell her by the flowered hat. Mama Puffin stood beside the table, holding a giant covered dish with the tips of her wings. I flipped the page. The dish now rested in front of Papa Puffin, who was about to wield a carving knife on its contents—not turkey, thank goodness, but an enormous smiling fish. The small Puffins jumped up and down in their seats, and even the main course looked implausibly cheerful, as if they hadn't quite gotten around to telling him exactly what role he was to play in the upcoming feast.

"I didn't realize she intended to be accurate," I said, flipping the page again and holding up a scene of the Happy Puffin Family sledding. "I mean, I'm sure she realizes that puffins don't actually wear little red mufflers and woolly caps."

"I'm not talking about the anthropomorphizing," the birder said. "That's silly, but not actually harmful, considering the age group. But look at their bills! And their plumage!"

A plump beringed finger, quivering with indignation, planted itself just below the picture of little Petey Puffin. I had to admit, I didn't like the look of him, but I had no idea what she thought was wrong with him. I noticed that, like bird guidebooks, the Puffin Lady never showed her subjects head-on. The Puffin Family invariably stood in profile. She must copy them from bird books, I realized. That would account for the strangely mechanical and puppetlike quality. But no; if she copied them from bird books, then they'd be accurate, wouldn't they? And then the birders wouldn't complain.

"I'm sorry," I said. "I'm not awfully knowledgeable about puffins. What's wrong with it?"

"This is not the picture of an immature puffin," the birder said. "An immature puffin looks like this." She plopped one of the ubiquitous blue bird guides open atop *Hark the Herald Puffins Sing* and pointed out a black-and-white shape. "And he's in breeding plumage. By Christmas, adult puffins have long since shed their colorful bill plates and their faces darken. Like this," she added, indicating yet another black-and-white shape.

I studied the page before me. Yes, the puffin in winter was a drab bird indeed compared to what he would look like in mating season. I'd almost have taken him for a different species. And all the Puffin Family were in breeding plumage, right down to diaper-clad baby Patty.

"I see what you mean," I said. I didn't add that I didn't see what was so important about the distinction. Perhaps they planned to haul Rhapsody before the Audubon Society on morals charges for turning an infant puffin into some kind of avian Lolita.

I was relieved when Michael joined us. Probably not an accident; we'd both become a little wary of the more rabid birders.

"Found something interesting," he said, holding up the back cover of another book: "Look familiar?"

He held out an oversized art book—a collection of Victor Resnick's paintings. On the back of the book was a picture of our gun-toting lunatic. Only in the picture, he wore a clean fisherman's sweater, his hair and beard were combed, and he looked quite distinguished. The picture was in three-quarters profile. Resnick's chin was lifted, and he gazed into the distance with a lofty, otherworldly look. He really appeared every bit the distinguished artist, already planning his next brilliant work.

"Yes, that's the jerk," I said. "Almost wouldn't have recognized him."

I turned the book over and began leafing through it. I sighed. The man might be a jerk, but he was definitely a talented jerk.

"Someone should do something about that horrible man," the birder said.

"Well, Mrs. Peabody, that's very difficult," Mamie said. "He's quite an important person. . . ."

"That's irrelevant," I said, glad to find a conversational topic other than puffins. "I don't care how important they are, people can't run around shooting off rifles or shotguns or whatever he's using."

"My God!" exclaimed Mrs. Peabody. "He's not shooting them, is he? I'd heard about the electric shocks; we've gotten up a petition about it. But this is beyond all belief! Shooting the birds!"

She whirled and ran for the door, knocking down a stack of stuffed puffins on her way.

"We can't let him get away with this," she shouted. "There's not a moment to lose!"

CHAPTER 9

Twelve Angry Puffins

"Wait," I called, starting after her. "I didn't say he was shooting the birds; I just said he was shooting at us!"

But Mrs. Peabody didn't hear me. And the electric lights chose that moment to flicker and die. In the sudden near darkness, I tripped over the fallen puffins and sent the rack of Rhapsody's books sprawling. Mamie scurried over to pick them up while Michael leapt to my side and spent rather more time than strictly necessary making sure I'd suffered no damage in the fall. By the time he finally relented and helped me to my feet, the birder had vanished.

"Don't worry about it," Michael said as we pitched in to put the book display back together again.

"She'll tell everyone Resnick is shooting birds," I said. "They'll probably all go hiking up to confront him."

"And either they'll lynch him or he'll shoot one of them, and either way, maybe you won't have to file charges against him."

"Are you going to file charges against him?" Mamie asked, wide-eyed.

"Yes, at least if Constable Barnes ever takes me seriously."

"Good," she said, patting my shoulder with approval. "Someone needs to do something about that man. He's absolutely beastly to poor Rhapsody. She had a one-woman show here last summer of some of her paintings from the books. You should have heard some of the things he said to her. Absolutely savage. Someone really ought to do something. Do you have any matches?"

I thought for a moment she was enlisting us to help burn

Resnick at the stake, but apparently she'd decided the power wasn't coming back anytime soon. She pottered through her drawers until she found some matches, then began lighting oil lamps.

I glanced back at the book of Resnick's paintings. I'd paused at a painting of the Black Head. He'd precisely captured the way the sky had looked all day; only slightly cloudy, but somehow full of vague future menace. I could imagine what he would have to say about poor Rhapsody's puffins.

"She went into quite a slump and almost missed her deadline for *Puffin in the Rye!*" Mamie said. "I really thought for a while she'd give up painting entirely."

I continued to leaf through the book of Resnick's work while Michael bought a puffin sweatshirt for his mom. I was torn. The more I looked at the paintings, the more I wanted to buy the book; Resnick had really captured the beauty of the island in a way that photographs couldn't quite manage. But I didn't want to risk the shopkeeper's disapproval. And for that matter, I had mixed feelings about giving any support, financial or otherwise, to the wild-eyed lunatic who'd fired a gun at me and built that horrible eyesore on one of my favorite parts of the island. Ironically, the book even included several paintings of the picturesque shack he'd demolished.

"Aha!" I cried, snapping the book shut. "I'll take this, please," I said to Mamie, handing over the book and fishing my Visa card out of my purse.

She looked at me as if I'd just declared myself a vivisectionist.

"Take a look here, on page one hundred and ten," I said. "See the caption—'View of Puffin Point from the Public Path.' That proves it."

"Well, of course," she said. "Everyone knows it's a public path."

"Yes, but this proves that he knows it. He said so in the

title of one of his very own pictures. I can use this in the court case; if Jeb Barnes won't take my assault charges, I'll file a civil suit."

"Oh, I see," Mamie said. "Your father was right; you have become quite the detective."

She rang up the book with enthusiasm, then waved cheerfully to Michael and me as we stepped outside again.

"Now where?" Michael asked.

"Back to the cottage, I think," I said. "Aunt Phoebe will try to put us to work, but we can get her to feed us first."

"Sounds like a plan," he said.

But when we neared the top of the hill, we saw Aunt Phoebe in heated conversation with several birders, including Mrs. Peabody.

"Oh damn," I said. "She's probably telling Aunt Phoebe a lot of inaccurate information about Resnick."

"You're probably right," Michael said. "And your aunt doesn't look too happy."

In fact, while we struggled up the last few feet of the hill, Aunt Phoebe broke away from the birders and began storming up the path toward Resnick's cottage.

"The man deserves a good thrashing," she called over her shoulder, brandishing her blackthorn walking stick.

"Aunt Phoebe! Wait!" I wheezed. She probably couldn't hear me.

"I'll show him a thing or two," she shouted as she disappeared around a bend in the road.

"Shouldn't we go after her?" Michael asked, puffing.

"Yes, but I don't think we could possibly catch her." I, too, was panting.

"True. She hasn't been hiking around the island all morning."

"Actually, she probably has, but never mind," I said. "Let's go tell the constable. It's downhill from here to the general store."

"And we can get those groceries your aunt wanted," Michael said.

While Michael gathered the items on Aunt Phoebe's list, I tried to convince Jeb Barnes to go after Aunt Phoebe. I wasn't having much luck.

"I'm sure there's no reason to worry," he said.

"Did you hear what I said?" I demanded. "She's going up there to confront Victor Resnick! She thinks he's been shooting birds."

"Probably has," one of the locals commented.

"I'm sure Phoebe can take care of herself," Jeb said.

"She probably can, but what about Resnick?" I said. "What if she carries out her threat to give him a good thrashing?"

"Call up and warn him," someone suggested.

"Phones are out," someone else said.

"Serve him right if she did," commented a third.

The lights flickered on at that moment, and everyone looked up with a hopeful expression. Then the lights winked out again and the locals sighed and huddled a little closer to the stove.

Just then, we heard the sound of a truck engine outside.

"That must be Fred," Jeb Barnes said. "I'll get him to take me up to Resnick's. We'll head her off."

He darted out of the store, flagged down Fred Dickerman, and the two of them roared off up the gravel road.

Michael and I watched as the truck careened off, scattering birders on both sides.

"Should we follow?" Michael asked.

"Let's go back and find Dad," I said. "Maybe he can figure out a way to calm her down."

We made rather slow progress, though. We had our arms full of grocery bags, and we had to push through throngs of birders, all of whom wanted to know if Victor Resnick was really slaughtering birds with his shotgun. At first, they seemed curiously unalarmed by the fact that Resnick had been shooting at Michael and me.

"We didn't actually *see* him shoot any birds," I said finally. "But he certainly shot at us. Probably thought we were birders trespassing on his land."

This tactic generated a satisfactory level of sympathy and outrage. Especially after one of the birders informed the rest that Resnick's land was the only place on the island where some rare bird had been sighted a day or two earlier.

Leaving the assembled birders debating whether the once-in-a-decade chance to add the bay-breasted warbler to their life lists was worth the risk that it might become the last bird they ever saw, Michael and I escaped and headed back to Aunt Phoebe's cottage.

We ran into Winnie and Binkie on the way.

"Meg, dear," Binkie called. "How are you enjoying your stay?"

"Well, it's not quite what we expected," I said. "We didn't expect to run into the whole family here."

"No, and I'm sure your mother and father weren't expecting that dreadful Resnick person to be here," Binkie said. "Terribly awkward, under the circumstances."

"Awkward?" I repeated. *Awkward* didn't even begin to describe the sensation of having a gun fired over one's head.

"Oh, leave it alone, Binkie," Winnie said. "It's all over and done with."

I felt a little miffed at their quick dismissal of our ordeal. Unless by "awkward" they meant some past conflict—perhaps this wasn't the first time Victor Resnick had taken violent measures against trespassers. Perhaps it wasn't the first time Aunt Phoebe had attempted to thrash him.

"And do be careful," Binkie added. "I've heard reports of an imposter running around the island."

"An imposter?" I echoed.

"Yes, someone carrying binoculars and a bird book and

pretending to be one of us, when he doesn't know a tern from a seagull," Winnie said, frowning. "Up to no good, whoever he is, if you ask me."

But before I could ask what possible harm the so-called imposter could do, Winnie and Binkie spotted another party of birders down the road and tripped off to compare notes.

I shrugged. The fake birder wasn't my problem; my family, on the other hand . . .

"I wonder if it was wise, letting Aunt Phoebe run off like that," I said, fretting.

"She's a grown woman," Michael said as we turned into the lane to the cottage. "She can take care of herself, and besides, the constable will referee. Let him take care of her."

"I suppose we'll have to," I said.

"Look, there's Rob," Michael said. "What's he doing there on the beach?"

"Posing," I said. "He probably saw us coming."

Rob stood on the narrow strip of beach, hunched against the cold, one hand jammed in his pocket, staring out to sea. Trying, no doubt, to achieve an air of picturesque, Byronic melancholy. Someone should break the news to Rob that blondes can't do Byronic. Michael, on the other hand, managed it without even trying; I particularly liked the way the breeze ruffled the lock of hair that had fallen over his eyes.

Then again, Michael wasn't handicapped by Spike. Rob held one end of a very long leash; on the other end, Spike was chasing the waves. When a wave fell back toward the ocean, Spike would pursue it, barking bravely, convinced he had terrified the water into flight. When the water turned and thundered back toward the beach, Spike would turn and run away, tail between his legs, howling in terror. Rob was pretending to be oblivious to the whole spectacle.

"Well, at least Spike's having fun," I said as I drew up beside Rob.

"Miserable little mutt," Rob muttered. "Sorry, Michael."

Michael shrugged.

"Don't look at me," he said. "The miserable little mutt belongs to my mom."

"You think he'd get tired of it," Rob said, frowning, as Spike chased the water back and forth again.

"I'm sure he will after a while," I said.

"I've been here two hours," Rob said. "He's not getting tired. Just hoarse."

"Well, hoarse might be an improvement," I said. "Why on earth have you been standing here for two hours? Is something going on?"

"Not much," Rob said. "Everyone's getting hysterical about some guy who's running around shooting the puffins. That's about it."

"He's not shooting the puffins; he's shooting us. At us anyway," I said.

"Us? You mean you and Michael?" Rob asked.

"Yes."

"Wow, are you going to file charges?"

"Yes," Michael said. "And when you've passed the bar, you can handle the civil suit, if you like."

"Cool," Rob said. "So what's going on with the puffins?"

"Nothing. They've left the island," I said.

"Lucky them," Rob muttered. "Here, take him for a while, will you?"

"No thanks," I said, backing away. "We've got our hands full of groceries."

Which was true, but Rob still glowered at me as he strode off down the beach, Spike skittering along at his heels. Michael and I headed back to the cottage.

"I wish Aunt Phoebe would come back," I said, glancing down the lane.

"Don't worry," Michael said. "Everything will be fine."

I always get nervous when people say that.

CHAPTER 10

The Puffin Before the Storm

"There you are!" Mrs. Fenniman said, pouncing on us the second we entered the cottage. "It's about time someone showed up to do some work around here!"

Before we knew it, Mrs. Fenniman had drafted us into hurricane preparations. Apparently, Dad had vanished shortly after Michael and I left, leaving her with only Rob to order around.

Fortunately, Aunt Phoebe's house was built along sensible lines, with working shutters. All you had to do was close them and make sure the latch was secure, thus sparing us the nightmare of boarding and taping that some residents had to do. Rob and Dad had apparently managed to deal with the shutters before they debunked. Probably took them all of half an hour.

Michael and I weren't so lucky with the lawn and deck furniture. Before dashing off to deal with Victor Resnick, Aunt Phoebe had left orders for us to bring every movable object inside. Mrs. Fenniman took her quite literally. The deck alone housed a dozen plastic chairs, three tables, a gas grill, half a dozen sets of wind chimes, and several dozen wooden planters or clay pots, with or without vegetation. The yard contained two picnic tables, three birdbaths, a rain gauge, a sundial, a second grill, a badminton net, a croquet set, a set of horseshoes, a pair of flagpoles, several dozen more flower boxes, an awesome assortment of lawn ornaments, and a never-ending supply of bird feeders and birdhouses. We finally convinced Mrs. Fenniman that the slate flagstones and the bricks bordering the flower beds could probably cope by themselves. And since the garden shed was already overflowing with junk not actively in use, we had to drag everything into the house and shove the furniture around until we could fit it all in somehow.

We had nearly finished and were looking forward to resting when Mother suddenly appeared on the upstairs landing, her hair falling down her back. She was wringing her hands, looking fit to give a bang-up performance of Ophelia's mad scene.

"Have you seen your father?" she demanded.

"Not since this morning," I said.

"Don't worry, Margaret," Mrs. Fenniman said. "He'll be fine."

"Where's Phoebe?" Mother asked.

"Up at the village," I lied, not wanting Mother to start worrying about Aunt Phoebe, too.

"You go back to your nap," Mrs. Fenniman put in. "She'll be back anytime now, and James, too."

"What if something has happened to him?"

"What could happen to him?" Michael asked.

"He said he was going to go out to Green Point and watch the hurricane hit the island," Mother said. "I told Phoebe not to let him go, and now she's gone, too."

"Oh Lord. I thought he was kidding about that," I said.

"You should know your father by now," Mother said pointedly.

"Well, at least he didn't go off with your aunt Phoebe to tackle Victor Resnick," Michael put in.

So much for not worrying Mother.

"Victor Resnick?" Mother repeated. "Is he on the island?"

"Yes, why wouldn't he be?" I asked. "He owns a house here."

"Oh dear," Mother said. "Your father doesn't know Resnick is here, does he?"

"Of course he knows, Mother," I said. "We all heard it from the Dickermans last night."

"Oh dear me," Mother said. She drifted down the stairs, looking preoccupied.

"Where did you say Phoebe was?" Mrs. Fenniman asked.

"Probably up at Victor Resnick's house, giving him a good thrashing," I said.

"I'm sure your father is doing no such thing," Mother said. "That's absolute nonsense."

She strode out into the kitchen, leaving the swinging door flapping wildly.

"Not Dad—Aunt Phoebe," I called after her. "Why on earth would Dad want to thrash Victor Resnick?"

"Well, he's a birder, too, isn't he?" Michael said. "Probably upset about what everyone thinks Resnick's doing to the birds."

"Birds! Don't be silly," Mrs. Fenniman said with a cackle. "The green-eyed monster, more likely."

"Green-eyed monster?" Michael and I said in unison.

"They were quite an item, your mother and Victor Resnick," Mrs. Fenniman said. "Of course, that was a few years ago, before she met your dad."

"Over forty years ago, if it was before she met Dad," I said. "What makes you think Dad would still be jealous of Victor Resnick after all this time?"

"Quite a famous man, Victor Resnick," Mrs. Fenniman said. "Bound to make a man a little nervous, his wife's old beau showing up like this. And still single."

With that, she disappeared into the kitchen.

"*He* didn't show up; Mother and Dad did," I said as the door swung to again.

I heard a smothered chuckle from Michael, who sat there as calmly as you please, flipping through one of the old family photo album. Men.

"Very funny," I said. "You don't really think Dad is off confronting Victor Resnick, do you?"

As if in answer, Michael held out a photo album, pointing to one of the pictures. I glanced down and saw Mother, posing arm in arm with a tall, gawky young man who looked dreadfully familiar. Something about the hawklike nose and the pugnacious expression. I flipped the page. And the page after that. Picture after picture of Mother with the same young man. In several, they were affectionately entwined in a manner that wasn't particularly shocking today but probably was back then. Particularly since the fashions and the ages of some of the younger cousins showed that Mother wasn't more than fourteen or fifteen. In one photo, he held a sketch pad and Mother had assumed an exaggerated cheesecake pose.

"Resnick." I said. "Damn."

The kitchen door swung open again.

"Meg, go and find your father at once!" Mother said. "Make sure he doesn't do anything foolish."

"Mother, he's probably just gone to Green Point to watch the hurricane hit the island," I said.

Mother looked at me in silence for a moment.

"*Anything* foolish," she repeated, and disappeared into the kitchen.

Mrs. Fenniman stuck her head out a few seconds later.

"Keep your eye out for Phoebe, too," she said. "She ought not to be out in this weather. Hurricane's moving again."

"Is it going to hit the island?" Michael asked.

"No, but it's going to come close enough to make things pretty nasty," Mrs. Fenniman said. "Don't forget your knapsacks; you may need some of that gear out there!"

With that, she popped back into the kitchen.

Michael and I looked at each other. For a moment, I could see a look of utter exhaustion on his face, and I felt a sudden surge of anger. Why on earth couldn't my family behave like sensible human beings for once? Then his face relaxed into a tired smile and he reached down to pick up his knapsack.

"Well, no one ever called life dull with your dad around," he said, turning to open the door. "Once more into the breach, my friends."

I sighed, picked up my own knapsack, and followed him out.

"So where do we go first?" he asked. "Green Point or Resnick's house?"

"It's the same general direction," I said.

We hurried through the village, asking passing birders if they'd seen Dad. No one had. We peered into the dimly lit general store and saw Jeb Barnes had apparently just arrived back. He was shedding his wet wraps by the stove.

"Have you seen my dad?" I asked.

"No, nor your aunt Phoebe, neither," he said. "I thought you said she'd gone up to Resnick's."

"She did."

"Well, she'd left by the time we got there, and he wasn't too happy to see us, either," Jeb said. "Mad as a wet hen about something, so we didn't stay long."

The electric lights flickered on and off again.

"Jim's not having much luck with that thing today, is he?" one of the locals said.

"Too much rain," Jeb said. "He might as well give up till the storm's past. Go ahead and light some more of those oil lamps, will you?"

"Come on," I said to Michael. "I guess we'll have to look for Dad by ourselves. Before he breaks his neck or something."

The men huddled by the stove looked uncomfortable, but none of them volunteered to help. I stomped outside. The rain was growing worse by the minute. The birders had all gone somewhere to roost, and the only local we saw as we passed through town was Fred Dickerman, trying to ease his truck out of a mud hole in the road. We gave him a wide berth and squelched up the road in the same direction we'd last seen Aunt Phoebe hiking.

"We're not really going back to Resnick's, are we?" Michael asked.

"We can claim we've come to rescue him from Aunt Phoebe," I said. "And we'll try to detour around the edge of his property."

Michael still looked dubious. I wasn't sure which prospect worried him more, meeting Resnick again or taking another of my detours.

The closer we got to Victor Resnick's house, the more anxious I felt. Michael reacted the same way, although since he didn't know the local landmarks, this meant he'd been in a constant state of anxiety since about five minutes after we left the village.

"Are we getting close to that lunatic's property line?" he kept asking.

"Yes," I said finally. "We'll start our detour in a few minutes. I just want to go a little farther up this path. There's a lookout point where we can see quite a way down the shore."

"Damn!"

I whirled, to see Michael sprawled facedown in the mud.

"Michael! What's wrong?"

"Tripped over another of these damned water pipes," he said. "Why don't they bury the damned things where they'll be out of the way?"

"Well, for one thing, half the places the pipes run don't have enough topsoil to bury a matchstick, much less one of these pipes," I said, pausing in the path to get my breath. "And for another, they take the pipes up in the fall to prevent them from freezing. They'd have a hard time doing that if they buried them."

"Take them up?" he echoed. "What do they do for water in the winter?"

"Use cisterns," I said. "And practice rigorous water conservation."

"When in the fall?" he asked. "They're not going to take them up while we're here, are they?"

"Not unless there's a freeze predicted," I said. "Make sure you didn't disconnect the pipe you tripped over, by the way."

"Right," he said. "You go on; I'll catch up in a second."

As Michael bent over to examine the pipe, still shaking his head in disbelief, I trudged up the path until I emerged from the trees into the open and could see along the shore to the end of the point of land on which Resnick's house and studio stood. I was hoping to see Dad, alive and well and ready to come back to the house to dry off and warm up.

Instead, I saw a dead body.

CHAPTER 11

From Puffin to Eternity

The body lay facedown in a shallow, rocky pool, but my money wasn't on drowning as the cause of death.

"Michael," I yelled. "Could you come up here a second?"

I stood looking down the slope at the tidal pool where the body floated. I was shivering, from nerves as much as the cold rain, as Michael scrambled out to the cliff's edge and stood beside me.

"Meg, maybe we should just go back to the house," he said, his voice raised to be heard over the wind and surf. "Your father's probably back there by now; I'm sure he was only kidding about wanting to stand on Green Point and watch the hurricane hit the island."

"I'm sure he wasn't, but never mind that now," I said. "Look down there."

"Oh my God," Michael said. He tried to pull me away so I couldn't see the body. "It's not him, is it?"

"You mean Dad? Heavens no! Look at all that hair."

"You're right," Michael said. "Sorry. I panicked for a second. So who is he?"

"I think it's Resnick."

Michael craned his head to look at the body from another angle.

"I think you're right. Well, that's a relief, for us at least."

"Not much of a relief, considering he was almost certainly murdered."

"Murdered! What makes you think that? I mean, why not drowned?"

"Look at that gash on the back of his head."

Michael peered through the rain.

"Oh," he said. "Not so much of a relief after all, I suppose; and before you say anything, I only meant a relief because it wasn't your dad. I didn't mean I was glad Resnick was dead or anything like that."

"Although I have a feeling a lot of people will be, even if they don't admit it."

We just stood there for a moment, staring at the body.

"We'd better go and tell somebody," Michael said. "The helpful Constable Barnes, I suppose."

"We'd better haul the body up first," I said with a shudder.

"We can't; we'd be disturbing a crime scene," Michael protested.

"I think the storm's going to do more than disturb the crime scene by the time we could get down to the village, much less bring anyone back. If we don't haul him up, he's going to wash out to sea."

As if to emphasize my point, the crest of a particularly big wave washed over the rocks into the tidal pool. The body rocked slightly, and the right arm moved back and forth, as if Resnick were waving to us.

"See, the tide's rising," I said. "We'd better hurry."

"Right," Michael said. He took a deep breath and then began easing himself over the side of the ledge, feeling for a foothold on the rocky slope.

"I'm sorry," I said.

"Not your fault," he replied, looking up with a reassuring smile.

"Yes, it is," I said. "I got us into this. Coming here was my idea. Some romantic getaway."

"Well, you never promised me a tropical paradise."

He gave me a hand over the edge of the cliff, and I began carefully following him down the slope. It wasn't all that steep; if there had been solid ground at the bottom, I'd have just slid and slithered down in a hurry. But considering what waited below—a dead body and a rapidly rising ocean—I very definitely didn't want to lose my footing.

"Getting him up again is going to be a real headache," Michael said, looking around. "I don't suppose there's another way back."

"There's a path that goes back toward Resnick's house," I said. "But I don't think the tide's low enough."

"You're sure?" Michael said. "Where is it? Maybe we can pick a time between waves."

I pointed to the narrow path hugging the side of the cliff. As we studied it, a wave sloshed over the path, stranding a wire-mesh lobster trap. A few seconds later, a larger wave broke over the path, crushing the trap against the side of the cliff and sucking the fragments back as it retreated.

"Okay, I guess the cliff's it," Michael said. He looked up at the cliff, frowning, and then back at the body. Water sloshed over our feet.

"Hang on a second," I said, pulling the knapsack off my shoulders. "I never thought I'd give Dad the satisfaction of hearing this, but for once this damned hiking emergency kit of his will come in handy."

I dug through the contents of the pack, passing up a hefty first-aid kit, a large bottle of SP35 sunscreen, plastic bottles of water and Gatorade, several packages of freeze-dried food, and a flare gun that probably dated from the Korean War. Sure enough, there at the bottom of the pack I found a long length of slender nylon rope.

"We can tie this to him and haul him up," I said. "There should be another rope in your pack, if we need it."

"He'll get a little battered," Michael observed.

"I think he's past caring."

"Yes, but it will complicate the autopsy, won't it?"

"Good point. We can hoist him up over there," I said, pointing a little to the right, where the cliff overhung the beginning of the submerged path. "We can keep him away from the cliff until the very top."

"I'll bundle him up," Michael said, taking off his parka and spreading it out on the rocks. "You find something up there to tie the other end of the rope to."

"Right," I said. But before I started scrambling back up the slope, I paused, took a breath, and tried to look around very methodically and fix the scene in my mind.

In the sunlight, the rocky shoreline would have looked rugged and picturesque, but in the gloomy half-light, I could think only what a bleak and cheerless place it was to die all alone.

Well, not quite all alone. Out of the corner of my eye, I saw the sudden bright flash as a beam of sunlight broke through the clouds and reflected off the lenses of a pair of binoculars. Somewhere, farther up the slope, birders were watching. I only hoped they had been watching long enough to see that Resnick had been dead when we found him. Awkward if they'd only seen us messing around with a dead body.

"Meg? Is something wrong?"

"No," I said. "Just looking around to see if there's anything unusual we should report to the police. I mean, you're probably right about this being a crime scene. Want me to help you pull him out?"

"It's okay," Michael said. "I can manage."

He didn't sound too happy about it, but if he wanted to play strong, protective male, I didn't plan to argue. It was one thing to talk about corpses and autopsies around the dinner table when Dad went off on one of his true-crime tangents and quite another to haul a body out of the briny deep.

Michael frowned down at the corpse.

"Michael, I'm—" I stopped myself. He looked up and raised an eyebrow. I couldn't help smiling; I loved the way he did that.

"Having promised that I wouldn't apologize for anything

that went wrong," I said, "I'm trying very hard to think of anything else to say right now."

He chuckled.

"I was just thinking what great research material this is for my acting," he said. "I had a part in a TV show once where I had to discover a murder victim. Had a tough time making it authentic, given the fact I'd never even seen a dead body. But since I've met you, I've seen more stiffs than a mafioso in training."

"Is that a good thing?" I asked.

"Well, it's useful."

With that, he bent down and began pulling at Resnick's body. I coiled the rope over my shoulder, replaced the pack on my back, and headed toward the cliff.

As I reached for the first rock in my climb, I saw a piece of paper fluttering on the ground at my feet. I stooped to pick it up. Force of habit—growing up with Dad, you tended to think the eleventh and twelfth commandments were "Thou shalt not litter" and "I don't care if you didn't put it there; pick it up anyway; it won't kill you to bend over."

I found myself staring at a familiar piece of paper; the map on which Dad had scoped out the best place on the island to watch the hurricane. It was soggy and some of the ink had smeared, but I recognized Dad's printing instantly. His handwriting achieved a degree of artistic illegibility that made him the envy of less accomplished physicians, but his printing was precise, elegant, more readable than most typefaces—and absolutely distinctive. I'd figured out the real scoop on Santa Claus one year when I realized that the note thanking me for the milk and cookies was in Dad's inimitable printing.

Oh damn, I thought. If anyone else found this, and figured out it belonged to Dad—and anyone who'd ever seen his printing would figure it out in a heartbeat . . .

"Meg?" Michael called.

"Sorry. I'm going," I said, stuffing the map in my knapsack and reaching again for the cliff.

"Hang on a second. Do you think we should take this, too?"

I glanced back. Michael had laid Resnick's body on a flat rock and was pointing down at something floating in the pool. I scrambled back down to see what it was.

A NO TRESPASSING sign, minus its post, bobbed just below the surface.

"It was under the body," he said.

"We'd better take it, I suppose," I said. "It could be evidence."

I tried a couple of times to snag it, using the rope so as not to touch it and leave fingerprints. But in the end, the only way we could manage to reach it without wading into the icy water was for Michael to hold on to my waist while I reached out and grabbed it, and even then both of us got half-soaked by the waves.

"Definitely time to make tracks," Michael said as I secured the sign to my backpack and he turned back to deal with Resnick.

Hauling the body up the slope took forever, and then we decided to put Resnick someplace out of the rain, since we'd moved him so far already. We picked him up—I took the feet, which seemed less personal somehow—and lugged him down the path to his house.

I didn't like the glass and steel monstrosity, but I couldn't help thinking it looked a little forlorn already. The wind had plastered the glass with wet leaves and mud, and the way the windows rattled made me glad I wouldn't be inside the house when the storm really broke.

We found room in the woodshed, put the body out of the storm, pulled a canvas tarpaulin over it, and stashed the sign in a corner.

Now that we were out of the rain, we paused for a moment. I took my flashlight out of the knapsack and played it over Resnick's face. In the struggle to get his body up above the tide line and under cover, I hadn't had much chance to inspect him. Now, in the harsh illumination of the flashlight, I had much too good a view. The angry gash on the back of his head didn't show, of course, since he lay faceup, but he had a nasty-looking bruise on his forehead, just at the hairline. And he definitely looked very dead. And very unhappy. Was the look on his face anger? Pain? Fear? Surprise? Probably a combination of all of them.

"Let's get out of here," Michael said, echoing my thought. "I mean, we need to get back to the village and report this."

As we stepped out of the shed, I tripped over something and went sprawling.

"Are you all right?" Michael asked.

"I'm fine," I said. "Just tripped over something Resnick must have left lying around."

"Even dead, that man's dangerous," he said.

Before I got up, I felt around to find whatever had tripped me—I didn't want to repeat the experience again immediately. My hands finally touched something—a thick, slightly damp nine-by-twelve envelope, curled up into a half cylinder. Was that what I'd tripped over? Odd that it was only slightly damp if it had been lying around in the rain for any amount of time. Perhaps the overhanging roof of the shed had sheltered it until I'd tripped over it. Or perhaps Resnick had carried it rolled up and stuffed into one of his pockets and it had fallen out when we moved him.

I stowed it in my knapsack for later examination; then Michael and I hiked back to the village, looking over our shoulders about every third step.

Jeb Barnes wasn't happy to see us again.

CHAPTER 12

A Puffin Is Announced

"We haven't seen your father," Jeb said, hunching toward the woodstove and holding his coffee closer to his face.

"Neither have we," I said. "That's not why we're here."

"Phoebe's not here, either," one of the locals said.

"We've come to report a murder," Michael said in his most resonant stage voice.

The group around the stove froze, and one dropped a coffee mug, which shattered on the gray wooden floor.

"Who did that crazy fool shoot?" Jeb Barnes asked when he finally found his voice.

"Resnick? He didn't shoot anyone," I said. "Someone smashed his skull in first."

I didn't imagine the faint sighs of relief from several of the locals.

"Who did it?" Jeb demanded.

"How should we know?" Michael said. "We just found him facedown in the water."

"In the water?" Jeb echoed.

"In a tidal pool a little down the shore from his house," I said. "We had to move him; the tide was about to wash him away, so we carried him up and put him out of the rain."

"My God," Jeb said. "What are we supposed to do now?"

Why does everyone look at me when people ask questions like that?

"I suppose you can't call the police over from the mainland until the storm's over?"

"The phones are down," Jeb said. "I could try radioing

the Coast Guard, but even if I got through, I doubt they could come till after the storm. It's headed our way now."

"No, it's not; it's going to miss us by at least fifty miles," another local put in.

"Fifty miles is nothing to a hurricane," Jeb said. "Why, in '24—"

"So aren't you going to do something about the body?" I interrupted. "To preserve it until the police get here?"

They all stared at me.

"Is there anyplace on the island with a working generator and a big refrigerator you can empty out?"

They looked horrified.

"One of the restaurants, maybe?" I suggested. "Most of them have closed for the season. And most of them have emergency generators, don't they? Because of the food?"

"Yes, but—" a local began, and then stopped. They looked at one another. I could read their thoughts. Having its refrigerator serve as a temporary morgue wouldn't enhance a restaurant's ambiance if it got out—and it would certainly get out in a community as small as Monhegan.

"I hear the Anchor Inn's probably going out of business unless the Mayfields get an extension on their loan," one said finally.

"Mayfields went back to the mainland, though," another said.

"They're having the Dickermans look after the place," Jeb Barnes said, looking relieved. "Fred, you've got a key, right? You take care of it."

Fred was tucked away behind the stove, nursing a mug with a protective air, which made me suspect it contained more than just coffee. He looked up, nodded, chugged the remaining contents of his mug, and slouched over to the coatrack beside the door.

"And someone official should take charge of the scene," I said, looking at Jeb. "Supervise bringing the body down."

Jeb sighed and began struggling into his raincoat and hat, as well.

"Sam, you see if you can raise the Coast Guard," he said. "I'll fetch the mayor and we'll go up to the crime scene."

"And can you have someone start a search for my dad and Aunt Phoebe?" I asked. "With a killer running loose on the island, I'm getting very worried about them."

"There's no way we can send anybody out right now," Jeb said. "If they have a lick of sense, they'll find someplace and stay put till morning. Can't have search parties risking their necks out on those rocks. Where did you say you left the body?"

"We'll show you," I said. Michael and I climbed in the back of the truck, which rattled over the gravel road and finally pulled up in front of a small gray saltbox house whose windows were tightly boarded against the storm.

"Why are we stopping here?" I asked nervously. "Doesn't the idiot even know where Resnick's house is?"

Jeb Barnes got out and began knocking on the door of the house.

"Mamie!" he yelled. "It's Jeb; we've got a problem."

The door opened, and the owner of the puffin-infested gift shop peered out.

"Problem?" she repeated. "What sort of a problem?"

"That damn fool Resnick's gone and gotten himself killed."

"Murdered, most likely," I called from my place in the truck.

"How awful!" Mamie said, her voice implying she didn't really think it was particularly awful at all.

"Those two found him," Jeb Barnes said, jerking a thumb over his shoulder at Michael and me. "We'd better secure the body until the mainland authorities can get here."

"Right," Mamie said. "Hang on a minute while I put on my rain gear."

Jeb climbed in the back of the truck with Michael and me.

"Why are we bringing Mamie?" I asked.

"Well, like you said, we need the local authorities to take charge of the body. She's the mayor."

Her Honor reappeared, dressed in a battered rain slicker, got into the cab of the truck with Fred, and we clattered off—this time, to my relief, in the direction of Resnick's house.

Jeb didn't say much—not that we'd have heard him, given the rising wind and the rough ground the truck rattled over. I had nothing to distract me from my thoughts, which were pretty grim. If the police didn't quickly figure out who had bashed Victor Resnick's head in, suspicion could start falling on far too many of my nearest and dearest. On Aunt Phoebe, last seen dashing off to Resnick's house, announcing her intention of giving him a good thrashing. On Michael and me, since we'd made no secret of our anger over Resnick taking potshots at us. And since we had no proof yet that we'd only discovered the crime, instead of committing it. And, worst of all, on Dad. Even though I'd pocketed the telltale map, I doubted if Mrs. Fenniman was the only one on the island who knew Resnick was an old beau of Mother's. And now that I thought about it, Dad had seemed in a rather strange, quiet mood after he'd heard that Resnick had returned to the island. What if some detective who didn't really know Dad jumped to the wrong conclusion?

Then again, with both Dad and Aunt Phoebe missing, I also had ample reason for worrying about what might be happening to them. I couldn't help fretting that if Hurricane Gladys didn't get them, the unknown killer would. And occasionally, just by way of a change, I glanced over at Michael and worried a little about what he thought of all this. Bad enough I'd dragged him off for a so-called vacation under cold, wet, primitive conditions that offered even less privacy than we'd had in Yorktown. Now I'd dragged him into the middle of another homicide.

Stop worrying, I told myself, though I might as well have told the wind to stop blowing. I come from a long line of Olympic-caliber worriers.

When we got to the gravel path to Resnick's house, Fred Dickerman stopped his truck and we all climbed out.

"We'll have to send someone up to the power plant to fetch Jim," Mamie boomed at us. "Hate to take him away from his repair work, but the Mayfields have a small backup generator; I think he can get that going to run the cooler."

"Can't Fred do that?" Jeb asked.

Fred shrugged.

"Jim's the one knows generators," he said.

"We'll fetch him," I volunteered. "You'll have no trouble finding the body; it's in his woodshed."

"You have to show us where you found the body," Mamie said.

"We can't," I said. She looked up with a frown. "Not until low tide anyway. We found him facedown in a tidal pool at the foot of the cliffs."

"Good thing you came along when you did, then," she said. "He'd have washed away by now if you hadn't brought him up."

I wondered if she was sincere or if, like me, she'd realized how much less trouble we'd have if Michael and I hadn't found Resnick. If the storm had washed his body away, they might never have found him. Or if they had, they'd probably have assumed the gash on the back of his head happened in the storm. Nonsense, I told myself; you've prevented a murderer from getting away with his crime.

"We'll show you tomorrow," I said. "After it's light. And after we find my dad and Aunt Phoebe."

"Good Lord, don't tell me they're still out there," Mamie said.

"Jeb says we can't send out search parties until the storm blows over," I said.

"No, we can't," Mamie said. "Let's go get the body."

As she headed down the path toward Resnick's house, I could have sworn I heard one of the three mutter, "Damn fool tourists." Maybe I was imagining things. Maybe not. And they needn't have muttered; I'd have agreed with them.

Michael and I toiled up the road a little farther, heading for the power plant.

"We should come back up here when the storm's over," I said as we rested before the final, nearly vertical stretch of road. "You get a beautiful view of this whole end of the island from up here. The village on this side, and the wild, unspoiled landscape on the other. At least you could the last time I came up here," I added with a frown. "Who knows—maybe between the power plant and Resnick's monstrosity, there isn't much unspoiled view left."

With that cheerful thought, we attacked the last hill. Up this high, we had little shelter from the wind, which blew the raindrops nearly horizontal at times. We could never have found the shed housing the power plant if not for the flickering lantern light in the windows. We felt our way around the side of the building until we came to a door, then began pounding as loudly as we could.

"I don't suppose it would occur to anyone to build a front porch to this thing," Michael shouted as we pounded.

"It's only a shed," I shouted back. Although I did think that even with a shed, any sane builder would have gone to the trouble of putting up gutters—so when it rained, you could get inside without walking through sheets of water running straight off the steeply slanted roof.

The door finally opened and a bearded face peered out

from considerably above my eye level. Could this be little Jimmy Dickerman?

"I'm working on it," he said, and started to shut the door.

"Wait," I said, inserting my foot in the frame. "What do you mean, 'I'm working on it'? You don't even know why we came up here."

He looked at me as if I were crazy.

"Same reason everybody else comes up here when the phones are out," he said. "To ask when the generator's going on-line again. And the answer's the same I'd give anybody: I don't know yet, and I'm working on it."

"Fine," I said. "Except that's not why we're here. Mamie sent us. Can we come in? It's pouring out here."

Jim looked at us for a minute, then nodded and turned to walk back into the shed. Michael and I followed.

"Good Lord!" Michael exclaimed, looking around. The shed contained a jungle of odd-shaped metal tools, parts, and machines. I remembered Jim, as a child, filling the Dickerman house with odd bits of half-assembled machinery that he was tinkering with or saving for some inscrutable purpose. He'd expanded the scope of his operations considerably since then. I once saw a picture of an elephant graveyard, littered with the skeletons and tusks of elephants who'd gone there to die. Jim had created the mechanical equivalent. No wonder Mrs. Dickerman had sounded so happy when she talked about her Jimmy up here tinkering with his machines. At least she had her living room back.

Jim had returned to pottering with one large machine. It looked old, but less abandoned than most of the objects in the room.

"That the generator?" I asked.

He nodded.

"What's wrong with it?"

Jim looked up.

"You really want to know?"

I had a feeling if I said yes, I'd regret it for at least the several hours he'd take to explain.

"Not really," I confessed. "Aunt Phoebe's not even hooked up to your power company yet, so it's academic to me how long it'll take to fix it."

"Good for you, then, 'cause it's going to take awhile," Jim said. "Specially if the mayor keeps sending people up here to pester me. What is it this time?"

His surliness irritated me.

"Murder," I said.

CHAPTER 13

Zen and the Art of Puffin Maintenance

Okay, it was a cheap trick, but Jim Dickerman got on my nerves. I enjoyed the way his head snapped around when I said that, and how he stared at me, openmouthed.

"Murder," he repeated finally. "Who?"

"Victor Resnick."

"Least it's nobody anyone's going to miss," he said, recovering his poise. "What's that got to do with me anyway?"

"The mayor wants you to go down and get the generator at the Anchor Inn going," I said. "They're storing the body there in the meat locker until the police can get here."

Jim chuckled.

"Mayfields know about this?" he asked.

"The Mayfields aren't here to object," I said. "The mayor's exercising her authority and commandeering it."

"Should have exercised her authority when the old bastard started putting up that eyesore of his," Jim commented. "Well, now he's gone, maybe the town can get it condemned, tear it down."

Not a very eloquent eulogy, but typical, I suspected, of what the townspeople would say when news of Resnick's death got around.

Jim poked around the shed for a while, gathering tools. I didn't mind the delay. I wasn't looking forward to going back out into the storm. And Jim's workroom was rather interesting.

The more I stared around, the more I could identify the bits and pieces. Over in one corner were the parts to an old lawn mower. Did anyone on Monhegan actually mow lawns? Another large pile would probably turn into a golf cart when reassembled. I saw two pair of binoculars, one more or less intact and the other in pieces. Or maybe it was the disassembled pieces of several sets of binoculars; I doubted all the parts would fit into one. The pile of radio parts also contained enough components to assemble two or three objects, as did the piles of fragments from televisions, VCRs, cameras, and outboard motors. He had a few intact things, too: propane tanks, Coleman lanterns, and, in one corner, a large glistening-wet coil of the familiar industrial-weight orange power cords Monheganites used when they wanted to borrow some electricity from a more wired neighbor.

"Your dad would love this place," Michael said.

Yes, he would. I shuddered at the thought of the havoc he could wreak.

"Don't want anyone barging in here right now when I'm working on the generator," Jim said, looking up from his tool bench.

"Don't worry," Michael said. "At the moment, Dr. Langslow's lost somewhere on the island. By the time he's found, you'll probably have the generator running again."

"Dr. Langslow?" Jim repeated, looking at me. "You're Meg, then?"

I nodded. Jim looked at me with a frown. I suppose he was trying to connect my thirty-something self with the teenager I'd been when he'd last seen me. He shrugged as he threw on several layers of wraps and rain gear. Then he picked up a tool box and stepped out into the storm.

Jim set off briskly, head down against the rain, ignoring us trailing behind him. When we got to the edge of the hill, I paused briefly to look around. Apart from my desire not to spend any more time than necessary with the mortal remains of the late Victor Resnick, I'd wanted to come up to the power plant because I knew it had a view of half the island. From this vantage point, I'd hoped I could spot Dad or Aunt Phoebe. But I could see only the occasional flickering lights of candles and oil lamps, and not many of those. I sighed and began scrambling down the slope after Michael and Jim.

When we got to the Anchor Inn, Jim disappeared into the back shed to tinker with the generator while Michael and I stepped into the front room to take a break before the rest of our hike back to the cottage.

A nice place, the Anchor Inn. Of course, the heat and power were off. But it was solidly built, and insulated well enough to keep out not only the wind but also a good deal of its noise. We stumbled past a number of tables with the chairs stacked upside down on their tops and peered into the shadowy kitchen.

Mamie had gone, but Jeb Barnes and Fred Dickerman still stood guard. Jeb stood beside the cooler door, looking around as if he expected body snatchers to leap out from behind the cabinets. Fred sat as far from the cooler as possible, smoking a cigarette. I wouldn't have pegged him for the squeamish or superstitious type, but I noticed that his hand shook a bit.

"You find Jim?" Jeb asked.

"He's out back," Michael said.

"Are the police coming over?" I asked.

Jeb snorted.

"In this weather? Hell no. Maybe tomorrow, but probably not till Monday."

A sudden rumbling noise filled the building. A light over in the far end of the kitchen came on, and the meat locker began humming.

"Well, that's taken care of anyway," Jeb said. He stood up and began donning his rain slicker. "You and Jim keep an eye on the place, make sure the generator's running."

"Right," Fred said. He still had all his rain gear on, and from the haste with which he buttoned his slicker on his way to the door, I had a feeling he'd keep an eye on the place from a distance.

"Shall we go?" Michael asked.

I started. I'd been lost in thought. If the police couldn't come out for a day or so, all the better, as far as I could see. I wanted time to find out some things before the authorities showed up. Like how Dad had managed to drop his map of the island at the murder scene. And where he and Aunt Phoebe were, and what really had happened when she confronted Resnick. After all, we were longtime summer people, but we were only summer people. Which in the local hierarchy put us only one step above day tourists, and considerably below lobsters and puffins. And I had a feeling that even the mainland police would rather have their internationally famous corpse bumped off by tourists or summer people instead of by some good, solid, salt-of-the-earth Monheganite.

The weather outside had gone beyond frightful. The wind drove the rain into our skin like cold needles, and at times we had to clutch fences and buildings to keep from being knocked down.

We seriously contemplated taking refuge for a while in the village church. Candlelight flickered invitingly in the windows, and the birders camping inside were having a splendid time, despite the lack of creature comforts. We could hear a spirited rendition of "Kumbayah" in three-part harmony.

"I'm not looking forward to going back to the cottage without Dad," I shouted over the wind as we struggled down the lane. Is the wind really that much worse, I wondered, or does it just seem that way this close to the water?

"Your mother will be frantic," Michael shouted back as we paused for a moment to steady ourselves.

"I'm already frantic," I bellowed back. "But there's no way we can keep looking when the storm's like this. We'll just have to hope that he's got the sense to—my God, what was that?"

Michael raised his arm instinctively to shield me as a gust of wind slammed a large metal object down in the road a few inches in front of our feet and then swept it over the side of the road and down toward the beach. I could hear a metal clanging noise as it hit the rocks of the breakwater below.

"An aluminum lawn chair, I think," Michael answered, staggering over to the edge of the road. "It almost—oh no!"

I struggled to his side and peered over the edge of the road. I could see someone crouching on the rocks, perilously close to the edge of the water.

Mother.

CHAPTER 14

A Long Day's Journey into Puffins

"Why on earth is she out in this weather?" I asked. Normally, we could barely coax Mother out on the deck on a perfect summer day, and even then she'd be well nigh invisible beneath the sunblock, the giant sunglasses, the parasol, and the mosquito hat. But for her to go out in the hurricane . . .

"She must be in a panic about your dad," Michael said, echoing my thought. "We'd better go rescue her."

We crawled down the breakwater toward her. She clung to a rock with one hand, but when she saw us coming, she waved at us with—What the devil did she have in her other hand?

An umbrella. Or what remained of one after the wind had turned the frame inside out and ripped away all but a few shreds of fabric.

"Hello, dears," she said when we reached her side. "I'm very glad to see you. I've hurt my ankle and I was beginning to wonder how I'd get home."

"What on earth are you doing out here?" Michael asked.

"Looking for James. Have you found him yet?" she asked. Beneath her usual calm tone was an edge of panic. Or was it pain? Either way, I'd have given anything to have some good news to tell her.

"Not yet, and there's no way we can keep looking at night, not in this weather," I said as calmly as I could manage. "I'm sure he's holed up somewhere and we'll find him in the morning."

She looked at me for a few seconds, and I tried to project calm, reassurance, and confidence. But after thirty-odd years, I should have known better than to try fooling her. She nodded slightly, and I could see her jaw clench.

"Let's continue this back at the house," Michael said. "Can you walk?"

"No, dear," she said. "I think I must have done something unfortunate to my ankle."

I twitched up the hem of her skirt and took a look. Yes, *unfortunate* was a good word; the ankle had swollen to the size of a grapefruit. I also noticed that she wore the battered remains of a pair of high-heeled leopard-print sandals.

"Good grief," I said. "It's no wonder you hurt yourself, wearing these things. Why didn't you put on a pair of sneakers or something? Something practical you could walk in."

"I walked all over Paris in these," she said. "They're the most practical ones I have with me."

"You should have borrowed a pair of mine."

"At least these fit," she retorted. She had a point; her feet were three sizes smaller than mine. But still . . .

"We'll have to carry her," I said, turning to Michael.

Just then a wave, slightly larger than the rest, lapped over Mother's foot.

"I think I'm ready to leave now," she said, clutching Michael's hand.

I couldn't help thinking, as we half-pulled, half-carried Mother home, how much easier it had been with Resnick—even though he'd been a deadweight and Mother helped as much as she could. But the storm had gotten so much worse in the last couple of hours. And then again, we didn't have to worry about hurting Resnick; Mother was fighting back tears of pain by the time we finally staggered up the front steps of Aunt Phoebe's cottage.

Mrs. Fenniman leapt up from the couch when we sloshed into the living room.

"Good heavens, Margaret," she exclaimed. "I thought you were upstairs napping!"

"Napping?" Mother snapped back. "Napping, with James out there in the storm, and for all we know—" She stopped, and settled for frowning at Mrs. Fenniman.

"Well, what do you two have to say for yourselves?" Mrs. Fenniman said, turning on us. "Have you managed to find anyone?"

"We haven't found Dad, we haven't found Aunt Phoebe, and someone knocked off Victor Resnick," I said.

" 'Knocked off'?" Mrs. Fenniman exclaimed. "As in murdered?"

"Oh my God," Mother murmured. "You should be out looking for your father."

"That's what we've been doing," I said. "But we can't possibly do any good right now; we'll go out again in the morning, assuming the storm has let up and there's a ghost of a chance of finding him without killing ourselves in the process."

"But we can't just leave him out there in the storm!" she protested, blinking back tears.

"Mother, he has his knapsack," I said. "Which means he's got supplies—food, water, Gatorade, flares, a flashlight, a first-aid kit, and even that silver blanket that's supposed to help you retain ninety-five percent of your body heat. He's got everything he needs to survive."

Except, of course, for the common sense that would have kept him from venturing out into the storm in the first place, but I wasn't going to bring that up.

Just then, the front door burst open and Rob stumbled in, bringing a gust of wind and spray with him. He had to struggle to close the door, then leaned against it, panting.

"It's impossible out there," he said finally. I glanced at Mother's face and had to look away.

"Come on, let's get you patched up," Mrs. Fenniman said, helping Mother toward the stairs. Mother stopped at the bottom step and fixed me with her sternest glance. She looked at me for a full minute, as if it were my fault Dad had gone off on another crazy expedition.

"First thing in the morning," she said. And then she shook off Mrs. Fenniman and limped up the stairs by herself, leaning heavily on the banister all the way.

Michael, Rob, and I fetched dry clothes and they chivalrously insisted I take first turn in the shower. I would have loved to stand under the spray for an hour, until I felt really warm again, but I knew the meager hot-water supply would barely let all three of us wash off our coatings of mud.

"I suppose I should fix something for us to eat," I said, slumping on the couch as I dried my hair.

"I'll do it after my shower," Michael said.

"Leave the cooking to me," Mrs. Fenniman said. "You come and tell me about the murder."

"Dinner sounds like a good idea," Rob said, disappearing into the bathroom. "I'll be out in half an hour."

"Don't you dare use all the hot water, Rob," I called. "Leave some for Michael."

"Don't worry about it," Michael said. "I'll manage."

"Rob's like Mother," I said. "You have to be firm with him."

"Like you are with your mother," he said with a smile, and disappeared into the kitchen.

Good point.

I slumped on the sofa and listened to the increasing wind, the rattle of pans, the rise and fall of Michael's voice as he narrated our day's adventures, and the occasional exclamation from Mrs. Fenniman. I couldn't actually make out Michael's words, thanks to the wind, which suited me just fine. I wanted to think about something other than lost relatives and dead bodies for a while. Not that I had the slightest chance of doing so. My brain was running like a hamster in a wire wheel, wondering where Dad and Aunt Phoebe were, and what they were doing, and whether they were all right, and occasionally, just by way of a change, wondering who had done in Victor Resnick.

Every few minutes, Mrs. Fenniman would pop out of the kitchen and bring me the next course of what was rapidly turning into an epicurean feast. I managed to put away a ham and cheese sandwich, a bowl of chili, a bowl of soup, a plate of mixed fruit, and a baked potato before I called a halt. Mrs. Fenniman didn't. She kept bringing out more food and insisting I needed to eat to keep my strength up. I got tired of arguing with her and started shoving the new arrivals under the coffee table. Spike was in ecstasy, alternating between devouring the food and licking my ankles. After an hour, Rob finally ceded the bathroom to poor Michael and settled onto the other sofa to be fed.

At one point, Mrs. Fenniman bustled upstairs. I could hear her and Mother squabbling about something, and then she stormed down again.

"Finally got her to take one of my Valium," she said. "Calm her down a little. Only way she's going to make it though tonight without going crazy."

As the night wore on, I became convinced that whoever had prescribed Mrs. Fenniman's Valium had actually slipped her a placebo. Mother didn't calm down in the slightest. Periodically, she would limp out of her room and lean over the balcony. She would stand motionless until she had attracted everyone's attention. Then she would look pointedly at the door and even more pointedly at me.

I should have just ignored her, but every time, I patiently explained that we had spent several hours searching all over the island before the storm made it too dangerous. That if Dad had any sense, he'd found someplace to hole up for the night. That as soon as it was light enough to see six feet in front of our faces, we'd go out and start hunting all over again.

She would look reproachfully at me, heave an enormous sigh, mutter something like "Your poor father!" and disappear. For about fifteen minutes. Then we'd go through the whole thing all over again.

Dad always says a person's true character comes through in a crisis. Judged by his own standard, Dad didn't come off too badly. Unless the crisis was a medical one, he was generally of no practical use and had a tendency to run around getting underfoot and making implausible suggestions. But he remained so cheerful and optimistic that no one really minded having him around. In fact, they almost invariably spoke of him afterward as a tower of strength and a real inspiration.

Mother ignored crises as long as possible, on the assumption that of course someone else would take care of them. Usually me. On those rare occasions when Mother felt a situation needed her attention, she would go into what Rob and I called the "off with her head" mode—making decisions and issuing orders with a ruthlessness that made Robespierre look benign. Once Mother took charge, crises tended to work themselves out quite satisfactorily—at least if you agreed with Mother's definition of a satisfactory outcome. That Mother could think of nothing to do except pace the floor and lay a guilt trip on me disturbed me almost as much as Dad's absence.

So far, Michael had shown a great deal of grace under pressure. He'd kept his sense of humor when the trip hadn't turned out to be the private, romantic getaway we'd planned, and if he was grumbling about the primitive conditions here on the island, he'd kept it to himself. Since Dad had gone AWOL, Michael had run himself ragged helping me search, all the while remaining supportive and upbeat, without displaying the sort of mindless, cheerful optimism that would have sent me over the edge. Over the last few weeks, Mrs. Fenniman had decided that Michael was, as she put it, "a keeper." Her habit of telling me this loudly, repeatedly, and in front of Michael had grown irritating, but I couldn't exactly argue with her.

I only hoped he felt the same way about me. I like to think that in a crisis I'm the cool, collected one who really gets things done with calm efficiency. I'm afraid that I'm really a lot more like Dad, with occasional touches of Mother at her worst. Well, I'd worry about that when the crisis was over; all I could do now was wait the storm out. For lack of something better to distract my mind, I picked up one of the bird books that perched on every available horizontal surface and began thumbing through it, trying to concentrate on the contents. Despite my agitated state, I couldn't help marveling at both the incredible variety of birds in the world and the incredible subtlety of some of the variations. I leafed through page after page of birds largely indistinguishable from one another unless you happened to have memorized minute differences in the amount of white on the head or red on the wing. And the way they were arranged—all the birds on the same page in the very same pose, like some avian chorus line—was particularly daunting.

"What's that?" Michael asked, sitting down beside me and handing me a cup of hot tea. He had a towel draped around his neck and smelled faintly of soap. He seemed in fairly good spirits for someone who had probably just taken a cold shower. I held up the bird book so he could see the cover.

"Thinking of taking up bird-watching?" he asked.

"Not on your life," I said. "I'd go crazy. Look at this!" I pointed to a page entitled "Small Hooded Gulls."

"Seagulls," he said. "Lots of seagulls. So?"

"Yes, but that's only one page of seagulls. There are five or six more, not to mention the terns. And look at these: the laughing gull and the Franklin's gull? Can you tell them apart? What if one of them gets a spot of tar on the red beak? You'd probably think he was a Bonaparte's gull, the one with the all-black beak."

"Does it really matter?" Michael asked, giving me an odd look.

"That's my point," I said. "I just don't get it. They're gulls; they eat garbage and scream at the ferry. Does it really matter that much which particular kind of gull they are? I can't figure out why the birders get so obsessive."

"See, I knew we had a lot in common," Michael said. "I promise I will never take up bird-watching."

"Here, take a look at this," I said, flipping to another page and pointing to a bird. Michael glanced at it.

"That's *not* a seagull," he said.

"No," I said. "It's our friend the Bohemian waxwing. *Bombycilla garrulus.* You know, the one those bird-watchers got so upset at us for scaring away this morning."

"If you say so," Michael said, putting his arm around my shoulder. "It seems like days ago, not this morning, and anyway, my mind wasn't on the damned bird at that point."

"I was just thinking about how fanatical some of those birders are," I said. "Do you think one of them could have lost all sense of proportion and attacked Resnick because of what they all thought he'd done to the birds?"

"It's possible," Michael said. "I think the lobstermen have a more down-to-earth reason."

"Oh, did you understand all that about the bill?" I asked.

"Not one word in ten, but I got the idea that they thought he'd spent a lot of money supporting a cause that would put them all out of business."

"It's a motive all right," I said. "And anyone who cares about preserving the unspoiled charm of the island has a motive every time they look at that horrible house of his. Anyone he's taken potshots at could have a motive. Somehow, I can't see the Puffin Lady of Monhegan bashing anyone's head in, but I wouldn't put it past Mayor Mamie."

"Yes, she's very protective of poor little Rhapsody," Michael said.

"I'm sure she sells a lot of her books."

"Is there anyone on the island who doesn't have it in for the guy?"

"Probably not," I said. "Maybe we're looking at a real-life reenactment of *Murder on the Orient Express*."

"Well, let's forget about it for now," Michael said. He used his bare toe to nudge aside some of the plates on the coffee table and then propped both feet up on it. "We can't do anything now, and we'll have to get up early to search. Let's unwind and get some rest."

It sounded like a good idea to me. I took a sip of my hot tea, leaned back into Michael's arm, and sighed. As long as I kept my eyes closed, I could pretend that everything was just the way I'd imagined it when I planned our getaway. Michael and I sitting warm and cozy on a soft couch in front of the fireplace, listening to the crackling of the fire and the pounding of the surf outside the cottage.

And my brother sneezing, and Mrs. Fenniman rattling plates in the kitchen, and, of course, the wind periodically slamming large objects into the side of the house. So much for cozy.

"You haven't had any coleslaw yet."

I opened one eye and saw a large, virtually untouched bowl of coleslaw floating just under my nose. I had given up telling Mrs. Fenniman that I hated coleslaw.

"No thanks," I said, closing my eye again.

"It was great, really," Michael said. "But I'm stuffed."

Mrs. Fenniman sighed and moved on to thrust the bowl under Rob's nose. I heard a sudden crash.

"What was that?" came a voice from above.

We all looked up to where Mother was standing on the balcony above us.

"I just knocked over another one of Phoebe's damned flowerpots," Mrs. Fenniman grumbled, picking her way through the shards of pottery toward the kitchen.

Mother disappeared back into her room.

I felt something cold and wet on my ankle. Spike,

having investigated the remains of the flowerpot and found them inedible, had returned to my feet and now resumed licking me obsessively. I discouraged his attempts to climb into my lap. For one thing, he'd probably bite Michael, and for another, if he'd eaten even half of the food I'd stuck under the coffee table, he'd probably start throwing up later in the evening. Better on my ankle than in my lap.

I looked around. The living room looked more like a consignment shop for used lawn and garden equipment than the cozy retreat of my vision. If I peeked over the forest of flowerpots and garden gnomes infesting the coffee table, I could see Rob reclining on the other sofa, reading a law book and adding to his thick sheaf of notes. Part of me wanted to shriek at him for being so lost in his role-playing game when we had no idea if Dad was even alive—and another part of me envied him.

His side of the coffee table was covered with plates and bowls containing samples of all the various foods Mrs. Fenniman had dished out. Mrs. Fenniman seemed to work on the theory that the hurricane wasn't going away until we'd emptied out the larder, but even Rob was long past the point where he could help her out.

She reappeared with a broom and dustpan, and a plastic ice-cream tub. She plopped the orphaned plant and some of its dirt into the tub and began sweeping up the rest of the dirt and the bits of broken pot. I jumped to move a birdbath out of the way before she knocked it over with the broom handle. Mrs. Fenniman continued flailing away with the broom, and I stood by, ready to rescue anything else that got in her way.

But she lost energy; with a final flourish, she swept a few more specks of dirt into the dustpan, then marched off into the kitchen, leaving a trail of potting soil behind her. I sighed and slumped down, shoving my hands into my pockets.

And my fingers encountered a piece of damp paper: the map.

I pulled it out and studied it. Traveling in my pocket had made it even more damp and wrinkled than when I'd found it, but you could still recognize Dad's distinctive printing.

"Meg? Is something wrong?"

Michael looked up at me with an anxious expression on his face.

"I need to talk to you for a moment," I said.

We both glanced upstairs, saw Mother limping dramatically past the railing, looked at each other, and shook our heads in unison. We could hear Mrs. Fenniman singing sea chanties out in the kitchen, so that was out.

"The garden shed?" Michael suggested.

"We're going to check how the shutters are holding up," I told Rob. He barely looked up as Michael and I donned our slickers. On the way out, I grabbed my flashlight and, remembering the envelope I'd picked up outside Resnick's shed, my knapsack. We trooped out the door and over to the garden shed and managed to clear enough space to squeeze inside and close the door.

"Alone at last!" Michael said, putting his arms around me.

CHAPTER 15

The Agony and the Puffin

Okay, we allowed ourselves a brief distraction from the original purpose of our visit to the garden shed. But—call me unromantic if you like—there are limits to how successfully I can be overcome with passion when I'm sopping wet and shivering in an unheated shed that I'm half-convinced won't survive the next strong wind.

"I hate to spoil the moment," I said, "but could you move a little to the left? There's a croquet mallet digging into my kidney."

"If I move to the left, I'll probably drown; the leaks are much worse over there."

"Sorry," I said.

"So much for my hopes that we'd found a hideaway suitable for romantic trysts," Michael said, shoving aside several life jackets and a lobster pot to clear a space for us to sit on a stack of old magazines in the driest part of the shed. "You wanted to talk about something? Or was that just an excuse to get me alone?"

"No, there was something. Here," I said, handing him the map as I perched beside him. He turned on his flashlight and peered down at the paper.

"Your dad's map of the island," he said. "Does this mean you've got some idea where he is?"

"Unfortunately, no."

"Then what's the big deal?"

I took a deep breath.

"I found it down on the shore. Near where we found Resnick's body."

"Damn," Michael said. He closed his eyes and leaned

against the side of the shed. "The police will find this very suspicious."

"The police!" I said, startled. "We can't give this to the police!"

"Meg, we can't not give it to them," Michael said, sitting up again. "That would be concealing evidence."

"Evidence that would make my dad the primary suspect in Resnick's murder. You saw how Jeb and Mamie reacted when they heard Dad had disappeared. For some stupid reason, everyone thinks Dad has some kind of grudge against Resnick because he used to date Mother fifty years ago, before she even met Dad. You heard them. The map will clinch it."

"That doesn't give us the right to conceal evidence. You do realize that, don't you?"

I sat staring at him. I felt betrayed. I'd trusted Michael with something that could hurt Dad, and here he was threatening to squeal to the authorities.

"Meg," Michael said, gently taking my hand. "I don't believe he did it any more than you do. But you have to see that we can't help him by concealing evidence. I mean, for all we know, that map could be what the police need to find and convict the real killer."

I sighed. I didn't like it. I didn't know the local police, wasn't sure I trusted them to find the real killer. But much as I hated the idea, I had to admit he was right.

"Okay," I said. "We'll turn in the map. But to the police, when they get here. Not to Constable Jeb or Mayor Mamie or anyone else on the island when Resnick was killed."

"That's sensible enough," he said.

"Which gives us a day or two to find the real killer," I said.

"You know, you're more like your dad than you want to admit," he said, grinning. "Never pass up a chance to play detective, right?"

"Michael, this is serious," I said. "We've all heard about

cases where the police find a likely suspect and don't look any further. We can't let that happen to Dad."

"Of course not," he said. "Though I'm curious how we're going to find the killer in the middle of a hurricane. Not to mention—well, never mind."

I suspected I knew what he hadn't said: that right now, finding Dad—alive—was more important than proving his innocence.

"I'll keep this safe for now," Michael said, folding the map and taking out his wallet.

"Don't trust me not to destroy it?" I said.

"I wasn't thinking that at all," he said. "But you can't keep carrying it around in your pocket; it'll turn to mush. And we can't just leave it lying around where someone could get hold of it prematurely, and, unlike your purse, my wallet almost never leaves my body."

"Well, that makes sense," I said, slightly mollified by his tone.

"Shall we go back in?" Michael asked. "Much as I'd enjoy being alone with you under other circumstances, this shed's getting colder by the minute. And damper," he added as a large drop of water splattered his nose.

"Hang on a second," I said, opening up my knapsack. "As long as I'm confessing to my crimes against humanity, I may as well make a clean breast of it. I found an envelope in Resnick's yard after we put his body in the shed— tripped over it, actually. It didn't seem wet enough to have been there long, and I wondered if it fell out of his jacket while we were moving him."

"Let's have a look at it, then," Michael said.

I pulled out the envelope and we both pointed our flash-lights at it. It was an ordinary nine-by-twelve brown clasp envelope, with no markings on the outside. Inside we found an inch-thick sheaf of papers held together with a giant binder clip as well as a smaller Tyvek envelope.

The top sheet of the papers held a title, centered, in all

caps: VICTOR S. RESNICK: UNHERALDED GENIUS OF THE DOWN EAST COAST. A BIOGRAPHY. By James Jackson.

"Wonder who James Jackson is," Michael said, flipping to the next page.

"I don't know, but the Tyvek envelope is addressed to him," I said. "In care of General Delivery at the Rockport Post Office."

"My God, listen to this," Michael said. " 'In this tome will be related the story of a great man whose genius has gone largely unappreciated in our century, a century in which the degradation of artistic taste has led to the exaltation of lesser artistic talents and those whose talents lie less in art than in publicity and the pursuit of notoriety, while alone, at the head of a small contingent of artists who still adhere to the tradition of representational art and the tenets of artistic quality that have prevailed, until now, since the Renaissance, Victor Resnick holds back the bulwark against the barbarians of popular culture and the deliberate obfuscations of an outworn academic community; unsung, unheralded, unappreciated, in recent years largely neglected, Victor Resnick nevertheless—' Arg!"

"Was that really all one sentence?" I asked.

"No, only about a third of one," Michael said. "I'm not sure which is worse, James's writing or his blatant toadying."

"I'll give you odds this is the authorized biography," I said.

"Definitely authorized," Michael said. "Our friend Victor has begun making some rather pungent comments on the first couple of pages. 'Small contingent of artists' used to be 'small contingent of artists, such as Andrew Wyeth and Edward Hopper.' Jamie boy might have crossed out the names himself, but only Resnick would scrawl 'Stupid! Don't mention those clowns!' Speaking of odds, I'll give you odds no one ever publishes it unless Jamie boy does a lot of rewrites."

"Looks like he already has," I said. "We've got draft seven, according to the footer. Oh my God!"

"What's wrong?"

"Jackson's got a time/date stamp in the footer—he printed this yesterday at six P.M. The ferry had stopped running by that time. He's on the island!"

"Lucky him, then; not every biographer gets a ringside seat at his subject's murder."

"We've got to find him."

"Why?" Michael asked. "To give him our editorial comments?"

"He's Resnick's biographer; he must know everything about his life," I said. "He'll know better than anyone who might have it in for Resnick."

"We've already decided that's a long list."

"Well, Jamie boy can tell us who's at the head of it. For that matter, we can probably get some ideas from the biography."

"Of course to do that, we'll have to read it," Michael said.

We both stared down at the manuscript in Michael's lap. I flipped over a page. Someone—Resnick, I suspected—had crossed out a paragraph with such violence that his red pen had torn the paper, and he had scrawled, "No, no, *no*!!!" in the margin.

"My sentiments precisely," Michael said.

"You know, we shouldn't lose sight of the fact that James Jackson is a suspect, too," I said.

"He's lucky he wasn't the victim," Michael grumbled. "Writing this badly ought to be a capital offense."

"Maybe Resnick finally realized that the guy can't write and so decided to fire him, or unauthorize him, or whatever you'd call it when you stop cooperating with a biographer.

And Jackson saw his years of hard work go down the drain, and he lashed out and killed Resnick."

"We'll keep it in mind," Michael said. "Meanwhile, I guess we should start reading. I'm sure it's no worse than some of my students' papers."

I read over Michael's shoulder for the first twenty or thirty pages. Okay, I confess, I skimmed a lot. When you chucked out the excess verbiage—was the man paid by the word, or only by the adverb?—and untangled the convoluted sentences, Resnick's story was really pretty simple. He'd grown up in a small midwestern town, a sensitive, misunderstood child, the butt of every bully and jester in town, until the day he first picked up a pencil and began to draw. At which point, to judge from James Jackson's account, the earth trembled, comets were seen in the skies, three-headed calves were born, and wise men came from the east bearing gifts in the form of a scholarship to study art at the Boston Conservatory. By the time we reached the detailed description of the physical ailments that had kept him, despite his intense patriotism, from serving in World War II, my head was spinning.

"I need a break," I said. "I think I'll see what's in Jamie boy's mail."

"It's a federal offense to open mail!" Michael protested.

"Well, I know that," I said, in exasperation. "It's already opened, and I've never heard it was a federal offense to read stuff that people leave lying around in their yards. So there."

"Sorry," he said. "Must be the demoralizing effect of Jamie boy's prose. Carry on."

I opened the envelope, to find another sheaf of papers— slimmer, fortunately, and not written by James Jackson. The first sheet was a cover letter to Jackson from a Boston private investigation firm, dated a few weeks earlier, stating that the information he had requested was enclosed and that if he required any other assistance, he should contact them.

I turned to the next sheet. A list of names, all with birth dates and some with dates of death. Some of them were people I knew—Mary Ann ("Mamie") Dawes (Benton). Elspeth ("Binkie") Grayson (Burnham). Lucinda Hart Dickerman. Others sounded vaguely familiar. Old island names, many of them. All women, born between 1925 and 1940. Some were crossed out in bright red ink. Others had question marks or checks beside their names. No clue what the list was for.

I finished scanning the first page and flipped to the second, shorter page. Along with the crossed-out, checked, and question-marked names, one was circled heavily in bright red pen: Margaret Hollingworth (Langslow).

What the devil was this list, and why was Mother on it, so prominently singled out?

I went on to the rest of the papers. A series of reports from the detective agency on the whereabouts of the women on the list during their teenage years.

How odd.

I scanned the reports, fascinated. Binkie had gone from a posh boarding school to an equally posh women's college, and from there to Harvard Law School. Not what James Jackson wanted, apparently; he'd crossed her name out on the main list. Several other names had similar histories—summer people, I noticed; their lives contrasted starkly with those of the year-round island residents, many of whom were married and had had several children by the time their wealthier counterparts graduated from whichever of the Seven Sisters they'd chosen.

I came across Mother's sheet, finally, and double-checked it. The private investigator had his facts correct, as far as I knew. Right address, and the dates she'd stayed on Monhegan seemed consistent with what Mother always related of her vacations on the island. High school and college data correct. And in the center of the report, the beginning and end dates of the two years she'd spent in Paris, living with Aunt Amelia, attending a French lycée, taking art and music lessons, and achieving a level of poise and sophistication I knew, even as a toddler, I'd never match.

I had sometimes wondered how different Mother's life (and mine) would be if when she was fifteen Grandfather hadn't finally given in to her pleas to see Paris. If instead he had, for instance, sent her to stay for a few months on Cousin Bathsheba's farm, learning to milk the cows and feed the chickens. That first trip to France was undoubtedly the watershed event in Mother's life.

So why had the private detective circled it in red? And printed five little exclamation points after it?

And why had the biographer clipped a Polaroid of Mother to the back of the page—the present-day Mother, stepping off the Monhegan ferry, wearing a scarf I'd given her three months ago?

I had a bad feeling about this.

"Michael," I said.

"Mmm?" he replied absently. I glanced up. He was lost in the manuscript.

"The biographer's style must be improving," I said.

"What's that?" he said, looking up with obvious reluctance.

"What's so fascinating? I thought it was a lousy book."

"Oh, it is! The writing anyway; but the contents— You've got to hear this. Wait a second; let me get back to the beginning of this chapter.

He flipped back several pages and began reading.

" 'It was at this formative stage of his life that young Victor Resnick underwent an experience, the impact of which would last for the rest of his life, an experience that, while producing no outward change in his demeanor or his countenance, would nevertheless affect the sensitive young artist in the most profound and permanent fashion imaginable. Who could have predicted this event, at once so joyous and so tragic? Who can calculate the import this occurrence would present upon his life and art? Who can possibly discern . . .' Well, you get the idea. It goes on like that for about another page and then Jamie boy finally gets around to dropping a few actual facts. Apparently, young Victor fell in love."

"Don't tell me; I know what's coming. She told him to get lost."

"No, apparently the attraction was mutual."

"That's a little hard to buy."

"According to this, young Victor was quite a hunk and a rising star of the art world to boot."

"According to the biographer, who we already decided was telling Resnick's decidedly one-sided version of events."

"Well, I suppose," Michael said, running his finger down the page. "Here we go: 'She saw beneath his gruff exterior the sensitive artist whose soul had been blighted by calumny and neglect; she alone appreciated not only the force of his artistic genius but also the inner light that he had previously shown only through his brushes, and, bravely scorning the rigid strictures of her upbringing, daringly risking the calumnies and slings and arrows of outraged society that would be flung at her if discovered, she at last surrendered to their mutual passion.' "

"Ick," I said. "So she slept with him. I suppose there's someone for everyone, even Victor Resnick."

"And no matter what the boomers may think, sex wasn't invented with the pill. Anyway, we now have several pages about the progress of the affair, a little light on concrete details, but heavy with descriptions of things heaving and throbbing—the sort of stuff that might be mildly titillating if better written."

"Let me see that," I said, looking over his shoulder.

"Be my guest," Michael said. "And if you should find any of it inspirational . . ."

"You can forget the rerun of the *From Here to Eternity*

surf scene," I said as I scanned the text. "It's vastly over-rated, even on a tropical beach."

"You know this from experience?"

"I know this from common sense," I said. "And do you have any idea how rocky the Monhegan beach is, not to mention the subarctic temperature of the water?"

"So we won't be doing Burt and Debbie this trip?"

"More to the point, I doubt Victor Resnick and his lady love ever did."

"We take this passage with a grain of salt, then. Want to bet the writer learned his—or, more likely, her—trade writing romances?"

"No—most romances are far better written. And most romance writers have a better grasp of reality; that, for example, is anatomically impossible," I said, pointing to one particularly florid paragraph.

"Are you sure?" Michael said, quirking one eyebrow.

"Positive, as I'll happily demonstrate later. He's obviously unreliable about the details—probably embroidered them over the years. This only tells us that some poor woman had the bad taste to sleep with Resnick, and he remembers her fondly, perhaps because that kind of thing was a rare event in his life. And then she came to her senses and broke his heart, or, more likely, dented his ego."

"It's a bit more than that," Michael said. "According to this, she was underage."

"Well, I'm not surprised," I said, fishing out my Gatorade and opening the bottle. "No woman old enough to have any sense could possibly fall for him. How underage?"

"Fifteen. Just barely."

"He's scum."

"Resnick was twenty-five," Michael added.

"Pond scum."

"And her parents forced them to part, then packed her

off to Paris to get over her broken heart. And then—Meg, are you all right?"

"I'm fine; you can stop pounding my back," I said, wheezing, once I'd finally cleared enough Gatorade from my windpipe to speak.

"You're not fine; I can tell," Michael said. "What's wrong?"

I handed him the detective's reports and sat back to cough a little more while he scanned them.

"Oh, damn," he said when he got to Mother's sheaf.

"He thinks Mother was Victor Resnick's secret love."

"Obviously," Michael murmured. He picked up the biography again and flipped over a few pages, frowning.

"It's ridiculous," I fumed.

Michael didn't say anything, and his eyes remained ostentatiously glued to the manuscript.

"Okay, it's not ridiculous; it sounds plausible enough. I certainly don't believe it, but people would if they heard it. And as long as Victor Resnick was alive, or even if he died of natural causes, the odds are no one would ever publish this travesty. But with his murder, they're going to want to drag all the skeletons out of his closet."

"Including a few that just might belong to your family."

We sat there for a few minutes, with me staring at the wall, trying to absorb what I'd read, while Michael continued to read the manuscript.

"Oh, bloody hell," he said suddenly.

"What's wrong?"

"Here," he said, handing me the manuscript and indicating a paragraph with his finger. "Read this."

I tried, but between the biographer's tangled grammar and his overly florid style, I couldn't make heads or tails out of the passage. Something flowery about a token of love, lost many years ago, that Resnick had sought ever since.

"I don't get it," I said. "What's this token thing anyway? Some kind of locket or something?"

"Sorry," Michael said. "It's a little hard to follow out of context. Back up and start reading a couple of pages sooner."

"I'd rather not," I said. "Since you've already suffered through it, why don't you give me the gist?"

"Okay," Michael said. "The biographer thinks Resnick fathered a child with his underage girlfriend. And she went to Paris to conceal her pregnancy."

"Impossible," I said.

"Impossible how?" Michael asked.

I knew what he meant. Impossible for Resnick to have fathered a child with his girlfriend? No. These things happened, even circa 1950. But impossible for the girlfriend to be Mother? Yes, if you asked me. I remembered all the tales Mother told of her years in Paris—the art and music lessons, the exhibitions, the galleries, the fashion shows, the opera, the ballet, the midnight meals in bistros, the flirtations in cafés. How could even Mother talk so blithely of that time if she'd spent the first nine months of it waiting out an unwanted pregnancy?

"I still don't believe it," I said. "But if he publishes that damned book, someone will believe it. Think of the embarrassment."

"Oh, I don't know," Michael said, the corners of his mouth twitching. "I'm not sure your Mother wouldn't like a wild unsubstantiated rumor that in her youth she was the mistress of a famous artist."

"She'd eat it up," I agreed. "But Dad would be mortified. And the cops would have yet another reason for suspecting him of Resnick's murder."

"True," Michael said. "Look, it's freezing out here; can't we finish reading this inside?"

"What if someone sees it!" I protested.

"I'll pretend it's a master's thesis from one of my students," Michael said. "I won't let anybody else read it, and I'll hide it in my suitcase, under the dirty socks, where no one would want to touch it even if they found it."

"Oh, all right," I said, smiling in spite of myself. "I have to admit, I'm not sure I can take much more of this cold."

And is Dad out in this cold? I wondered as we walked back to the house. Or has he hung on to his knapsack, with the chemical hand warmer and the body heat–conserving blanket? Is he curled up warm and dry somewhere? Is he . . .

No, I'd worry about that tomorrow.

When we arrived back in the living room, Rob had disappeared. Michael settled down with the manuscript. I picked up the photo albums and leafed through them until I found the pages that showed Mother and the young Victor Resnick, and brooded over the smiling black-and-white images.

Mrs. Fenniman appeared occasionally with plates of food, sighed when she saw our third helpings of everything were untouched, and clomped back out into the kitchen without speaking.

Suddenly, a shower of plaster rained down on our heads. I looked up, to see a large muddy Reebok protruding from the ceiling.

"Oh damn," came Rob's voice from beyond the Reebok.

"Rob? Are you all right?"

The Reebok wiggled slightly, dislodging more plaster. I adjusted my plate to make sure my unwanted coleslaw got its fair share of debris.

"Yeah, I guess so."

"Do you need any help?" Michael called.

"No, I'm fine," Rob answered.

The Reebok gyrated wildly for a few seconds, then dropped down another six inches and was joined by its mate.

"Actually, I guess I could use a little help after all," Rob said.

Michael and I abandoned our plates, grabbed our flashlights, and climbed upstairs, where, at the end of the hallway, the trapdoor in the ceiling gaped open and a small rickety ladder led up into the attic.

The attic didn't have a floor, just a rolling meadow of fluffy pink insulation crisscrossed by the two-by-fours that formed the rafters. Here and there, large flat pieces of plywood placed across the rafters formed storage spaces for boxes and trunks. None of them anywhere near the ladder, unfortunately. Evidently, Rob had stepped on a piece of plywood too light to hold his weight. Both feet disappeared into a rough-edged hole in the plywood, while he lay sprawled backward on the pink insulation.

"I see you found the jigsaw puzzles," I remarked. Several cardboard puzzle boxes lay nearby, and Rob lay half-covered by the brightly colored pieces of several enormous puzzles.

"I was looking for something to do," Rob said. "I saw the puzzles up here when I fetched the photo albums."

"You're lucky you didn't fall through," Michael said. "You're in the part of the attic over the living room. It'd be a long way down."

Rob shuddered.

"What's going on up there?" came Mrs. Fenniman's voice.

We extricated Rob from the plywood, helped him back to the trapdoor, and watched as he limped away to be patched up and cosseted by Mrs. Fenniman. Michael was about to follow him, but he turned to see why I wasn't coming.

"I'll be down in a little bit," I said.

"You've found something?" Michael asked eagerly.

"No, but it occurs to me that there's an awful lot of old junk in the attic besides the photo albums," I said. "I'm just going to poke around for a while and see what turns up."

"I'll go down and guard the manuscript," Michael said.

Nothing much turned up in the first dozen boxes I opened. Actually, I'd have found some of the stuff fascinating at another time. Vintage clothes, trinkets, and souvenirs of bygone eras. More photos, this time in boxes. Even letters and diaries. A collection of taxidermy, including a stuffed squirrel wearing a jeweled collar and a wolverine in a Groucho Marx nose and a neon Hawaiian-print shirt. Fascinating stuff, really. But most of it more than fifty years old and none of it relevant.

At the bottom of the last box I found about a dozen faded brown manila file folders, tied in a packet with some string. I was struggling to untie the knot when I suddenly heard a commotion down in the main part of the house.

Now what? I thought, tucking the file folders under my arm and carefully walking along the rafters to the trapdoor. I heard Mother's voice wailing.

"I don't believe you; she's lost, too!"

I stuck my head down out of the trapdoor. Mother stood at the edge of the upper hallway, one hand clutching the railing, the other pressed to her forehead, and her eyes raised heavenward. Vintage Sarah Bernhardt.

"How could you let her do it, Michael?" she asked mournfully. "How can you sit there when Meg is out there in the storm, frantically searching for her father?"

"Because I'm not out there in the storm, Mother," I said. "I'm up here in the attic."

Mother turned, looked at me, and blinked.

"Well, what are you doing in the attic?" she asked in an aggravated tone. "Why aren't you doing something useful? Looking for your father, for example?"

I could see her working up to another dramatic scene, and I was tired of the game. I'd been calm, patient, and reassuring the last million times she'd popped out of her room. So by way of a change, while she continued to wail about poor Dad out in the storm, I stuck the folders under my arm, climbed down the ladder, and went downstairs, where I stepped over a pile of croquet mallets, dodged around an upended picnic table, and jerked open the front door.

A gust of wind burst in, carrying with it a half-crushed lobster pot, sending Rob's papers flying like giant snowflakes, knocking flowerpots and other breakable objects onto the floor, and spraying showers of rain halfway across the room.

"Damn it, Meg, close that door!" Rob shouted, snatching at his notes. Mrs. Fenniman and Michael tried to grab as many breakable objects as they could and hold them down. Mother simply sighed and limped back into her room.

Having presumably made my point about the impossibility of searching for Dad in the middle of a hurricane, I stuck the folders under the umbrella stand, got a better grip on the door, and began forcing it closed. But suddenly, I suddenly noticed something outside.

There was a body on the porch.

CHAPTER 16

Travels with My Puffin

I let the door crash open again and staggered outside.

"What the hell are you doing out there?" Rob shouted.

"Michael, Rob, come here and help," I said, crouching over the still form on the porch. "It's Aunt Phoebe."

Aunt Phoebe moaned slightly at the sound of my voice.

"Meg?" she whispered.

"It's all right," I said. "You're home."

Rob, Michael, and I carried her in and laid her on the sofa. She was soaking wet, her clothes were ripped and filthy, and after the first dozen I gave up counting the cuts and bruises on her face and arms.

"I'll get her some clean, dry clothes," Mrs. Fenniman said, knocking over a stack of plastic lawn chairs on her way to the stairs.

"Phoebe!" Mother cried, looking down from the balcony. "What's wrong? Where have you been? Have you seen James?"

"James? Why, isn't he here?"

Mother limped down the stairway and over to the sofa. She sat there patting Aunt Phoebe's hand and giving the rest of us orders to go and do what we'd already started doing—fetching blankets, clothes, hot tea, the first-aid kit.

"You boys come out in the kitchen while she changes," Mrs. Fenniman said.

"A nip of brandy in this wouldn't hurt," Aunt Phoebe said, inhaling the steam from her tea.

"Good idea," Mrs. Fenniman said, crashing her way toward the kitchen.

"And some of that leek and potato soup, while you're there," Aunt Phoebe added.

"And some toast?" Mrs. Fenniman asked.

"Is there jam left?"

I relaxed a little. Aunt Phoebe's injuries couldn't be that bad if she showed such an interest in food. Rob, Michael, and Mrs. Fenniman clattered about in the kitchen and Mother supervised while I helped Aunt Phoebe change, cleaned her wounds, and wrapped an elastic bandage around her hugely swollen knee. I hoped she hadn't dislocated it or done something else serious, since we couldn't possibly get her to the hospital for a day or two.

"So where have you been all this time?" I asked when Michael and Rob had returned and Aunt Phoebe, under Mrs. Fenniman's approving eye, was making serious inroads into a six-course banquet.

"Damn fool thing to have happen," Aunt Phoebe said, plopping a generous dollop of homemade jam on her toast. "Slipped on the path up above the Dickermans' and fell into a gully. Took me forever to crawl out."

"Why didn't you call for help?"

"I did, but who can hear a thing in all this wind? Finally got myself back on the path, then had to half-crawl home. Lost my walking stick."

"Well, why didn't you stop and ask for help at the Dickermans'?" I asked. "Or those people next door, whoever they are?"

"Didn't want to impose on strangers," she said. "My own damn fault, falling in that gully; didn't want to cause them any bother."

"The Dickermans are hardly strangers," I said in exasperation. "You've only known them thirty or forty years."

"Now, Meg," Mother said.

"What were you doing gallivanting up that way anyway?" I asked. "The last time we saw you, you were running up to Victor Resnick's to give him a piece of your mind."

Everyone else in the room froze and looked anxiously back and forth between me and Aunt Phoebe. She paused in the middle of helping herself to another pint of potato salad and cackled.

"I gave him a bit more than a piece of my mind," she said. "Scoundrel had the nerve to wave that blunderbuss of his in my face. Had to take it away from him."

"You did *what*?" Rob said.

"Oh lord," Michael muttered.

"Took away that fool gun of his," Aunt Phoebe said through a mouthful of potato salad. "Threw it off the cliff."

"I'm not sure she should say any more," Rob said.

"Cool it, Rob," I said. "Now's not the time to play lawyer."

"I'm not playing; she may need a lawyer."

"Why, has that fool complained about me?" Aunt Phoebe said. "That rap on the noggin I gave him when he tried to take the gun back is nothing. Look at this bruise where he grabbed my arm! And this cut here—I got this when he tripped me."

"Self-defense," Rob said. "She has a very good case for self-defense."

"Aunt Phoebe," I said, "exactly what happened when you went up to Resnick's house?"

"Why, what does he say happened?" she asked.

"Just tell us."

Aunt Phoebe thought for a moment.

"All right," she said. "I walked up and knocked on his door a couple of times, and nobody answered. I was about to leave when he came charging around the corner of the house, waving his gun. Wasn't aiming it at me, but the way he was waving it around, who knows what could have happened. So I grabbed it, and we played tug-of-war for a bit, until he lost his grip. He tried to twist my arm to make me give it back, so I whacked him sharply on the noggin, and he let go, and I ejected all the shells and threw the thing off the cliff. After that, he yelled for a while, and I yelled back, and then he stomped back into his house and tried to slam the door."

She shrugged and bit into a large ham and cheese sandwich.

"And that was the last you saw of him?" I asked.

She nodded as she chewed and swallowed, then chuckled.

"Fool hadn't put up a single board or a scrap of tape, as far as I could see when I was up there. Wonder if he's still up there trying to ride the storm out in that fishbowl."

"No," I said. "Actually, he's down in the meat locker of the Anchor Inn."

Aunt Phoebe stopped chewing.

"What's he doing there?" she asked through a mouthful of sandwich.

"Waiting to be autopsied," I said. "Michael and I found him floating facedown in a tidal pool earlier today."

Aunt Phoebe swallowed hard and then coughed a few times.

"Are you saying he's dead?" she asked when she could finally speak.

"That's generally a prerequisite for autopsying someone."

"Good Lord! You think that rap on the head killed him?"

"We won't know what killed him until the autopsy," I said.

"He was fine when I left him," Aunt Phoebe said. "Just as loud and obnoxious as ever."

"Maybe he had a delayed reaction," I said. "Or maybe you had nothing to do with it. Was he bleeding very badly when you left him?"

"Didn't see that he was bleeding at all," she said. "I didn't smash his skull in, just rapped him sharplike to let him know I wasn't going to stand for him trying to lay hands on me."

"Rapped him with what?" Michael said.

"My walking stick, of course."

"Well, they can examine the walking stick and compare that to the wound," Michael said. "Maybe someone else hit him later. It's not as if the guy didn't have other enemies."

"If I still had the stick," Aunt Phoebe said. "I told you— I lost it."

"In the gully?" I asked. "We could go look for it in the gully."

"No, somewhere between Resnick's house and the gully," she said.

"That only covers half the island," I said. "I don't suppose you could widen the search area a little?"

"I wasn't thinking about my stick," she said. "I was hopping mad, and I took the long way around to blow off steam. I know I'd lost my stick by the time I got to the gully, because I remember thinking I wouldn't have fallen in if I'd had it. Careless damn fool thing to do."

Or incredibly clever, if the walking stick was the murder weapon. She had only to toss it off the cliff and no one would ever see it again. Except that I couldn't quite picture Aunt Phoebe as a murderer.

We were all silent for a few minutes.

"There's no way they could prove first-degree murder," Rob said, finally.

"Not now, Rob," I said.

"I mean, manslaughter's probably the most they could even hope to—"

"Shut up, Rob!"

"You didn't see James on your way home, did you?" Mother asked.

"Haven't seen him since he took off for Green Point to watch the hurricane hit the island," Aunt Phoebe said. "Have you looked there?"

"Yes, that's how we came to find Resnick's body," I said.

"I'm sure something has happened to him," Mother said.

"He'll be fine, Mother," I said. "He'll turn up in the morning, full of enthusiasm about what an exciting adventure he's had."

I tried to sound as if I really believed it. I wasn't sure I'd fooled anyone. Probably not, since Michael chose that moment to take my hand and give it a reassuring squeeze. Aunt Phoebe had fallen very silent, and, worse yet, she'd stopped eating. Definitely a bad sign.

"Well, I'd better get myself off to bed," Aunt Phoebe said, startling us by thumping the floor with her makeshift walking stick—a flagpole we'd dragged in from the porch— as she struggled to her feet. "I want to look my best when I turn myself in tomorrow."

"Oh, Phoebe, no!" Mother cried.

"No help for it," Aunt Phoebe said. "I can't keep quiet any longer and run the risk that someone innocent will suffer for my crime."

"Ought to give you a medal, considering who you bumped off," Mrs. Fenniman remarked.

"It doesn't matter," Aunt Phoebe said, striking a noble pose. "I must pay the consequences of my actions."

"Ingrid Bergman," I said.

Everyone looked at me as if I were crazy. Except for Michael.

"In *Joan of Arc*?" he asked.

I nodded.

"I can see that," he said. "Although actually I thought more of a Katharine Hepburn."

"In what movie?" I asked.

"I hadn't quite figured out yet. It'll come to me."

"*Sylvia Scarlett*, maybe," I said. "Or, better yet, *Mary of Scotland*."

"Oh, that's the ticket. Definitely *Mary of Scotland*."

"You're both crazy," Mrs. Fenniman announced. "Rob, come help your aunt and your mother with the stairs; they both need their rest."

Michael leapt up to help as well, and after they'd hauled Aunt Phoebe and Mother upstairs, everyone drifted off to bed. Just as well. I was exhausted, too. I retrieved the folders I'd left by the umbrella stand, but then I stuffed them in my suitcase to look at in the morning and took myself to bed. I wasn't sure I could manage dawn, but I knew I'd have to get up pretty early to resume the hunt for Dad. And I wanted to tag along when Aunt Phoebe turned herself in. I didn't for a minute believe she'd murdered Resnick. I couldn't exactly say why, but her story sounded phony to me. Maybe I'd figure out why in the morning, after a good night's sleep.

Of course, a good night's sleep was exactly what I didn't get. The first couple of times I woke up, the storm had definitely gotten worse, as if the cottage were in a wind tunnel, with a herd of elephants pounding on the walls and tap-dancing on the roof. And Michael either had the world's worst case of insomnia or thought he could avert some danger by patrolling the cottage half the night, checking doors and peering out of windows. After about 2:00 or 3:00 A.M., either the hurricane started moving again or I got used to the noise, and I finally got a few hours of sleep.

Mother woke me up at dawn.

"Time to get up and start looking for your father again," she said, leaning over me.

Spike, sleeping on my chest again, growled at her. For once, I agreed with him.

"I don't dare get up till he does," I said, and closed my eyes again.

A few minutes later, I heard the refrigerator door opening and closing several times, followed by pots and pans rattling, and then the crinkling noise of a cellophane wrapper.

Spike lifted his head.

Mother appeared in the doorway, massaging a half-empty potato chip bag.

Spike jumped off my chest and ran over to her, wagging his tail. He followed her back into the kitchen and then out again. She no longer held the potato chip bag, and from the look on Spike's face, I doubted he'd gotten any of the contents.

"You could at least feed him, if you're going to torture him like that."

"I'll feed him after you're gone," she said.

"Don't leave without me," came Aunt Phoebe's voice from above. She stumped down the stairs with her flagpole. Michael and Rob, both half-dressed, trailed after her, trying to help and being firmly shooed away.

"I'm going down to see the constable now," she announced when she reached the ground floor.

"It's only six A.M.; does the store open this early?" I asked.

"It doesn't matter; Jeb Barnes lives behind it," she said. "I don't want to put it off any longer."

"And what about the hurricane?" I asked.

"Moving out to sea," Mrs. Fenniman said. "We're just seeing the tail end of it now."

She could be right, I thought; I hadn't actually heard the wind slam anything into the side of the house for the whole ten or fifteen minutes I'd been awake. Probably a good sign.

"I can't let a little rain stop me," Aunt Phoebe said.

"I think you should have a good last meal first," Mrs. Fenniman announced, knocking over a clump of pink plastic flamingos on her way to the kitchen.

"No, I can't think of food right now," Aunt Phoebe said. "I just want to look around one last time. Who knows when I'll see my own hearth again?"

I wasn't sure she could see the hearth now, considering

the amount of junk in the room, but I suppose she was speaking metaphorically.

"Hang on a minute while I throw some clothes on," I growled. "I won't let you go into the lion's den alone."

I suppose that struck the right melodramatic note; at any rate, she waited, tapping her foot, until I had dressed, gulped down a few ounces of coffee, and grabbed my knapsack. Then she, Michael, and I set off for the village.

Of course, we had to clear quite a bit of debris off the deck before we could escape the house. Leaves, twigs, branches, limbs, and even whole trees were strewn about everywhere, and the number of smashed lobster pots littering the landscape made me worry about how the fishermen would manage next season.

"What a morning," I grumbled as we preceded Aunt Phoebe down the path, moving the worst of the debris out of the way as we went.

"Oh, come on; think what an interesting adventure we're having," Michael said.

"Are you usually this cheerful in the morning?" I asked.

"Why? Is cheerful in the morning a good or a bad thing, in your opinion?"

"Cheerful's fine, as long as it's quietly cheerful until I'm completely awake."

"I'm not awake at all myself," Michael said. "Never am before ten. I'm only this cheerful because I'm sleepwalking."

"That's much better. Sleepwalking I can understand."

"Come on, you two!" Aunt Phoebe called out. "Look sharp up there! Can't keep the law waiting!"

"In a hurry to hang herself, isn't she?" Michael said.

"Do you mean that literally?" I asked. "I mean, does Maine actually have capital punishment?"

"Guess we'll find out," Michael said.

The worst of the storm appeared past, but Hurricane Gladys couldn't have gotten all that far away. It was still raining and blowing heavily, and we had trouble keeping upright. Aunt Phoebe let us help her over the rough spots until we got to the door of the general store. She insisted on walking up the steps and into the store on her own, with the help of the flagpole. Michael opened the door and Aunt Phoebe limped dramatically into the store.

Jeb Barnes already stood behind his counter, despite the early hour, and the usual collection of locals had already gathered around the stove, listening to a battery radio. Or perhaps they'd never gone home last night. Mayor Mamie sat among them, sipping a cup of coffee.

"I've come to turn myself in," Aunt Phoebe announced in ringing tones. "I killed Victor Resnick."

CHAPTER 17

The Return of the Prodigal Puffin

When the commotion died down, Aunt Phoebe described her confrontation with Victor Resnick with a great deal of gusto. Perhaps she had been too tired to go into much detail the night before, or perhaps she found the gang at the general store a more congenial audience. At any rate, she produced a great many more details than she had the first time around. The bit at the end, where she left Resnick lying senseless in the middle of his yard with the hurricane howling around him, was particularly effective. By the time she got to that part of her story, everyone in the general store was speechless with amazement. I was surprised no one applauded. Back home, my family would have.

"Well, I guess that about wraps it up," Jeb Barnes said, when he finally found his voice.

"So you might as well arrest me now," Aunt Phoebe said.

The constable frowned. I suspected he was wondering what to do. I doubted the island had a jail.

"Why don't you have her go back to the cottage and consider herself under house arrest?" I said. "It's not as if she can go anywhere before the ferry starts running."

"Just what I was thinking," Jeb Barnes said. "Consider yourself under house arrest, Miss Hollingworth. Don't leave the island."

"You'll know where to find me, Constable," Aunt Phoebe said. She turned and limped across the room, head held high. Her grand exit was a little spoiled by the blast of wind and rain that burst into the room when she opened the door, nearly knocking her over, but she recovered rapidly and slammed the door behind her.

"What a grand old lady," Jeb Barnes said.

Murmurs of agreement came from the crew around the stove.

"Yes, she is," I said. "She's not your murderer, of course; but she did make a grand confession. I almost believed it myself. But ever since she told us last night, something about her story's been bothering me, and I finally figured out what's wrong with it."

"So what's wrong with it?" Jeb said, giving me a wary look.

"You heard what she said: They were struggling over the gun, and she rapped him on the noggin."

Jeb looked blank.

"Oh, I see," Michael said. "Allow us to demonstrate."

He plucked two umbrellas from a stack dripping by the front door and handed one to me with a flourish.

"My umbrella represents Resnick's gun, and Meg's is her aunt's stick," he said.

Jeb nodded.

Then we pretended to grapple over the gun umbrella. Michael allowed me to wrest it away from him and then, when he tried to grab it back, I rapped him lightly on the head with the top of the walking-stick umbrella.

The crowd around the store was entranced. To my satisfaction, scattered applause greeted the conclusion of our reenactment.

"Notice anything?" I asked.

"Looked pretty authentic to me," Mamie said, sipping her coffee. "Pretty much as she described it.

"Exactly," I said. "So if they were struggling like that, how did she hit him on the back of the head? That's where the wound was; in fact, it was pretty far down the back of the head. I can manage the forehead—like this."

I tapped Michael on the forehead. Just at the hairline,

where I remembered seeing the bruise on Resnick's face.

"I can even manage the top of the head," I continued, demonstrating.

"But there's no way I can manage the back of the head unless he turns his back to me. Her confession doesn't hold water."

"Then why'd she do it?" Mamie asked. "Confess, I mean."

"She probably feels guilty over having hit him on the head," I said. "She's had all night to stew about it; by this time, she probably really believes she killed him. You know my family; by tomorrow, she'll be convinced that she left him lying in a pool of blood with her stick stuck through his heart like a stake."

The nods and chuckles from the locals around the stove showed I'd hit home. I didn't mention the other possibility: that Aunt Phoebe might be covering for someone. Mamie and Jeb looked at each other.

"Go look at Resnick's wounds if you like," I offered. "I'm sure you'll see what I mean."

"No, no," Mamie said. "I think you're right. We'll pass that along to the police."

"And another thing. Jeb, remember we told you Aunt Phoebe was going up to Resnick's. And you went dashing up in Fred Dickerman's truck, right?"

He nodded warily.

"So why didn't you see this supposed murder? You couldn't have gotten there before she did, or you'd have seen her come storming up a few minutes later. And if she really left him lying dead in the middle of the yard, you'd have found him there. But you found him alive, remember? And madder than a wet hen; I believe that was the expression you used. And according to Aunt Phoebe, she left him lying dead in his yard. So how did he end up floating in the tidal pool?"

"That's right," Jeb said. "Guess it's not her after all."

"No problem," one of the locals said. "Not as if they have to look far for a suspect."

Murmurs of agreement followed this statement, and I could see my worst fears coming true. By the time the police arrived, the locals would have Dad tried and convicted in the court of public opinion.

Of course, at the moment, they were doing it in absentia, which reminded me of my real mission, now that we'd defused Aunt Phoebe's confession.

"By the way," I began, but before I could get much further, the door burst open, letting in another blast of wind and water. We all turned to see who was coming in.

"Dad!" I cried, and ran over to hug the wet, bedraggled figure staggering into the store. I felt as if someone had just lifted an enormous weight from my shoulders, and I heard Michael sigh with relief.

Dad was covered with mud and had bits of leaves and twigs stuck in his eyebrows and clinging all over his clothes. The bandage was half off his head, and the gash had opened up again.

"Meg!" he said. "And Michael! I thought I saw you two in here. What are you doing out in the storm?"

"Never mind that; where have you been?" I asked.

"I got lost and had to spend the night under a bush on the far side of the island," he announced, as if he'd managed to pull off something clever. "Did you miss me?"

"You have no idea," I muttered.

"Meg, you should have seen what it was like, watching the hurricane hit!" he cried, waving his arms as if trying to imitate a gale-force wind. "It was awe-inspiring! Invigorating! Absolutely breathtaking! I feel reborn!"

"That's nice," I said. "Now come down to earth for a while; a lot of things have happened while you were out being reborn."

"Was anyone hurt?" Dad asked, no doubt sensing my serious mood.

"Victor Resnick's dead," I said.

"Oh dear," Dad said. "I suppose I should take that as a lesson. I've been so busy enjoying the hurricane, I haven't stopped to think that it can be deadly as well as beautiful."

"Well, actually—" Jeb began.

"And now I shall always regret having parted on unfriendly terms with him," Dad went on.

"Parted on unfriendly terms?" I said while the rest goggled.

"Yes, I ran into him on my way to Green Point," Dad said. "I couldn't understand why he kept trying to invite me in for a drink. I'm afraid I treated him rather rudely. Never liked him much, actually; and I was in no mood to waste time on him when I could be watching the hurricane. Ironic, isn't it?"

"What is?" I asked.

"Well, at one point when I was stumbling around, trying to find my way back, I began to regret how uncivil I'd been to him. I promised myself that when I got safely back to the village, I'd go and have that drink with him and apologize for the way I'd acted. And now I'll never have the chance, with him taken by the very storm that spared me."

"Actually, he wasn't," I said. "Taken by the storm, that is. He was murdered."

"Murdered!" Dad exclaimed. "How dreadful!"

He didn't sound as if he thought it dreadful. In fact, he sounded suspiciously enthusiastic. I hoped Jeb and the rest wouldn't take his tone the wrong way. I made a mental note to explain to the police about Dad's obsession with murder mysteries.

Then again, maybe I should wait until the police caught the real murderer. They might not realize I was talking about fictional murder mysteries. No sense letting them jump to any more false conclusions.

"How was he killed?" Dad asked.

Several of the locals around the store guffawed.

"He was hit over the head," Jeb said. "But we don't know whether the blow actually killed him or just knocked him unconscious into a tidal pool, causing him to drown."

"Well, we'd better examine him to see if we can find out," Dad said.

"Examine him?" Jeb exclaimed.

"Yes," Dad said. "Of course, you'll need the coroner for the actual autopsy, but—"

He suddenly yawned prodigiously and blinked slightly.

"Sorry, where was I?" he went on. "Oh, yes: Examining the body early on could be very important. Have you done anything to preserve it?"

"You don't expect us to let a suspect just mess around with the body," Jeb said.

"A suspect?" Dad repeated. His face lit up. I should have known. For a mystery buff like Dad, being a suspect in a real, live mystery was probably the next best thing to playing detective.

"Everyone on the island's a suspect," I said.

"Why so they are!" Dad exclaimed. "It's like a classic locked-room mystery! How exciting! Still, it could be important for someone with medical knowledge to observe the body early on. There might be another doctor or two among the bird-watchers. Perhaps we could get together a panel and do a noninvasive examination, under close supervision, before the body deteriorates. Take pictures. And—"

He yawned again, even more broadly.

"Dad, the body's in a refrigerator, and it isn't going anywhere. You need some rest—why don't you take a nap while Jeb considers your suggestion?"

"Yes, but—"

"And Mrs. Langslow's worried sick about you," Michael put in. "Have you seen her yet? Does she know you're all right?"

"Oh, goodness!" Dad exclaimed. "I never realized. I'll go right up there. Meg, do explain to them how important the examination could be. I'll—" He yawned again, and made no protest as Michael and I hustled him out the door. Michael stood, watching him trot up the street while I turned back to Jeb.

"You know, he does have a point. You could do worse than have some doctors examine the body."

"Like I said, we can't have a suspect messing with the body," Jeb replied.

"Why not?" I said. "We did last night, when you and Mamie and Fred fetched it down to the Anchor Inn. Are you trying to tell me that none of you had any possible reason for disliking Resnick?"

Jeb looked taken aback, and chuckles from the locals confirmed that I'd hit the mark.

"Yeah, Jeb," one of them said. "Bet you killed him just to get him off your back."

"Off your back?" I repeated.

"Bastard wanted to buy my store," Jeb said. "I told him to take a hike, of course. Been in the family since my grandfather's day; not likely I'd want to sell it. And even if I did, I wouldn't have sold it to him. Wouldn't take no for an answer, always hanging around here, waving his damned checkbook."

"You see," I said. "You need to protect yourself from suspicion, as well. Of course, it's your jurisdiction, but if I were you, I'd think very carefully about seeing if you can't find another doctor or two among the bird-watchers, as Dad suggested, and letting them all examine the body to verify its condition."

"I'll think about it," Jeb said. I wasn't sure if this really meant he'd think about it or if, like beleaguered parents, he used "I'll think about it" as a gentle way of saying "Hell no!"

"And you may want to stop making such a big deal about any person in particular being a suspect," I said. "Of course, I'm not a lawyer, like my brother, but I imagine people do get sued for that type of thing. Especially since you have so many possible suspects."

"You ask me, Fu Manchu there did it," one elderly local piped up from his place by the stove. "They were having a big set-to just before he died."

"Fu Manchu?" Jeb repeated.

"Ayah," the old man said, and buried his nose back in his coffee.

"Ayah," Michael murmured to me. "They really do say that, then?"

"Only to amuse the tourists," I whispered back. "Fu Manchu?"

Michael shrugged. Jeb didn't seem very impressed with the revelation that Sax Rohmer's sinister pulp villain was alive and well and plotting on Monhegan. Could dacoits and Thugs be far behind? And then I saw someone passing outside the store windows, and enlightenment struck.

"Well, if I were you, I'd think about finding those doctors," I said. "Meanwhile, we'd better run along," I added, tugging at Michael's sleeve. After one plaintive glance at his coffee mug, he sighed and followed me outside.

"What's up?" he asked.

"We're going to interrogate Fu Manchu," I said.

CHAPTER 18

East of Puffins

"Interrogate Fu Manchu?" Michael said. "You're not serious."

"I think the old guy meant the Asian man we saw quarreling with Resnick yesterday," I said.

"The one too well dressed for a birder?"

"Exactly. And if I'm not mistaken, that's him right now."

I pointed across the street to the front porch of the Island Inn, where the Asian man was stamping his feet and shaking himself. He had a brightly colored bag with the name of the other, upscale grocery on it. With a bottle of wine inside, from the shape of it.

"You could be right," Michael said.

"I'm positive," I said. "If we had to find a middle-aged Caucasian woman with binoculars, we wouldn't have a chance in the world of figuring out which birder it was. But Monhegan in flyover season isn't exactly a hotbed of ethnic diversity."

The Asian man had disappeared by the time we entered the hotel lobby, but the desk clerk looked up.

"Good grief, he's fast," I said. "Sorry, but you know the man who just came back into the lobby?"

"Mr. Takahashi?" the owner said.

"Yes," I said. "He forgot to mention which room he's in, and we need to give him back something."

I pointed vaguely back at my knapsack.

"He's in room twenty-three," the clerk said. "You want me to call him?"

"We can just take it up, if that's all right," I said. "Won't be a minute."

Mr. Takahashi looked surprised when he opened his room door and saw Michael and me.

"Yes?" he said. I had to look up to see his face. He was young—thirty-five at most—and taller than I expected—he nearly matched Michael's six four.

"Mr. Takahashi, I hate to bother you, but it's very important," I said. "Yesterday, you were overheard in . . . well, in a rather heated discussion with—"

"Oh, good God," Takahashi said. "Just tell the bastard to lay off, will you? I won't harass him, I'll do my damnedest not to even see him, but I can't very well leave the island until this damned hurricane blows over."

I was surprised to notice that he had a faint southern accent. And obviously he had mistaken us for someone official. I decided not to enlighten him.

"I assume you're talking about Victor Resnick?" I asked.

"Well, who else?" Takahashi said. "You don't mean someone else has filed a complaint about me? If they have, I guarantee you Resnick's behind it."

"Just what is the nature of the relationship between you and Mr. Resnick?" I said.

"Relationship? We don't have a relationship; I came to see him on business."

"What's the nature of your *business* relationship, then?" I persisted.

Takahashi looked at me with exasperation. He glanced behind me at Michael, who tried to look stern and official while dripping audibly on the floor. Michael seemed to rattle him a little. Men Takahashi's size don't often run into people taller than they are.

Takahashi sighed and turned to pick up something from the bedside table. A card case. He handed each of us a business card. Very nice cards, engraved on heavy off-white textured paper so thick, it was almost cardboard.

"Kenneth N. Takahashi," I read. "Vice President, Coastal Resorts, Ltd."

Takahashi nodded as if that explained everything. About the only thing it explained for me was his accent, since the firm was headquartered in Atlanta.

"What is Coastal Resorts, Ltd.?" I asked.

"What is it?" Takahashi's drawl got a little thicker when he got excited. "It's only the country's second-largest developer of luxury resort properties. Don't tell me you haven't heard about the hotel project?"

"Hotel project?"

"I came all the way up here from Atlanta in good faith to negotiate with Mr. Resnick about the purchase of some land that my company had planned to develop as a luxury resort," Takahashi said.

"A luxury resort? Here on Monhegan?" Michael asked, glancing at the window, which Gladys was pelting with sheets of cold, icy rain.

"I'm told it's very pleasant in the summer," Takahashi said, following Michael's gaze.

"Not much room here on the island for another hotel," I said.

Takahashi shrugged.

"I didn't put the deal together," he said, frowning. "I'm just here to try to keep it from falling apart."

I got the feeling he would have a few interesting things to say to someone back in Atlanta.

"No offense," I said, "but the whole thing sounds a little far-fetched to me. I mean, does this look like the kind of place that could support a big hotel?"

"We weren't planning a big hotel," Takahashi said. "A very small one, in fact; very luxurious, very secluded. The sort of place where high-profile people could come with absolute assurance of their privacy."

"You mean over-the-hill movie queens recuperating

from plastic surgery, reclusive, paranoid billionaires, people like that?" Michael asked.

"Exactly," Takahashi said. "People who appreciate the kind of tight security you can maintain in a place this isolated."

We must have still looked dubious. He walked over to the small rustic table under the room's one window and unrolled a large sheet of paper.

"Look, here are some of the project plans."

We gathered around and looked down at a three-foot-by-five-foot map of Monhegan. Only this wasn't the Monhegan we knew. A giant, sprawling building occupied the top of the hill where the lighthouse now stood. Labels indicated where the restaurant and the indoor pool would be located. A nine-hole golf course had been carved out of the undeveloped ocean side of the island. The meadow where the Central Monhegan Power Company's modest generator now chugged housed a sprawling complex of equipment and support buildings. I wondered if the owner of the Island Inn knew that one of his guests was plotting to raze his hotel and replace it with a heliport? Or if Aunt Phoebe had any intention of having her cottage torn down to make room for a set of indoor tennis courts?

"A lot of people would be pretty ticked with Resnick if they knew about this," Michael said, looking at me with one eyebrow raised significantly.

He was right. And one of them might have gotten mad enough to murder him. I couldn't decide whether to rejoice that we'd already discovered another plausible motive for Resnick's murder or feel depressed at the incredible number of possible suspects Takahashi had just revealed. I ran my hand through my hair in frustration, managing to shower Takahashi's map with drops of water in the process.

"I'm sorry," I said. "I forgot I was still wet."

"I don't think I'll ever be dry again," Takahashi muttered. "Don't worry, you can wave the damned thing out the window, for all I care; it's useless now."

Michael nodded, but my radar went on the alert. Useless? How could Takahashi know his maps were useless unless he already knew about Victor Resnick's death?

"What do you mean, 'useless'?" I asked.

"The bastard backed out of the deal," Takahashi said, rolling up the map. "Going with the competition. So the whole thing's completely useless. Would you like a souvenir of what Coastal Resorts could have done to bring this place into the twenty-first century?"

"I wouldn't give up yet," I said. "If he hasn't actually signed the deal, who knows, maybe you can win over Resnick's heirs, whoever they are. Of course, the whole thing could get caught up in probate for years."

"Heirs?" Takahashi said. "What do you mean, 'heirs'? The bastard was perfectly healthy yesterday."

"Yes, but someone bashed his skull in late yesterday," I said.

"Oh, damn," Takahashi said. He sat down heavily on the bed and buried his face in his hands. "Damnation. That's all I need."

"You sound awfully upset for someone who claims he hardly knew Victor Resnick," I said.

"Why shouldn't I be upset?" Takahashi said, looking up. "My boss will probably make me stay here to negotiate with the heirs. Do you know who they are?"

I winced, thinking about the damned biography. It didn't sound as if Resnick had much family left, apart from the long-lost illegitimate child. What if his death led to a massive, well-publicized search for the missing offspring? I fervently hoped he'd made a will leaving his estate to some second cousin. Or maybe his favorite charity. The Society for the Relief of Indigent Curmudgeons, perhaps.

"I don't imagine we'll find out until they probate his will," I said. "Guess you'll have to stick around for a while to find out."

"Not when the storm lets up," Takahashi said, glancing at the window. "As soon as that damned ferry starts running, I'm out of here. They can send someone else to clean up the deal."

"I know how you feel," Michael said.

We left the disgruntled Takahashi sitting in his room, staring out the window and muttering curses in the drawl that grew deeper when he got more upset. And struggling to open a bottle of pricey Chardonnay with one of those makeshift bottle openers they sell for people to take on picnics.

"Now what?" Michael asked.

"Now, if you're up for it, we're going to burgle Resnick's house," I said.

By the time we left the inn, the birders had started to emerge from shelter, although the absence of any birds to watch reduced them to wandering around marveling at the storm damage. Michael and I pretended to do the same as we strolled nonchalantly out of the village and up the path to Resnick's house.

"Would you look at that?" I said, pausing on a hilltop to look down at the glass monstrosity. "It's a good thing Resnick isn't here."

"You mean, apart from the fact that he'd have a clear shot at you standing there?" Michael said, joining me on the crest.

"No, I mean imagine how he'd feel if he saw what's happened to his house."

A large branch had crashed through one of the ten-foot square glass walls flanking the front door. I counted at least two more cracked panes, and we hadn't even seen the more exposed ocean side yet.

"People who live in glass houses . . ." Michael began.

"Should have some way of protecting them in nor'easters," I replied. "I wonder if he was killed before he had a chance to board it up, or if he was really fool enough to think all that glass would survive a hurricane."

"We'll never know. But he strikes me as the kind of guy who'd call his insurance company five minutes after it happened, demanding that they send someone out immediately to fix it."

"Only there wouldn't have been any phone service."

"True," Michael said. "That would really have set him off."

"Come on," I said very loudly as I started down the path. "We need to take care of this."

"Take care of what?" Michael called after me.

"Resnick's house."

"I thought that's what we were here for," Michael said. "To burgle—"

"Shh!" I hissed. "Not so loud; there could be birders lurking in the bushes."

"Oh, I get it," he hissed back, and then said more loudly, "The storm's passing; it's not likely to break any more windows."

"Yes, but there's enough wind and rain to do considerable damage to everything inside," I said. "Someone should make sure anything valuable is safely stowed away."

"Someone also wants to snoop around and see if there's any useful evidence," Michael added more softly as he caught up with me.

"Well, that's the whole idea of burgling his house, isn't it? You didn't think I'd suddenly decided to turn daring international art thief, did you?" I asked as I picked my way carefully through the leaves and glass shards to the gaping hole by the door where the glass panel used to be. "It's not as if anyone else is doing anything useful."

"Everyone else is wisely waiting until the mainland authorities arrive," Michael said, following me.

"By which time, anything could happen." I said, stepping into the house. "The wind and rain could reduce any important documents to papier-mâché. Or break any valuable antiques. And he's sure to have paintings—"

Yes, he had paintings. I stopped just inside the hallway and stared open-mouthed at the one I saw there. Michael bumped into me.

"Sorry," he said, grabbing me to keep from knocking me over. "If you're going to snoop, better not get cold feet just inside the door, where your accomplices might trample you on their way in."

"Oh my God," I said. "Michael, look!"

Michael followed my finger with his eyes. He looked puzzled for a moment, and then I had the satisfaction of seeing his jaw drop in amazement.

"Is that who I think it is?" he asked.

"It can't possibly be," I said.

Resnick was mostly famous for his landscapes, but, if the picture before us was anything to go by, not from any lack of talent at painting interiors or the human figure. You could almost have warmed yourself at the roaring fire in the painted fireplace, and the way the half-filled champagne flute reflected the firelight was extraordinary. You could all but feel every hair of the white bearskin rug on your own skin, and I suspect had I been a man, I'd have felt an erotic response instead of envy at the flawless skin and perfect figure of the nude blond woman sprawled on the rug. Under other circumstances, I'd have admired the painting enormously. As it was . . .

"That can't possibly be Mother," I said finally.

CHAPTER 19

Nude Puffin Descending a Staircase

"It certainly looks like your mother," Michael said, tipping his head to scrutinize the painting. "Or at least looks like what I gather she would have looked like at that age, from the photo albums we looked at last night. The face anyway; I wouldn't know about the rest of it."

"Well, yes, that's what she looked like at that age," I said. "As far as one can tell from pictures of her in swimsuits. But surely you don't think Mother would actually have posed for something like that?"

"It's definitely got her attitude."

He was right. The woman in the picture lay full length on the rug, facing the viewer, her head and shoulders propped up by a couple of pillows covered with Oriental fabric. One hand was behind her head and the other held the champagne. One leg was bent slightly at the knee and the other outstretched fully, with a high-heeled fur mule dangling from the toes. Her face showed no sign of awkwardness or embarrassment, only an expression of pride and absolute confidence. I couldn't imagine Mother posing nude for a painting, but if she had decided to, I'm sure she would have stared out at the artist with just that air of arrogant self-assurance.

"She'd never wear a tacky fur slipper like that," I said defensively. "And the bearskin's pretty clichéd, too."

"He could have done it from photos," Michael said.

"Of course he did it from photos," I snapped. "*Clothed* photos. But why? And when?"

"Let's make sure it's out of the rain," Michael said. "We can worry about the rest later."

We took the nude down and carried it with us into the living room.

Michael gasped. "What a view!"

I frowned at him. My mind was still on the picture we carried, and it took me a second to realize he was talking about the room we'd entered.

A giant wall of glass gave a sweeping view of the shore and the sea—a very gray and turbulent view, at the moment. The inside was a mess, too. The panes of glass forming the wall were slightly smaller than the ones beside the door—perhaps because this was the ocean side of the house. Even so, something had bashed one of them in, and mud and leaves littered the room. Several paintings on the wall were getting a bit damp. Only landscapes, I noted with a sigh of relief.

We hauled the paintings to the driest corner of the living room and continued our explorations.

"Impressive kitchen," Michael said. "You could run a small restaurant out of this place."

"Pretentious," I said. "I bet he hasn't cooked a dozen meals here since he moved in. Look how spotless everything is."

"Maybe he's just a good housekeeper."

"No," I said. "There's a difference between spotless from regular cleaning and spotless from disuse. This is disuse. Trust me—I know what disuse looks like from the occasional flying visit to my own kitchen."

"Well, pretentiousness has its advantages," Michael said. "Take a look at this wine cellar."

"Pretentious is right," I said. His wine cellar was probably larger than all my closets combined. "But what use is it? Unless you're suggesting that we take advantage of Resnick's wine collection, since he's not around to complain?"

"It's a tempting thought," Michael said, examining the labels of a few bottles with obvious interest. "Actually, I thought we could stash the paintings in here. No windows, and the walls are designed to protect the contents."

"Good idea," I said. We stowed the nude safely along one wall, then put the slightly damp landscapes from the living room along the other.

The dining room would have seated a dozen people easily, although all the chairs except the one closest to the kitchen had a thin film of dust on them. The guest room was expensively furnished but rather cheerless. And long unused. Despite the shortage of rooms on the island, obviously Resnick hadn't offered his spare bed to anyone, and I doubted anyone had even asked. I suspected the birders we'd heard singing in the church the night before were happier there than they would have been here anyway.

The master suite rivaled the kitchen for pretentiousness. But the lush white carpet was already dingy from lack of cleaning. And strewn with wet leaves, which had probably blown in from one of the broken windows.

"Fancies himself quite the ladies' man," I said, frowning at the ornately canopied king-size bed. "I'm surprised he resisted the ceiling mirror."

"He ran out of mirrors after he finished in here," Michael's voice echoed from the bathroom.

I poked my head in.

"Ick," I said, stepping inside to gape at the interior. "It's like a fun house. Imagine having to look at yourself in all these mirrors first thing in the morning."

"The view doesn't look that bad to me," Michael said, coming up behind me and putting his arms around my waist.

"Thanks for the vote of confidence," I said, leaning back against him. "But now try imagining you're Victor Resnick."

"No thanks," he said, sighing. "I know it's stupid, but poking around in here actually makes me feel sorry for him."

"Me, too," I said.

Actually, until Michael said that, I'd been thinking what a pity the one place we'd managed to find five minutes alone together all weekend was the house of a murder victim. If Victor Resnick had been merely missing, I'd have suggested to Michael that we make ourselves at home and, if anyone ever caught us later, pretend that we'd taken refuge here during a bad part of the storm. But since an army of forensic experts would soon begin swarming all over the house, I knew we shouldn't do anything we couldn't explain away as part of our quest to minimize damage and secure the contents of the house.

Although I couldn't help noticing the extralarge sunken tub. More like a small wading pool, really, all lined with gold-flecked turquoise-colored tiles. There was even a small adjoining fireplace, though that showed little sign of use.

Like something out of *Lifestyles of the Rich and Famous*. Which Resnick was, of course. No sensible person would use a tub like that for ordinary daily bathing, especially on an island with a chronic water shortage. But fill it up, add lots of bath oil, set several dozen candles around the periphery, light the fire, and send Michael to the wine cellar to pick out a bottle or two of Resnick's undoubtedly expensive wine . . . I shook myself. This was not the time for erotic fantasies.

"Depressing," I said, reluctantly pulling away from Michael.

"Gee, thanks," he said.

"I mean this place," I said. I stepped over to the wide vanity counter and, using the corner of my shirt to avoid smearing—or leaving—fingerprints, popped open the medicine cabinet.

"Why the medicine cabinet?" Michael said. "He wasn't poisoned."

"You can learn a lot about someone from his medicine cabinet," I said as I poked through the bottles, jars, and tubes in the cabinet.

"Remind me to clean my medicine cabinet before you get another chance to rummage through it," Michael said, peering over my shoulder. "Anything suspicious?"

"No," I replied. "Apart from having an ulcer or some other serious stomach problems for a couple of decades, he was pretty healthy for someone his age."

"A couple of decades? How can you tell?"

"Fifteen-year-old leftover Tagamet pills; Zantac prescriptions from four and seven years ago—obviously he was one of those suicidal idiots who never threw out old medicine."

"On second thought, remind me to put a padlock on my medicine cabinet," Michael said. "Is this significant?"

"Probably not," I said. "The rest of the drugs are normal over-the-counter stuff. He wasn't on medication for anything like epilepsy or heart problems, anything that would account for his falling down into the tidal pool from natural causes."

"Well, we knew that from the gash on the back of his head."

"True," I said. "Well, one good thing: If he was this much of a pack rat about medicine, maybe there's a desk somewhere crammed with interesting papers."

"I think it's out in the living room," Michael said. "I noticed it while we were hauling the wet paintings down."

"Well, why didn't you say something?" I said, going back out into the bedroom. "Let's go and—"

"What now?" Michael asked, seeing that I'd stopped in the middle of the room.

I indicated the bearskin rug in front of the fireplace.

"Yes, the man liked bearskin rugs," Michael said. "They have their charms."

"He must have liked this one anyway," I said. "It must be older than God. Look how ratty it is."

"He probably had it for years."

"But he didn't have it lying here very long."

"The house hasn't existed very long," Michael said.

"Yes, but look at those paler areas of the carpet," I said. "Here, you can see it better if we move the bearskin."

I peeled back the bearskin rug and pointed to a rectangular area of white carpet still more or less the original snow white.

"I see," Michael said. "From the shape of the clean spot, he had another rug, a rectangular one, lying here up until very recently. And then he replaced it with the bearskin rug."

"After the storm began, most probably," I said. "See, a couple of wet leaves stuck to the underside of the bearskin."

"Which brings up the question of whether he did it or someone else?"

"Why on earth would someone sneak in here and unroll a ratty old bearskin in front of Resnick's bedroom fireplace?"

"Bloodstains on the other rug?" Michael suggested. "Maybe he wasn't killed outside; perhaps he was killed here and then the murderer replaced the bloodstained rug with the bearskin."

"It's possible," I said. "But I think it's more likely that Resnick did it himself. Shortly before he died, which would account for the wet leaves under it."

"And why would he do that?" Michael asked.

"To make Dad jealous," I said. "We know the bearskin rug hasn't been here all that long. How long has that picture been in the entryway?"

"Possibly as long as the house has been here. How many people brave the shotgun blasts to visit him?"

"Yes, but he had to have workmen, delivery people. I'm sure if it had been there any time at all, someone in the village would have seen it, and they would have said something about it by now. Mrs. Fenniman practically broadcast the news that Resnick was Mother's beau before Dad came along, and I'm sure other people know about it."

"But would they recognize who it was?" Michael said. "No offense; your mother's in wonderful shape for a woman her age, but would anyone really recognize her in the picture?"

"A stranger wouldn't, but at least a dozen people on the island right now knew her then. Maybe more. And that's not counting anyone who's leafed through Aunt Phoebe's photo albums; she's always dragging them out at parties."

"Well, that's true," Michael admitted. "They'd know it was a Hollingworth, at any rate."

"I bet he put it there deliberately, to make sure someone saw it and spread the word," I said. "Heck, maybe he planned to invite Mother and Dad for dinner and hope the sparks flew."

"There's another possibility," Michael said. "Maybe he wanted to stir up another kind of spark."

"What do you mean?"

"What if he planned to invite just your mother over? Show her the picture, claim he'd kept that ratty old bearskin all these years as a souvenir, and try to rekindle their romance?"

"I'm sure Mother has more sense," I said.

"Yes, but did Resnick?"

I pondered it for a while and sighed.

"I wish we wouldn't keep finding evidence that points at members of my family."

"Cheer up," Michael said. "Let's go through Resnick's desk. We're probably already on the hook for trespassing and interfering with a murder investigation; let's not stop before we find something useful."

"We're just making sure nothing's getting damaged," I repeated.

"Or we could always pretend we were taking advantage of the empty house to get a little privacy in which to . . . misbehave."

"You think they'd believe that?"

"They will if we show them that sunken tub," Michael said, quirking one eyebrow. "If the town decides to raze the house, do you suppose they'd give us the tub?"

"I'm not sure it would survive the move," I said.

"True. In fact, it may not have survived the hurricane," he said. "Perhaps we should check it out."

"Maybe later," I said, "when we've finished burgling."

"And when you're feeling less frantic about clearing your father," Michael said with a sigh. "Just a thought."

"Well, hold the thought, but let's worry about the desk for now."

CHAPTER 20

The Puffin Who Liked to Quote Kipling

Michael led the way back to the living room and pointed out Resnick's desk.

"Good work," I said. "I'd overlooked it somehow."

"Overlooked it?" Michael said, staring at the huge antique rolltop desk. "How could you overlook that thing? It's over five feet tall."

"I'm afraid my idea of a desk is a mound of papers with legs sticking out from under it," I said. "I never imagined that anything that tidy could be a working desk."

"You're describing your own desk, aren't you?" Michael said.

" 'Fraid so."

"And yet I'll bet you're going to say that, despite its messy appearance, you can find any piece of paper you need in five minutes."

"Are you kidding? Five days, working full-time, and that's if I'm lucky. Now that's more like it," I said as we rolled up the top, revealing a desktop computer and a reasonably promising quantity of paper. "A little too tidy for my taste, but at least there are signs of life here."

"Luckily, the desk is awfully close to that cracked window," Michael said. "See, it's getting wet already."

"I don't suppose we could possibly lift the desk," I said.

"I don't even want to try," Michael said. "We'll have to move the contents to safety. The wine cellar, I should think."

Most of the contents weren't all that interesting. We studied his bills and bankbooks as we transported them, but we didn't find any dirt. Victor Resnick was a rich man who spent a great deal of money on his own pleasures, but then, he had a great deal of it to spend.

Or did he? He didn't have a very large balance in any of his accounts. Maybe he had a broker somewhere managing the bulk of his money. Then again, we found an awful lot of dunning letters from creditors. Was he simply, like so many wealthy people, careless about paying on time, or was he going broke?

We found an entire drawerful of papers related to the publication of the book of his paintings I'd bought—contracts, proofs of the photographs, and about fifteen drafts of the text, each annotated lavishly in a bold, angular handwriting. Along with corrections, we saw a great many scathing remarks about the intelligence and ancestry of the writer. If by chance we found the writer on Monhegan, I'd add him to the top of the list of suspects.

"The handwriting on these matches the edits on the biography," I pointed out. "Resnick was definitely cooperating with James Jackson."

"Did Jackson write this, too?" Michael asked as he perused one of the drafts.

"No, someone named Edwards. Who can actually write. I don't know where Jamie boy came from, but he can't write for beans."

"Resnick didn't realize that," Michael said, flipping through a fat sheaf of papers from another drawer. "And Jackson's definitely a pseudonym. Here's another copy of the biography—dated a couple of weeks ago, with the author listed as James Jones; and Resnick crossed the name out, with these orders: 'Sounds too phony—pick another alias!' "

"And the biographer thought James Jackson sounded more plausible?"

"I suppose; tell that to the publishers of *From Here to Eternity*. Resnick edited this version with just as heavy a hand; the whole manuscript looks as if it has the measles.

But he's not as hard on Mr. Jones/Jackson as on poor Edwards."

"Another draft or two and I bet he'd have started ripping Jamie boy's liver out, too," I said.

"He didn't like the galleries that handled his work, either," Michael remarked.

We found several files of letters to and from various galleries. Resnick evidently considered the owners of several of the most prestigious New York and Boston galleries either fools who had no idea how to sell his work or scoundrels trying to take him for a ride. More suspects, if they were on the island, which I doubted, but I grabbed a piece of paper and jotted down their names anyway.

"You suspect the gallery owners?" Michael asked.

"I suspect everybody," I said. "Besides, haven't you heard that the value of an artist's work triples when he dies?"

"I don't suppose we could buy a few before word gets out on the mainland," Michael suggested.

"Probably not," I said. "And anyway, I don't know about you, but it's not as if I have fifty or a hundred thousand dollars to do it with."

Michael whistled.

"They sell for that much?"

"Well, that's nothing compared with what you'd have to pay for a painting by someone really famous. A major Wyeth, for example. I think they go for a million or two."

"But still, it's a motive. I wonder how we could find out who owns his paintings."

"Ask and ye shall receive," I said. "See, he keeps a list of everything he sells. Most artists do."

"That's great! Although I suppose they won't all still belong to the original buyers anymore."

"On the contrary, artists usually keep pretty close track of where all their paintings are. See, here's a painting he sold to someone in 1962, and a note that it was resold in

1970, with the selling price and the new owner's name. And here's one that was sold about the same time, then donated to the Cleveland Art Museum in 1981."

"Want me to help you copy the names down?" Michael asked.

"No," I said. "He printed out three copies; we can take one and still leave two for the cops."

Michael studied the list, looking over my shoulder.

"Notice anything odd?" he asked after awhile.

"Only that he wasn't selling very many paintings these days," I said, frowning. "And other people haven't been selling them much, either. Look at all these entries for the fifties and sixties. And in the eighties and nineties—practically zip."

"Maybe he stopped keeping track of sales and resales?"

"No," I said. "See, here's a sale from two years ago. And a resale from three months ago. He's keeping track, but there's not much to keep track of."

"Makes you wonder how he could afford to live like this," Michael said, looking around. "Imagine how much this house must have cost."

"We don't have to imagine," I said. "We've got the files right here."

From the house construction files, we deduced that Resnick had gotten along about as well with his architect and his general contractor as he had with the rest of humanity. He had withheld some of the money he owed them until they fixed various minute flaws. Strangely enough, though, considering the local uproar about the house, we found almost no paperwork on approval for the construction—just a standard building permit for "renovations" signed by Mrs. M. A. Benton, Mayor.

"Renovations?" Michael exclaimed. "Who did he think he was kidding? He definitely got special treatment. Wonder if he had some kind of hold over the mayor?"

"Pay dirt!" I shouted, holding up a stack of files. "Here's the stuff on the resort project."

I'd found a file marked "Coastal Properties, Ltd." and another marked "New England Development Associates." Both full of correspondence that would no doubt fascinate a corporate lawyer but which only reminded me how little sleep I'd gotten the night before. A third file was more interesting; it contained a map of the island, with all the property boundaries marked and a number assigned to each plot. Parts of the map were colored in solid blue, parts in blue and white stripes, and a few in pink. Behind that was a list of numbers from the map, with people's names written beside them.

"What's this supposed to be?" Michael said, studying the map.

"If I'm reading this list correctly, the blue is property he owned. See, here's where we are now, in blue. The gift shop by the dock, that's in blue, too. And the blue and white stripes are places where he'd negotiated some kind of option to buy."

"And the pink?"

"I'm guessing there are places he'd tried and been turned down flat. Yes, there's Jeb Barnes's store in pink. Remember what Jeb said? That Resnick had tried to buy the general store and Jeb told him to take a hike?"

"Yes, but isn't that your aunt Phoebe's cottage there?"

"You're right," I said, frowning.

"I think she'd have mentioned it if he'd tried to buy the place."

"Maybe it just means places he expected to have problems buying," I suggested.

"That sounds logical," Michael said. "He colored your aunt Phoebe's lot a particularly intense pink, compared with some of the others."

We went on through the rest of the files, which were all marked with the names of local citizens. Some of them—

Mamie Benton's, for example—contained bills of sale. Apparently, Mamie had once owned the building in which her gift shop was located, but now she rented it from Resnick. Other files—including Frank Dickerman's file—contained long documents in legalese. Options to buy, as far as I could tell.

But he had a file on everyone on the island, not just the property owners. And along with the contracts or details of any negotiations he'd been conducting, all the files contained notes—sometimes pages and pages of notes—about the owners, including any dirt Resnick had dug up about their personal and financial peccadilloes.

"Michael, the man was a monster," I said after browsing in a few files. "He was blackmailing people into selling him their property."

"Well, he's a dead monster now, and these files could very well contain the motive for his murder," Michael said. "We have to turn these over to the proper authorities."

"You mean to Mayor Benton, who, according to her file, had to sell her building to him to pay off her gambling debts and then rubber-stamped the building permit for this house to keep him quiet? Or Constable Barnes, who hadn't yet agreed to sell the store, but might have changed his mind if Resnick had threatened to tell his wife about that fling he had with Candi, the hairdresser over in Port Clyde?"

"I see your point," Michael said. "The mainland authorities. Well, this is interesting."

"Whose file are you reading?"

"The Dickermans'. One of those blue-striped pieces is their house, and it was about to go solid blue."

"Why?" I asked. "The power company isn't making a profit?"

"The power company's doing fine, but they're probably going to lose that, too. Mr. Dickerman senior borrowed money from Resnick to bail two of his sons out of jail on charges of grand theft auto. And assault. Our charming friend Fred and a brother named Will, whom we probably won't be meeting, because he skipped out on his bail, bringing the whole family economy crashing down in ruins. Resnick threatened to foreclose on the loan in a few weeks."

"Now, there's a motive."

"And the assault consisted of Will hitting someone on the head with a lug wrench."

"Ooh, I like it!" I said. "I mean, it's terrible, of course; but I'm sure the mainland police will find it fascinating, having someone with a motive and a history of bludgeoning his victims."

"And consider Will Dickerman a far more likely suspect than any of your relatives."

"Him or Fred, either one," I said. "I've never met Will, at least not since we were kids, but if you asked me who of all the people I've met on Monhegan in the past few days was the most likely to have bashed someone's skull in, Fred Dickerman would be my number-two choice."

"Only number two?" Michael said, raising one eyebrow. "Who's number one?"

"The victim himself."

"And, unfortunately, he's out of the running."

"True," I said. "Suicide by blunt instrument's pretty hard to accomplish. Oh, good grief!"

"What's wrong?"

"Is there anyone on this island who doesn't have a guilty secret in their past?"

"I see you're holding your aunt Phoebe's file; don't tell me he dug up any dirt on her!"

I scanned her file quickly.

"No, thank goodness. The only charges he's logged against her are a complete lack of tact and caring more about birds than humans."

"Guilty on both counts, if you ask me," Michael said with a chuckle.

"Agreed. But I've never heard either of those is even a misdemeanor. Besides—"

"What's that?" Michael said, pointing to the glass wall behind me. I saw only the rain-soaked shrubbery outside.

"What did it look like?" I asked, going over to the window.

"I thought I saw someone behind that bush."

Just then, I saw a flicker of motion at the edge of the yard and caught a glimpse of someone disappearing into the woods.

"Rhapsody," I said. "Wonder what she's doing here?"

"Maybe she's researching her latest book," Michael said.

"To Kill a Puffin," I suggested. *"The Happy Puffin Family Solves a Grisly Murder."*

"Or *Silence of the Puffins*?" Michael countered.

"I know!" I said. *"The Puffin of the Baskervilles!"*

"You're right; that's it," Michael said as we dissolved into laughter.

"Ah, well," I said. "Maybe we should wrap things up here before someone else comes along snooping. I think we've found as much as we're going to. At least until the power comes on and we can get into his computer."

"By the time that happens, we'll have police all over the place," Michael said.

I didn't answer. He was right, of course.

"Let's check the studio," I said.

We locked the last of the papers up in the wine cellar and went back out the smashed window in the front hall. Unfortunately, the studio had weathered the storm far better than the house. The only broken glass was in the roof, way beyond our reach.

"I think if we had a rope, we could let ourselves down through that hole from one of those trees," I said.

"Aren't we supposed to have ropes in our knapsacks?"

Michael asked, shrugging his off his shoulder.

"Yes, but we used them hauling Resnick's body up, remember? And we never got them back."

"That's right," Michael said, hefting the knapsack back onto his shoulders. "Not that I especially want those particular ropes back. We'd need the rope to get up into the tree, too. Not to mention a really good story in case we get caught."

"We have to," I said as my stubborn streak kicked in. I glanced over at Michael. He was looking down at the ground, and from the expression on his face, I suddenly feared that we were on the brink of an argument. That he would refuse to do any more unauthorized snooping, and try to stop me from doing it, too. And I couldn't exactly blame him; it wasn't his family.

Then he looked up, caught my eye, and sighed.

"Okay, let's go back to the house and get some ropes, then," he said.

CHAPTER 21

A Cat Among the Puffins

When we came to the intersection where Resnick's private path joined the main gravel road, I insisted that we lurk in the bushes for a few moments to make sure no one was around.

"I told you we wouldn't run into anyone else," Michael said as we finally stepped out into the road.

"We have to be careful," I said. "After all—"

"Hello!" called several voices from behind us. We whirled, to see half a dozen birders striding energetically down the path.

"Did you hear about the murder?" one of them asked eagerly.

"Yes, we found—" Michael began.

"Yes, but what's the latest word?" I asked, interrupting him before he could reveal our close connection to the case.

The birders swept us into their midst and, as we panted to keep up with them, talked nonstop and simultaneously all the way down to the village. Other birders joined us in progress, and by the time we reached the main square of the village, we formed part of a milling, chattering crowd that must have included half the birders on the island.

When the police arrived, they'd have a lot of fun interrogating all the birders. Not surprisingly, since they'd wandered all over the island since their arrival, their ranks contained possible witnesses to nearly everything that had happened over the past several days.

The police would find witnesses to Resnick shooting at Michael and me, and several witnesses who would testify, truthfully or not, that he'd shot at them. Witnesses to the fight with Ken Takahashi, several of whom had taken photographs. Witnesses to Aunt Phoebe's struggle with Resnick. I was relieved to hear confirmation that he had still been standing—actually jumping up and down, yelling his head off, according to the witnesses—when Aunt Phoebe stormed off. Of course, that didn't prove that he hadn't collapsed later on as a result of the rap on the head, but it was encouraging. Eyewitnesses to Aunt Phoebe pulling up at least one of Resnick's NO TRESPASSING signs and throwing it violently over the cliff, which could answer the question of how the sign ended up floating in the tidal pool. Though not, of course, the question of whether the murderer had used the missing signpost as a weapon. And from what we heard, the sign couldn't have landed on Resnick's head by accident when Aunt Phoebe had thrown it; too many witnesses had seen him alive and well afterward. Witnesses who saw Jeb Barnes's subsequent arrival and summary dismissal. Witnesses who saw Dad have some kind of altercation with Resnick a short time later, which terrified me, until I managed to extract the information that though they'd exchanged harsh words, Resnick had been very much alive when they parted. Witnesses who saw Resnick afterward, patrolling his borders in search of trespassers. Witnesses who saw him pottering about by the shore, throwing a few stones at the gulls. Even witnesses who'd seen Michael and me when we'd found the body. I'd have felt better if some of the witnesses were a little more reliable on the matter of time. They tended to think less in hours and minutes and more in terms of "before we saw the bay-breasted warbler, and just after I got that snapshot of the crested grebe feeding." But just by circulating through the crowd and listening, we could more or less put together a time line of exactly what Resnick had done up until shortly before Michael and I found him.

We also encountered potential witnesses who claimed they had actually seen Resnick shooting down puffins, which I took with a grain of salt under the circumstances, since we had it on good authority that the puffins had all long since departed for the Arctic Circle. And then there were the witnesses who claimed they'd seen a sinister stranger skulking about the island, pretending to be a birder, despite an almost complete lack of birding knowledge. I made a note to ask Rob what kind of pranks he'd been playing over the past day or so.

The one thing we didn't find was a witness who could explain Resnick's transformation from a live misanthrope strolling along the seashore with a small bump on his forehead to a dead body with a bloody gash on the back of his head. During the critical period, which, depending on the feeding schedule of the crested grebe, ranged anywhere from fifteen to forty-five minutes, no one had seen anything out of the ordinary.

"Well, our killer certainly picked his time well," I said to Michael in an undertone.

"Yes," Michael said. "Almost every birder on the island passed by his house sometime yesterday, and not a single one of them saw the murder."

"Where's your father?" someone asked. I turned, to see Jeb Barnes and Mamie Benton looking very stern.

"Up at Aunt Phoebe's cottage, recovering from his ordeal," I said.

"I got through to the police briefly," Jeb said. "They're going to want to talk to him."

"Talk to Dad?" I said, feigning innocence. "Why?"

"I'd say he's their prime suspect," Mamie said, sounding rather smug. "No alibi for the time of the murder, and everyone knows there was no love lost between him and the deceased."

"Oh, and everyone else on the island adored the old curmudgeon and has an ironclad alibi?" I said. "I can think of a few other possibilities. You might tell them to keep their eyes out for the missing Will, for example."

"What, Resnick's will?" Jeb asked.

"How do you know it's missing?" Mamie asked. "And what's the problem if it is? Far as I know, he used a mainland law firm; they'll have a copy on file."

"Not Resnick's will," I said. "Will Dickerman."

"Haven't seen him on the island in months," Mamie said.

"No, not since he skipped bail on those grand theft auto and assault charges, I expect," I said.

"What the devil—," Jeb began.

"How on earth did you find out about that?" Mamie asked.

Not wanting to admit that we'd rummaged through Victor Resnick's files, I settled for looking inscrutable.

"Well, he's not on the island anyway," Mamie said. "I'd have seen him get off the ferry."

"How do you know he didn't come over on a private boat before the hurricane hit?" I said.

Mamie blinked. Jeb chuckled.

"Yeah, normal weather, he could have come over most anytime," he said. "But even if he had, what does that have to do with the murder? I mean, you're not thinking that just because he's had a few brushes with the law, he's got to be the killer, are you?"

"No," I said. "But he's definitely someone we want to keep an eye on, considering that he's a fugitive from justice with a reason to hate Victor Resnick and a history of whacking people with blunt objects."

"Reason to hate Resnick?" Jeb echoed. "I'm sure he didn't like Resnick any more than the rest of us, but what reason does he have to hate him? With all those steam baths and cattle prods and such Resnick has up at that house, he's the Dickermans' best customer. *Was* their best customer. Why would Will want to spoil that?"

"Because Resnick had bought up Mr. Dickerman's loans and was about to foreclose on them," I said. "About to take away the power plant. So if you see Will Dickerman, he's a suspect all right. For that matter, I'm sure the police will take a very close look at everyone who has had adverse financial dealings with Victor Resnick."

I looked at Mamie Benton when I said it, and felt a guilty satisfaction at seeing her turn pale.

"Take a damn long time to do that," Jeb Barnes said. "Not a person on the island the bastard didn't try to rook sometime or other. Me included. Liked to run a tab with me, and then when I'd try to make him pay, he'd argue. Claimed he'd never gotten things. I finally cut him off, and now the bastard does—well, did—all his shopping over on the mainland."

"Then I suppose they'll cross-examine everyone on the island," I said.

"I suppose they will, which means you don't have to go poking your nose in it," Jeb retorted as he and Mamie turned to leave. "You just let us handle it until the police get here."

I stepped forward, about to tell them just what I thought of how they were handling things, but Michael grabbed my arm, pulled me back, and gave me a warning look. I fumed silently until Jeb and Mamie were out of earshot.

"I don't suppose there's any chance you're going to take that advice?" Michael asked.

"Not when they're trying to railroad my Dad, no," I said. "Let's get out of the rain a minute; I need to think."

We shook the standing water off two metal Adirondack chairs on the front porch of the Island Inn and sat down. The birders continued to mill about in the square in front of us, trading bird news and crime rumors.

"Okay," I said when I felt a little calmer. "Let's make a mental list of the things we need to do."

"A pity, you didn't bring along the notebook that tells you when to breathe," Michael said, referring to the organizer I normally took everywhere. For some reason, people interpret my attachment to my organizer as a sign that I am unnaturally organized. I'm not, really; just the opposite. I long ago accepted the fact that if I write something down, I'll probably get it done, and if I don't, all bets are off.

I'd left the organizer behind, though; which shows you just how complete a getaway from my day-to-day life I'd been planning. A pity, as I could have used it now. But before I could even begin my plan for the afternoon, Rob appeared out of the crowd, dragging Spike, who was making heroic efforts to bite unwary passing birders.

"Could you hang on to Spike while I run into the general store?" Rob asked, holding out the leash.

"They don't mind dogs in the general store," I said.

"They mind Spike, ever since he took a chunk out of that woman who runs the gift shop," Rob said. "And Mother sent me to fetch some cream for Dad's coffee when he wakes up."

"Oh, all right," I said.

I watched as Rob ambled across the muddy square and disappeared into the general store.

"Help me keep an eye out for Rob," I said.

"Why?" Michael asked. "Is he in danger?"

"He will be if he tries to sneak off and leave me with Spike," I said. "If the general store had a back door, I wouldn't have let him out of my sight."

But while we stared at the door, watching for Rob's reappearance, a commotion elsewhere in the square distracted us. Mrs. Peabody, the stout birder, had intercepted Jeb and Mamie and was haranguing them. She was thrusting something at them, and they were backing hastily away from her. After several attempts to give them whatever she was holding, Mrs. Peabody shook her finger at them.

"What's got them all fired up?" came a voice from behind us. I glanced up, to find Ken Takahashi looking over our shoulders. I deduced from the little bits of cork all over his clothes that he hadn't had much fun opening his Chardonnay.

"The murder, of course," Michael said. Takahashi shuddered.

"Do you have any idea if the ferry's running today?" he asked, zipping up his parka.

"No, but I bet they know over at the general store," I said. "Let's go and ask."

"Are we really that interested in the ferry's whereabouts?" Michael asked as the three of us strolled across the street.

"I'm more interested in Rob's whereabouts," I said. "He's been in there long enough to buy a case of cream. If he's gone off and left us with Spike, Jeb may have another homicide on his hands."

"She's only kidding," Michael said quickly. Takahashi looked as if he didn't quite believe him.

The locals all looked up when we entered, and several of them actually nodded. I stayed near the door, where they'd be less likely to object to my bringing in Spike. Evidently, Takahashi hadn't quite given up the idea of charming the locals out of their real estate. He pasted a bright smile on his face.

"My God, it's like the North Pole out there," he said, shoving back the hood of his parka and shaking himself.

A couple of the locals huddling around the fire frowned. I suspected that any second we'd start hearing mutters about "weak-livered city folk."

"What brings you here, Mr. Takahashi?" Jeb Barnes asked.

"Do you know if the ferry's running today?"

"Doubt it," Jeb said. "Why?"

"I'd like to know how much longer I have to stay in this hellhole," Takahashi said, his charm slipping for a moment.

The native Monheganites bristled visibly at this. Even

Takahashi noticed, and he returned to full-blown salesman mode.

"I mean, it's all very well for you hardy New England types, but I'm from Atlanta," he said. The drawl was heavier than before; he made it sound as if the name Atlanta had at least twelve syllables. "I can deal just fine with ninety-eight in the shade and near one hundred percent humidity. But this kind of weather—call me a wimp, but I just don't understand how y'all can bear it. I'd have double pneumonia half the time if I lived here. In fact," he said, sniffling audibly, "I think I am coming down with something now. I don't suppose I could buy a cup of hot tea?"

"I can put the teakettle on," Jeb said. "We don't have fancy herbal teas, though, like they do down the street. Just plain old supermarket tea."

"As long as it's hot," Takahashi said.

"I wouldn't mind some myself," Michael said. "What about you, Meg?"

"Actually, we're just looking for my brother, Rob," I said. "You haven't—"

Just then, the door flew open and a swarm of birders burst into the store.

"That's him! That's him!" they shouted, pointing to Ken Takahashi.

CHAPTER 22

Tell Me How Long the Puffin's
Been Gone

I was afraid the birders planned to lynch Takahashi, for some unknown reason. And when I looked around for Jeb Barnes, I found that he'd slipped away into the store's back room. Ostensibly to put the teakettle on, I supposed, though surely he could hear the commotion out here in the store. Takahashi quailed behind Michael. I was relieved to see a few familiar faces entering at the tail end of the birder mob, including Winnie and Binkie.

"Now then, let's calm down," Binkie called out in a surprisingly penetrating voice. "Let's have a little order here!"

The shouting died down, and the birders stood back as Binkie pushed her way to the front of the crowd.

"One of you tell me what's going on here," Binkie ordered. "Just one!" she added as several birders began to speak.

Mrs. Peabody stepped forward and pointed a quivering hand at Ken Takahashi.

"He's the one!" she said.

"What one?" I asked. "Do you mean you think he's the murderer?"

"Well, that's for the police to find out, isn't it?" Mrs. Peabody said. "All I know is, he's the one pretending to be a birder."

"Pretending to be a birder?" I said. I glanced at Takahashi, somewhat disappointed. I'd hoped the phony birder would turn out to be our missing biographer. Ken Takahashi seemed too down-to-earth to have written that much purple prose. Still, a way of testing the possibility occurred to me.

"Walking around, pretending to be one of us, when he doesn't know a tern from a seagull," Mrs. Peabody said. "Probably in league with that lunatic who was trying to wipe out the bird population of the island."

Considering what Takahashi and Resnick had planned for the island, she wasn't that far off the mark.

"That's ridiculous," Takahashi said. He reached inside his coat, probably to pull out his business cards. "I'm—"

"Mr. Takahashi!" I snapped. He froze. In fact, everybody froze.

"Hold on a second," I told Mrs. Peabody, the ringleader.

"If you don't mind . . ." I said to Binkie. She looked puzzled, but nodded.

I handed Spike's leash to Michael, drew Takahashi aside, and spoke to him in an undertone.

"Are you sure you want to tell them what you do? These are rabid environmentalists. They're very militant about development."

Takahashi turned pale.

"What am I supposed to tell them?" he asked.

A thought struck me.

"What do you know about the *Unheralded Genius of the Down East Coast*?" I asked, recalling the subtitle of Resnick's biography.

"It's another of those birds, isn't it?" Takahashi said without enthusiasm.

" 'Who could have predicted this event, at once so joyous and so tragic?' " I quoted. " 'Who can calculate the import this occurrence would present upon his life and art?' "

Takahashi began edging away from me. Okay, so he wasn't the biographer. Just checking.

"Inside joke," I said. "Just leave it to me."

"What's going on anyway?" Mrs. Peabody asked, tapping her foot with impatience.

As Takahashi continued to sidle farther away, I beckoned Mrs. Peabody to join me—which took her out of earshot of the other birders.

"You can't reveal this to a soul," I said in a low voice.

"No, of course not," she said eagerly.

"Are you familiar with the *Unheralded Genius of the Down East Coast*?" I said.

"No," Mrs. Peabody said, looking at Takahashi. "Is that him? What's he supposed to be a genius at?"

Okay, so neither of the Peabodys was masquerading as James Jackson, either. It was worth a shot.

"Well, I can't say too much—but would it surprise you to learn that a certain environmental organization had taken an interest in Victor Resnick's less savory activities?"

Takahashi looked as if it would surprise the hell out of him, but he managed a feeble smile when Mrs. Peabody put on her reading glasses and inspected him at length.

"Well, that's quite a different kettle of fish," she said finally. Takahashi must have passed muster; she grabbed his hand and shook it vigorously for several seconds. "Carry on, then!" she ordered before turning on her heel and beginning to shoo the other birders out of the room.

"No, it's not what we thought," I heard her telling several people. "I can't talk now, but I'll tell you all about it later."

So much for not telling a soul.

"What am I supposed to do now?" Takahashi asked.

"As little as possible, until the ferry comes," I suggested.

"Right," Takahashi said, looking around nervously. "You really think one of them would harm me?"

"I have no idea," I said. "But if I were you, I wouldn't take chances. For all we know, one of the birders could have knocked off Victor Resnick. If some kind of environmental vigilante is running around loose on the island, you don't want to make yourself the next target, do you?"

"But what am I supposed to do if they ask me why I'm here?" Takahashi said, looking perplexed.

"Tell them you're under orders not to reveal that information," Michael said.

"Whose orders?" Takahashi persisted.

"Mine," I said. "But don't tell them that, of course. Just say orders."

"Right," Takahashi said.

"And stop the masquerade; just carrying around a pair of binoculars isn't going to make anyone think you're a birder."

"Binoculars? I don't even own binoculars."

Well, that was odd. Had the birders imagined the binoculars, or was there another imposter masquerading as a birder?

But before I could interrogate him further, Mrs. Peabody burst back into the room.

"Is there something else wrong, Mrs. Peabody?" I asked.

"There certainly is," she boomed. "Look at this!"

She thrust something under my nose.

For a split second, I wasn't sure what it was. And then I realized that it was a puffin. Not one of the plush stuffed puffins from Mamie Benton's shop. Right general size, shape, and color. But even a stuffed puffin left out overnight in the hurricane wouldn't be quite such a limp, bedraggled mess. This was the real thing. Or had been, when it was alive.

"I thought the puffins were long gone by now," Michael said. "Out to sea for the winter or something."

"Well, this one obviously wasn't in any shape to make the trip," I said. "Where was it anyway?"

"Down by Victor Resnick's house," she said. "Near that tidal pool you found him in. The poor thing was probably his last victim."

"And when did you find it?"

"An hour ago," she said.

"An hour ago?" I echoed. Something about this didn't make sense. "Would you mind showing us where?"

"Not at all," said Mrs. Peabody. To my relief, she whisked the dead puffin out from under my nose and began striding toward the porch steps. "It's about time somebody did something about this! Clearly the local authorities aren't going to take any action!"

I looked around for Rob, but he had fled, and Mrs. Peabody was rapidly disappearing.

"Arg!" I exclaimed, taking the end of Spike's leash. "Come on, you little monster."

He followed me, barking with glee. As I expected, I had to pick him up and carry him after about fifteen feet—although, to his credit, he managed to pick up a remarkable amount of new mud during his short time on the ground.

To my dismay, other birders began following Mrs. Peabody as she strode through town. I suppose, given the weather, there wasn't all that much else for them to do, since most of the birds remained sensibly out of the rain. We had collected fourteen or fifteen stragglers by the time we reached Resnick's house. Mrs. Peabody led us past the house and down to the tidal pool, along the path the rising tide had prevented Michael and me from using yesterday.

"Right there," she said, pointing to a large flat rock. "It was lying right there."

"Lying how?" I asked.

"I'll show you," she said, reaching for her knapsack. For a second, I thought she was about to shed her knapsack and arrange herself on the rock in the place of the dead puffin. But instead, she pulled out a camera.

"I took pictures of the body," she said.

"The puffin's body, you mean?" I asked.

"Well, of course," she said. "What other body could I mean?"

"Victor Resnick's?" Michael suggested.

"Him," she said, shrugging. "Why would I bother? Here, I'll show you."

"Great," I said as she held out her camera. "We can have the film developed."

"You don't need to develop any film," Mrs. Peabody said with a scornful look. "This is a *digital* camera. Here."

She pressed a switch on the camera, looked at it for a few seconds, then turned it so we could see. The back of the camera had a little display screen, on which I could see a picture of a small evergreen tree.

"That's fantastic!" Michael said, looking over my shoulder. "You can see the pictures as soon as you take them! Does it use film?"

"No, it saves the pictures on a computer chip," Mrs. Peabody said.

"The things they do with computers these days," another birder said, shaking his head.

"And if you don't like what you've taken, you can erase them and try again," Mrs. Peabody said.

"Amazing!" Michael said.

"How much does a thing like that run anyway?" another birder asked.

"Later, guys," I said. "I thought you said you had a picture of a puffin. That's not a puffin; it's a cedar."

"No, it's a wren," she said. "See there, he's roosting inside the cedar.

"If you say so," I said. "What about the puffin?"

"Just press this button," she said.

I put down Spike so I would have my hands free. He galloped off to bark at the waves, which were creeping closer and closer; we'd have to adjourn to the top of the hill soon. I took the small camera, pressed the button Mrs. Peabody had indicated, and waited for several seconds as another picture of the cedar tree scrolled onto the screen.

"Keep going," she said. "It's been an hour; I may have taken quite a few pictures."

I kept pressing the button and waited while several more pictures of the cedar loaded. These were followed by pictures of other shrubbery, presumably containing other wrens. Interspersed with the nature photos were occasional off-center shots of the sky or of Mrs. Peabody's muddy hiking boots, which I assumed she'd taken by mistake. Michael and several male birders looked over my shoulder, exclaiming at the high quality of the pictures, and Mrs. Peabody explained how she took the electronic pictures and e-mailed them to her sister in California.

Finally, a puffin appeared on the tiny screen. It lay on its back on the flat rock, with its toes pointing straight to the sky, its wings neatly folded by its side, and its feathers carefully groomed and reasonably clean. It looked a lot better in the photo than it did now that Mrs. Peabody had hauled it around for an hour. It looked as if it'd been laid out for viewing at a wake, and I didn't for a minute believe it had landed in that position by accident.

"There's something odd about this," I muttered, glancing from the puffin on the camera screen to the flat rock. I took off my knapsack, fished around in it, and pulled out a small pamphlet called *The Pocket Guide to Monhegan*.

"Was the puffin there when you found the body?" Mrs. Peabody asked.

"No," I said, still leafing through the guide.

"How can you be sure?" she insisted.

"Well, in the first place," I said, "that was the rock where we put Resnick's body after we hauled him out of the water; if the puffin had been there, we'd have stepped on it."

Several birders who were leaning against the rock shuffled a few feet away from it.

"And, in the second place, I took a good look around for clues, and I'd have noticed something as unusual as a dead puffin. In the third place, that rock's underwater at high tide, so even if it had been there yesterday when we found the body, it'd have washed away by this morning.

The tide came in after we found Resnick's body, you know. This whole place was underwater between ten P.M. and two A.M."

I waved the pocket guide, held open to the page with this year's tide tables on it.

"That's true," a birder said.

"Perhaps it washed out to sea after the murder and then washed back in again this morning," Mrs. Peabody said.

"Does it look as if it was washed in?" I said, pointing at the little screen. "It looks as if someone posed it there. Deliberately. But why?"

"Maybe the murderer did it," Michael said. "To confuse us."

"He's wasting his time, then," I said. "We're already as confused as we're ever going to get; he should save it for the mainland cops."

"Maybe someone's trying to give us a subtle clue to the murder?" Michael said.

"Well, they're going to have to try a lot harder, and be a lot less subtle," I said.

"This is all very odd," Mrs. Peabody announced, frowning at Michael and me as if the whole mess were our fault and we should do something about it.

"And speaking of odd," I said. "There's something else rather odd about that puffin. Let me take a look at it."

"Yes, of course," Mrs. Peabody said. She tried to hand me the small carcass. Spike growled and leapt up, trying to attack it. I backed away, happy to settle for a visual inspection. Yes, there was definitely something unusual about the puffin.

"Strange," I said. "I wonder why anyone would bother to keep a dead puffin around all this time."

"I beg your pardon! I'm not keeping it around, as you put it," she said. "I only brought it along to show what that horrible man was doing."

"I didn't mean you," I said. "I meant whoever had it before you."

"No one had if before me. I found it today, not even an hour ago, right here on this rock."

She pounded the rock with one plump fist by way of emphasis.

"Well, you may have found it there, but I doubt if it died there; and it didn't die today, or yesterday, for that matter," I said. "That is not a recently deceased puffin."

"Nonsense, it's still quite fresh," Mrs. Peabody said, thrusting it under my nose by way of proof.

"Possibly," I said, backing away. "I suppose whoever put it there could have had it in his freezer for the last couple of months."

"In the freezer?" she said. "Whatever makes you think someone had that poor puffin in a freezer?"

The other birders were muttering, "The freezer?" and looking at me as if I'd announced my intention of serving them southern-fried puffin with a side of pickled puffins' feet.

"This puffin is wearing mating plumage, or whatever you call it," I said. "I mean, that is what the white face and those bright orange-and-yellow plates on the beak mean, isn't it? That when this puffin died, he was still looking for his soul mate? Unless I've completely misunderstood all the puffin lore everyone's babbled at me, he would have shed the white feathers and the pretty little plates by the end of the spring, right? So he must have died before that."

The birders looked at each other and then at the puffin.

"She's right," one of them murmured. "She's absolutely right."

"Do you mind if we keep your camera for a while?" I asked Mrs. Peabody.

"Not at all," she said. "Or if you want to come by the Island Inn, I can have my husband transfer the pictures onto diskettes for you."

"Thanks," I said. "We'll probably do that."

"I've got some digital pictures, too," another binoculars-toting man said, bounding up holding his camera. "I've got pictures of that lunatic shooting at you!"

"That has nothing to do with the murder!" Mrs. Peabody said, elbowing him aside.

"Well, neither does your puffin," said the second birder. I almost expected him to say, "So there!"

Michael tried to defuse the confrontation by taking the man's camera and exclaiming over the pictures, but the two birders were squaring off for a verbal donnybrook, when a voice rang out from above us.

"What's going on here?"

I glanced up and saw Jeb Barnes, hands on hips, stumbling down the last few feet of the path.

Inspired by the interest we had shown in the puffin, Mrs. Peabody strode over and, with a flourish, tried to present it to Jeb, who began backing up the path to escape her.

I flipped through Mrs. Peabody's pictures of the puffin again. The remaining birders, sensing that I wasn't going to do anything else amusing, followed Jeb and Mrs. Peabody.

"This puffin is evidence!" Mrs. Peabody shouted.

"Nonsense!" Jeb shouted back.

"Mind if I take a look at the puffin?" I asked, looking up at the two.

"No," Jeb said. "I mean yes. I'm impounding it. As . . . as . . . as a danger to public health."

With that, he snatched the puffin from Mrs. Peabody's hands and, holding it at arm's length, fled up the path.

Mrs. Peabody frowned.

"I think he's going to lock it up for the police," I said.

"Well, that's all right, then," Mrs. Peabody said.

"And you people stay away from the crime scene," Jeb called from the top of the cliff.

"Yes, we'd better get off the beach before the tide gets any higher," Michael suggested.

We stowed our two borrowed digital cameras safely in my knapsack and headed for the path.

"So, what has the defrosted puffin told you?" Michael said as we picked our way up the side of the cliff.

"Not a thing; he's keeping his beak shut," I said in a passable imitation of a thirties movie gangster. "But give me a few minutes alone with our feathered friend and I'll make him sing like a canary."

Well, Michael thought it was funny. Mrs. Peabody said, "Humph!" and strode off ahead of us.

"Seriously, I don't know if the puffin tells us anything useful," I said in a more normal tone. "So far, it's just another puzzle: Why would someone keep a dead puffin around for months, then leave it at the scene of a murder the day after the body was discovered? It makes no sense."

"Maybe it's symbolic," Michael suggested. "That he was killed to revenge his crimes against puffinkind?"

"Possibly, but it doesn't narrow down our suspect list," I complained.

"Maybe it does," Michael said. "Whoever left the puffin here has to be a local with a freezer to keep it in, right?"

"Not necessarily," I said. "One of the birders could have brought it over on the ferry. Can you swear there wasn't a cooler containing a dead puffin somewhere in that mountain of luggage on the dock when we arrived?"

"True," he said.

"And even if a local put the puffin there, we don't know for sure that the puffin has anything directly to do with the murder."

"What other reason could anyone have for putting it there?" Michael asked. "To throw us off the scent?"

"When we find whoever put it there, we'll ask," I said.

"When *you* find whoever put it there?" Jeb echoed from above. "I thought I told you to keep your nose out of this."

"Well, I assume when the police find out who put the puffin there, they'll let all of us know," I said as I reached the top of the path. "Surely there's no harm in being curious."

Michael chuckled.

"Well, at least Jeb's taken custody of the puffin," Michael said in an undertone.

"Even if he's only doing it because he thinks we want it," I answered. "Whereas the only one who really wants the damned thing is Spike."

"Speaking of Spike, where is he?"

"Oh damn," I said, turning around. "Still down by the rock, chasing the waves, I suppose. I'd better get him before the tide carries him away."

"I don't see him down there," Michael said, frowning.

"Oh bloody hell," I said. "Your mother will kill us if anything happens to him."

"Well, with any luck, she'll only kill Rob," Michael said. "But it would break her heart. Let's go down and look for him."

We called back Jeb Barnes and Mrs. Peabody, and the four of us scrambled around the area by the tidal pool, frantically calling Spike's name and looking in every crevice. The waves started to wash over the rocky, flat area, drenching us and narrowing our search with every passing minute.

"We'll have to give it up," Jeb said finally. "The tide'll cover the path in a minute."

"No, we have to find him!" I said.

"Meg, he's right," Michael said.

He half-dragged me up the path behind Jeb and Mrs. Peabody. We had to wait for a moment between waves to cross one spot, but we made it up to the top of the hill and stood looking down at the churning mass of water occupying the spot where we'd been standing—well, wading anyway—only a few minutes before.

"I'm so sorry about the poor little dog," Mrs. Peabody said. She sounded genuinely sympathetic, probably because she hadn't known Spike very well. And probably never would now.

"Oh damn," I said. I was astonished and embarrassed to find tears welling up in my eyes.

CHAPTER 23

Puffin, Come Home

Of all the stupid things, I told myself as I scrubbed at my eyes with the back of a sleeve that was already sopping wet. I take everything in stride—a dead body, a murder, my own aunt confessing to the crime, both parents nearly managing to get themselves killed in a storm. And now I break down over Spike, of all things.

"Don't worry; he'll probably turn up," Michael said, putting his arms around me. "And if he doesn't, we'll figure out some cover story to tell Mom."

"No, we'll tell her the truth," I said, standing up straight and bracing my shoulders. "That I carelessly took him out in a hurricane and callously ignored him while the surf carried him away and it's all my fault."

"It's not your fault," Michael began.

"No, it's all my fault, and I'll never forgive myself," I said. "Please, let him turn up somewhere. If we could just find him safe and sound, I promise I'll—"

Just then, a familiar yapping broke out somewhere behind us.

"Spike!"

We all whirled, and I was relieved to see Spike running toward us.

"What was it you were about to promise if Spike turned up safe and sound?" Michael asked.

"Not to feed him to the sharks on the trip home," I said. Michael chuckled.

"Good dog!" I added, rather pointlessly, as Spike arrived at my feet, panting and still yapping.

His normally sleek black-and-white fur was now a uniform muddy grayish brown, and I didn't envy whoever had to wash him before Michael's mother saw him again. Not me, I vowed, no matter how glad I was to see him undrowned.

I quickly noticed that he wasn't just barking. He was running back and forth between my feet and a pile of rocks at the edge of the cliff, yapping all the way.

"Are you trying to tell us something?" Michael asked, leaning down toward Spike the next time he arrived at my feet. Spike growled at him and turned back to me.

"You're both watching far too many *Lassie* reruns," I said as Spike ran off again. "The bit where Lassie finds the lost child is an overdone cliché; and besides, we've already found all our lost relatives."

"Oh, you're no fun," Michael said, pretending to sulk. "Can't we just go see what he's found?"

"Dead fish washed up from the storm, I expect," Jeb put in.

"Never mind, then," Michael said.

"Let's head down and see how Dad's doing," I said. "And then—"

I heard a low rumble down by my ankles.

"Cool it, Spike," I said.

Spike growled again, then butted my ankle with his head. I glanced down and started.

"What the hell has that fool dog got there?" Jeb asked.

"Aunt Phoebe's walking stick," I said.

Noticing we were paying attention to him, Spike began wagging his tail and trying to bark, his efforts a little muffled by the walking stick in his mouth. He held it at one end—the lower, narrower end. The stick had been pretty battered and gnarled to begin with, but I could see several obviously new chips and scratches. And was I imagining the telltale dark stain on the top third?

"Is that blood on one end of it?" Jeb Barnes asked.

"Could just as easily be mud," Michael said.

"Careful!" I said as Jeb reached down toward the stick. "He bites!"

"Well, not with that stick in his mouth," Michael said. "But he could choke himself trying."

"We don't want him to run off with it," Jeb said.

"How fast can he run?" Michael said. "The thing's so heavy, he can barely drag it."

"Someone give me a handkerchief," I said. "I'll try to get it away from him."

Holding Michael's handkerchief behind my back with my right hand—fluttering cloth sometimes spooked Spike— I knelt in the mud and extended my left hand.

"Here, Spike," I called, fixing an insincere smile on my face. "Here, boy. Come here, boy."

Spike paused six feet away and looked at me, then at the others.

"Back away some more," I said, not taking my eyes off Spike.

"If we back any farther away, we'll fall off the cliff," Jeb said.

"Here boy," I called to Spike. "Come and give me the stick, you miserable little fur ball."

"You're not going to get him to come to you, calling him names like that," Jeb said.

"He doesn't care what names I call him," I said in my most coaxing voice, eyes still locked on Spike's. "It's the tone he's listening for. I could call him a mangy little cur, and as long as I smile when I say it, he won't care. Will you, Spike?"

Spike wagged his tail.

"Here, you ornery little mutt," I said, smiling harder and beckoning. "Come to Aunt Meg. Don't make me wring your wretched little neck."

Spike wagged harder, then staggered over to me, dragging the stick behind him.

"That's a good little monster," I said, patting him. Spike

had to drop the stick to begin his usual pastime of licking me obsessively, which gave me the chance I needed to grab the walking stick with the handkerchief and hand it over to Jeb Barnes. I reattached Spike's leash while Jeb juggled the puffin and the stick.

"Yes, that's Phoebe's cane," Jeb said.

"Stick, not cane," I corrected. "Don't let Aunt Phoebe hear you calling it a cane; she'd kill you. Not literally," I added, seeing the startled expression on Jeb's face. "That was a figure of speech."

"Right," he said. I wasn't sure he believed me. "I thought she said she'd lost the . . . stick when she fell."

"No," I said, starting down the trail toward the village. "She told us she lost it before she fell."

"It could be evidence," Jeb said, falling into step beside me. "After all, she did confess to the murder this morning."

"She did?" Mrs. Peabody said with a gasp. "Well, I never!"

"Yes, but you'll remember I pointed out exactly why her confession didn't hold water."

"Good," Mrs. Peabody said. "I can hardly imagine a dedicated environmentalist like Phoebe committing murder."

"Not even of someone like Victor Resnick?" Michael asked.

Mrs. Peabody didn't answer. I glanced back. She had paused at a fork in the trail and seemed to be seriously thinking over the question. Much too seriously.

"That dark stuff on the stick really looks like mud to me," Michael said.

"We'll let the police decide that," Jeb said.

"Exactly," I said. "Let's just get the stick safely locked up until the police can do a forensic examination."

"Locked up where?" Jeb asked.

"In the locker with the body, I suppose," I said. "Bodies, if you include the puffin. After all, the damned stick's survived a hurricane; a little cold won't hurt it."

"Yes, that would work," Jeb said.

We watched as Jeb trudged off toward the Anchor Inn with the puffin and the walking stick in hand. Mrs. Peabody trailed after him, presumably to keep her eye on the puffin.

"Let's go get a rope and do our burgling," I said. Michael nodded and fell into step beside me as we headed back to Aunt Phoebe's cottage.

"Aunt Phoebe did say she lost her stick before she fell into the gully," I said. "She just didn't say how long before."

"Still, it doesn't look good, her walking stick turning up so near the scene of the crime. And with blood on it."

"You're the one who keeps saying it's mud."

"Could be mud," he said. "Could be blood, too."

"True," I agreed. "And that makes two possible murder weapons that have some association with Aunt Phoebe."

I brooded on that a while longer.

"Of course," Michael put in, "The sheer improbability of the story she told goes in her favor."

"Yes, except that if she were guilty and knew all the details of the crime, she could make up an improbable story better than anyone."

"Is she that devious?"

I had to think about that one.

"I don't think so," I said finally. "Normally, I tend to think of Aunt Phoebe as abrupt and straightforward. But if she'd brooded a lot about the crimes she thought Resnick had committed against the birds . . . who knows?"

"Or if she's particularly good at thinking on her feet."

"Exactly. And then again, there's the question of why she would tell such a howler in the first place."

"Because she's covering up for someone else?"

"Yes," I said. "And people would naturally assume that someone is Dad. Which isn't an idea we want to encourage."

Just then, I saw Jim Dickerman shambling along the path toward us.

"Afternoon," I said as he drew near.

"Yeah, I know," he snapped. "Give me a break."

"Pardon?"

"Look, I'll get it running as soon as I can, damn it. I stayed up all night trying to fix the damned thing. I'm going back up now, but I had to get a couple hours of sleep."

"Hey, calm down," I said. "Aunt Phoebe isn't even hooked up to your generator, remember? I wasn't asking when you'll have the thing fixed or giving you a hard time; I just said good afternoon."

"Sorry," he said, fighting a yawn. "Bad night."

His eyes were bloodshot, and he looked as if he hadn't shaved, combed his hair, or changed his clothes in several days.

"You look as if you could use a lot more sleep," I said. "Let the generator wait a few more hours."

"Too many people complaining," he said, stifling another yawn.

"One less than there used to be at least," I said.

"Yeah," he said with a startled laugh. "I guess so. And the bastard was the biggest complainer of all. Course, he was our biggest customer, too. Pity."

"I don't suppose you saw anything useful," I asked. "Any possible clues or anything?"

"I wasn't down by Resnick's yesterday," Jim said, shrugging. "Too busy with the generator."

"What about your windows?" I asked. "I should think you have a pretty good view from there."

"When they're not shuttered up," he said. "Got 'em nailed shut for the storm right now."

"That's true," I said. "When did you do that?"

He thought for a few seconds.

"Day before they stopped the ferry," he said. "That'd be Thursday afternoon."

"So I don't suppose you saw much of what went on around the island yesterday and today, then?"

He shrugged.

"Only when I went outside," he said. "Damn birders all over everywhere."

"You don't like the birders?"

"Can't see what the big deal is, but I've got nothing against them. Mess up the island less than most damn tourists."

What a relief to see that Resnick's death wouldn't completely deprive the island of curmudgeons. I wondered if Jim and Victor Resnick had actually gotten along in their own gruff way. And then a thought hit me. . . . Jim . . . James—what if Jim Dickerman was the phantom biographer?

"Tell me," I said. "Do you know anything about the *Unheralded Genius of the Down East Coast*?"

"The what?" Jim asked.

" 'Who could have predicted this event, at once so joyous and so tragic?' " I quoted.

" 'Who can calculate the import this occurrence would present upon his life and art?' " Michael added.

"If that's one of those word games, I don't get it," Jim said in a voice that suggested he didn't much care, either. If he wasn't the biographer, he was a phenomenal actor. Ah, well. I tried another angle.

"Before the storm. You could see what went on at Resnick's, right?"

"Yeah, I guess."

"Was he really electrocuting birds?"

"Yeah, but he wasn't killing them."

"Then what was he doing?"

"Running a low-voltage current through some of the metal struts in his roof. Give 'em a hotfoot, scare 'em away so they'd stop crapping on his glass. Town made him stop, though."

"You mean he actually did what they asked?"

Jim snorted.

"Yeah. Well, he wouldn't have, except that it didn't really work anyway. Gulls just sat on the glass. Funniest thing you ever saw, watching him jump up and down in his yard, yelling at the gulls. Couldn't throw anything without breaking the glass."

"When did he stop?"

"May, maybe June. Before the tourist season anyway."

That made sense; the puffin could have still been in breeding plumage in May or June, as far as I could tell from the bird books. Maybe puffins were more sensitive to a hotfoot than gulls. Or maybe Resnick had experimented with higher voltages before the town pulled the plug on his bird-control program.

"Have you seen your brother recently?" I asked finally.

"Fred? Yeah, he's down in the village somewhere, I guess."

From the tone of voice, I got the feeling there was no love lost between the brothers.

"No, I actually meant Will."

Jim frowned but said nothing.

"Monhegan's own candidate for America's most wanted," I went on. "You haven't seen him around recently, have you?"

"No, not since—" Jim began, then stopped.

"Not since when?" I asked.

"Not since before they got arrested," he said slowly. "What does he have to do with anything? Will wasn't even on the island when . . ."

His voiced trailed off, as if something had just occurred to him.

"Well, if you find out he's on the island, tell him to see his lawyer," I said.

"Even if he didn't do it," Michael said.

"Especially if he didn't do it," I added. "Do you think

the police will look far for another suspect if they find someone right under their noses with a prior history of whacking people over the head?"

At least I hoped that's what the police would do. I must have sounded pretty convincing. Jim frowned.

"I have to get back to the generator," he said, and strode off.

"Okay, I'll bite," Michael said. "What was last bit all about?"

"I'm not sure," I said. "I'm hoping if Will Dickerman is on the island, Jim will go and see him."

"To warn him, or to give him hell for jumping bail and jeopardizing the power plant?"

"Either one will do," I said.

"Shouldn't we do something? Like maybe follow him?"

"He knows every inch of the island; I think we'd be slightly conspicuous?"

"So we stir things up and then just sit around and wait to see if something happens?"

"No. Like I said, we get the rope and burgle Resnick's studio."

But before we got to the cottage, Winnie and Binkie came hiking briskly up behind us. Predictably, after we exchanged greetings, they asked if we'd heard any more news about the murder.

About ten seconds after we told them about Mrs. Peabody and the puffin, Michael and Winnie were deep in conversation about digital cameras. Binkie and I fell in step a little behind them.

"I have the awful feeling I'm going to hear a great deal about digital cameras over the next few months," I said with a sigh.

"Dear me, yes," Binkie murmured. "And, if your young man is anything like Winnie, spending a great deal of time saying, 'Yes, dear, that's a lovely picture.'"

I shuddered. I had no doubt she was right.

"Speaking of pictures," I said, "what do you think of Resnick's painting ability?"

Instead of answering, Binkie looked over her glasses at me and frowned. Was I just imagining things, or had I touched a nerve?

CHAPTER 24

The Puffin Who Knew Too Much

"Resnick's painting ability?" Binkie asked warily. "Why, what's that got to do with his death?"

"I don't know that it has anything to do with it," I said. "Unless you know of a reason."

"No, of course not," Binkie said. A little too quickly perhaps? "Well, anyone on Monhegan can tell you about Victor Resnick. He's probably the most distinguished local landscape artist—"

"The real scoop, not the Monhegan Chamber of Commerce spiel."

She looked over her glasses at me. I tried to look innocent, earnest, and discreet. Apparently, I pulled it off.

"Second rate, at best," she said. "A shame, really. He showed such early promise, but then he never developed."

"I'm no art critic," I said. "His paintings seem pretty good to me."

"Oh, they're good, of course," she said. "But they're no better today than they were fifty years ago. In fact, they're not the slightest bit different. Not the style, not the technical skill, not even the subject matter."

"Always landscapes, yes," I said.

"Always Monhegan landscapes," Binkie corrected.

"I thought he'd spent most of the last twenty years in the south of France," I said.

"Yes, and did nothing the whole time but paint pictures of Monhegan. What kind of artist could live for twenty years on the Côte d'Azur and never once paint the Mediterranean?"

She frowned and shook her head. I followed suit, while

privately thinking that it might take more strength of character than I possessed to pick up a brush at all if I were living on the Côte d'Azur.

"Maybe he was homesick," I suggested.

"If he was homesick, why didn't he come home a little more often, then?" Binkie said. "Lazy, more like. Did it from snapshots, of course. Only came home when he wanted more snapshots. If he were still alive, you'd see him running around with that Polaroid of his right now, taking pictures of the storm."

I had a sudden vision of Victor Resnick standing in his expensive greenhouselike studio, ignoring the glorious view as he peered at a curling Polaroid clipped to his easel.

"And honestly," Binkie went on, "if I have to look at one more painting of those eerie, foreboding, calm-before-the-storm skies . . . well, I suppose now I won't have to."

"You'll probably think I'm a total philistine for saying this," I said, "but I bought a book of his paintings down at Mamie's store largely because of those skies. I thought he did them rather well."

"Oh, he did do them well. Superlatively. It's just that he did them all the time. He figured out the technique early on, dazzled everybody, and couldn't let it go. Flip through that book of yours and see. Every other painting's got that same gray-green sky. That or the gnarled tree."

"Gnarled tree?"

"He used to have this charmingly gnarled tree on a rock near where his house is now," Binkie said. "I've lost count how many of his paintings I've seen it in, from one angle or another. The poor thing blew over in a nor'easter eighteen or twenty years ago, and I remember thinking, What a relief—no more gnarled tree; or at least he'll have to find another gnarled tree."

"Let me guess: He had photos of it."

"Hundreds, I imagine; from every conceivable angle. I don't think he even noticed it was gone for a year or two;

and then only because he went out to take more snapshots. That's one reason why his sales are in such a slump. In his early days, when he was hot, every museum and major collector had to have a Resnick or two. But that's all you need, really. A seascape with the gnarled tree and the gray-green sky, and maybe a weathered saltbox with waves crashing on the beach behind it, and you've pretty much got Resnick covered."

"And that's not the case with most artists, right?"

"Oh, no," Binkie exclaimed. "Take someone like, oh, Picasso. There's no way you could mistake a painting from his twenties for one done in his fifties. With Resnick, you couldn't tell if he didn't date them. Of course, the critics took awhile to realize he wasn't going any further, but he'd fallen pretty well out of the mainstream by the eighties, which means he missed out on all the real money, back when the Japanese started buying."

"So he wasn't all that wealthy, then?"

"Well, he hadn't made as much money as people like Wyeth, for example, but I shouldn't think he was broke, if that's what you mean," Binkie said. "I suspect he invested well enough to live quite nicely. No reason why he shouldn't have; apart from that eyesore of a house, he never spent much money on anything that I can see."

"And he never married or . . . um . . ." I said, bogging down with embarrassment in the middle of my attempt to pry into Resnick's love life.

"He never married, no; and as for uming—well, if he bedded any woman around here, she had the good sense to keep quiet about her bad taste. Of course, I have no idea what he might have gotten up to in France," she added with a slight frown.

"Mrs. Fenniman said he was an old beau of Mother's, before she met Dad," I said.

"Well, I don't know that you'd call him a beau," Binkie said, her frown deepening. "He was quite smitten with her, of course; all the young men were. But I don't think she took him seriously. Or any of them back then. She'd pretend to, of course, if she thought it would shock your grandparents. I think that's why she took up with Resnick, really. He was the most unsuitable young man she could find. Any of the older girls, I think your grandfather would have stuck them in a convent school after that, but your mother managed to wangle that trip to Paris she'd always wanted."

Binkie shook her head, as if in admiration of Mother's cleverness.

"Well, this is your turnoff," she said, stepping up to take Winnie's arm as we arrived at the foot of Aunt Phoebe's lane. "We'll see you later, dear. Don't worry. I'm sure it will all work out much better than you think."

With that cryptic encouragement, the Burnhams strode up the hill toward the Dickermans' house.

"So," Michael asked when they were out of earshot. "Did you learn anything useful?"

I sighed.

"Not really," I said. "Nothing we didn't already know. Damn, I'm getting tired of this. We come here for a little peace and quiet, to get away from it all, and we land right in the middle of another murder. This whole thing has been a disaster from start to finish."

"I'm crushed," Michael said, reeling back in mock dismay. "You don't think it's romantic, us trapped together on a remote island, like the Swiss Family Robinson?"

"More like a remake of *Ten Little Indians*," I said, and then instantly wondered if my answer had been a little too honest. Michael didn't seem insulted, though. "What a pity Mother and Dad didn't just stay in Europe for a few more weeks," I added, trying to change the subject.

"Yes, I think you might rather enjoy all this if you weren't worried that the police will suspect your family."

"Exactly," I said. "Besides, I always enjoy it anytime Mother's off traveling."

"That's rather a rotten thing to say about your own mother," Michael said.

"I don't see what's so rotten about it," I said a little defensively. He was kidding, wasn't he?

"Saying you don't want her around? That's not rotten?"

"I didn't say I don't want her around; I said I enjoy it when she's traveling," I corrected. He smiled, and I relaxed. Okay, he didn't think me an ungrateful daughter after all. "She sends home such interesting stuff," I added.

"What kind of stuff?"

"You never know with Mother," I said. "She thinks of traveling largely in terms of shopping, so of course she always sends home lots of loot. Though you never know when you open a package whether you're going to find a present for you, something she bought for herself, or some laundry she decided was easier to send home than get washed."

"Not much shopping on Monhegan," Michael said. "Unless you're into puffin-related tchotchkes."

"True. I wonder why on earth she agreed to come here."

"Your dad wanted to come," Michael said. "Isn't that reason enough?"

I glanced up. Michael was looking casually out to our right, apparently enjoying the view of the churning surf and dripping rain. But I had this sneaky feeling that was some kind of test question, as in "Wouldn't you do something like that for me?"

I hate that kind of test question. I always assume I've flunked them—even when it turns out later that I didn't, or that it wasn't a test question after all.

"Reason enough?" I said. "I guess it would be for most normal people. For Dad, certainly, or Rob, or just about anyone I can think of. But Mother?" I shrugged.

"You don't give your mother enough credit; I think she's very devoted to your dad."

She was certainly very intent on letting him get his rest.

Before we even got in the door, she sent Mrs. Fenniman running out to shush us.

"Your dad's asleep," Mrs. Fenniman hissed. "And your aunt Phoebe's resting up for her ordeal."

"Ordeal?" I asked.

"When the mainland police come to haul her away," Mrs. Fenniman said.

I decided not to spoil Aunt Phoebe's grand drama just yet. Her idea of resting involved sitting in the kitchen with her injured knee propped up under an ice pack, helping empty the larder. Perhaps she thought they wouldn't feed her in jail. I inquired after the knee, dodged her questions about what we'd been up to, and settled down in the living room with two heaping plates of food—one for myself and one for Michael, who had gone upstairs to change.

As I sat there with my eyes closed, munching a ham sandwich, I felt a sudden, surprisingly intense surge of relief and pleasure. I hadn't felt this happy about things since arriving on the island—since shortly after setting foot on the ferry, for that matter. Illogical, I thought. The storm still rattled the windows. We might still see Dad or Mother or Aunt Phoebe arrested on suspicion of murder. And even if we escaped the forces of nature and the long arm of the law, we still had the ferry ride back to the mainland to dread.

"You look very cheerful," Michael said, plunking down beside me.

"Things are looking up," I said.

"You've solved the mystery?" he asked eagerly.

"No, but for the moment, we're all safe and sound under the same roof, the whole family. And we're warm and dry and fed."

"Some of us are fed," he said, frowning.

"Here, I brought you a plate, too."

"Thanks," he said. "So warm, dry, and fed is enough to make you happy?"

"For now," I said. "Later, we'll work on warm, dry, fed, and free of all suspicion in the death of Victor Resnick. Speaking of which . . ."

CHAPTER 25

Puffin or Tiger?

I rummaged through my suitcase until I found the files I'd dragged down from the attic.

"You're not going to slog away at that while we're eating?" Michael asked.

"There're only a few of them," I said. "I just want to get to them before something else interrupts us."

Michael rolled his eyes and returned to his sandwich.

Most of the files were pretty boring. My grandfather Hollingworth's correspondence with a contractor about renovations to the cottage. Bills from someone named Barnes—Jeb's father or grandfather, presumably—for groceries and supplies.

I came close to giving up on the files and sticking them back in the attic, when I ran across a file marked "Resnick."

I was relieved at first to see that it contained only a series of increasingly angry letters from Grandfather to Resnick. Apparently, Grandfather had bought a painting, which Resnick had procrastinated about delivering. How odd; as far as I knew, my grandfather had a reputation as a canny businessman, but he wasn't exactly a patron of the arts. Perhaps he'd been canny enough to recognize Victor Resnick as a young artist on the rise and had bought a painting as an investment. Then again, having seen the painting in Resnick's house I could think of another reason for the transaction. Especially when I found the last documents in the files: a canceled check for ten thousand dollars, made out to Victor Resnick, and two copies of a bill of sale.

"Michael," I said. "Where's that book of Resnick's paintings?"

"Good question," he said, looking around the living room.

"Help me find it, will you?"

After a prolonged search, we finally found the book behind a stack of flowerpots, sitting on a coiled garden hose. I flipped through the first chapter, searching for dates.

"What's up?" Michael said, leaning over my shoulder. I lost track, just for a moment, of why I was looking through the book. Oh, right, Resnick's paintings.

"Aha!" I said, when I found the right page. "Victor Resnick made his first major sale in 1956. For the princely sum of five thousand."

"Think what a bargain that would be today," he said. "Now that he's selling for a hundred times that much."

"More like twenty times, maybe, but yes, it's a bargain. But up till 1956, his sales were for peanuts. Where's that sales log of his anyway?" I asked, fishing through my knapsack. "Aha. See. Nothing over a thousand until 1956."

"True."

"So what would you say if I told you that in 1953, someone paid Resnick ten thousand for a painting?"

"I'd say the buyer was either very gullible, very farsighted, or buying something more than just a painting."

"And that it wasn't recorded in the sales log?"

"Scratch out gullible and farsighted."

"Right," I said, handing him the canceled check. "Take a look at this."

"R. S. Hollingworth—let me guess, your maternal grandfather," he said. "It doesn't say, but I'd bet anything we've seen the painting in question."

"The nude."

"So how does this relate to the murder?" Michael asked.

"I have no idea," I said. "Not at all, I hope. Though if the police start poking into the case, I'm sure it will all come out, whether it's related or not."

I began reading the letters in the file again. I looked up

when I heard a snort of laughter from Michael. He was playing with the digital cameras again.

"What's so funny?" I asked.

"Nothing," he said, pressing a button on the camera.

"Let me see the camera," I said.

I had to wrestle with him for it, which would have distracted both of us from my original request if Mrs. Fenniman hadn't kept wandering in and out. He finally let me have the camera, and I turned it on to see what he was looking at.

This was the second camera, the one whose owner claimed to have photos of Resnick shooting at us. He had indeed caught some interesting shots of the confrontation. First, a none-too-flattering view of my rear end as Michael and I scrambled over the top of the hill. Then a shot or two of Resnick waving his gun around. And one of me looking very Neanderthal, standing on the top of the hill, threatening Resnick with my rock.

"I think I'll ask for a copy of some of these," Michael said.

"Very funny," I said, pressing the button to remove my picture from the little screen. "I really don't see why . . ."

I found myself staring at the next picture in the camera.

"What's wrong?" Michael said, looking over my shoulder.

"Look at this," I said.

"It's the tidal pool," he replied. "So?"

"You can see part of a figure there in the corner."

"Since we have no idea who it is, what's the use?"

"It's Rhapsody," I said.

"Rhapsody? How can you tell?" Michael asked, peering more closely at the camera.

"The lilac and black clothes, combined with that hunched-over, 'Please don't hurt me' posture."

Michael studied the photo.

"You could be right," he said. "But it looks pretty light

in this picture. Must have been taken fairly early in the day."

"It was, obviously; before the pictures of us confronting him anyway."

"Then what's the point?"

"I don't know," I said. "I just think it's funny that she was there at all. And she was hanging around the house again today; I'm sure that it was Rhapsody we saw through the windows. We need to find a way to ask her about it."

"I'm sure you'll manage," Michael said.

"Oh, there you are, dears," Mother said, looking down from the balcony above. "Your father isn't up yet; I'll keep you company until he's awake. Let me just find my embroidery."

She disappeared again.

"Your mother does a great deal of embroidery, doesn't she?" Michael said.

Was that simple admiration in his voice, or was there some kind of subtext? As in "Why don't you do something decorative and feminine, instead of dragging me all over the island in the rain while you play sleuth?"

"She doesn't actually *do* a lot of embroidery," I said. "She carries it around all the time, but if you watch, she takes a stitch only occasionally. I don't really think she's that keen on it."

"Then why does she do it?"

Before I could answer, Mother limped into the room. She settled herself on the sofa opposite us. We watched as she laid out several dozen skeins of brightly colored embroidery thread on the sofa beside her and covered half the coffee table with the contents of her sewing basket. She fussed with the items for a while, like a decorator primping a floral arrangement. Then she picked up her hoop and her needle and looked at us with a smile, one eyebrow raised, as if asking whether the stage set looked just right. Or possibly hinting that we should entertain her while she worked.

Out of the corner of my eye, I could see Michael's mouth twitching.

"How's the new embroidery coming, Mother?" I asked.

She cocked her head to one side, like a wren, and studied the cloth on her lap.

"Slowly," she said with a sigh.

Michael made a strangled noise, and Mother took three or four leisurely stitches before stopping to examine her progress from several angles. Michael now sat with his elbow on his knee and his hand over his mouth, a very serious look on his face. In fact, he looked rather like the Thinker come to life, except that I somehow couldn't imagine the Thinker ever wheezing with suppressed chuckles.

I hated to put a damper on his fun, but something preyed on my mind. I glanced around to make sure no one else could overhear before turning to Mother.

"Mother," I said. "We found an interesting painting up at Victor Resnick's house. A portrait."

I should have known better than to expect a dramatic reaction from Mother.

"Oh?" she said, pausing, her needle poised gracefully over the embroidery hoop.

"I didn't know he even did portraits," Dad put in, peering down from the balcony. So much for my carefully chosen moment. "Thought he only did landscapes."

"Well, apparently he did in his youth," I said.

"I've never heard of any," Dad said, rubbing his eyes as he ambled down the stairs. "And there weren't any in that book about him."

"Are you sure, Dad?" I asked.

"Well, yes, of course," he said. "I'll show you. Where's that book anyway?"

"Out in the kitchen, I think," I said, shoving the edge of the book in question out of sight under the couch. Dad trotted out to the kitchen.

"I doubt if he ever exhibited this painting," I said, my

voice too low for Dad to hear in the kitchen. "I think it was done for his own private enjoyment."

Mother looked up again.

"Oh really?" she said. "What makes you think that?"

"The subject was . . . rather unconventional."

To my amazement, Mother smiled.

"Yes, he was rather unconventional as a young man," she said. "And terribly wild."

My jaw dropped.

"Gifted with an overactive imagination, of course," she said. "And not very honest, I'm afraid."

"Yes," I said. "Taking payment for something and then never delivering it isn't very honest, is it?"

"Well, he did deliver it eventually," Mother said. "I rather wish he hadn't; I was so provoked when your grandfather burned it."

"Burned it!" Michael and I echoed.

"Yes, can you imagine it?" Mother said. "Burning a genuine Victor Resnick! Of course, we didn't know then how famous he'd become, but still. I would so like to have that painting. It would bring back such fond memories."

Michael and I looked at each other in consternation. What kind of fond memories? I wondered. Memories of an affair with Resnick? Or just of the days when she looked the way she looked in the painting?

"Well, you may be in luck," I said. "Apparently, he painted at least one more portrait of you."

"Another portrait?" Mother asked, looking very interested. "What was it like?"

"Well," I said, and then froze. I looked at Michael for assistance.

"Not a painting I can imagine Meg's grandfather would approve of," Michael said.

"No, I imagine not," Mother murmured. "Well, that explains a lot."

"A lot of what?"

"I think he expected someone to come over and collect it this weekend," she said. "Perhaps you and Michael could take care of that?"

"No, at least not without some kind of proof that we're not pulling a million-dollar art heist," I said.

"Oh, well," Mother said. She dropped the embroidery into her lap, reached over to the end table for her purse—an impractical scrap of velvet, lace, and satin that would probably survive five minutes if I tried to carry it—and pulled out a small envelope.

"Here," she said, handing it to me.

There was no stamp. "Margaret Langslow" was written on the front in the same bold, angular hand I recognized from Resnick's files. I hesitated before opening it, and Mother gestured impatiently.

"My dear Maggie," it began.

"Maggie?" I said aloud.

"I never liked that nickname," she said, shrugging.

"I have something of yours that I'd like to give you—that painting your father admired so much. Come and see me; we can talk about old times. Vic."

It was dated Friday—the day after she'd arrived on the island. He hadn't lost much time.

"How did you get this?"

"Your aunt Phoebe found it slipped under the door sometime after we arrived."

"Did you go to see him?"

"Of course not," Mother said. "I had no interest in seeing him, and even if I had, why would I want to walk that far in this weather? And I thought he was lying about the painting."

"Maybe Grandfather lied about burning it."

"Oh, no," Mother said. "He made me watch while he burned it."

Somehow I could picture the scene: Grandfather sputtering like a firecracker while Mother coolly pretended indifference to the fate of the painting.

"Well, Resnick has this one hanging in his hallway," I said. "I don't think he'd had it there long, though, or everyone on the island would have heard about it."

"Is it still there?" Mother asked. She didn't look alarmed, just interested.

"No, we put it and some of the other paintings away where the rain couldn't damage them."

"That's nice," she said. "Well, go along and collect it. I'm sure it would cause all kinds of confusion if the police found it."

"It's not out there," Dad said, popping in from the kitchen.

"Oh, I'm sorry," I said. "I just found it here under the couch."

For the next half hour, I had to keep my composure while Dad thumbed through the book with one hand and ate with the other. And he commented all the while, with his mouth full, on what a genius Resnick was and what a shame such a great artist had been such a difficult person, and what a pity it was he had come to such an untimely end. Mother continued to fuss over her embroidery and practice her patented Mona Lisa smile, occasionally reminding Dad not to drop food on my new book.

Well, it wasn't as if Dad had ruined my chance to find out more about the painting. Mother had obviously said all she planned to say about it. Whether she had posed for it or whether Resnick had done it from memory or imagination, I'd probably never find out. In fact, I wasn't even sure I wanted to know.

I decided not to worry about the painting until tomorrow. In fact, I wasn't going to worry about anything until tomorrow. As soon as possible, I was going to go to bed. I might even take a nap right now, I thought, leaning back into Michael's arm and closing my eyes with a contented sigh. I felt Michael shift his weight and then felt his breath in my ear. Yes, I thought, a very nice time to whisper a few sweet nothings in my ear.

"Things would be a lot easier if we didn't have all these damned birders underfoot," he murmured.

"Yeah," I agreed. Not to mention my family. I opened one eyelid to check on what our unintentional chaperones were up to. Dad was studying a photo with a magnifying glass. Mother was contemplating her embroidery with a dreamy expression on her face.

"I mean, they're very useful for establishing the time line, but there are just too many of them, and any one of them could be the murderer. In fact . . . What's so funny?"

Mother and Dad both glanced up, wondering what the joke was, and Michael and I fled to the kitchen, where we could talk with more privacy.

"I thought you were talking about our situation, not the latest homicide," I said, giggling.

"Yeah, well, that, too," he said, sheepishly. "But you've got to admit, it's intriguing."

"It's completely baffling," I said. My sleepy mood had vanished. "Too many suspects, all with motive, means, and opportunity."

"I like Will Dickerman for it," Michael said. "Perfect casting for the murderer."

"Well, if you like Will, don't forget about Fred," I said. "To know him is to loathe him, and he'd have had much the same reasons Will had for doing Resnick in. And for all that southern-fried charm he puts on, I wouldn't put it past Ken Takahashi to do the old boy in. For ruining the deal, or just for dragging him out here in a hurricane."

"I don't know," Michael said. "I rather like Takahashi. I'd hate to see him turn out to be the one."

"Well, I'd hate for the police to suspect Dad or Aunt Phoebe."

"Perhaps it will turn out to be someone we don't know,"

Michael said. "One of the birders, or a local we haven't really met."

Just then, we heard the front door slam. We peeked out of the kitchen door to see what was up.

"This place is absolutely impossible," Rob said, striding in.

"What's wrong, dear?" Mother asked.

"They won't let me use the power in the Anchor Inn, even though they've got that generator going, doing nothing but running the freezer," Rob complained. "And then I tried to talk to the guy who does the generator, and all he wants is free legal advice."

"Let me guess," I said. "Was he asking what happens if someone who's jumped bail gets turned in? Or what happens to a foreclosure if the note holder dies while it's in progress?"

"Both, actually," Rob said. "What are you, psychic?"

"She's a very fine detective," Dad said, beaming.

"I'm just using the brain God gave me," I said. Well, that and the information from Resnick's files. "What did you tell him?"

"Basically, that I had no idea," Rob said. "I mean, that's the kind of stuff you don't know off the top of your head unless you work with it every day. And even if I did know, I'd know how it worked in Virginia. This is Maine. Things could be completely different here."

"He shouldn't ask for free legal advice," Dad said. "It's unfair; like asking me for free medical advice just because I'm a doctor."

"Not that I've ever heard you turn anyone down," I commented. "Or, for that matter, that you usually wait to be asked."

"Well, he should talk to a Maine lawyer," Dad said. "I don't know why he doesn't ask Binkie Burnham. She's an old friend of the Dickerman family; I'm sure she'd give him any legal advice he needs."

"That's right; Binkie's a lawyer," I said, remembering the private investigator's report. "Harvard Law School!"

"Oh, yes," Dad said. "Quite a famous litigator, too. She does environmental cases, mostly, plus the occasional criminal case. Of course, she's semiretired these days."

I pondered this fact for a moment.

"Let's get some fresh air," I said to Michael.

"Fresh—" he began, looking at the drizzle outside. "Oh, right, fresh air," he said. "Good idea."

What an actor, I thought as I grabbed my knapsack and stuffed some rope into it. I could almost believe him myself.

CHAPTER 26

Round Up the Usual Puffins

"Fresh air?" he repeated as we finished fastening our rain gear.

"The game is afoot," I said. "Let's go up to the Dickermans' for a minute."

"I can manage that far," Michael said as we turned down the road. "Barely. But why?"

"Every time I've seen Winnie and Binkie for the past few days, they've been going up or coming down the road from the Dickermans'," I said. "I just assumed it was for bird-watching purposes. Or because they've all been friends for decades. But now that we know Binkie's a crack criminal lawyer, it strikes me as odd that she would spend so much time near the house of the only two criminals on the island whose identity we already know. Let's go see what's up."

In the light of day, the Dickermans' house looked rather more run-down than usual, even for Monhegan. Signs that they could no longer afford the upkeep? Or just my overactive imagination?

I knocked on the door, and we waited awhile—I had a feeling someone was inspecting us from behind a curtain. Then the door opened and Mrs. Dickerman peered out.

"May we come in?" I asked.

She hesitated for a moment, then stepped aside. I walked into the living room, where Winnie and Binkie sat holding teacups. Mr. Dickerman stood before the fireplace, looking anxious.

"Meg, dear, how nice to see you," Binkie said, looking

up with a smile. "And Michael. Mamie says you two are trying to play detective."

"We're trying to keep them from railroading my Dad, if that's what you mean," I said. "Just because Mother knew Victor Resnick half a century ago does not make Dad suspect number one."

"Quite right, I'm sure," Binkie said. "And how's your sleuthing going along, then?"

Chalk it up to tiredness, but I had no patience for drawn-out verbal fencing.

"Coming along about as well as you'd expect," I said. "I don't suppose I can persuade you to come clean about Will?"

The Dickermans started, and even Winnie looked mildly disconcerted. Binkie only smiled and sipped her tea.

"Come clean?" she said with a shake of her head. "My, that sounds so melodramatic. I can almost hear Cagney saying it, or Bogart. What on earth could Will Dickerman have to do with the events of the past few days?"

"Quite a lot, if he was on the island for the past few days," I said.

"I can assure you, Will Dickerman is not on the island today, and was not on the island at the time of Victor Resnick's death." Binkie said.

"How can you be so sure, if he's on the lam?"

Binkie sighed.

"Because just before Winnie and I came over to the island, I accompanied Will to the Port Clyde police station, where he surrendered himself to custody," Binkie said in a brisk, businesslike tone of voice. "Needless to say, there was no possibility of bail."

I thought for a moment.

"I notice you were very careful to say when Will wasn't on the island," I said. "Just for the sake of argument, suppose he had been on the island sometime after he skipped bail and before he went to the mainland to turn himself in."

Binkie raised an eyebrow but said nothing.

"Suppose he had hidden himself by camping out on the far side of the island, and Michael and I had found the remains of his campsite."

Mr. and Mrs. Dickerman started.

"I mean, if we were absolutely sure it had nothing to do with the murder, Michael and I wouldn't have to go out of our way to report the campsite to the police," I said. "In case they got the idea that someone on the island was aiding and abetting a fugitive by bringing Will food and beer."

Binkie thought for a moment.

"Hypothetically, if I were representing any parties involved in the situation you describe, I would work with the district attorney to arrange immunity from prosecution on the aiding and abetting charges in return for providing vital evidence in a homicide."

"But if what you say is true, the campsite isn't vital evidence, is it?"

"To the extent that a defense attorney might use the campsite to muddy the waters in a trial, the police might find the true explanation of its origin rather vital, now wouldn't they, dear?" Binkie smiled gently.

I gazed at her round weathered face and wondered how many sharp young district attorneys had, over the years, come to grief by mistaking Binkie for a harmless, well-bred New England matron.

"So in the unlikely event that we found this hypothetical campsite, we could safely assume it had nothing to do with the murder?"

"I imagine you could safely assume it was abandoned three or four days before the murder," Binkie said.

And from the look on her face, I doubted we'd pry any more information out of Binkie. I stood up to go.

"Sorry to barge in," I said, looking at the Dickermans. I felt sorry for them. Not their fault, really, how Fred and Will had turned out; or if it was, they were certainly paying for it now. "I hope you can work things out with the power plant and all. I know Aunt Phoebe's not sold on it, but I'm sure a lot of people around here would hate to see it shut down or change hands."

"Don't worry, dear," Binkie said. She smiled—not the gentle smile I'd seen previously, but the sort of smile that made me feel very, very sorry for anyone who might attempt to take the Central Monhegan Power Company away from the Dickermans.

Just then, we heard frantic knocking at the door. Both of the Dickermans leapt to answer it, then returned almost immediately with Mamie and Dad at their heels.

"Ah, Mamie thought we'd find you up here!" Dad exclaimed. I was about to ask what he wanted me for, but then I realized he was looking at Binkie.

"Dr. Langslow suggested that we might want a couple of doctors to examine Resnick's body," Mamie said. "Just in case there's anything significant that doesn't . . . uh, last. Seemed like a good idea."

"Yes," Binkie said. "Provided you have some responsible witnesses to supervise the proceedings, of course."

"We thought perhaps you could do that," Mamie said.

"Of course," Binkie said. "Shall we go now?"

"Well, first we have to find John Peabody," Dad said. "He's the only other doctor we know of on the island, and we haven't seen him all day."

"Off finding a bit of peace and quiet, I imagine," Winnie said. Having met Mrs. Peabody, I imagined he was right.

"Winnie and I can find John, then meet you at the Anchor Inn," Binkie said. "We'll see you later, then," she told the Dickermans, and shooed the rest of us out. She and Winnie hiked off in search of Dr. Peabody while Mamie, Dad, Michael, and I took what Mamie assured us was a shortcut to the Anchor Inn.

"Oh, Meg," Dad said as we strolled. "Mrs. Peabody said you had her digital camera and could take some pictures."

"What a great idea," Michael said.

I rolled my eyes, wondering whether I really wanted to be involved in this.

Just then, we rounded a turn in the path and I caught sight of a cottage I hadn't seen before.

"Mamie," I said. "That's Rhapsody's cottage, isn't it?"

"Why yes," she said, beaming. "How did you know?"

"Just a lucky guess," I murmured.

CHAPTER 27

Touch Not the Puffin

Unlike Aunt Phoebe's cottage, which was just a small weathered saltbox, this really looked like a fairy-tale cottage. Rhapsody had painted it various shades of lilac and lavender, with blue trim. The blue tile roof hadn't weathered the hurricane well, and several of the blue-and-lavender shutters had come loose, revealing, rather than protecting, the small diamond-shaped windowpanes. Dead vines covered the front. The vines probably bore purple flowers during Monhegan's brief summer, but they looked pretty stark now. Still, the effect was charming, in a cloying sort of way. I half-expected to see Hansel and Gretel walk around from the backyard, munching on chunks of marzipan windowpane and gingerbread woodwork. The door knocker was shaped like a unicorn's head, complete with a wickedly sharp horn, and I wondered how many people had impaled themselves on it.

"Isn't it cute?" Mamie said.

"Very cute," I said. Mamie smiled and Michael looked puzzled. Only Dad had known me long enough to realize that I'd just uttered my ultimate insult, but even Dad wasn't tactless enough to say so.

"Look, we'll catch up to you in a bit," I said. "I want to talk to Rhapsody."

"What about?" Mamie snapped.

Damn. I'd forgotten how protective Mamie was of her pet artist.

"Mother's interested in a painting," I said. Well, it wasn't a complete lie; if Mamie chose to think I meant one of Rhapsody's paintings, that was her problem.

"I'll come with you, then," Mamie said. "She's very shy, you know."

"I'd like to meet her," Dad said, falling into step beside Mamie.

We slipped and slid up the cobblestone path—nature never intended cobblestones for use in hurricanes—and Mamie knocked very gently on the front door.

After half a minute, I saw motion out of the corner of my eye. The curtain in the window to the left of the door fluttered slightly. I deliberately avoided looking at it, and pasted what I hoped was a friendly, harmless smile on my face.

Mamie had raised her hand to knock again when the door opened slightly, with the sort of creak they use in movies to suggest that maybe this is a door you'd be better off not entering. But there wasn't a monster or a wicked witch hiding behind the door. Just poor Rhapsody, who peeked through the narrow opening as if she were the one expecting monsters.

"Rhapsody, we're so sorry to intrude, but Meg's parents want to buy a painting," Mamie said.

Rhapsody didn't seem reassured by Mamie's words, but after staring at us blankly for a few seconds, she opened the door a little wider and scuttled back to let us pass.

"I'll make tea," she murmured, and fled down the tiny hallway while Mamie led us into the living room. I instantly wished I'd suggested inviting Rhapsody down to the general store or to Mamie's house. Her decor gave me galloping claustrophobia. Not so much the furniture, although she had too much of it—fussy little chairs that would collapse instantly under anyone over a hundred pounds; rickety-looking tables about to overturn under their loads of knick-knacks; spindly cabinets whose glass fronts bulged outward from the further hoard of knickknacks within. You could have sewed all the frayed antimacassars and antique doilies together to make several bedsheets, and from the number of puffin-related items among the knickknacks, I gathered that Rhapsody was Mamie's best customer.

And apart from the black and white of the puffins and the various wood tones, everything in the room was colored some shade of lavender, purple, or lilac.

Everything also carried a visible coating of dust. I sneezed four times while poking around the room to find a chair I would feel safe sitting on.

Mamie beamed with pride at the decor. Dad gazed at me, clearly awaiting brilliant deductions. I could tell Michael wanted to make a break for the wide-open spaces. I tried to stifle my sneezes by concentrating on the pictures on the wall. She had about thirty of them, all book covers or illustrations from the Puffin Family series. At the lower left-hand corner of every painting was Rhapsody's signature—a fussy, overelaborate design, barely recognizable as the letter R, in luminous purple paint.

Rhapsody emerged from the kitchen, wearing a frilly lavender dress that served very well as camouflage, considering her decor. She carried a tray, from which she handed out tea in eggshell-thin antique china. The idea of actually grasping the delicate gold-and-lavender handle of the cup was more than I could manage; I was sure to break it. Besides, I could tell from the smell that she'd made some kind of odd-tasting herbal muck. So I cleared a space among the fragile-looking knickknacks on the doily-covered end table, set down my cup, and tried not to watch what Dad was doing with his.

"By the way, before we talk about the painting, I have a question about puffins," I said.

"I don't really know that much about them," Rhapsody said, her voice hardly more than a whisper. "I just paint them."

"Yes," I said. "That's what I wanted to ask you about."

She smiled nervously. I got the idea that four people were almost more of an audience than she could handle. I felt a sudden surge of impatience and claustrophobia and decided not to waste time beating around the bush.

"You had a dead puffin you used as a model, right?" I asked. "You kept it in your freezer."

She stiffened but said nothing.

"Oh, come on, Rhapsody," I said. "We saw you down by Victor Resnick's house on the day of the murder and—"

Rhapsody shrieked, burst into tears, and threw herself on the sofa. Mamie Benton hurried over and began patting her back.

"There, there," she said, glaring at me. "That wasn't a very funny joke, but I'm sure Meg didn't mean anything by it."

Mamie acted as if she'd caught me torturing a small child, which I suppose wasn't far from the truth. Dad had that "I'm disappointed with you" look, and even Michael seemed rather uncomfortable.

"I didn't do it on purpose!" Rhapsody wailed. "It was an accident! Honestly!"

Rhapsody lapsed into hysterical sobs. The others gaped when they heard her words, and Mamie froze, her hand still outstretched toward the sobbing woman's shoulder.

"You don't mean—" She gasped.

"Aha!" Dad said. "I knew you'd solve this!"

"She can't possibly have done it!" Mamie wailed. "Oh, this is awful!"

"Oh, for heavens' sake," I said. "Stop carrying on; what she's done may be perfectly legal."

"Perfectly legal!" Mamie exclaimed. "I'm sure you could argue that killing Resnick was morally justified, but even if it was self-defense—"

"Oh, do be quiet for a few minutes and let Rhapsody talk," I said. I strode over to the sofa and nudged Mamie aside so I could take her place beside Rhapsody.

"Rhapsody," I said in a firm, matter-of-fact tone.

She continued to sob. Dealing with sobbing members of

my own sex isn't my forte. I began to wonder if we should send for someone better equipped to deal with the situation—though I had no idea who that might be. Mrs. Fenniman or Aunt Phoebe would only scare Rhapsody to death, and Mother would enjoy the drama and encourage her to sob for a few more hours. We had no time for that.

"For heaven's sake, stop sniveling and sit up," I said, pulling her upright and giving her a firm shake. "No one cares about the stupid puffin; we just want to know the whole story so we can clear this thing up."

She collapsed back on the sofa with such violence that she knocked over the end table. I could hear the tinkle of breaking glass and china. So much for the knickknacks and antiques.

Michael suddenly appeared, kneeling at our feet.

"Let me try," he murmured. I scooted aside to let him sit closer to Rhapsody.

"Now Rhapsody," he said, in soothing tones, taking her hands in his. "It's all right. No one wants to hurt you. We just need to know what happened so we can take care of things."

He went on in much the same vein while gently chafing her hands. He was making progress; her sobs grew less violent. She finally sat up, took the tissues Michael had ready, and began swabbing at her face with them.

"They'll arrest me," Rhapsody moaned, looking at Michael with an expression of adoration. I resisted the impulse to knock her down and jump up and down on her, yelling, "Mine! Mine!" Michael was, I reminded myself, an actor. The expression of tender concern on his face wasn't real. Still, I was irrationally relieved to see that Rhapsody was not one of those women who can cry charmingly. Her entire face was beet red, and I upped my estimate of her age by a decade.

"Arrest you for what?" Michael asked.

"They'll think I killed the poor little p-puffin," Rhapsody

said, sniffling slightly. "They'll arrest me for harming an endangered species."

"Puffins? Nonsense, they're not endangered," I said.

"But there are only twelve puffin nests on Egg Island," she said.

"And a couple million healthy puffins flying around northern Canada and Greenland," I said. "Isn't that right, Dad?"

"Oh, yes," he said. "It's threatened in this habitat, of course; they've all moved farther north, where humans don't impinge on their breeding grounds. But it's not endangered. Not in the least."

"But I can see your point," I said. "The birders around here wouldn't take kindly to anyone killing a puffin. But of course you didn't, did you?"

"N-no," she said. "That horrible man did, with his electric-shock things. I was trying to sneak past his house to go down to the point, where I could watch the live puffins, and I saw the poor thing die when it landed on the roof, and it fell off and was just lying there, and I couldn't resist. He was always calling my drawings lifeless and mechanical, but all I ever have to work with are photographs and bird books. I thought maybe if I used a real puffin, it would help."

"And did it?" I asked.

"No," she said. "I couldn't even look at it without wanting to cry. But by the time I found that out, they'd made him stop using his electric-shock things, and he was chasing people out, and I didn't have a chance to take it back."

"So you kept it."

"Why didn't you just leave it somewhere else on the island?" Michael asked.

"Because Puffin Point's the only place on the island where anyone ever sees puffins," she said.

"And certainly the only place on the island where you'd expect to find one electrocuted," I added.

"Yes," she said, sniffing. "And when the hurricane came along, I thought I could just leave it there, and people would think it had washed up in the storm, and even if they figured out it had been electrocuted, they'd think he was at it again. I didn't even know he was dead until after I did it."

"That must have been quite a shock," I said.

"I was so terrified someone had seen me and would think I'd done it," Rhapsody said.

"Well, you should never keep quiet about something like that," I said in my sternest tone. "These things always come out in a murder investigation, and you're always better off if you tell the truth from the start."

Michael quirked one eyebrow. I rolled my eyes to show I realized how stupid and pretentious that sounded. But Rhapsody, Dad, and Mamie all nodded with great enthusiasm.

"So," I said. "Tell us more about the puffin."

CHAPTER 28

Anatomy of a Puffin

And so for the next half hour, Rhapsody told us about the sad fate of the puffin. Now that she'd confessed her dread secret, she was pathetically eager to spill everything. I waited patiently and let Michael respond to her description of how she'd found the puffin and what had occurred while she'd had it in her custody. I cared more about her two most recent visits to Resnick's house.

"So anyway," she said finally. "I hid the puffin under a cloth in the bottom of my wicker basket and went up the path toward that horrible man's house."

"Weren't you afraid of meeting him?" I asked.

"Oh yes!" she said. "So I found a place to sketch where I could overlook the path and see when he went down to the village. I think I ruined my sketchbook, sitting out in the rain all that time."

She gestured toward the fireplace, where a book bound in lavender velvet stood on end, its pages fanned open toward the thin warmth of her fire.

"I was just looking around the house, trying to decide where to put the puffin, when I heard a noise down on the shore. I thought at first it was Mr. Resnick, coming back from another direction, but when I ran back down the path, I almost knocked him over. So he hadn't been down on the shore after all."

"Probably the murderer," Dad said with obvious relish.

Rhapsody looked stricken, and her hands flew to her mouth, stifling a shriek.

"Nonsense," I said. "Probably only a birder, taking advantage of Resnick's absence to look for that rare whatsit that's nesting by his house."

"Yes, I'm sure that's all it was," Michael said, patting Rhapsody's shoulder again. I braced myself for more hysterics, but our reassurances—well, Michael's anyway—did the trick.

"Do you really think so?" she said, gazing up at him with an expression of frail, helpless innocence that would have looked perfect on the face of a Victorian maiden. For that matter, it had probably served Rhapsody rather well in her twenties.

"After all that, I'm amazed that you managed to go back the next day," I said. "That took a lot of courage."

"Well, I had nightmares all night," she said. "I knew I just had to return the poor little puffin so he could rest in peace. I decided that even if that dreadful man tried to stop me, I was going to march right down there and put the poor little thing somewhere near Puffin Point, where he belonged. And I did. Not near the house, of course; but I thought he belonged by the shore."

A pity she hadn't chickened out again; if she had, we wouldn't have wasted so much time on a red herring.

Rhapsody had no other useful information to offer, at least none we could extract during another twenty minutes of questioning, so I decided to call it quits.

"Well, we'd better run along," I said, standing up. Surely Winnie and Binkie would have found Dr. Peabody by this time. My head felt far too near the ceiling—doubtless an optical illusion created by the busy lavender-and-white-patterned wallpaper overhead.

"Oh, can't you stay a little longer?" Rhapsody said. To her credit, she was looking at me, with barely a sidelong glance toward Michael. "I could make more tea."

"No," I said. "But if you like, come down to the cottage if the rain lets up a little. We can talk more, and Mother would enjoy the company. She gets out so little in this kind of weather."

As we all milled about in the tiny front hall, poking one another in the noses with our elbows as we struggled into our rain gear in the confined space, a thought hit me.

"Oh, by the way," I said. "May I borrow your sketchbook?"

"My sketchbook?"

"Yes, the one you had the day you staked out Resnick's house. Who knows, perhaps something you sketched may give us a clue."

"Staked out Resnick's house," Rhapsody repeated. "Oh, yes, of course! Let me find something to wrap it in!"

We set out finally, with her battered velvet-covered sketchbook wrapped in several layers of plastic in my knapsack. Rhapsody stood in her doorway, waving a fond goodbye to us.

"Now look what you've done," Michael said. "I'm sure she'll come down to the cottage in a few hours, panting to know what clues you've discovered in her sketchbook."

"The sooner the better," I said.

"Do you really want her hanging around?"

"I want to get her into Mother's clutches as soon as possible," I said. "Now that Dad's home safe, Mother will start getting restless and looking for something to do. I think Rhapsody's just the thing."

"And what's your mother supposed to do with Rhapsody?" Michael asked.

"Well, either Mother will decide to take Rhapsody in hand or Rhapsody will be overwhelmed with Mother and begin imitating her. Preferably both. Rhapsody's an attractive woman, but I get the feeling she's been stuck in that Haight Ashbury Pre-Raphaelite-style garb since the late sixties. She could do worse than pick up some of Mother's style. And Mother would love to have a docile, cooperative protégée; she's certainly had no luck working her magic on me."

"Thank goodness," Michael said. "Much as I adore your mother, I like you just fine the way you are."

Well, those were encouraging words, I thought. Not to mention the look that went with them, which went well past encouraging. As a teenager, I'd always resented how easily Mother charmed my boyfriends. With some of them, I'd never shaken the feeling that they only took up with me in the hopes that ugly duckling Meg would eventually blossom into a swan like Mother.

Just then, Mamie, who had stayed behind to talk to Rhapsody, came out of the lavender cottage. She saw us standing there and strode up.

"I heard Jeb tell you to keep your nose out of this," she began.

"Yes, but when Mrs. Peabody insisted on dragging that miserable puffin up, I knew we had to do something," I said. "I mean, if we hadn't cleared this up, Rhapsody might have had to talk to the police!"

I tried to give my voice an authentic quaver, calculated to create the impression that Rhapsody was in genuine danger of being beset by the minions of the law, bearing handcuffs, rubber hoses, and truncheons. Whatever truncheons were. Mamie frowned, then nodded and walked off.

"Bring the damned camera," she said over her shoulder.

We followed Mamie to the Anchor Inn, where Jeb, Binkie, and Dr. Peabody already waited.

Considering how cold, wet, and miserable conditions still were outside, I found myself surprisingly reluctant to step inside the Anchor Inn. Get a grip, I told myself. It's dry, warmer than outdoors, and solidly built. Compared with some of the island buildings, the Anchor Inn, I felt sure, could withstand whatever huffing and puffing the departing Gladys could manage outside.

Yes, quite solidly built, and rather well insulated. Once

we all stumbled inside and slammed the door shut behind us, the noise of the storm was a lot less overpowering. Almost muted. For some reason, that wasn't comforting. In fact, it was downright spooky.

"Quiet as a tomb in here," Jeb remarked. He sounded nervous.

"Let's not waste time, then," Dad said.

"This really isn't my specialty," Dr. Peabody said apologetically. "I'm a dermatologist."

Smart man, I thought. In grade school, when Dad had managed to give us the impression that as Langslows we were doomed to medical careers, Rob and I had debated at length what kind of specialist to become, our main criteria being the ease of avoiding dead bodies and large quantities of blood. I'd opted for psychiatry, but I had to admit dermatology seemed a reasonable choice for someone like Rob, who fainted at the sight of rare roast beef. Fortunately for the skins and minds of our countrymen, neither of us had actually allowed Dad to bully us into medical school. Evidently, Dr. Peabody's parents had found him more malleable. He looked greener than any of us, and we hadn't even gotten near the deceased yet.

Jeb led the way through the silent front room of the restaurant and back into the kitchen. We stood around looking at the door to the meat cooler as he fumbled through his pockets and finally located the key to the padlock holding the door closed.

"In here," he said after he'd unlocked and opened the cooler door.

Dad and Dr. Peabody peered in. I looked over their shoulders at the blanket-covered bundle on the floor of the cooler.

"Well, let's get him out here where we can take a look at him," Dad said.

Jeb and Michael looked at each other. Having taken my turn carrying Resnick's body when Michael and I first found it, I decided I could honorably wimp out this time and let the men do the heavy lifting.

"You'll need more light," I said. "I'll see if I can find some lanterns."

I uncovered a stash of oil lamps in a cabinet, and enough lamp oil to fill half a dozen of them. While I bustled about trimming wicks and lighting lamps, the four men, after a bit of nervous hemming and hawing, picked up Resnick and laid him on the long wooden table I had cleared. Binkie stood watching them with her arms crossed, looking stern and vigilant.

Dad whisked back the blanket to reveal the late Victor Resnick. He didn't look much like the distinguished figure on the back of the book I'd bought. From our brief acquaintance, I suspected the angry expression on his face was a lot more characteristic than the lofty, noble, far-seeing expression the photographer had captured. His face was pale and had a sort of weird bluish color to it. His eyes were open, and his hair and beard wildly disheveled. The impulse to run screaming out of the room fought in my mind with an irrational urge to close his eyes, smooth his hair, and remove a little bit of seaweed tangled in his beard.

"Hmm," Dad said. That knocked some of the fright out of me, and replaced it with irritation. I hate it when doctors do that. "Hmm" can mean just about anything. "How soon can I get this disgustingly healthy person out of my office and go on to someone with an interesting ailment?" or "Yikes! How can I possibly break it to her that she's got maybe six weeks to live?" or "Chinese or tacos for lunch?" Give me a doctor who babbles out exactly what he's thinking.

Dr. Peabody looked faint. He examined the body visually, but from rather a distance, with his hands clasped tightly behind his back. Dad was doing his Sherlock Holmes act, inspecting every inch of Victor Resnick with great attention. Jeb scrutinized the Anchor Inn's kitchen fixtures as if he planned on buying the joint. Michael was snapping pictures frantically. Only Binkie and I paid attention to Dad's examination. I wondered what he found so interesting about Victor Resnick's fingernails.

"Let's turn him over," Dad said after a while.

Binkie and I supervised again while the men did the turning.

Dad repeated his detailed inspection on this side of Resnick, with particular attention, naturally, to the head wound, which didn't look all that bad now. I thought I had seen quite a lot of blood on Resnick's head when we first found him floating facedown in the pool, but there wasn't much when you looked at it close-up. Had a lot of it washed off while we were hauling him up here to the Anchor Inn? Or had I overreacted when I first saw him—when I thought, for a heartbeat, that it might be Dad. Close-up, the wound looked so small that I wondered how it could have been fatal.

"Very interesting," Dad said at last. "Let's turn him over again."

"So, did he die of drowning or from getting hit on the head?" Jeb asked when the body was right side up again.

"Neither," Dad said.

"Neither? Then how the blazes did he die?"

"Electrocution."

CHAPTER 29

I Am the Only Running Puffin

"Electrocution?" we all chorused.

"How can you tell?" I asked.

"See this small burned spot?" Dad said, indicating the corner of Resnick's mouth. "And this discoloration?" He pointed to the fingernails.

"Don't tell me those tiny burns killed him."

"No, undoubtedly the ventricular fibrillation killed him."

"The what?" Jeb asked.

"Ventricular fibrillation?" I echoed, stumbling over the half-familiar term. "Isn't that what they do in emergency rooms to revive people?"

"That's defibrillation," Dad said. "If a person's heart has stopped or is irregular, you can use a controlled electrical current to get it started, or steadied. But if you take someone with a normally functioning heart and subject them to an electrical shock, it can slow or stop the heart, or mess up the rhythm. Can be fatal."

"So that's why in emergency rooms they always yell, 'Clear!' and make sure no one's touching the patient before they try to defibrillate," I said.

"Oh, right," Jeb said, nodding. "I've seen that on TV."

"Essentially, yes," Dad went on. "Most people who die in low-voltage electrical accidents don't die from burns; it's the v-fib that kills them."

"Dr. Peabody, what do you think?" Jeb asked.

"Oh, Langslow's diagnosis sounds fine to me," Dr. Peabody said. "Electrocution, definitely."

"You can really tell that, without an autopsy?" I asked.

"Well, not for certain," Dad said. "We won't really

know for sure until the local ME does a formal autopsy. But I'd put my money on electrocution."

Dr. Peabody nodded vigorously and glanced at his watch.

"What about the wound to the head?" Jeb asked.

"Superficial," Dad said. "If he walked into my office with that, I'd have given him a few stitches and had his family watch for signs of concussion."

"Can you tell what did it?"

"A rock, most probably," Dad said.

"Not a stick?" I said, thinking of Aunt Phoebe's walking stick and the NO TRESPASSING sign reposing back in the cooler. "Or a board?"

"Oh, no," Dad said. "Much too jagged for either of those."

"Could the blow have knocked him out?" Jeb asked.

"It's not impossible," Dad said. "But unlikely, I'd say. And even if it did knock him out, it wouldn't have caused his death. Unless he fell on a live wire when he lost consciousness."

"And he didn't fall on a live wire; he fell into the tidal pool," Jeb said.

"Unless someone put him there," Michael suggested. "To make it look as if he'd drowned."

"Or unless there was an electrical charge in the tidal pool," I said. "Remember how the birders accused Resnick of shocking the puffins to scare them away from his land? According to Jim Dickerman, he did run a charge through some of the metal parts of his roof to keep the birds from sitting on it and messing it up. But I only saw seagulls on his roof. Puffins are waterbirds—so maybe he ran a wire along the shoreline."

"And the gash could have happened if he was thrown back by the shock," Dad said. "In fact, considering the angle, I'd say it was probable."

"Good heavens," Jeb said. "Maybe it wasn't murder after all. Maybe the whole thing was a horrible accident. Probably reached in to retrieve his precious NO TRESPASSING sign, not realizing that the power was on."

He suddenly looked very cheerful. Obviously an accident, however horrible, would cause the town a lot less trouble than a murder.

"I don't suppose you could rule it a death by misadventure," he said.

"The coroner may, when he or she gets here," Dad said. "I have no jurisdiction. Still, I shouldn't be surprised."

He looked so downcast that I was almost tempted to pat him on the back and say, "Never mind, Dad; I'm sure we'll find you another murder soon."

"It's possible," I said instead. "But until they're positive, I'm sure the police will take every precaution. Treat it as a possible homicide until they're sure it's not."

"She's quite right," Dad said, brightening again at the thought that the investigation would continue, even if it was only pro forma.

"And while you're at it, why not take a look at the dead puffin?" I asked.

"The puffin?" Dad echoed. "Why?"

"Evidence," I said. "I'm sure the police will want to know how and when it died. Just to confirm Rhapsody's story."

Jeb pulled out the puffin and Dad bent over to examine it.

After blinking once in surprise, he shrugged and began giving the puffin the same careful scrutiny he'd previously given Resnick.

"Good thing Meg already figured out that Rhapsody had it in her freezer, or I'd worry about him," he said, jerking his thumb over his shoulder at Resnick.

"I think he's past worrying about," I said.

"I mean, from the point of view of an accurate autopsy," Dad said. "Could complicate things if you'd been running the meat locker cold enough to freeze the body. But, of course, you already figured out that the puffin was frozen elsewhere."

"Because of plumage," Michael put in.

"The plumage?" Dad said, looking blank.

I explained about the breeding plumage.

"Oh, very good!" Dad exclaimed. "Actually, I wasn't thinking of the plumage at all; it was the texture."

"Your medical expertise confirms Meg's deduction, then?" Michael asked.

"Actually, it's my culinary expertise," Dad said. "From my bachelor days. You can tell by the limpness that it's been thawed," he said, waggling one of the puffin's legs in a disgusting fashion. "And from the smell that it wasn't thawed recently enough to be safe," he added, bending over to smell the puffin and wrinkling his nose.

"It's not an entrée, Dad; it's evidence," I said with exasperation.

"Although I do hope we're not having poultry tonight," Michael murmured.

"Can you tell how the puffin died?" I asked. "Was it electrocuted, for example?"

"Can't really tell without an autopsy, which I don't suppose you want me to do," Dad said, looking around with an eager expression. Jeb shook his head, and Dad sighed.

"Could be electrocution," Dad said. "Could be a lot of things."

"Well, it's probably irrelevant to Resnick's accident anyway," Jeb said.

"Look, about this accident idea," I said. "How do we know it was an accident? I mean, even if you assume he had the bad luck to touch something electrified during one of the rare moments yesterday when we had power, what was the something? And if you think he had some kind of electrical bird trap hooked up among the shoreline, where is it?"

"Probably washed away with the storm," Jeb said.

"Possibly, but why didn't Michael and I see it when we found the body?"

"You saw the wound, and you were looking for something that could have hit him," Dad said. "You probably didn't see the bird trap."

"I'd have noticed," I said. I glanced at Michael for support.

"She did look around," he said. "She said that the tide was about to cover up the crime scene, and she looked around very carefully so she could describe it later."

"A really strong electrical shock could have thrown him back some distance," Dad said. "Maybe whatever shocked him wasn't all that nearby. If he touched something, got a shock, and fell back into the pool, landing on a rock that caused the gash, and then floated to the other side of the pool . . ."

"Hell, maybe it was a lightening bolt from the storm," Jeb put in.

"It was a hurricane, not a thunderstorm," I said.

Jeb shrugged.

"Well, whatever it was, it's gone now," Dad said, patting my shoulder.

"Maybe the waves got it and washed it away just before we got there," Michael said. "They were awfully close to washing Resnick away by the time we found him."

"We'll let the mainland authorities worry about it," Jeb said.

Everybody took that as a signal that the examination was over. I followed them out of the cooler, still irritated.

"You don't look very pleased," Michael murmured to me.

"Oh, I'm thrilled," I said softly. "Dad's just removed any need for us to run around the island investigating the murder."

"What's wrong with that?"

"We still haven't found James Jackson, the biographer, remember? Even if they rule the death accidental, he'll probably try to capitalize on it. If it really was accidental."

I tried not to take my irritation out on him, but I suspect it still showed. Was it just hurt pride, because I'd failed to notice Resnick's electrical contraption lying around? Or was there something to my feeling that this was suddenly turning out much too easy?

Jeb secured the meat locker again and we left the Anchor Inn. Dad and Dr. Peabody strode ahead, eagerly sharing the news with everyone they met.

"I'm sorry," Michael said as we followed along more slowly.

I shrugged.

"Well, maybe after this, Dad will stop bragging about my detective abilities," I said.

"Not necessarily," he said, with a chuckle. "You did figure out about the puffin."

To my relief, Michael had the good sense not to keep trying to cheer me up, and we hiked back to Aunt Phoebe's cottage in companionable silence.

Word of Dad's and Dr. Peabody's findings spread throughout the island, and within half an hour people began turning up at the cottage for a spontaneous celebration. People swarmed up and down the stairs, carrying all the lawn furniture and yard ornaments up to the bedrooms, which would make bedtime a whole lot of fun. Jeb Barnes was one of the first to arrive, and he brought along a case of cheap champagne.

"I got through to the Coast Guard!" he announced over the popping corks.

A ragged cheer went up from the twenty or so people gathered around the crate, and Rob asked, "When's the ferry going to start running?"

"Maybe tomorrow, maybe Tuesday," Jeb said. "They're going to wait and see. But the Coast Guard will bring the police over from the mainland tomorrow so we can tie up all the loose ends about Resnick's death."

Another cheer, this time accompanied by clinking glasses.

Death. No one was calling it a murder any longer. Even Dad seemed to have gotten over his disappointment that our homicide had turned into death by misadventure. Jim had the generator running again, and Dad put a collection of big band music on the portable player. I was the only one not in high spirits. After all, even if the police declared the death an accident and eliminated the danger of assorted members of my family being arrested for murder, Resnick was still news. James Jackson, the biographer, was still here on the island, sitting on the latest draft of his manuscript. And I suspected that whether he'd uncovered the truth about Mother's past or jumped to a totally wrong conclusion wouldn't matter to a pack of reporters hungry for sensational headlines. We had to find Jackson and deal with him, somehow, before he made his story public.

Dad was telling a group of birders some kind of story. From his gestures, I deduced he was describing Resnick's wounds.

"Absolutely understandable," I heard him say during one of those chance lulls in the general noise level. I saw several of the birders glance my way. "Electrocution is remarkably hard to—"

Drat. I'd hoped no one had noticed my ineffectual attempts to play detective, but from the looks on the birders' faces, I suspected they had all noticed. Irrational of me to resent that. Equally irrational to resent Dad's not being around earlier to give his verdict on the cause of death.

I glanced around the party, trying to convince myself that everyone present wasn't pointing at me and snickering at my failure. I saw that Rhapsody had arrived and, as I expected, had immediately become enthralled with Mother. She followed Mother around, literally sitting at her feet, absorbing her every word and gesture as if the fate of the world depended on it. She had already picked up some of Mother's mannerisms. Mother, of course, was eating it up and acting even more charming and elegant than usual.

Damn. On top of everything else, I didn't need to feel like one of Cinderella's ugly stepsisters.

"Don't be so gloomy," Michael said, handing me a glass of the champagne. "Aren't you glad it turned out to be an accident?"

"It isn't an accident until the police say it is," I said. "Sorry, I don't mean to take it out on you."

"I understand," he said. "It's not as if you can take it out on your dad; he didn't mean to get lost just at the one moment when we really could have used his expertise. Look, don't worry so much about Jackson; I'm sure we'll figure out some way to—"

"Great news," said Kenneth Takahashi, appearing beside us. "I mean, I'm sorry the old goat's dead, but thank God it was an accident."

I noticed that Takahashi had learned one thing from the birders at least. He had grasped the concept of protective coloration, and now he wore clothes as faded and mud-stained as the best of them.

"Well, don't let your guard down yet," I said. "Some of the birders would still give you quite a hard time if they knew why you came here."

"Oh, that's all right," he said, waving his glass genially. "If they ask me what I do, I'll tell them I'm in land use. Sounds vaguely conservationish. They seem to like that. They keep trying to feed me."

I had a sudden mental image of birders trying to coax him out of a tree with handfuls of sunflower seeds and cracked corn.

"Pity there isn't a decent restaurant on the island," he added.

"Is that your latest development project?" I asked, fearing the worst.

He shuddered.

"Good heavens, no!" he exclaimed.

"That's good," I said. "I think the people who come here like roughing it a little."

"Obviously," he said. "Each to his own; me, I plan to do everything I can to make sure I never have to come back here in my entire life. Up till now, my idea of roughing it was staying at a hotel without a four-star restaurant nearby."

Somehow, I had a feeling that Ken Takahashi's rather jaundiced view of Monhegan would soon make the rounds to every real estate development firm on the East Coast. Which should do much, I thought with satisfaction, to discourage any other developers who might have their eyes on the island.

"That reminds me of something," Michael said. "Could I have a word with you?"

He dragged Takahashi off into the corner and the two of them began an animated discussion about something. I leaned back and tried to concentrate on a yoga breathing technique that was supposed to improve one's mood.

"Meg?"

Of course, you had to do the breathing for a little more than ten seconds before it started to have any effect. I bit back an oath and opened one eye. Rob stood in front of me.

"Dr. Peabody and that other birder want their digital cameras back," he said.

"We have to give the photos to the police," I said.

"But if it's not a murder . . ."

"We don't know that until the police say so," I said.

"But can't we just—"

"No."

"I could download the photos if you like," Rob offered.

"Then we could just give the data files to the police."

"Good idea," I said. "Want to do it now, since the power's on?"

Rob looked plaintively at his champagne glass.

"Then I'll hold on to them until you're ready," I said. I picked up the knapsack containing cameras in question then stormed into a corner, where it was quieter.

Get over it, I told myself. What harm would it really do to let them have their silly cameras? I took the other birder's camera out of my knapsack and began flipping through the photos. I was brooding over one that showed the fateful tidal pool when Mother came up behind me and looked over my shoulder.

"Oh, what a lovely view of the shore," she said. "You should print that out and have it framed, dear."

I wondered if I should tell her that this picture showed where we'd found the body of her late beau. Better not, I decided. I flipped to the next photo, one of the tidal pool from a slightly different angle.

"I liked the first one better," Mother said. "More unspoiled."

I peered at the photo. It looked much the same as the first, except that in one corner you could see a tiny flash of orange.

"I know the electricity makes it so much easier, especially for the islanders who live here year-round," Mother said. "But I do wish they'd find a way to bury the wires, instead of having all those blue pipes and orange extension cords all over the place. So . . . untidy, really."

I opened my mouth to explain the impossibility of burying pipes and wires in the island's rocky terrain, then closed it again.

Mother was right. An orange extension cord.

I flipped through the rest of the photos. The extension cord appeared in several, snaking down toward the tidal pool. No wonder all the birders thought Resnick had been killing puffins. They *had* seen some kind of electrical gadget near the tidal pool.

I closed my eyes and thought back to how the pool had looked when Michael and I had found the body. No, I thought. I'd have seen an orange extension cord. It hadn't been there.

Who had moved it? And when? And for that matter, exactly where had the extension cord come from? Hard to tell from this angle. For all I knew, it came from out in the ocean.

I had to go back to Resnick's house and see.

CHAPTER 30

The Scene of the Puffin

I grabbed two flashlights, snagged one of Dad's hiking knapsacks, stuffed the digital cameras inside, and went in search of Michael.

I found him backed into a corner, enduring a lecture from two birders.

"—vital for every educated citizen to take action!" one of them was exclaiming as I walked up. He shook his finger in Michael's face. "We cannot afford to sit idly by and watch these large corporations—"

"Sorry," I said, coming up and taking Michael's arm. "Hate to interrupt you, but we have to be somewhere, remember?"

Michael started and looked at his watch.

"Oh, sorry . . . yes . . . have to run," he said as we backed away. From their expressions, I could tell the birders wanted to ask what kind of urgent appointment we could possibly have elsewhere on the island at this time of night.

"Hurry!" I stage-whispered to Michael.

We made it to the front door, grabbed two ponchos from the pile of several dozen identical drab, damp ones, and slipped out onto the front deck. Michael looked surprised when I turned on my flashlight, pulled up my hood, and headed for the driveway.

"We're not really going anywhere, are we?" he asked.

"Oh, would you rather stay here and talk to the bird-watchers? I got the distinct impression you didn't mind being rescued."

"I would rather be with you any day, even if it means circumnavigating the island again," he said with an exaggerated bow. "Only it's night, not day; and it's still rather cold and wet out here. Couldn't you have found some way to rescue me that didn't involve going outdoors?"

"We need to go back to Resnick's house," I said. "Something's bothering me."

"What?"

"I'll show you when we get there."

We hiked along in silence. I concentrated on not tripping and falling down, or at least not landing in any large puddles when I did so.

Maybe I shouldn't have dragged Michael out on this wild-goose chase, I thought. For all I knew, he might be getting tired of my amateur attempts to solve the murder and protect my family. But I felt better with his tall form striding along beside me. Not safer, really—I wasn't expecting any danger—just more natural. The idea of going back to Resnick's house, or anywhere else on the island, for that matter, and not having Michael along seemed unthinkable. Quite a remarkable change in attitude for me; stubborn independence and the need for a certain amount of solitude had always been my hallmarks. How odd, I thought, then put the subject away for further consideration after the present crisis. We'd arrived at Resnick's house.

It definitely hadn't fared well. Rain had ruined the finish on the polished wood floor of the entry, and the wood itself had buckled in several places. When we entered the living room, we startled several birds roosting on the exposed high beams of the cathedral ceiling.

"We should chase the damn things out," I said.

"They'd only get back in again," Michael said. "Besides, I thought you hated this place. Wanted it torn down."

"Yes, but I feel bad just seeing it fall apart like this. Even if it is a pretentious eyesore."

"Is that what we came back for? To make sure Resnick's place isn't falling apart? Or something about the biography?"

"No, it's about the murder."

"I thought we found out it was an accident, not murder."

"We found out it was electrocution instead of a blow to the head," I said. "The accident or murder question is still open. Very open."

"Okay," he said. "So what are we looking for?"

I pulled out the digital camera and showed him the best shot of the tidal pool.

"See that?" I asked, pointing to the orange cord.

"So what?" he said. "They're underfoot all over the island, as the state of my poor mistreated shins can testify. Along with those pestilential pipes."

"Yes, but there wasn't one there when we found the body," I said. "And I don't remember seeing one when we searched the house before. I want to make sure."

"We came up here in the middle of the night to search the house for orange extension cords?"

"Humor me," I said. "Please."

Was my idea so off-the-wall that even Michael wouldn't take it seriously? To my relief, he smiled, shrugged, and began rummaging through the hall closet.

Searching the house didn't take that long. I took the kitchen, while Michael did the rest of the house. Sooner than I expected, we met again in the living room, empty-handed.

"Nothing here," I said.

"The shed!" Michael said, snapping his fingers. "We forgot the shed."

"I hadn't forgotten it," I said. "I'm working up my nerve."

"Strikes you as a little creepy, does it?" Michael said.

I nodded as I pulled my hood over my head and turned for the entrance.

"No reason to feel that way," he said, following me. "Just because Resnick's body was there for—what, half an hour? No reason to get squeamish about the place."

"You're right," I said. "Then I assume you'll have no problem dining at the Anchor Inn if we come back to Monhegan next summer? It's probably the best restaurant on the island."

"On the other hand," Michael said, "who am I to criticize a perfectly normal human reaction?"

"I thought so," I said, throwing open the shed door.

It took us only five minutes to make sure the shed concealed no orange extension cords. Stumbling around the yard with our flashlights took more like half an hour, but still no extension cords.

"Tide's still fairly low," I said. "Let's go down to the shore."

It was still a little wet, but we reached the tidal pool, and after a great deal of peering back and forth between the photo and the landscape, I identified the place where I'd seen the orange electric cord in the picture. I wasn't surprised to see that instead of running along the shore toward Resnick's house, it would have climbed up the cliff toward the center of the island.

"That's odd," Michael said.

"Very odd," I said. "For one thing, it was on the inner side of the pool, so how could it have washed away before his body?"

"And for another, what was it connected to?" Michael said. "Do you suppose the old skinflint ran the extension cord up there and tapped into the power line before it hit his meter?"

"I don't think he ran that extension cord anywhere," I said, craning to look up. We were out of sight of the village, and Resnick's house was dark. The only light I could see was a thin ray shining down from high above us. Probably from the ridge at the top of the island. It reminded me of the glint of light I'd seen when we'd found the body; the glint I'd thought was the reflection from a birder's binoculars.

"Of course," I said. "It's obvious who did it; I'm an idiot not to have seen it sooner."

"I still don't see it, whatever it is," Michael said. "Care to give me a clue?"

"Jim Dickerman," I said. "He's the only one who could have done it. When we thought someone had whacked Resnick on the head, we had too many suspects. Anyone on the island could have done that. In fact, Aunt Phoebe did. But now that we know he was electrocuted, there's only one possibility. Jim. No one else could possibly have arranged for the power to come on just when Resnick reached into the tidal pool. He could wait until Resnick touched the water and then flip the switch to turn the generator on. He may have boarded his windows up, but I bet he left enough chinks to see through."

"And his motive?" Michael asked quietly.

"He was afraid of losing the power plant, of course. He didn't know about Binkie negotiating restoration of bail. All he knew was that Resnick was going to take away his precious power plant, and all his mechanical toys. He could easily have rigged the extension cords going down; no one would pay any attention to Jim doing something electrical. Maybe he was the imposter the birders kept talking about, if he slung his binoculars around his neck when he came down here to do it. He probably planned to wait until Resnick picked up the cord. Aunt Phoebe throwing in the sign was just another fantastic bit of luck. Remember how at least one time that day the power came on for only a few seconds? I bet that was him, throwing the switch that killed Resnick."

We stood there for a few moments, watching as the receding waves uncovered more and more of the rocky ledge.

"You're right," Michael said. "It's the only logical solution. Brilliant."

"Thanks," I said. "Come on, we've got work to do."

"Are we going up to the power plant to confront Jim?"

"Are you crazy? You're definitely watching *way* too much TV," I said. "That's the sort of stupid thing that gets people killed, or at least gets them into the kind of trouble that they can't get out of until just before the last commercial. We'll tell the police tomorrow and then let them confront Jim."

"Then what are we doing?"

"Burgling Resnick's studio," I said, opening my knapsack and pulling out the ropes I'd brought.

"But why?" Michael asked. "If we're sure Jim is the murderer—"

"We still haven't found James Jackson," I said. "I want at least a chance to talk him out of mentioning Mother in his wretched biography. And the studio's the only place we haven't looked where Resnick might have left some clue to Jackson's identity, and tonight's probably the last chance we'll have to search before the police arrive tomorrow. With the press hot on their heels, no doubt."

"Let's get it over with, then," Michael said.

CHAPTER 31

Abandon Puffins, All Ye Who Enter Here

I'd spotted a useful tree next to Resnick's studio. One branch spread over the yard, where we could throw a rope over it and shinny up, while another was perfectly positioned for using the same rope to climb through the broken pane of glass in the studio roof.

Actually doing all this proved a lot harder than we expected.

"I hadn't realized how long it's been since I've climbed a tree," I said as I examined the knees, elbows, and palms I'd skinned during our travels.

"Obviously, there are significant gaps in my fitness program," Michael said from where he sat on the floor, puffing. "Please tell me we're going to figure out a way to leave at ground level."

"We can probably unlock the door," I said, limping over to it. "Damn, I think it needs a key on both sides."

"Try that," Michael said, pointing to a key on a hook a few feet from the door.

"Perfect," I said. "Voilà! Our exit."

"Unlock it, and leave the key in the lock," Michael said. "In case we need to make a quick getaway."

"Good idea," I said. "And let's take the rope down, too, so no one passing by will spot us."

"The place has glass walls," Michael said. "Anyone passing by will spot us even without the rope. Even if we only use our flashlights."

"Well, if we take down the rope, at least we can pretend we found the door open and we didn't actually break into the place."

"That's what I like about you," Michael remarked. "Your finely honed sense of deviousness."

We teased the rope out of the tree, and I buried it in the very bottom of my knapsack, where you could hardly see it beneath the Gatorade, first-aid kit, flare gun, water, and candy bars. Michael was groping around the walls of the studio.

"What are you looking for?" I asked.

"The light switch," he said. "If we're going to pretend we found the door open, we may as well search in comfort, instead of creeping around with our flashlights like burglars. Ah, here it is."

The lights came on, and we both turned to survey the studio.

And saw Mother. Two Mothers, in fact; both nude and staring straight out of their canvases at us. One stood, her weight resting on one hip, her head cocked to one side, and a petulant look on her face, as if she were about to open her mouth and complain about how long she'd been standing there, and ask how much longer was this going to take. The other sat on the side of a bed, her arms raised, her hands either putting up or, more likely, taking down her hair, and judging by the look on her face, any words she was about to say would be edited out for broadcast on network television.

"Oh my God," I moaned. "More of them!"

We continued to search the studio, under Mother's watchful eyes, and turned up several more nude Mothers, stacked against various walls. Mother lying on a red velvet couch with a black velvet ribbon around her throat, rather reminiscent of Manet's *Olympia*. Mother, seen from above, sprawled in a giant claw-footed bathtub. Mother holding an old-fashioned large porcelain doll that somehow just barely managed to avoid covering any erogenous zones.

After a while, I began turning the paintings to the wall.

The cumulative effect of so many naked Mothers unnerved me.

"Somehow I don't think we're going to have much luck hushing this up," I said, sitting down in the middle of the studio and burying my head in my hands. "Between the damned biographer and these ghastly paintings—Oh!"

"What?" Michael asked, looking up from another painting.

"Well, we've solved the mystery of the disappearing bedroom rug anyway," I said, pointing to the Oriental rug beneath me. "Of course, we still have the mystery of why he dragged it out here."

"Are you sure it's the same rug?"

"Well, I see little bits of white carpet fuzz sticking to the underside," I said, examining the back of the rug.

"Redecorating, I suppose," Michael said, shrugging.

"All my best clues turn out to be useless," I complained.

"This is weird, too," Michael said. He had pulled out another painting and was staring at it with a puzzled frown.

"What?" I asked. I glanced over. Michael stood between me and the painting, but I could see that this nude Mother was waving a gauze scarf, which I somehow suspected would emphasize, rather than conceal, anything of potential prurient interest.

"Would you look at this!" he said.

"Do I have to?" I replied. "I'd really rather not. I've seen enough. Much more than enough, actually."

"You haven't seen anything like this," he said, stepping aside so I could see the latest painting.

I glanced up, expecting to see another smiling, unblushingly nude Mother. I was right about the scarves; they left absolutely nothing to the imagination. But instead of Mother's face, I saw a patch of blank canvas.

"Has he painted out her head in that one?" I asked.

"More like he never painted it in at all," Michael said.

"Or could he have taken the face off with turpentine or something?"

I went over and looked at the head. Or rather, the lack thereof.

"No, if he'd wiped off the head, he'd have taken the background, too," I said. "But that's still perfectly fine."

"All ready to paint the head in," he said. "This is really weird."

"And she's standing on the migrating rug," I pointed out.

Michael nodded. He moved the nude with scarves aside, revealing yet another headless nude, this one posing brazenly in a clearing in the woods. Resnick had finished the background in elaborate detail, right down to a bee hovering above a clover blossom in the grass and the delicate fluff of a dandelion in the nude woman's hand. But again, no head. The coloring of the skin and body hair made it obvious that the woman was blond, and she definitely had Mother's tall, slender build. But the head was completely missing.

"What the devil's going on here?" I muttered.

Michael began to move the latest painting aside. A piece of paper fell from behind it, and he stooped to pick it up.

"You know," he said, glancing at what he'd picked up. "This may sound crazy, but—"

"Put your hands on your heads!" barked a voice from behind us. "And don't move!"

Since the two halves of that order were obviously contradictory anyway, I decided to risk turning around as I raised my hands.

Jim Dickerman stood in the studio doorway, holding a gun.

Assuming we survived the night, I was going to have a long talk with Dad. He was always so excited at the idea of my investigating a real murder case. But here, I would explain to him, we had a perfect example of why this was such a stupid hobby. If you go around trying to hunt down criminals, some of them resent it, and sooner or later they take matters into their own hands.

"Should have known your snooping would cause trouble," Jim said.

"Don't be a fool, Jim," Michael said in his most earnest, persuasive tones. "You'd never get away with it. Just put it down."

It sounded sensible to me; I'd have dropped my gun in a heartbeat. Jim wasn't buying it.

"If I have to shoot you, I'll just put the gun back in my brother's truck and they'll think he did it," Jim said.

"You'd set up your own brother for a murder rap," I exclaimed. I still felt guilty enough over setting my brother up for a disastrous blind date, and that was years ago. Jim, however, shrugged casually.

"If I have to. Back up a bit," he added, gesturing slightly with the gun. "And lie down. Facedown. And stick your hands up behind your backs."

We followed orders. Then he walked over to Michael's side. I braced myself. Was he going to shoot Michael? Should I throw myself at Jim? Then he dropped something by Michael's head. A roll of duct tape.

"You," he said, obviously meaning me. "Tape his wrists."

He backed up and pointed the gun at me while I did as he ordered. And then he made me lie back down again, and he taped my wrists.

I should have been terrified that I was probably about to die, but instead, I found myself fuming over the fact that he'd taped my arms behind my back. Don't male thugs ever stop to think that although lying on your stomach on a hard wooden floor may not be relaxing for men, it's downright torture for any woman with larger than an A cup? Obviously not. I growled to myself and shifted slightly so I could see what Jim was doing. I had a hard time looking over my knapsack, which lay open just in front of my face.

The knapsack—was there anything in it I could use to get us out of this?

Jim puttered about the studio, looking for things. I noticed he was wearing work gloves, which meant he wouldn't leave any telltale fingerprints.

Not worth worrying about, I told myself. If things got to the point where the police were looking for fingerprints, I'd be past caring.

He dragged something out in the middle of the floor—a rather ancient-looking kerosene space heater. He rummaged about some more until he found a large tin can. He unscrewed the can, filled the heater most of the way, then dropped the can. Some kerosene spilled out, but apparently not enough for his purposes. He picked up the can, poured the remaining kerosene on the floor, then dropped the can again.

While Jim did this, I scanned the contents of the knapsack for possible weapons. Gatorade, rope, compass, first-aid kit—alas, Dad's emergency survival plans had never included exchanging gunfire with armed desperadoes. I could try the flare gun, of course, but I had no idea if it would do any damage, even assuming I got a chance to snatch it up. And I wasn't even sure I could fire it, since my hands were taped behind my back. Still, I had to try. First, though, I'd need to distract him.

"You're not really going to burn down the studio, are you?" I asked.

"Why not?" Jim said. He was rummaging through the trash can, pulling out paint- and turpentine-stained rags and scattering them about the studio. But not at random—he was making a path. Toward the back of the studio, where I could see what looked like a gas generator.

"You'd destroy the work of a great artist," I said. Yes, definitely a path; now he took a can of turpentine and shook splashes of it along the path.

"Yeah, right," Jim said. "They've got museums full of

his art; they won't miss what's here. All looks alike anyway; the old bastard hasn't painted anything new in forty years."

Michael began laughing.

"Oh no?" he said. "Take a look at one of those canvases before you light the torch."

The sight of his bound, helpless captive convulsed with laughter must have roused Jim's curiosity. He glanced around at the canvases—all of which I'd turned to face the wall. He went over to one of the easels and turned the canvas around. It was the picture of Mother taking down her hair. His eyes widened, his jaw dropped, and I seized my chance.

I rolled over so my bound hands could reach the knapsack, scrabbled until I had the flare gun, and then rolled the other way and fired when I thought I had the gun pointed in his general direction. I missed—big surprise—but the flare passed close enough to his head to startle him.

Unfortunately, firing a flare gun in a room filled with spilled kerosene and paint-covered rags wasn't exactly a move that would endear me to fire-safety experts. The flare hit one of the easels, then skittered into some of the spilled kerosene, setting it on fire and splashing Jim's jeans, which also caught fire.

He yelped with pain and began beating at his pants with both hands. Not the best idea when you're holding a loaded gun; the gun went off, though, to my disappointment, he didn't actually shoot himself in the foot.

He turned and ran to the door. Michael and I were awkwardly struggling to our feet. Jim fired several wild shots in our direction—causing us to fling ourselves back on the floor—then yanked the key out of the lock, opened the door, and ran out while Michael and I were still struggling to our feet again.

"We've got to stop him, damn it!" Michael cried, and ran for the door like a charging bull.

Too late. I heard the key turn. Michael twisted at the last minute and threw himself at the door, trying to break it down with his shoulder.

"Oww!" he yelled as he fell over.

"Are you all right?" I called.

"I think I've broken my shoulder," he said. "Please tell me that the door cracked or something."

"It looks the same as before," I said, jumping as something—an aerosol can, I think—exploded across the room.

"That always works in the movies," he said, lurching to his feet again.

"They use wooden doors in the movies," I said. "Not metal ones. Maybe we should tackle the glass."

"And impale ourselves on glass shards?" Michael said. "Maybe we can kick the door in."

He began trying, but I could tell from his expression that the effort hurt him a lot more than it did the door.

"Maybe we need a battering ram," he muttered, looking around, without success, for something large enough to serve.

The fire was spreading rapidly. I had to dodge a few stray patches of flame to make my way to the largest canvas—the standing portrait of Mother. I backed up to it, got a grip on it, and began dragging it toward the nearest glass wall.

"Don't worry about saving the damned art," Michael said.

"We're not saving it; we're sacrificing it to save ourselves," I said. "Here, help me wedge it up against this glass wall.

"What good will that do?" he asked.

"It may keep me from being impaled on shards when I try to break the glass," I said.

"Brilliant," he said. "But let me do it; I'm heavier."

He backed up and ran again, this time at the painting. I

noticed he led with his other shoulder. I heard a cracking noise.

"Let me take a turn," I said.

Instead of running, I gave the painting a few swift karate kicks. I could hear glass shattering; after half a dozen kicks, we pulled the painting away and found a space large enough to climb through.

"After you," Michael said.

"Keep your eye open," I said. "Remember, Jim's out here somewhere with the gun."

We both managed to climb out, then crouched down and ran for some nearby bushes. Starting nervously at every stray noise, we sat back-to-back and I pulled the duct tape off Michael's hands. He was just untaping mine when something exploded. The flames, which had grown steadily, suddenly shot ten feet into the sky at the back of the studio. We both leapt to our feet and backed up some more.

"Reached the kerosene stove, I guess," Michael said.

"That or the generator," I agreed.

"Are you okay?"

"I'm fine," I said. "I'm a mass of cuts, bruises, scrapes, and burns, and I think I singed off a few inches of hair on one side, but I'm alive."

"We're both alive, thanks to you," Michael said.

I had hoped for a more enthusiastic demonstration of gratitude, but Michael stood there for a moment, looking at the fire, frowning. Then he reached in his back pocket and took out his wallet.

What on earth?

"With any luck, the fire will destroy all of those very interesting paintings," he said. "But we still have a few loose ends to tie up."

He took a piece of paper out of the wallet. I recognized it: the map, the one with Dad's printing on it that I'd found at the murder scene.

"We don't need this anymore," he said, and he wadded it up and threw it at the fire.

"Michael!" I said, launching myself at him.

"Watch the shoulder," he said.

Making allowances for his injuries, I found the demonstration of gratitude that followed quite satisfactory. At least the beginning of it; after a few minutes, the Monhegan volunteer fire department arrived and we postponed any further celebrations until their departure.

Chapter 32

Much Ado About Puffins

"I think the coast is clear," Michael said as he shook me awake.

"Or as clear as it's going to get," I said, peering out the door of Resnick's garden shed, where we'd taken refuge until the crowds died down. Jeb Barnes had drafted most of the spectators into the search parties that were, even now, combing the island for the missing Jim. Only two people stood guard by the studio, and both of them were swathed in wraps, huddled against a tree, and, most important, facing in the other direction. We slunk across the lawn and paused in the shadows outside the entry to make sure no one had seen us. The guards hadn't moved.

"Some guards," Michael muttered. "Probably asleep. And why did they have to leave guards at all; do they really think Jim's likely to come back here?"

"No, but given the way everyone feels about Resnick's house, I think they want to make sure it doesn't go up in smoke, too."

"And this would be a bad thing?"

"No, as long as we get one more chance to snoop around before it happens. After all, Jim proving himself the murderer only solves one of our problems. There's still the biographer to deal with. Before he or she tries to capitalize on the notoriety of Resnick's death. Maybe if we can get into Resnick's computer, we can find a clue to the biographer's identity."

"Actually, I think I know his identity," Michael said, giving me a hand through the broken glass into Resnick's front hallway.

"You do!" I exclaimed. "Who?"

"I'll tell you in a second. Stay here while I check out something."

"But—"

"Humor me, just this once," he said.

So I stood in the hallway while Michael padded softly into the living room.

"Aha!" he called back. "I thought so."

"Thought so what?"

"Resnick's biographer is no longer in any condition to reveal anything," Michael called back.

"You don't mean—"

"Yes," Michael said. "Come and see who is—or rather, was—writing the biography."

I took a deep breath and walked into the living room, expecting to see a bloody corpse lying on the floor. Instead, I saw Michael. He held up an eight-by-ten print of a photo—the photo of Resnick that had appeared on the back of the book of paintings.

"You mean Resnick?" I said. "He's the biographer?"

"Bingo," Michael said, setting down the photo.

"How do you know?"

"Well, right at the moment, it's sort of a hunch, but now that the power's on, I bet we can find the drafts of the thing in his computer."

"Okay," I said, reaching for the switch to turn on the computer. "So you think it was an autobiography?"

"No, I think he wanted it published under a pseudonym, so it would look like a genuine critical biography."

"Fat chance," I said. "Only one person in the world has that high an opinion of Victor Resnick. That should have given us a clue right there."

"Too true."

"Yeah, and I guess if he planned to reveal the scandals of his youth, it was a lot easier to pretend that someone else had dug it up, instead of having to face the criticism if anyone like Mother objected. It makes sense, but I still don't understand what gave you the idea that Resnick was the biographer."

"The paintings," Michael said

"The paintings? What about them?"

He held up his hand to show me a smear of blue paint on the palm.

"He did those paintings recently," Michael said. "Recently enough that the one we used to help escape from the studio was still wet—I got this on my hand helping you carry it."

"You're sure it wasn't just melting from the fire?"

"No, the painting wasn't hot when we picked it up, and it wasn't wet on the surface—I put my finger on a blob and paint squished out. That's what happens when you put on a thick layer of oil paint; it dries from the outside in."

"But how does that explain the headless paintings?" I asked. "He was getting them ready, but he couldn't do the heads until Mother showed up? It's not as if he could use the present-day Mother as a model, you know."

"I also found this," Michael said, plucking something out of his shirt pocket.

A faded photograph of Mother as a teenager. Clothed. In fact, she wore the same bathing suit we'd seen in Aunt Phoebe's photo album.

"I suspect we've just solved the mystery of the missing photos," he said. "And maybe he only recently managed to get into your aunt Phoebe's cottage to filch these."

"Everyone kept telling us he painted from photos," I said, shaking my head.

"Yes, and that his style hadn't changed appreciably during his whole career," Michael said. "So if he just waited until they dried, who would have any doubt that they were older paintings?"

"I think they have ways of figuring out the age of a painting," I said. "For example, do you really think they're still manufacturing the same oil paint, canvas, and varnish he used forty or fifty years ago, with no modern improvements that would show up in an analysis?"

"But why would they even bother if they got it from the artist and it was clearly in his style?"

"Yes, and why would anyone bother to forge a Resnick when for the same amount of effort they could forge the work of someone a lot more famous? And for that matter, does it really count as forgery if the only thing false is the date he painted it?"

"I don't understand why he painted them in the first place," Michael said. "Was writing about his youth making him nostalgic? Or did he think he had to have some paintings of the people involved to prove the truth of his biography?"

"More likely, he just wanted to stir up trouble," I said. "That's perfectly in character. In fact—my God, that's it!"

"What's it?" Michael said.

"Consider the detective's report."

"You're right," Michael said, his shoulders slumping. "That doesn't add up. I can see why he would have the detective's report on your mother, maybe to try to find out what she'd done with her life after they'd parted. But why those other women—unless maybe it was camouflage," he added, looking up with a hopeful expression.

"No, I think the detective's reports were just what they looked like—he wanted to find out more about those women to see who could be his long-lost sweetheart."

"But surely he knew who she was."

"Not if he invented the whole love affair," I said. "And wanted to find out which woman had a gap in her life that would match the story he'd made up."

"Made up? But why? That's an absolutely crazy idea!"

"Crazy like a fox," I said. "I know exactly why he did it. Just look at that stack of books on his desk."

"Books?" Michael said, glancing over. "They're art

books; wouldn't you expect a painter to have them?"

"Yes, but these aren't books with pictures of paintings. They're biographies. The one on top's a dead giveaway: a biography of Andrew Wyeth."

"So?"

"So remember the whole Helga thing? When Andrew Wyeth revealed that for fifteen years he'd been painting this beautiful redheaded model without his wife knowing it? And suddenly, he's on the cover of *Time* and *Newsweek*. Of course, I don't know if it did Wyeth's career good or harm in the long run, and I don't suppose it would ever have occurred to Resnick that Wyeth might be a better painter. All Resnick saw was that after the Helga paintings came out, Wyeth got more media attention than he could handle. And Resnick wanted some."

"And what better way to get it than to rake up an old scandal and suddenly reveal that he's got a collection of highly erotic paintings featuring a beautiful underage model," Michael said, shaking his head. "It's tailor-made for the tabloids."

"And I bet there's not a word of truth in it anywhere. Look, there're also books about van Gogh, Picasso, Franz Liszt, and even Byron, for heaven's sake. He was going for notoriety."

"So let's search his computer and see what we find," Michael said, hitching a chair up to the desk.

What we found was six earlier drafts of the book, stretching back over a period of two years.

"Obviously practice doesn't always make perfect," I said. "I don't think his drafts were getting any better."

"Oh, I don't know," Michael said. "I don't recall seeing this bit about her turquoise eyes rolling on the floor in the draft we found. Sounds more like a game of marbles than a love scene."

"Sounds painful, if you ask me. Yes, and some instinct for self-preservation made him take out all the bits about him nurturing other artists' careers. I somehow doubt that he even met Keith Haring and Basquiat, much less nurtured them."

"I think we've pretty well established who the biographer is," Michael said. "Now we have to decide what to do about it."

I sighed. For my part, I wanted to reformat the hard drive and burn every scrap of evidence that the biography had ever existed. But I had a dreadful feeling Michael wouldn't consider this ethical.

"What do you think we should do?" I asked, and braced myself for an answer I wasn't going to like.

"Reformat the computer and burn every scrap of paper," Michael said readily. "Don't you agree?" he asked, seeing my jaw drop. "I mean, we have to reformat it; you can recover deleted files with a good utility program. We can back up the nonbiography stuff to diskettes before we do it."

"Sounds great to me," I said. "But I wasn't sure you'd see it that way."

"We know Jim Dickerman killed Resnick," Michael said. "At best, all this stuff will only embarrass your family. At worst, Jim's lawyer could use it to cast doubt on his guilt."

"What about the painting?" I asked.

"We'll take it with us."

"Take it with us?"

"The old coot owes us something," Michael said. "After all, we solved his murder, at considerable personal risk."

"And if someone catches us with it?"

"We've got the bill of sale from your grandfather's files, remember?"

"I like the way you think," I said, grabbing an armload of papers and heading for the fireplace. "Let's do it."

"No, no!" Michael said. "Not that fireplace; do you want everyone on the island to see? We'll use the one in the bathroom—there's no window in there. You work on the computer; I'll take care of the fire."

I sat and watched the computer grinding away, first backing up Resnick's other files—there weren't many— then reformatting. Michael ferried armload after armload of papers back to the bathroom fireplace.

"How's it going?" he asked, coming up behind my chair and putting his hands on my shoulders.

"Nearly there," I said. "How's the fire?"

"It'll take a while," he said. "But I figure we'll have to hang out here until all the firemen go home or fall asleep, so that's no problem." He straightened up and went out into the kitchen.

Checking for papers there, I assumed. Probably not a bad idea.

I heard a sudden loud *pop* from the kitchen.

"Michael?" I called. "Is something wrong?"

"Everything's fine," he said, reappearing with two filled champagne flutes. "Absolutely fine."

"Isn't that Resnick's champagne?" I asked.

"Yes, and a very fine one at that," he said, handing me one flute. "Like I said, the old coot owes us one. To our host!"

"To our host!" I echoed, and sipped the champagne.

"Why don't you take these in and keep an eye on the fire?" Michael said, handing me his flute. "I'll see what we have in the pantry. Oh, and I found a jar of bath salts; goodness knows what Resnick wanted with that."

The bathroom was warm and wonderfully scented. Steam rose from the tub, and the fire blazed away merrily. From the size of the paper mound, I knew we'd need quite a few hours to burn them all. And who knows how many glasses of champagne.

"To our host," I said again, raising my glass. And then I fed a few more pages of the biography into the fire and kicked off my sneakers.

CHAPTER 33

Hair of the Puffin

"You'd think after all we went through to steal the damned painting, we'd get a little gratitude," I muttered.

Gaahhh! replied the seagull to whom I was speaking. I sighed and fed another handful of trash into the rusty barrel that served Aunt Phoebe as an incinerator. Given Monhegan's astronomical trash-removal fees, most residents only paid for hauling away things they couldn't possibly burn or feed to the gulls. As a kid, I'd always adored the giant trash fire that marked our last day on the island.

Of course, as a child I'd never had to burn the trash with a raging champagne hangover. Or all by myself. The police had dropped in to question us far earlier than I'd planned on getting up. Then Dad hauled off both Michael and Rob to help him with a project, leaving me stuck with all the chores and errands that Mother, Aunt Phoebe, and Mrs. Fenniman together could think up. At least as long as I stayed down here at the water's edge burning trash, they couldn't dump any more work on me. And it was relatively quiet. And I was getting very, very good at feeding trash into the fire without moving my throbbing head or, for that matter, opening my eyes.

Pyromania was a lot more fun last night, I thought, examining my fingers, whose tips still looked faintly prune-like, although the garbage and kerosene had long since overpowered the faint lingering scent of the bath salts.

I closed my eyes. Yes, the aspirin had begun to work. I'd given up trying to recall last night's rapture; all I asked was a slight lessening in the severity of my headache.

"Good Lord, there's more trash now than when I left,"

came Michael's voice, startling me out of my concentration.

"Last day's like that," I said, stirring up the fire in the barrel and managing a feeble smile. "Heard anything more from the police?" He shook his head, and I breathed a sigh of relief. Luckily for us, the police had found searching for Jim much more interesting than poking though Resnick's house; they'd taken at face value our story of rescuing papers and paintings by hauling them into the wine cellar. And I suspected he'd had a word with the younger of the two detectives to explain the still-damp sunken tub.

"Your Dad's been running us ragged, going all over the island taking pictures with the digital cameras and downloading them into your brother's laptop," Michael said, massaging his shoulder. He'd been at the aspirin bottle, too.

"Pictures of what?"

"Resnick's house, the Anchor Inn, the place where we found the body—everything. Documenting your latest detective triumph, as he calls it."

"Good Lord," I muttered. "He does remember that those aren't his cameras, doesn't he?"

"Yes, eventually we filled up Rob's hard drive and had to give the cameras back to their owners," he said. "And by the way, it's still looking good for the ferry tomorrow, or possibly even this afternoon," he added. "In fact, your Dad went up to the cottage to get everyone started packing. We should probably head up there, too."

"Give it a few minutes," I said. "I want to stay out of Mother's way right now."

"Why?"

"She's presenting Dad with a late wedding present, and I'm wondering how he's going to like it."

"A late wedding present?" Michael echoed. "What?"

"The painting."

"The painting—my God, you've got to be joking!"

"No. Hang on, here they come."

They strolled out onto the deck, Mother limping gracefully, with the support of Dad's arm. Dad was beaming from ear to ear.

"Oh, good," I said. "I think he likes it."

"She must not have presented it yet."

"Yes, she has; see, I can see the back of the easel through the window; the cloth's thrown back."

"Your father's a strange bird," Michael said, shaking his head. "This is not how I would react under these circumstances, a fact I hope you'll keep in mind if any lecherous painters express an interest in immortalizing your charms quite that completely, with or without your cooperation."

"I'll definitely keep that in mind," I said. "Shove another wad of trash in the barrel, will you?"

"In fact," Michael said, warming to his subject, "I'm not even sure—What the devil's this?"

He held up a piece of paper and stared at the half-dozen giant purple letter *R*'s writhing and curling across its surface.

"Well, what does it look like?" I asked, suppressing a smile.

"It looks like Rhapsody's signature."

"Yes, it does, doesn't it?"

"Dozens of signatures," he said, picking up another stray piece of paper.

"Yes, it took quite a few tries before we got it right," I said.

"Got what right?"

"Rhapsody's signature, of course. Mother and I worked at it for several hours before we finally decided I could do it well enough to try it on the canvas."

"By canvas, I presume you mean the portrait of Mother?"

"Naturally. How could Dad possibly object to Mother commissioning a female painter to do a glamour portrait of her as a young woman as a present for him?"

"Oh Lord," Michael said, closing his eyes.

"Of course, that does leave us with one small problem," I said.

"Dare I ask?"

"We haven't quite figured out what to do with the painting we bought from Rhapsody," I said. "I mean, we needed it to copy the signature from, and we bought the biggest one she had so we can pack the two paintings together and sneak the portrait off the island that way. But we haven't quite figured out what to do with it when we get it home. I don't suppose you'd like a larger-than-life portrait of a puffin, would you?"

"What's he doing—sledding, trimming Christmas trees, mowing the lawn?"

"Nothing silly like that. It's a nature study, not an illustration from one of her books. He's just sort of loitering about on the rocks, with a dead fish dangling from his beak. Very picturesque."

"No thanks," he said. "Unless, of course, you have developed an inexplicable fondness for the thing and want to see it on a regular basis."

"No," I said. "I'd be just as happy never to see it again."

"I'll pass, then," he said. "Although if you need a place to hide it, I'd gladly offer my attic. Or my basement. When I have an attic or a basement again."

"I'll keep it in mind," I said. "Oh my God!"

"What?" he asked, whirling about. With Jim still loose somewhere on the island, everyone startled easily.

"Rhapsody's coming," I said. "Help me stuff the rest of the forgeries in the trash barrel!"

We were backing away slightly from the roaring blaze that resulted when Rhapsody reached us. And, unfortunately, Dad spotted her and came dashing down the path. Mother fixed me with a gimlet eye and raised an eyebrow in a signal for me to deal with the situation.

"What a wonderful painting!" Dad exclaimed as he reached us. "I can't tell you how much it means to me!"

"Why . . . thank you," Rhapsody replied. She was pleased, although obviously a bit taken aback by the force of Dad's enthusiasm.

"It's a masterpiece," Dad said, taking both of her hands in his and shaking them vigorously. "It really transcends everything else you've ever done."

"Do you really think so?" Rhapsody said. "I wasn't sure it worked, really. It's the first time I've done anything like it, and the first time I've worked from life, so to speak."

"Well, you should do more like it," Dad said. "Truly astounding. The skin tones are absolute perfection!"

"Skin tones?" Rhapsody echoed in a puzzled voice.

"Of the feet and the beak, I suppose," I murmured in an undertone. "He tends to anthropomorphize."

"And the way you've captured the fur!" Dad went on.

Rhapsody's confusion deepened.

"Fur, feathers—he gets them mixed up when he's this excited," I stage-whispered.

"I know we'll always treasure it as a reminder of a special time in our lives," Dad said.

"Yes, it has been quite a weekend—" Rhapsody began.

"Dad," I broke in. "When are you going to show us the painting?"

"Show us?" Michael repeated, his voice so strangled, it was almost a squeak.

"Why—" Dad's jaw suddenly dropped, and he blushed bright red. "No," he said, finally. "It's . . . well, it's rather personal. I'm sure your mother would rather not. You understand," he said, looking at Rhapsody and then retreating back to the cottage. Mother smiled her thanks at me as she followed him inside, and for the next few minutes we could hear the fuss and bother Dad kicked up as he ransacked the cottage in search of a quiet, discreet place to hide the painting.

"Personal," Rhapsody repeated.

"He's very sentimental about presents Mother gives

him," I improvised. "Hides them away where he thinks no one but the two of them can find them. And keeps them forever; she's learned the hard way never to give him anything edible. Bottles of vintage wine turned to vinegar in their closet; ten-year-old chocolate truffles petrifying in the bureau drawers. A nuisance, I suppose, but we've always thought it rather sweet."

"Yes, I see," Rhapsody said. "I'm sure that's very nice for your mother. So many men aren't sentimental at all. Well, I must be going. Oh, I almost forgot. Mamie sent me up here to tell you that the ferry's definitely going this afternoon, and she has your tickets, but you'd better come down soon and claim them before someone else does."

"Right, thank you," I said. Rhapsody headed back to town, looking back now and then as if she wasn't quite sure what to make of us.

"Will you consider me an oaf if I confess that I ate the chocolate dinosaur you sent me last week?" Michael asked.

"I'd consider you an idiot if you hadn't," I said. "You didn't really buy that nonsense about the ten-year-old chocolate, did you?"

"Just checking," Michael said. "And if I ever bring you a bottle of vintage wine, I'll bring a corkscrew, as well."

"Now you've got the idea," I said. "Let's go down and claim our tickets before the birders filch them."

CHAPTER 34

A Farewell to Puffins

We hustled everyone down to the docks, only to find that the ferry wasn't taking off quite as soon as originally planned. Another Coast Guard cutter had arrived, carrying more police to join the search for Jim. A dozen or so police and Coast Guarders swarmed all over the docks, inspecting every piece of luggage larger than a hatbox and affixing stickers over the latches and fastenings of the containers when they finished. Loading the ferry would definitely take longer than usual.

Michael, Dad, and I arranged the family's luggage in a giant mound along one side of the dock and ordered Rob to guard it.

"I wish we could persuade him to relax a little," I said, glancing over to where Rob sat.

"Rob or Spike?" Michael asked, following my gaze.

Rob had perched on top of a trunk, with the strap of his laptop over one shoulder and Spike's leash wrapped around the other wrist. He clutched the wooden crate containing Mother's portrait and Rhapsody's puffin painting—clutching it so tightly with both hands that his knuckles had turned white. Spike strained at the leash, barking at a seagull that seemed to enjoy sitting just out of his reach, on top of another larger crate that someone was shipping some paintings in. And someone with more courage than sense had managed to paste one of the police inspection stickers to the back of Spike's head.

"Spike's a lost cause," I said. "But you'd think Rob could control his nerves better."

"Yes," Michael said. "Someone should explain to him

that the key to pulling off a daring daylight art heist is to look nonchalant and unconcerned."

"I did," I said. "Several times. We'll just hope they chalk up that anxious, furtive look to worry about his computer."

"I wouldn't count on it," Michael said. "Luckily, with Spike around, even the police won't want to get close enough to question him."

"I just wish Rob would move away from that other crate," I fretted. "It's so obviously a painting-shaped crate; what if someone notices the similarity in shape and makes the connection?"

"Don't worry; we do have bills of sale that will serve for both paintings, remember?" Michael said.

"I'm not worried that they'll think we're stealing it; what if they insist on unwrapping it out here on the dock?"

"We'll insist they take it inside, out of the rain," Michael said, jerking a thumb at the ramshackle baggage shed near the end of the dock. "Oh, hang on a minute; there's Ken Takahashi. I need to ask him something."

He strolled over to the other side of the dock and greeted Takahashi. I wondered what they kept finding to chat about. Suddenly, they both glanced over at me. Takahashi pulled something out of his inside jacket pocked, scribbled on it, and handed it to Michael. Then they laughed and shook hands.

No one talked to me, of course. I'd blown the whistle on Jim, and apparently some of the birders had dubbed him a hero. An environmental warrior, doing battle against a bloodthirsty bird-killer. I more than half-suspected they might help him hide. I hoped the police realized this; they'd have to keep a sharp eye out when the ferry began loading, in case someone tried to sneak Jim aboard in their party.

The birders were also taking up a collection, although the reason for donating varied from birder to birder. Some thought they were contributing to Jim's defense fund, others to a fund to rescue the Central Monhegan Power Company, and a few to the expense of tearing down Resnick's house and restoring Puffin Point to its natural, unspoiled condition.

I found myself resenting the great outpouring of sympathy for Jim and the Dickermans. After all, no matter how nasty Victor Resnick had been, that didn't give anyone the right to kill him. Not to mention trying to kill Michael and me, which they were all conveniently overlooking. And had it dawned on anyone that if I hadn't already fingered Jim as the murderer, they'd probably all still be stuck on the island being questioned and investigated? Or maybe they didn't resent me for fingering Jim, just for losing him. Yes, that was it; they thought it was my fault we were looking over our shoulders nervously every five minutes while the police ransacked our luggage.

And then there was Michael. He was astonishingly cheerful about leaving. Granted, this hadn't exactly been an ideal vacation. And looking back, I realized that I had rather neglected him, taken him for granted while we chased up and down the island looking for miscreants and lost relatives. But still, did he have to look so damned happy about escaping? Had last night made up for the several miserable days before it, or would this weekend manage to kill our grand romance before it really got off the ground?

"Hello!" came a soft voice from my elbow.

Rhapsody. With luggage.

"I didn't know you were leaving the island," I said. "I thought you stayed here year-round."

"Well, usually I do," she said. "But the puffins are gone for the winter, and who knows when they'll manage to arrest that horrible murderer? So when your mother invited me to visit all of you in Yorktown, I thought, Why not?"

"How nice," I said with as much sincerity as I could muster. Had Mother gone mad? For that matter, had she completely forgotten how many stray relatives we already had staying with us? And with Rhapsody underfoot, how could she continue to pull the wool over Dad's eyes about who had painted the nude?

"I'm so excited," she said. "I'm so looking forward to studying you."

"Studying us? Why?"

"Well, you mostly."

"Me?"

"Yes," she said, beaming. "You've inspired me!"

"Inspired you how?"

"I'm planning a whole new series of books based on you!"

"On me?" I squeaked.

"Yes!" she said, clasping her hands. "You'll be a friend of the Puffin Family, a brave and clever girl detective! Can't you just see it?"

Unfortunately, I could. Did she really mean a girl detective, or did she plan to puffinize me? Either way, I could see it all too clearly: a tiny, round Meg conversing stiffly, in profile, with little Petey and Patty and all the beady-eyed members of the Happy Puffin Family. Probably carrying a magnifying glass and wearing a deerstalker hat. I supposed I should have been happy that someone wasn't mad at me, but the idea of becoming a badly drawn cartoon character filled me with despair. *The Puffin of the Baskervilles* didn't sound so funny now that I thought it might become a reality.

Rhapsody must have noticed my lack of enthusiasm.

"Don't you like the idea?" she asked.

She looked so fragile that I couldn't bring myself to confess how much I hated it, so I settled for saying, "Well, I'm having a hard time seeing myself as a puffin."

"So was I," Rhapsody confessed. "So I've decided to branch out. I'm going to make you an owl! A wise, clever owl!"

Well, marginally better than a puffin, I thought.

"And Michael will be a falcon!" she added, eyes shining.

I managed to keep a straight face, but I suddenly felt very sorry for Rhapsody's editor—she had an editor somewhere, didn't she, seeing that she never went beyond a certain level of inanity? I had a feeling the editor would have quite an eye-opening experience when Rhapsody's first owl and falcon adventure landed on his desktop, no doubt seething with barely repressed eroticism.

"Don't you think murder's a little much for a kid's audience?" I asked.

"Oh, yes," she said. "So I'm going to start with having them find Patty Puffin's little lost kitten."

Did she have any idea what a real owl or falcon would probably do to a little lost kitten if they found it? Oh, well. Editor's problem, not mine.

I glanced down. Rhapsody was making a few tentative sketches of her owl detective. They were, alas, enough like me to be identifiable. In fact, if I crossed my eyes and pasted feathers all over my face, the likeness would be uncanny.

I made a solemn vow to evict the sculptor squatting in my studio within the next two weeks, even if I had to break the doors down and hire a forklift to move his fifteen-foot work in progress.

"Well, I guess we'll see you back for the trial," Jeb said, coming up to shake my hand.

"Assuming they ever find Jim," I said.

"He'll turn up sooner or later," Michael said, rejoining me.

"That's so," Jeb said. "Hard to hide that long on an island this small. Course, they'll probably have the trial over on the mainland. Don't want to inconvenience all the summer folk."

"I'm sure we summer folk will all be properly grateful," I said.

"Well," he said, clearing his throat. "Some of you aren't so bad. Time comes that you want to get away from the craziness over there, you call one of us up. Someone'll have a room free."

With that, he nodded and stumped away up the hill.

"I'm not entirely sure, but I think that counts as an extravagant compliment," I said.

"Sounded that way to me," Michael said.

"A pity we couldn't just convince Mother to leave the painting here until the trial," I said. "When there won't be quite so many police swarming around."

I glanced back at Rob, who still crouched by the painting, looking so guilty that I wasn't surprised several Coast Guarders had already come up to check his ID. Spike was still barking obsessively at the seagull.

No, actually the seagull had flown. Several other seagulls perched nearby, but Spike ignored them. He was barking obsessively at the crate.

The crate. I strolled over, trying to look casual, and inspected it. About six feet tall, four wide, and maybe a foot deep. I glanced from it to several of the Coast Guard officers and then back again. Tight quarters for a grown man, but if he was desperate enough . . . I glanced at the label. One of the New York galleries whose name I'd seen in Resnick's files. No return address. No official stickers or labels to indicate what shipping company would claim it on the mainland, though it did have one of the ubiquitous inspection stickers plastered rather haphazardly on one side.

I flagged down the officer in charge of the Coast Guard squad.

"Did your people really open this to inspect it?" I asked.

"Didn't need to," she said, frowning at me in irritation. "It was in the baggage shed over there. Been locked up there all night. Can't you keep that thing quiet?" she added, gesturing at Spike.

"I'd check that one again," I said. "Guy you're looking for has a brother who does a lot of the local baggage hauling. I wouldn't be surprised if he had a key to that shed."

Her head snapped around. I could see her measuring the crate with her eyes. And then she barked orders at several of the enlisted men around her. They lowered the crate gently on its flat side and then, with a couple of police standing by, weapons drawn, two of the Coast Guarders began prying at the top with their chisels.

With a snap, the lid popped open and the Coast Guarders shoved it aside. Jim Dickerman lay sprawled in an X shape, like a giant squashed bug, blinking in the sudden light.

"Jim Dickerman?" asked one of the police.

"That's him," Jeb said.

"Miserable mutt," Jim growled. I almost opened my mouth to point out that I, not Spike, had finally convinced the Coast Guard to open the crate, then thought better of it. I'd made it my new policy never to annoy suspected murderers—at least not ones with whom I still shared a planet.

Jim had obviously hidden in the box for hours; he was so stiff that several of the police had to help him up.

"You have the right to remain silent," the policeman began as mingled cheers and catcalls from the crowd drowned out the rest of the Miranda warning. Several over-exuberant birders came to blows and fell into the water in the excitement, which gave the Coast Guard something to do while the police handcuffed Jim.

"A flighty bunch, these birders," Michael remarked. "A few minutes ago, they were all calling Jim an environmental martyr, and now some of them are happy to see him arrested."

"Well, they're not stupid," I said. "They may sympathize with what they think he's done, but they're not eager to have an armed fugitive running around the island."

"Look what I've got!" Dad said, trotting up, beaming.

"Puffins," I said, closing my eyes. He carried an assortment of plush stuffed puffins in all sizes.

"A souvenir of your latest adventure!" he said.

"Where do you want me to put the rest of them?" Mamie Benton said. I could see two local men behind her, both carrying boxes of stuffed puffins.

"What a splendid idea!" Mrs. Peabody trumpeted. "Do you have any left?"

"A few," Mamie said. "And of course I can always take your orders and have them shipped directly to your homes."

The birders, led by Mrs. Peabody, began swarming into the gift shop and trickling out with large parcels for the Coast Guard to inspect.

Adding half the contents of Mamie Benton's store to the already-substantial load destined for the ferry made it doubly difficult for the captain and his crew to embark. We took off a full hour later than planned, close behind the Coast Guard cutter carrying Jim, and even then, one woman came running up the gangplank at the last minute, clutching an armload of puffin coasters and tea towels.

I spent the intervening hour, and most of the crossing, being congratulated by the birders, having my picture taken with them, and autographing their stuffed puffins. I think I had liked it better when they avoided me. Spike took a violent dislike to the entire puffin tribe, and he barked whenever he saw one. I could see his point of view. The birders finally gave me some peace and quiet when I managed to drop a rather large stuffed puffin down where Spike could get hold of it. He immediately pounced on it, buried his teeth in its neck, and spent the rest of the trip noisily trying to dismember it. The birders all found this either so shocking or so entertaining that they finally left me alone.

"Good Lord," I said as we approached the Port Clyde docks, where the Coast Guard cutter had just landed. "It's a media circus over there."

We could see three or four television sound trucks and a police line holding back several dozen people laden with cameras and notebooks.

"Well, the man wasn't completely unknown," Michael said.

"Unheralded Genius of the Down East Coast," I muttered, shaking my head.

Luckily for the rest of us, the press latched onto the police, their prisoner, and Binkie Burnham. The older cop said about two sentences, and then Binkie took the floor, making a folksy but no-nonsense statement. The reporters scribbled and filmed madly. Most of the birders stood around watching, some of them hoping, no doubt, to use their proximity to a notorious murder to capture their allotted fifteen minutes of fame.

Michael and I collected our baggage and crept round the edge of the crowd, hoping to make it to his convertible before anyone spotted us.

"Oh, there you are," Dad said, appearing at our side with a double armload of stuffed puffins. "Can you find some space for a few of these?"

We piled our luggage in the trunk, then filled the remaining space, as well as the space behind the seats, with puffins.

"I might have a few smaller ones that could fit in the crevices," Dad said, and headed back for the docks.

"There you are," Rob said, appearing on the driver's side of the car just as Michael opened the door. "Why don't you take him back with you?"

"Well," Michael began.

Spike, spotting the pile of puffins behind the seat, began barking and straining at the leash.

"With all these stuffed puffins?" I said. "You've got to be kidding. Besides, we're not going directly back to Yorktown. Michael has to get back for his classes, and I have to evict that damned sculptor."

Rob tried on his patented pitiful look. Impressionable coeds eat it up, but Michael and I were immune.

"See you," Michael said, getting into the driver's seat.

"Later," I added, taking the passenger's side.

Rob slouched off, dragging Spike behind him.

"Good thinking," Michael said. "By the way, what do you say to a small detour on the way home?"

"What kind of a detour?"

"Well, did you know that Coastal Resorts owns a small but very exclusive hotel outside Rockport? About an hour south of here."

"Oh, is that what you and Kenneth Takahashi were talking about?"

"Yes, and Ken feels very grateful to us," Michael added as he started the engine. "So he gave me a voucher for three nights' stay. I think we should drop by on the way home and check the place out. See if we want to come back and stay there sometime."

"Not tonight, of course," I said. "Because you have to get back to teach your classes."

"Oh, no; we'll just cruise by and check it out, and then head straight on home. Assuming we don't have car trouble again, of course. I really don't like the sound of that knocking in the engine."

"What knocking?" I said, cocking an ear. I heard only the usual smooth purr of a well-maintained engine.

"You're not getting into the spirit of the thing," Michael complained as he guided the car through the rut-infested gravel parking lot, heading toward the exit. "I'm sure if you try, you can hear it."

"Now that you mention it, I do hear a funny noise," I said with a chuckle. "Although I would have called it more of a ping than a knock."

"You're right," Michael said. "It's pinging and knocking. Do you think it's safe to drive?"

"Well, let's try it on the road for a while," I said.

"Maybe an hour," Michael said. "I think if it's going to break down, it won't do it before we get to Rockport at least. Why don't we—Oh my God!" he said suddenly, jamming on the brakes.

"What?"

"Look at that!"

He pointed out toward the harbor, beyond the crowded, noisy dock. I followed his finger and saw . . . a puffin. Even a bird-watching amateur like me could recognize it. It flew so clumsily, I was sure it would fall at any second. In fact, I thought it had when the stocky black-and-white figure plummeted toward the choppy water just beyond the end of the dock. But instead of falling in, it skimmed along the top of the waves and then rose again with a wriggling fish in its beak.

"Shall we go tell the bird-watchers?" Michael asked. We both glanced at the docks. The cluster of reporters had broken up and spread out in search of new camera fodder. Birders happily offered themselves up to the cause. Mother and Aunt Phoebe, sitting on a pile of luggage with their injured legs elevated, had already collected a quorum. Aunt Phoebe gestured wildly with her makeshift walking stick while Mother smiled and looked elegantly enigmatic.

"They're bird-watchers," I said. "If they did their jobs, they'd spot it."

The puffin headed toward the open ocean, wings flapping madly, looking as if at any moment it might lose the battle with gravity and plunge into the water. None of the birders noticed.

Except for Dad, who stood a little apart from the pandemonium. He glanced around, saw us, smiled, pointed at the puffin, and turned back to the harbor. The three of us watched until the puffin disappeared.

And as Michael eased out of the parking lot, I could see Dad in the rearview mirror, still standing at the edge of the crowd, waving cheerfully at us with a toy puffin in each hand.

READ ON FOR AN EXCERPT FROM
THE NEXT BOOK BY DONNA ANDREWS

Revenge of the Wrought-Iron Flamingos

COMING SOON
FROM ST. MARTIN'S MINOTAUR

"I'm going to kill Michael's mother," I announced. "Quickly, discreetly, and with a minimum of pain and suffering. Out of consideration for Michael. But I am going to kill her."

"What was that?" Eileen said, looking up and blinking at me.

I glanced over at my best friend and fellow craftswoman. She had already unpacked about an acre of blue-and-white porcelain and arranged it on her side of our booth. I still had several tons of wrought iron to wrestle into place.

I scratched two or three places where my authentic Colonial-style linsey-woolsey dress was giving me contact dermatitis. I rolled my ruffled sleeves higher up on my arms, even though I knew they'd flop down again in two minutes. Then I hiked my skirts up a foot or so, hoping a stray breeze would cool off my legs.

"I said I'm going to kill Michael's mother for making us do this craft fair in eighteenth-century costume," I said. "It's absolutely crazy in ninety-degree weather."

"Well, it's not entirely Mrs. Waterston's fault," Eileen

said. "Who knew we'd be having weather like this in October?"

I couldn't think of a reasonable answer, so I turned back to the case I was unpacking and lifted out a pair of wrought-iron candlesticks. Eileen, like me, was flushed from the heat and exertion, not to mention frizzy from the humidity. But with her blond hair and fair skin, it gave the effect of glowing health. I felt like a disheveled mess.

"This would be so much easier in jeans," I grumbled, tripping over the hem of my skirt as I walked over to the table to set the candlesticks down.

"People are already showing up," Eileen said, with a shrug. "You know what a stickler Mrs. Waterston is for authenticity."

Yes, everyone in Yorktown had long ago figured that out. And Martha Stewart had nothing on Mrs. Waterston for attention to detail. If she'd had her way, we'd have made every single stitch we wore by hand, by candlelight. She'd probably have tried to make us spin the thread and weave the fabric ourselves, not to mention raising and shearing the sheep. And when she finally pushed enough of us over the edge, we'd have to make sure our lynch mob used an authentic Colonial-style hemp rope instead of an anachronistic nylon one.

Of course, my fellow craftspeople would probably lynch me, too, while they were at it, since I was her deputy in charge of organizing the craft fair. And in Mrs. Waterston's eyes, keeping all the participants anachronism-free, was my responsibility. When I'd volunteered for the job, I'd thought it a wonderful way to make a good impression on the hypercritical mother of the man I loved. I'd spent the past six months trying not to make Michael an orphan. Speaking of Michael. . . .

"Where's Michael, anyway?" Eileen asked, echoing my thoughts. "I thought he was going to help you with that."

"He will when he gets here," I said. "He's still getting into costume."

"He's going to look so wonderful in Colonial dress," Eileen said.

"Yes," I said. "Lucky we don't have a full-length mirror in the tent, or we wouldn't see him for hours."

"You know you don't mean that," Eileen said, with a frown. "You're crazy about Michael."

I let that pass. Yes, I was crazy about Michael, but I was a grown woman in her thirties, not a starry-eyed teenager in the throes of her first crush. And Michael and I had been together a little over a year. Long enough for me to fully appreciate his many good points, but also long enough to notice a few shortcomings. The thing about costumes and mirrors, for example. And the fact that getting dressed to go anywhere took him two or three times as long as it took me.

Not that I complained, usually; the results were always spectacular. But at the moment, I'd have traded spectacular for available to help. I wrestled an eight-foot trellis into position and sat back, panting.

"Maybe I will wait until he gets here to finish this," I said.

"But Mrs. Waterston wants us all set up by ten!" Eileen said. She rummaged in the wicker basket she was using instead of a purse, then shot a guilty glance back at me before pulling out her wristwatch.

"It's 9:30 already," she said, thrusting the watch back out of sight beneath the red and white checked fabric lining the basket. Familiar gestures already: the furtive glance to see if anyone who cared—like me, theoretically—was looking before someone pulled out a necessary but forbidden modern object. And then the hasty concealment. Eileen should have figured out by now that as long as nobody else spotted her, I didn't give a damn.

Then again, we'd found out this morning that Mrs. Waterston had enlisted a dozen assistants, whom she'd dubbed the Town Watch. In theory, the watchmen were under my orders, available to help with crowd control and prevent shoplifting. In practice, they were the reason I was running late. I'd spent all morning trying to stop them from harassing various frantic craftspeople about using modern tools to set up, and keeping them from confiscating various items they'd decided were "not in period." The crafters had started calling them the Anachronism Police.

"I'm nearly finished with my side," Eileen said. "If you like, I could—"

A loud boom interrupted her, seeming to shake the very ground. Both of us jumped; Eileen shrieked; and her pottery rattled alarmingly. We could hear more shrieks and oaths from nearby booths.

"What on earth!" Eileen exclaimed, racing over to her table to make sure none of her ethereally delicate cups and vases had broken.

"Oh, Lord," I muttered. "I thought she was kidding."

"Kidding about what?" Eileen asked.

"What the hell was that, a sonic boom?" shouted Amanda, the African American weaver in the booth across the aisle.

"The artillery," I shouted back.

"Artillery?" Eileen echoed.

"The what?" Amanda asked, dropping a braided rug and trotting over to our booth.

"Artillery," I repeated. "For the Siege of Yorktown. That's what this whole thing is celebrating, you know."

"Yeah, I know," Amanda said. "October 19, 1781. The British finally throw in the towel and surrender to George Washington and the Revolutionary War is over. Whoopty-do. Let freedom ring, except for my people, who had to wait another eighty years. So what's with the sound effects?"

"Another of Mrs. Waterston's brainstorms," I said. "She hired a bunch of guys to fire a replica cannon to add to the authenticity of the event."

"You mean, like a starter's gun to open the fair?" Amanda asked.

"Demonstrations for the tourists, maybe," Eileen suggested.

"Actually . . ." I said.

Another thunderous boom shook the encampment. This time we heard fewer shrieks and more angry yells.

"Actually," I began again. "She's going to have them firing continuously. To simulate the siege. Washington's troops shelled the British nonstop for a couple of weeks before attacking their entrenchments."

"She's going to have them doing that all day?" Eileen asked.

"Probably all night, too, unless someone can find an obscure county ordinance to stop it." Someone like me, probably. I'd already promised half a dozen townspeople who'd seen the artillery setting up that I'd find a way to silence the cannons at bedtime. Now that the shelling had actually begun, I'd be swamped with complainers—and no matter how irate they were, none of them wanted to tackle Mrs. Waterston directly.

"Bunch of loonies," Amanda muttered.

No argument from me.

"Bad enough I have to dress up like Aunt Jemima," she said, as she returned to her own booth. "And now this."

"Oh, but you look . . . wonderful," Eileen called. "So authentic!"

Amanda looked down at her homespun dress and snorted. She was right, unfortunately. I'd always envied Amanda's stylish urban wardrobe, with its vivid colors and offbeat but sophisticated cuts. I'd never before realized how well her chic outfits camouflaged a slightly plump figure. And when you threw in the cultural associations an African American woman raised in Richmond, Virginia, was bound to have with Colonial era clothing . . .

"Oh, dear," Eileen murmured. From the sudden crease in her normally smooth forehead, I could tell that the last point had just dawned on her. "This must be awful for poor Amanda! Do you think we should—"

"Look sharp!" hissed a voice nearby. "Here she comes! Put away your anachronisms!"

"Oh, dear, Mrs. Waterston will be furious that you're still unpacking!" Eileen exclaimed.

"I still have fifteen minutes," I said, turning to see who'd given the warning. Just outside our booth I saw a man, a little shorter than my 5'10" and slightly pudgy, with a receding chin. I had the feeling I'd recognize him if he were in, say, blue jeans instead of a blue Colonial-style coat, a white powdered wig, and a black felt hat with the brim turned up in thirds to make it into a triangle—the famed Colonial tricorn hat.

"Oh, you look very nice, Harold," Eileen said.

Harold? I started, and peered more closely.

"Cousin Harold," I said. "She's right; you look great in costume. I almost didn't recognize you."

Cousin Harold looked down at his coat and sighed. Normally he loved costume parties—in fact, he assumed (or pretended) that every party he attended was a costume party, and would invariably turn up in his beloved gorilla suit. Usually even Mother had a hard time convincing him to take the ape head off for group photos at family weddings. I wondered how Mrs. Waterston had managed to browbeat him into putting on the Colonial gear.

"It's just one of the standard rental costumes from Be-Stitched," he said, referring to Mrs. Waterston's dressmaking shop. "You'll see dozens just like it before the day is out."

"Well, it looks very nice on you," Eileen said.

"Meg, you have to talk to Mrs. Waterston," he said. "She listens to you."

News to me; I hadn't noticed that Mrs. Waterston listened to anyone—except, possibly, Michael. What Harold really meant was that no one but me had enough nerve to tackle Mrs. Waterston.

"Talk to her about what?" I said, feeling suddenly tired. Cannons? Anachronisms? Or had some new problem arisen?

"Now she's going on about talking authentically," he added. "Avoiding modern slang. Adopting a Colonial accent."

"Oh, Lord," exclaimed Amanda from across the aisle. "Who the hell does that witch think she is, anyway?"

Harold glanced at me and skittered off. Eileen looked pained.

"Who died and made her queen?" Amanda continued.

"Great-aunt Agatha," I said. "Who didn't actually die; she just decided that at 93, she didn't have quite enough energy to continue chairing the committee that organizes the annual Yorktown Day celebration. Mrs. Waterston volunteered to take her place."

"Yeah, she's got enough energy," Amanda said. "It's the common sense she's lacking."

"We'll probably be seeing a lot of Mrs. Waterston," Eileen said. "She's Meg's boyfriend's mother."

"Oh," Amanda said. "Sorry."

"Don't apologize on my account," I said. "You can't possibly say anything about her that I haven't said over the past year. Though not necessarily aloud," I added, half to myself.

"Take my advice, honey," Amanda said. "Dump him now. Can you imagine what she'd be like as a mother-in-law?"

Unfortunately, I could. I'd spent a lot of time brooding over that very prospect. But for now, I deliberately pushed the thought away, into the back of my mind, along with all the other things I didn't have time to worry about until after the fair.

"Oh, but you haven't met Michael!" Eileen gushed. "Here, look!"

She walked across the aisle to Amanda's booth, digging

into her wicker basket as she went, then pulling out a bulg-
ing wallet. She flipped through the wad of plastic photo
sleeves and held up one of the photos. Amanda peered at
it, her face about three inches from the wallet.

"Not bad," she said.

"He's a drama professor at Caerphilly College," Eileen
said. "And a wonderful actor, and we all think he's just
perfect for Meg."

"If you could lose the mother," Amanda said. "Is he
going to be around today?"

"Of course," Eileen said. "He and Meg are inseparable!"

Well, as inseparable a couple can be, living in different
towns, several hours' drive apart and trying to juggle two
demanding careers that didn't exactly permit regular nine-
to-five hours. Another reminder of problems I was trying
to put on hold until the damned craft fair was over and
done with.

"Okay, I'll try not to say anything too nasty when Blue
Eyes is around," Amanda said. "If I recognize him. My
glasses are banned," she said, with a disapproving glance
at me. "Not in period. Only wire rims allowed."

"Sorry," I said, shrugging. "Anyway, Michael's pretty
hard to miss."

"Everyone's a blur from two feet away," Amanda grumbled.

"He'll be the six-foot-four blur in the white French uniform with violet cuffs and gold lace trim," I said.

"You're right," she said, with a chuckle. "I think I'll
probably manage to pick him out of the crowd."

"That's my son Samuel he's holding," Eileen said. "It
was taken at the christening. Here's another one we took
at the reception afterward."

"Very nice," Amanda said. She glanced nervously at Eileen's wallet, beginning to suspect how much of its bulk
came from baby pictures.

"And here's one of Samuel with his daddy," Eileen continued, flipping onward. I could see a trapped look cross Amanda's face.

"Not in period," I sang, clapping my hands for attention as our first-grade teacher used to do. And when Eileen turned with a hurt look, I added, "Come on. Help me out; we're supposed to be setting a good example for the others."

Eileen sighed, stowed her anachronisms, and returned to our booth. I don't know why I bothered. She'd pull the photos out the minute my back was turned. Amanda would have to fend for herself if she wanted to dodge Eileen's hour by hour photographic chronicle of the first two months of young Samuel's life.

Don't get me wrong; I've got nothing against kids. I love my sister Pam's brood, all six of them—although I prefer them one at a time. As young Samuel's godmother, I was perfectly willing to agree with his parents' most extravagant boasts about his winsome charm and preternatural intelligence. I could even see that producing an offspring or two might be something I'd be interested in doing eventually, under the right circumstances and with the right collaborator.

But, I'd already seen Eileen's pictures several dozen times. At least she'd left the infant prodigy himself home with a sitter. I was getting very, very tired of having people dump babies into my arms and warble to the immediate world what a natural I was. Especially when they did it in front of Michael. Or his mother.

Speaking of Mrs. Waterston, if Harold was right, I probably would need to straighten her out about the accent problem, before she browbeat all the crafters into mute terror. But at least I could postpone the ordeal until she dropped by my booth. I peered outside to see how close she was. And breathed a sigh of relief. She was still a good way off, standing in front of her tent, in the middle of our temporary, fictional town square.

We'd set up all the tents and booths of the fair like the streets of a small town, its aisles marked with little street signs painted in tasteful, conservative Williamsburg colors with names taken from Yorktown and Virginia history, like "Jefferson Lane" and "Rue de Rochambeau." Thirty-four street signs, to be precise—I knew, because I'd had to think up all the names, arrange for Eileen's cabinet-maker husband make the signboards, and then forge the wrought-iron posts and brackets myself.

In the center we had what Mrs. Waterston called the town square, complete with a fake well and a working set of stocks that I was afraid she had every intention of using on minor malefactors. Not to mention her headquarters tent, which she'd decorated to match some museum's rather ornate recreation of how General Washington's tent would have looked.

Mrs. Waterston turned to look our way, and I winced. She wasn't dressed, like the rest of us, in workday gowns of wool, cotton, or linsey-woolsey. She wore a Colonial ball gown. The white powdered wig added at least a foot to her height.

"What the hell is she wearing on her hips?" Amanda said, from her vantage point across the aisle.

"Panniers," I said, referring to the semi-circular hoops that held out Mrs. Waterston's dress for at least a foot on either side of her hips. "Don't the historical society folks ever wear panniers up in Richmond?"

"Not anyplace I've ever seen," she answered. "Remember, Richmond didn't do too much worth bragging about in the Revolution; they're all running around in hoop skirts fixated on the 1860s and St. Robert E. Lee. And I thought Scarlet O'Hara looked foolish," she added, shaking her head. "She must be three feet wide, and no more than a foot deep."

"That was the style back then," I said. "Like Marie Antoinette."

"Looks like a paper doll," Amanda said. "How's she going to get up if she ever falls down?"

"You could trip her and we could find out," I suggested.

"Don't tempt me," Amanda said, with a chuckle.

Mrs. Waterston still stood in the town square, turning slowly, surveying her domain. A frown creased her forehead.

"Oh, Lord," I muttered. "Now what?"

"What's wrong?" Eileen asked.

"Mrs. Waterston's upset about something."

"Mrs. Waterston's always upset about something," Eileen said. "Don't worry; I'm sure it's not your problem."

Probably not, but that wouldn't stop Mrs. Waterston from making it my problem. I'd worked like a dog to make the craft fair successful. I'd twisted crafters' arms to participate. Begged, browbeaten, or blackmailed friends and relatives to show up and shop. Harassed the local papers for publicity.

And it worked. We'd gotten a solid number of artists, and their quality was far better than we had any right to expect for a fair with no track record. Especially considering the requirement for Colonial costume. Most of the best crafters were old friends, some of whom had passed up prestigious, juried shows to help out. I hoped Mrs. Waterston understood the craft scene well enough to appreciate that without my efforts, she'd have nothing but amateurs selling dried flower arrangements and crocheted toilet paper covers.

And wonder of wonders, with a little last-minute help from Be-Stitched, they were all wearing some semblance of authentic Colonial costume. And by the time the barriers opened, and the crowd already milling around outside began pouring in, I'd have all the anachronisms put away, if I had to do it myself.

So why was Mrs. Waterston frowning?

"Miss me?" came a familiar voice in my ear, accompanied by a pair of arms slipping around my waist.

"Always," I said, turning around to greet Michael more properly. I ignored Eileen, who had developed a maddening habit of sighing and murmuring "Aren't they sweet?" whenever she saw us together.

"No, shall I set the rest of this stuff up?" Michael asked, eventually.

"Please," I said, and stood back to give him room. Maybe I'd be set up on time after all, and could take a last run around the grounds to make sure everything was ship-shape.

I caught Amanda sneaking a pair of glasses out from under her apron and shook my finger at her, in imitation of Mrs. Waterston. She stuck out her tongue at me, put the glasses on and watched with interest while Michael shed his ornate, gold-trimmed coat, rolled up the flowing sleeves of his linen shirt, and began hauling iron. Then she looked over at me and gave me a thumbs up.

"What on earth is that!"

Mrs. Waterston's voice. And much closer than I expected. Though not, thank goodness, quite in our booth. Not yet, anyway. Still, I started; Amanda ripped her glasses off so fast that she dropped them; and Eileen began nervously picking at her dress and hair.

Michael alone seemed unaffected. I wondered, not for the first time, if he was really as oblivious to his mother's tirades as he seemed. Maybe it was just good acting. Or should I have his hearing tested?

"Put that thing away immediately!"

Eileen and Amanda both looked around, startled, to see what they should put away. Michael continued calmly trying to match up half a dozen pairs of andirons on the ground at the front of the booth. I peered around the corner to see who or what had incurred Mrs. Waterston's displeasure.

"Oh, no," I groaned.

"What's wrong?" Michael said, putting down an andiron to hurry to my side.

"Wesley Hatcher, that's what," I said.

"Who's that?" he asked.

"The world's sneakiest reporter," I said, "And living proof that neither a brain nor a backbone are prerequisites for a career as a muckraking journalist. Wesley," I called out, as a jeans-clad figure retreated into our booth, hastily stuffing a small tape recorder into his pocket. "If you're trying to hide, find someplace else."

Wesley turned around, wearing what I'm sure he meant as an ingratiating smile.

"Oh, hi Meg!" he said. "Long time no see."

Actually, he'd seen me less than two hours previously, when he'd tried to get me to say something misquotable for a snide story on how craftspeople overcharged and exploited their customers. With any other reporter, I'd have seized the opportunity to give him the real scoop on the insecure and underpaid lives so many craftspeople led. But I knew better than to talk to Wesley. I'd made the mistake of talking off the record to him years ago, when he was earning his journalistic reputation as the Yorktown Crier's most incompetent cub reporter in three centuries. Like the rest of the county, I'd been puzzled but relieved when he'd abandoned our small weekly paper, first for a staff job with the Virginia Commercial Intelligence, a reputable state business journal, and then, returning to character, for the sleazy, but no doubt highly paid, world of the Super Snooper, a third-rate tabloid. Why couldn't he have waited until Thanksgiving to come home and visit his parents?

"So, got any juicy stories for me?" Wesley asked.

"Get lost, Wesley," I said.

"Aw, come on," he whined. "Is that any way treat your own cousin?"

"He's your cousin?" Michael asked.

"No," I said.

"Yes," Wesley said, at the same time.

"Only a distant cousin; and about to become a little more distant—right, Wesley?" I said, picking up a set of andirons as I spoke. It wasn't meant to be a physical threat, but if Wesley chose to misinterpret it as one . . .

"I'll stay out of your way; just ignore me," Wesley said, sidling a little farther off.

Which meant, no doubt, that Wesley thought he could pick up some dirt hanging around my booth. Or possibly that he knew about the orders my mother had given me to "find poor Wesley a nice story that will keep his editor happy." Wesley was a big boy; why was helping help him keep his job suddenly my responsibility? I'd taken him on a VIP tour of the festival last night, hoping he'd find something harmless to write about. I'd even shown him the stocks and let him take some pictures of me in them, pictures I knew he'd find a way to misuse sooner or later. What more was I supposed to do? And what had he done to upset Mrs. Waterston?

I peered out again. To my relief, Mrs. Waterston had returned to the town square. Her head was moving slowly, as if she were scanning the lane of booths leading up to ours. And she was frowning. Maybe she saw something unsatisfactory about our entire row of booths—but no, that was unlikely. This row and the adjoining one were the showplaces, closest to the entrance, where I'd put the best craftspeople with the most authentic Colonial costumes and merchandise. I'd kept the weirder stuff toward the back of the fair. More likely she was watching someone walking down the row. Someone who was about to pass my booth, or maybe even enter it . . .

"Hi, Meg! Has anyone asked for me?"

My brother, Rob.

"No, not yet," I said, eyeing him. I couldn't see anything wrong. His blue jacket, waistcoat, and knee breeches fit nicely; his ruffled shirt and long stockings were gleaming white; both his shoes and the buckles on them were freshly polished; his hair was neatly tied back with a black velvet ribbon, and a tricorn hat perched atop his head at a jaunty but far from rakish angle. Not for the first time, I envied the fact that he'd inherited our mother's aristocratic blond beauty.

"Meg?" he asked. "Is there something wrong? Don't I look okay?"

"You look fine," I said. "Help Michael with some of my ironwork."

"I'm supposed to be meeting someone on business, you know," he announced, for about the twentieth time today. "I don't want to get all sweaty."

"Well, work slowly if you like, but try to look busy."

"Why?" he asked, shoving his hands in his pockets.

"Because Mrs. Waterston is coming this way," I said, glancing over my shoulder. "Would you rather help me out, or do whatever chore she has in mind for you?"

"Where do you want these?" Rob asked, snatching up a pair of candlesticks.

"I've got nearly everything out of the crates and boxes," Michael said. "I should probably go check on the rest of my regiment."

"Fine," I said. "Rob can help me finish."

"I'll bring back some lunch," he said, leaning down to kiss me. "You'll be here, right?"

"Actually, I'll probably be running up and down all day, keeping the crafters and the Anachronism Police from killing each other," I said. "And if things get slow, I need to go down to Faulk's booth for a while."

"Can't Faulk mind his own booth?" Michael said, frowning.

"I'm sure he can," I said. "But he's supposed to inspect my dagger."

"Oh, have you finished the dagger?" Eileen exclaimed. "The one with the falcon handle? Let me see it!"

So, now, of course, I had to show Eileen the dagger. Not that she had to twist my arm too hard—I admit, I was proud of the dagger. Eight months ago, Faulk, the friend who'd introduced me to iron working when we were in college together, had come back to Virginia after working for the last several years with a world-renowned swordsmith in California. He'd been burning to share what he'd learned about making weapons, and, I confess, I'd caught the bug.

The last couple of months, I'd been working on a dagger, with an intricate ornamental handle and a highly functional steel blade. I'd finished it—at least I hoped it was ready for prime time. But Faulk was the expert. I'd been looking forward for weeks to showing him the dagger

Eileen oohed and aahed over the dagger so loudly that Amanda came over to see what was going on. Michael, I noticed, was standing aloof, still frowning. I realized, suddenly, that this wasn't the first time over the last few months that he'd shown a certain coolness, even irritation, whenever I'd mentioned my dagger. What was the matter with him, anyway? He didn't seem to feel threatened by my blacksmithing; what was so different about making swords?

I turned my attention back to the dagger in time to grab Amanda's hand before she touched the blade.

"Careful!" I said. "It's razor sharp; you could slice your finger off."

"You get much call for working daggers?" Amanda asked.

"There's a growing market for period weapons," I said. "Renaissance Faires, Society for Creative Anachronism folks—you'd be surprised."

"They let people run around at Renaissance Faires with sharpened swords?"

"No, but this is my journeyman piece," I said. "Proof that I've learned the swordsmithing craft. I had to hand-hammer the steel blade, just the way they would have in the 1500s, and sharpen it to perfection."

"Can't you just buy the blades somewhere these days?" Rob asked. "From Japan or something? That'd be a lot easier."

"Yes, and you can get them pretty reasonably from India and Japan, and most people couldn't afford a hand-hammered steel blade. But even if you're usually going to buy your blades and just make the handles, Faulk says it's important to learn how they're made, the traditional way, so you really understand the steel. You're much better able to choose a good blade if you know how they're made."

Michael frowned again when I mentioned Faulk's name. Aha! Maybe it wasn't swords that bothered him—maybe it was Faulk. As I realized that, he smiled—was it a genuine smile, or was he just making an effort?—and disappeared into the crowd with a slight wave.

"Mr. Right not keen on the swordsmithing project?" Amanda asked.

I shrugged. Damn, she had sharp eyes. I'd only just picked up on it myself.

"Well, you seem to be in good shape," boomed a voice from outside the booth.

Mrs. Waterston. We all whirled, and Rob, who had been testing the blade of my dagger, yelped as he cut himself slightly.

"I told you to be careful," I said, taking the dagger back as Rob sucked his finger with a martyred air.

Mrs. Waterston fixed her gaze on Rob. And frowned.

"Haven't you got anything useful to do?" she asked. She was, I noticed, speaking with an accent that might be mistaken for British, but only by someone who'd never heard the real thing.

Rob looked uncomfortable, and tugged at the ruffled neck of his shirt.

I found myself resenting Mrs. Waterston's immediate assumption that Rob was loitering about with nothing to do. Irrational, since that's just what he would have been doing if I hadn't scared him into action. But then, he was my brother. I might disapprove of his character in private, but I wasn't about to give Mrs. Waterston the privilege.

"He's been helping me unpack," I said. "Put the stand for the dagger right in the middle of the table, Rob."

"Besides, I'm meeting someone here," Rob said. "A business meeting."

"A representative of one of the software companies that's interested in buying Lawyers from Hell," I added. "You know, the computerized version of the role-playing game he invented."

"Oh. I see," Mrs. Waterston said. "By the way, I've been meaning to speak to you about people's accents."

"Don't worry; I've already given orders about that," I improvised. "Since the fair's located behind American lines, we're going to represent Colonial crafters, not British ones. The town watch has orders to arrest anyone speaking in a British accent and put them in the stocks, as suspected Tories."

"I see," Mrs. Waterston said, blinking. "Well, then, carry on," she added, in something closer to her normal accent.

She scrutinized Rob once more, as if she still hadn't quite gotten used to the notion of him as capable of inventing something for which grown-ups would pay good money. Then she turned and sailed off. Though not without difficulty. The lane had grown more crowded, and she had to turn sideways every few feet to squeeze her panniers through the crowd. Instead of a galleon in full sail, she looked like a barge being towed through a crowded harbor.

"Wow," Cousin Harold said, peering around the edge of the booth. "That was great."

"So go tell the town watch about arresting Tories," I said. Harold disappeared.

"Thanks," Rob murmured, his eyes still on Mrs. Waterston's retreating form.

"No problem," I said. "I thought the guy wasn't supposed to come till noon, though."

"I didn't want to miss him if he came early," Rob said.

Two hours early? Well, it was important to Rob.

"You're welcome to stay as long as you keep out of the customers' way. Or, better yet, make yourself useful. Bring some more stuff out from the back."

"Of course," Rob said, nodding vigorously, and disappeared behind the curtain concealing the storage area in the back of our booth.

"Are you really meeting the software company guy here?" Eileen asked.

"Yes," Rob said, dragging out one of my metal storage boxes. "It solves the problem of what to wear."

Eileen looked puzzled.

"The first time Rob met with a software company, he got all dressed up in a three-piece suit," I elaborated. "They all showed up in jeans and t-shirts."

"And sandals," Rob said. "I felt like an idiot. So the next time, I showed up in jeans and a t-shirt."

"And I bet they were in three-piece suits," Eileen said.

"Bingo," I said. "So when we heard the latest guy was coming today, while the fair was on, I told Rob to meet him at my booth. He can scope out what the guy's wearing, suggest that they meet at someplace less crowded in half an hour, and change into the uniform of the day, whatever that turns out to be."

"What if he shows up in costume too?" Rob asked.

"Then drive him up to Colonial Williamsburg and eat at one of the taverns," I said.

"That might work," Rob said. "Thanks. Where should I put these?"

I turned to see him holding up a pink wrought-iron flamingo.

"Back in the box, quick," I said.

"Why?" he said. He was holding the flamingo out at arms length, inspecting it.

"Put it away, now," I said, dropping a set of fireplace tongs to race over to the box. "Mrs. Waterston will explode if she sees it."

"I don't see why," he said, as I snatched the flamingo from his hands. "It's kind of cool in a weird way. I like it."

"You would," I said, opening the case to shove the flamingo inside. "It's a complete anachronism and—"

"And you've got a lot of them," Rob said, peering into the case. "Any chance you'd give me—"

"Meg!"

Mrs. Waterston was back. I slammed the lid of the case closed and sat on it, hard, for good measure, ignoring the yelp of pain from Rob, who didn't quite move his hand fast enough to avoid getting nipped by the closing lid. And the small crash to my left, where a customer had dropped one of Eileen's vases and was now cowering against the curtain at the back of our booth.

"Yes?" I said, ignoring Rob, who was grimacing and shaking his injured hand. "What's wrong, Mrs. Waterston?" I couldn't quite manage a smile, but I think I achieved a polite, interested expression.

"These people you brought are impossible!" she exclaimed.

"Which one in particular?" I asked. Eileen had gone to the customer's side and was making reassuring noises, I noted. I stood up from the chest, warning Rob, with a glance, not to open it again.

"That female glassblower," she said. "She's wearing men's clothes."

"Merry's giving glassblowing demonstrations at noon, two, and four" I said. "She can't wear skirts for that."

"Why on earth not?"

"Because it would be a serious fire hazard," I said. "Burning was one of the leading causes of death for women in the Colonial, or any other historical era, before we developed cooking and heating methods that didn't involve open flames. One good spark and these skirts could go up like so much kindling," I said, shaking my own skirts with resentment. "So unless you really like the possibility of Merry reenacting the death of Joan of Arc in front of all the tourists, I suggest you overlook her gender for the time being."

"She could at least wear proper clothes when she's not demonstrating."

"I'll see if that's possible," I said.

"Why wouldn't it be possible?"

"She may not have brought another costume, and it might be hard for her to make any sales at all if she's spending all her time either demonstrating or changing in and out of costume."

"That's no excuse," Mrs. Waterston fumed. "Don't these people realize we're trying for authenticity here? Don't they understand—"

Doesn't she realize that these people are trying to make a living, I thought; and I was opening my mouth to say so, and no doubt precipitate the argument I'd been avoiding for so long, when I realized that Mrs. Waterston was staring, open-mouthed, at something behind my back.

What now, I wondered?